HIGH ART

HIGH ART

Rubem Fonseca

Translated from the Portuguese
by Ellen Watson

1817

HARPER & ROW, PUBLISHERS, New York
Cambridge, Philadelphia, San Francisco, London
Mexico City, São Paulo, Singapore, Sydney

Designer: C. Linda Dingler

Library of Congress Cataloging-in-Publication Data

Fonseca, Rubem.
  High art.

  Translation of: A grande arte.
  I. Title.
PQ9698.16.0'46G713   1986   869.3   85-45635
ISBN 0-06-015572-8

86 87 88 89 90 10 9 8 7 6 5 4 3 2 1

I
PERSEV

IT WAS a tool like no other. It was made of high-quality material and its use demanded a long and difficult apprenticeship. Not to mention the use it was put to by its owner. He was familiar with all the utensil's functions, and capable of executing the most difficult maneuvers—the *in-quartata,* the *passata sotto*—with unsurpassable skill, but he used it to write the letter *P,* nothing more, to write the letter *P* on various women's faces.

The woman was lying beside him talking banalities. He looked around. The walls were green, like certain hospitals. A record player with a dusty plastic cover sat beside a portable TV. A can of ordinary talcum powder lay on the bed and he nudged it with his bare foot.

No point in wondering why. It was a waste of time to speculate why particular things give us pleasure. The *P* had no literary resonance, nor did he consider himself a puritan psychotic bent on exorcising the inborn depravity of the female.

That the women were prostitutes had no bearing whatsoever on his resolve. He was merely minimizing the risk; for this reason he chose individuals society considered dispensable. But now, looking at the woman's face curved over his naked body, he had to admit that perhaps he was lying to himself. She really was a featureless woman, it truly would be no loss. The pleasure she could give was minimal, easy to find, imagine.

The woman ran her tongue up his chest, lingering at the nipple. Feeling the ache in his groin, he pulled away from her and got up, standing beside the bed. The woman kneeled in front of him, adaptable, functional.

He grasped her around the neck and threw her to the floor, adding the weight of his body to the strength of his

3

hands. The woman opened her mouth, trying to breathe, grunted hoarsely, her eyes wide and fixed on his, arms raised, fingers trembling, reaching for anything that would save her from sinking into the darkness that was rapidly overtaking her.

It was all over in seconds.

The gleaming object was slipped from its leather sheath. He held it firmly, positioning himself *en garde*, muscles tense—an amusement he permitted himself in that moment of euphoria and sensuality. But before long, altering his grip on the haft, he sat down beside the woman on the floor and carefully traced on her cheek the letter *P,* which in the ancient Semitic alphabet signified mouth.

He picked up the clothes he'd left on a chair and dressed, alert, efficient, in spite of his mind's refusal to stop imagining, remembering. When he was ready, he inspected the bedroom and bathroom; checked through the spy hole that the hallway was empty. On the way out as he wiped the doorbell with a handkerchief, it rang—the only slip, though irrelevant, in his painstaking procedure.

There would be no fingerprints, no witnesses, no clues to identify him. Only his penmanship.

I did not become aware of these facts in a chronological way. Lima Prado's Notebooks came into my possession long before the conversations with Miriam that helped me to understand the relationship between José "Iron Nose" Zakkai and Camilo Fuentes. The reconstruction of incidents occurring in Roberto Mitry's apartment is based not only on my own deductions and discoveries but on information supplied to me by the weapons dealer Monteiro (not his real name).

These events became known and comprehensible to me through direct personal observation, or through the testimony of those involved. At times I have interpreted events and behavior. Am I not a lawyer professionally accustomed to the practice of hermeneutics?

1

THE HOUSES were being demolished to make room for a place to be called New Town. They were one-story houses, with blue wooden shutters opening directly onto the sidewalk. One entire side of the street was still intact, the last of the old red-light district. You could hear the noise of machines knocking down walls. Fine yellow dust from shattered bricks floated in the hot air. To think that prostitutes would no longer be seen at their windows flirting with the men passing by.

I stepped out of Madam Miriam's place, and together we walked to Saboia's bar. We sat around a white marble-topped table drinking beer.

"They told me they're going to build an overpass over this place. You think it's true?" asked Saboia.

"Maybe."

"What do they need another overpass for? Isn't the automobile industry in a slump?"

I had come to tell my client that he was about to be dispossessed. Saboia was not surprised to hear it. He hadn't expected to win his case against the government.

"There's nothing more we can do, Saboia. We lost on the last appeal. Miriam may have a little more luck. City Hall's trying to find a place for the girls."

I remembered the first time I'd visited that street. It had looked to me like a cheery outdoor market—men weaving from one side to the other, smoking and talking on street corners or stopping in front of the houses to check out the women. A redhead standing in a doorway had called to me: "Playing hooky, kid?" She was young, with large

5

breasts and thick arms, and when I looked at her indecisively she made a nasty face, sticking out a tongue the color of her hair.

"I knew it would turn out this way." Saboia set another bottle on the table.

"I've got to go." I touched Miriam's hand lightly. "See you soon."

I walked along the Mangue Canal until finally finding a cab. The polluted water in the canal gave off a disagreeable odor. From the taxi window I gazed out at billboards that filled the spaces left by the demolition: cigarettes, televisions, cars.

As soon as I got to the office, Wexler, my partner, came in to talk to me.

"There's a woman here with a weird story. I've come to the conclusion that she's a little wacko. Why don't you have a talk with her."

She was sitting on the sofa in Wexler's office, staring at her nails. A woman in her early twenties with two bright splashes of blush on her cheekbones to brighten her sallow skin. Her name was Gisela.

"This is my partner. I'd like you to tell him the story you just told me."

She stared at her nails.

We waited.

"I already told you."

"Right," said Wexler. "It seems she's being threatened —that's it, isn't it?—by a man whose name she doesn't know."

"His name is Frenchy."

"You said you didn't know his name."

"That's what Danusa calls him."

"Who's Danusa ?"

"Danusa's my friend, she's the one who brought him over. She's got a place in Santos Vallis, on Rua Senator Dantas."

"And why is this man threatening you?" Besides being

6

laconic, Gisela would not stop staring at her nails. They were brilliant red. The word that came into my head was scarlet.

We waited. You need to have patience to make people talk.

"I have something that's his."

"He threatened you because you have something that is his and you won't give it back, isn't that right?"

"Mmm-hmmm."

"And why don't you give it back?"

"I'm scared."

"What is it?"

"A videotape."

"What's on this videotape?"

"I don't know. I don't have a machine to play it on."

"The tape is his. So give it back and that's that," said Wexler.

"But I'm scared. When I called to tell him I had the tape he told me I was crazy, he told me I'd seen something I shouldn't have seen."

"What was this guy Frenchy doing at your house in the first place?"

We waited.

"Well . . ."

We waited.

"Well, I'm a masseuse." Pause. "With a certificate—I'm registered and everything. He came over to my place with Danusa. And left this black box. Then he called, all upset."

Wexler looked at me and made a face registering disenchantment with humanity which only Jews know how to make. "And you asked him for money to get back his box, which you opened and saw contained a videocassette."

Staring at her nails, she nodded her head affirmatively.

"Look, miss, we don't work for blackmailers," said Wexler. "There's nothing we can or are willing to do for you."

For the first time she raised her head and looked at us. She was frightened, all right. Clearly she wasn't intelligent enough to put on an act this good.

"Who sent you here?"

"Miriam. She said you could help me."

"But we can't."

From the door she looked back at us for the last time. Certainly not much of a talker. She left without a word. Dejected.

"Dejected, nothing. You just don't know how to be firm when it comes to women. As if we had time to waste on such sleazy stuff," said Wexler.

Innocents and criminals of all types had passed through our office. Gisela was one of the least communicative of all. A few hours later I had already forgotten she existed. Later that day Sônia, our secretary, announced that a man named Roberto Mitry was there to speak with me.

He must have been around forty and dressed with the careful negligence of the rich.

"The question which brings me here regards some personal property of mine that is in the possession of one of your clients."

"One of my clients?" I had completely forgotten about Gisela.

"I'm afraid that this Gisela woman, she, well . . . Since I'm a man about society, with my name appearing in the columns and such, she, well . . . Once she realized who I am, she wanted . . ."

I waited.

"You see, poor people . . ."

I waited.

"Poor people are fascinated by the well-to-do. It's the poor who read the social columns."

"And the rich."

"This is a democracy. And the rich, granted. The rich do what they do. I think it's only fair that we all have the same opportunities." Mitry pretended to yawn. It seemed like he had something in his mouth. His jaws rotated back and forth slowly. "It's all so tiring." Another yawn.

"Excuse me for just a moment, would you?"

I went to talk to Wexler.

"There's a guy named Mitry in my office who I think is none other than Frenchy, the guy with the videotape that girl was talking about this morning. Apparently she told him she's our client."

"I knew that woman was a liar. Fill him in."

"Don't you want to see him? He's a real character. Dripping with gold chains."

I made the introductions. Wexler got right to the point.

"The woman in question is not a client of ours. She simply came here and told us she had something of yours, a videocassette, and that you were threatening her."

"It's a lie, it's a lie. I never threatened her." Mitry furtively popped something into his mouth, and the subtle rotating movement continued. He swallowed saliva in tiny gulps. "The truth of it is that I'm the one feeling threatened."

"By her?"

"No, not her. But I have reasons or—better—*feelings,* which lead me to . . . I believe I'm in danger. I'm being followed."

I was accustomed to people's paranoia.

"Could you explain that a little further?"

"No, it's just intuition. It's not that I have enemies, understand, but I feel I'm in danger. It's very subjective, I know. But I really want you to believe me."

We were all silent for a while. I lit a panatela. Suerdieck's dark panatela has a dense, dark ash and can be smoked any time, unlike those Cuban cigars which have to be smoked on a full stomach. Pimentel No. 2, another of my favorites, is rather ordinary and foul-smelling. Its offensive odor clings to curtains, upholstery, women's dresses. The Americans make a sort of green cigar that comes with the little hole made in it already.

"I would like you to represent me," said Mitry finally.

"What for?" asked Wexler.

"I'm being blackmailed." Mitry made a gesture in my direction. "And I know you're a very competent professional. I made a few inquiries before coming here."

"I'm a regular blue chip," I said. He impressed me as the type who might have struck it rich playing the stock market.

Mitry smiled. "I'm prepared to cash in a couple of my own blue chips to pay your price. And anyone else's, any others involved. Not price—sorry. What do you call it?"

"Retainer." Wexler.

"Retainer." He laughed. Wexler and I exchanged looks.

"Fine. Just give us power of attorney and we'll try to resolve the situation without police interference."

"Don't telephone or enter into any contact whatsoever with the woman," said Wexler.

"It's a pleasure to have you as my attorney, Dr. Mandrake—if I may call you by your sobriquet."

"As you like." The phone rang. It was Ada.

"It's a year today," said Ada.

"I'd like to get that videocassette back as soon as possible," Mitry said to Wexler.

"Do you remember the first time we met?" asked Ada.

"If we have to, we'll ask for police assistance," said Wexler.

"No police," said Mitry, "at least not for now."

I remembered. Evening, walking down Avenida Ataulfo de Paiva. Looking up at the brightly lit windows of an exercise club. Ever since the days of Eva Cavalcanti Meier I'd been fascinated by women exercising. But that's another story. Inside the studio on Ataulfo de Paiva a group of women were running in line, to the beat of some music that couldn't be heard out on the street. In front, in a black leotard, a tall, thin woman with long, powerful legs, her neck slightly curved forward, moved effortlessly. I waited for the class to be over and for her to come out. Approached her on the street. "I was watching you exercise. You looked like a horse in a canvas by Ucello," I said. "I know Ucello," she said, "in the Uffizi." It wasn't the one in the Uffizi, but in the Louvre, the black horse in the center, hooves raised, chomping at the bit, his muzzle twisted toward the left. She wasn't in the habit of talking to strangers, but my face inspired confidence in all the women of the world. Besides, it was the first time anyone had told her she looked like a horse.

"What's on the videotape?" asked Wexler.

"To tell you the truth, I don't know. It belongs to a third party," said Mitry.

Ada's reminiscences made me uncomfortable. Women love to relive the past.

"Is there some way to identify this tape?" asked Wexler.

"I'm in a meeting, sweets. I'll call you later."

"It's in a black case, a cassette case, but without a label," said Mitry.

He signed the power of attorney. "Should I pay something now? I'm heading out to Angra today, to an island that belongs to a cousin of mine."

"We can leave that for later."

"Then, adieu. I'll call in a few days. I have faith in you."

"I don't like him," said Wexler afterwards. "Obviously the type who made his fortune swindling millions of poor fuckers. His weekend begins on Monday."

" 'A waycher mentsch diment.' Isn't that what Figenbaum told you?"

"Figenbaum is dead."

Maybe so.

Gisela's real name was Elisa de Almeida. By the time we tried to reach her the following day, it was already too late.

"Who's calling?" asked a man's voice.

"A client," I said.

"She went out and asked me to take her messages. Leave me your name and number and she'll call you later."

"I'll call back." I hung up. If there was anything I recognized right off it was the voice of a cop.

Wexler called and listened to the same routine.

"Maybe, maybe not," he said. "Is it worth giving Raul a call?"

"Not yet."

"Talk to Luizinho."

11

Luizinho was the crime reporter for *O Dia*.
Luizinho had stepped out. I left a message.

I stopped by the courthouse. Wexler handled civil suits; criminal cases were my territory. But whenever necessary we helped each other out. When I got back to the office, Wexler informed me that Luizinho had called. Elisa de Almeida, otherwise known as Gisela, had been murdered in the apartment on Avenida Beira Mar where she lived and practiced her profession as masseuse. The body had been discovered that morning.

"We should get hold of that friend of hers, Danusa."

"Exactly what I was thinking."

Wexler had already made a few phone calls and located a Danusa on Rua Senator Dantas.

"How do you know it's her?"

He didn't.

I picked up the phone and dialed.

"Danusa? I'm interested in a massage, how about if I stop by?"

"No, not here. I only do massages at the client's place. Or a hotel."

"Isn't Gisela a friend of yours? She's the one who gave me your name."

"Sure. Gisela. She lives on Beira Mar, and has clients up to the apartment. I don't. Only very special cases."

"I could be a very special case."

"No you couldn't. I don't know you."

"Then you'll come to me? Praça Marechal Floriano, in Cinelândia." I gave her the address.

"What's the phone number there?" asked Danusa. The world was full of jokers and she didn't want to waste the trip.

A few minutes later the phone rang: "I'll be there in half an hour."

"I'd better leave," said Wexler. "She might be scared off if there were two of us here." Sônia had already gone home. On the dot of six she always gathered up her things and left.

12

Danusa looked slightly over twenty. Chunky, with short brown hair and a chipped front tooth.

"What's this? An office? Where are we going to do the massage?"

"How about the sofa?"

Danusa shrugged her shoulders.

Some people sigh their way through life.

Danusa stripped down to her bra and panties. I left my shorts on. "I'd like a massage with oil," I said.

"Oil?" Her plans obviously hadn't included a massage. What kind of client was this? "I didn't bring any oil."

"Powder, then."

"I didn't bring any powder."

"What did you bring?"

"Nothing."

"Too bad."

Danusa studied me thoughtfully. Was I just a jerk? Or someone who wanted to give her a hard time?

"How about if we play a little game?"

"I want a massage."

"Then it'll have to be dry," said Danusa, irritated. It was the first time a client had actually wanted a massage instead of something more substantial. "Lie down over there."

I lay down on the sofa. Danusa grabbed a toe and twisted. She twisted each one.

"How about if we take off this little pair of shorts?"

I took them off.

"Do you want me to give him a little kiss?"

"Do you have a friend named Elisa?"

"Of course. I already told you that, didn't I? On the phone?"

Her eyes met mine. She clenched my leg, hard; her hands were sweating. She seemed overwhelmed by a sudden flood of fear. Her eyes darted to the drapes, as if she thought someone might be hiding behind them.

"I've got to go. I'm sorry, but my mother's home alone. She's sick."

"I think you're lying to me."

"Okay. It isn't my mother. It's my husband."

13

"Your husband."

"He works in a restaurant on Uruguaiana, near Rua Larga. His name is Gilberto. I swear to God." People long to be loved, even by their executioners.

"I'm not going to strangle you. Do I look like a strangler?"

"No. Not at all, no."

"I just want to talk to you."

"Okay, yes, okay." Her fingers in her mouth. She was trembling. Without taking her eyes off me she slipped on her pants.

"As I was leaving I asked the doorman in my building how to get here. He gave me directions but I had a hard time finding it, because I forgot and left the address with him."

This one was no dummy. But why the sudden fear? She didn't even know yet that Gisela had been murdered. Feminine intuition?

"Let's go have a drink," I said.

We went to Amarelinho's, a bar on the corner of Alcindo Guanabara. After we'd come down in the elevator and she'd had a chance to observe me, Danusa seemed to relax.

In Amarelinho's, Danusa ordered a *caipirinha*. The place had no drinkable wine, so I asked for a beer.

"Do you remember a man named Roberto Mitry? You brought him to Elisa's apartment. Elisa told him her name was Gisela. Remember?"

"Roberto who?"

Danusa had made short work of her *caipirinha*. A pleasant warmth radiated up from her stomach and through her whole body. She smiled at me. "Can I have another?"

"A guy wearing lots of jewelry, a gold watch, always seems to be chewing on something, maybe his own tongue. You two girls were with him together."

"A threesome? Let me think. . . . He chews his tongue?"

The second *caipirinha* was gone even faster than the first. She asked for another.

"What's he look like?"

"Very white, frail, languid, flabby, suave. Rawhide, bullwhack, switch, rod, crop, scourge, knout, quirt."

"What's all that supposed to mean? You're weird. Hey, waiter, bring me another." Her voice more and more confident.

"A whip," I said.

"A whip? Yeah, he had a whip. Sure, it's Frenchy, I remember him. Paid good bucks, but gave us hell. He's got a whip."

"And afterward?"

"Also a leather mask, and a chain. He brought everything in a suitcase. No, it was just a big bag."

One more *caipirinha*.

"He gave us hell."

"You already said that. And afterward?"

"Afterward I said to Gisela, Elisa, I said, never again, not this little Carlota."

"And afterward?"

"I mean like I even enjoy a couple nice little bites, some pinches, a little hair-pulling, but a whip!"

"Did he leave anything behind?"

"No, I don't think so. He put everything in a bag and took off."

People were streaming out of office buildings. The bar began to fill.

"There was a minute, though, when he grabbed me by the neck and started pressing, he was hissing and foaming at the mouth—nothing but maniacs around here."

Pressing, hissing, and foaming. Too much television.

"If he calls you again, let me know, okay?"

We sat in the bar a little while longer. When we left we were reeling, Danusa/Carlota hanging on my arm, each of us laughing, entertained by the other.

15

2

"WE YEARN for voluptuous consummation."

"What else?"

"Bodies and souls fructifying, with no thought of the outcome."

"What else?"

"The utter splendor, the faust of the fuck."

"What else?"

"What more do you want, woman?"

"I want to be your friend, too."

"You are my friend."

Me and Ada in bed. We were leafing through a magazine of naked women.

"Do you think this represents infantile, unrepressed behavior, or a more serious pathological syndrome?" she asked.

"Orgasm is an accident."

"That's no answer."

"There's nothing infantile, or sick, about you. Or me."

"This stuff gets me excited. Imagining you and me in bed with another woman. Make a mark on my breast."

I sucked the smooth flesh of Ada's breast with such force that my gums ached. "You know, I bet you'd like it if I were an angler fish, which lives in the dark depths of the sea. The male bites into the female and attaches himself to her body, becoming a parasite for the rest of his life; all his organs, except those of reproduction, degenerate and become totally mingled with hers, even the vascular systems."

"You've got bags under your eyes, my . . . What's the fish called again?"

16

"An angler. *Mine is a land of palm trees where sings the sabiá.*"

"You're afraid to be romantic. So you pretend to be cynical."

We examined our faces in the bathroom mirror, trying to decide whose was more haggard. In the early-morning light seeping through the curtains, our skin looked fragile and sick. Two long hairs emerged from Ada's nose like live insects.

"Remember when you told me you were going to give me the key to your apartment?" I asked.

"Why bring that up now?"

"You said: I'm going to give you the key to my apartment."

"You're acting crazy."

"But you never had time to make a duplicate."

"I really didn't."

"Because of this, that, and the other thing. You never had time to have a key made."

"You really are acting crazy."

"How can I love a woman who doesn't trust me? Love is trust."

"Is this a serious conversation?"

"All the other women trusted me."

"Don't expect me to believe you cried about it."

"Not fat, juicy tears like yours. My eyes are smaller."

"You big jerk."

"Is there any wine?"

"There's coffee and *campesino* cheese. Also wheat germ and yoghurt."

I listened to the noises coming from the kitchen. The first time: Ada walking across her living room, appreciating herself through my eyes, as if my eyes were the mirror in the studio in which she made love to her own body. That was how Ada had walked toward my embrace; and, sensing her narcissism, I had turned my body away slightly, to prevent the embrace from becoming more intimate. Noticing my standoffishness, Ada had asked, surprised, What's wrong? I breathed in the smell of her skin, felt the heat of the solid, muscular body between my arms.

17

Against my will, I was flooded with a wave of emotion. Later, just a little later, in bed, surprise: *virginatas intactus.*

The phone woke me.

"It's Wexler. He wants to talk to you," said Ada.

"Have you read the paper?" Wexler sounded upset.

"What time is it?"

"Don't you have a watch?"

"Noon." Ada, from the kitchen.

"They killed Danusa. the one you had up to the office yesterday."

It occurred to me that she had left my address with the doorman.

"Her husband came back and discovered her strangled. The police are suspicious, they think he killed her, figuring the timing was good because the cops would assume it was the same pervert who killed the other one. But they haven't picked him up yet. As usual, they're sucking air."

"Anything else?"

"The husband's a waiter in a restaurant downtown."

"Carlota. Poor kid."

"Right, Carlota Ferreira. How did you know?"

"She eventually gave me her real name." I told him the story of how she'd given my name to the doorman.

"You're not serious."

"Don't get excited. Are you at the office?"

"Yes."

"Call Mitry to see what his reaction is."

I opened the fridge. Yoghurt, cheese, oranges, papaya, squash, peas, broccoli.

"Berta always used to keep a bottle of white wine on ice for me."

"Yoghurt and wheat germ are better for you."

"Berta had big breasts."

"Why don't you go back to her? Drink wine and play chess all day. Should be a thrilling life. Especially with a woman who's got big breasts."

18

"Berta wasn't cross-eyed."

Ada knelt down in front of me. "Marry me and come live here."

The restaurant where Gilberto worked was one of those luncheonettes with stools around a U-shaped counter. A few waiters were eating, lunchtime was already over. Standing at the door was a muscle-bound mulatto, looking more like a mechanic than a waiter, who said, "We're closed."

"Gilberto?"

"Over there."

White-skinned, bald, with a long nose and sad eyes.

"I'd like to talk to you."

Gilberto was eating stewed beef and rice. He stuffed huge forkfuls into his mouth and chewed with his front teeth. The molars are always the first to go.

"You're Gilberto?"

"Right."

Gilberto gripped his knife tightly. Looked scared.

"I've got a .38 in my belt," I said. Toothless people believe anything you tell them.

Gilberto set down his knife. Wiped his mouth with the backs of his hands. "I'll be done in a minute."

Gilberto emptied his plate and mopped up the sauce with a piece of bread. "I didn't do it. I went to her apartment, and soon as I opened the door I could see something had happened, the living-room furniture was upside down, and there she was on the floor. We were always fighting. I don't know why I married such a kid. But I'd never want this to happen to her. Sure, Carlota threw me out, but I wasn't even mad. She had a right to, she paid the rent and everything. Six months I was unemployed, and she picked up the slack. She was just a kid. It's the other one who put ideas in her head."

He wiped his eyes with the backs of his hands, the same gesture as when he wiped his mouth.

"What other one?"

"Are you going to bust me?"

"I'm not a cop. I'd suggest you make yourself scarce for a couple of days. Find a lawyer."

"I don't have the money for a lawyer."

I took a card out of my wallet and gave it to Gilberto. "Give me a call."

The muscle-bound mulatto came toward us. "Hey, Gilberto, give me a hand with the trash."

Wexler was waiting, nervous. My partners have all been nervous. L. Waissman, the king of torts. Figenbaum. Now Wexler. Someone, someday, would pay for what they did to Figenbaum.

"The trash consisted of leftover food in two big cans, like oil drums, and it smelled nauseating. They took the trashcans out the back door, which opened onto Rua Teofilo Otoni. Several beggars were waiting. The men in the bunch shoved the women aside savagely, plunged in their arms up to the elbows and began digging out the best stuff, chicken bones, scraps of beef, any kind of half-devoured meat. Once they had filled their plastic sacks, they left. Then the women and children attacked what remained, bits of vegetables, rice, gummy pasta. Think of it. At that hour, at back doors of restaurants all over the city, other bands of the down-and-out were gathering leftovers of meals served to those who can pay."

"And Gilberto?"

"I was so absorbed watching those people make off with the trash, when I turned around he had disappeared. I could kick myself for letting him get away without telling me who the 'other one' was that he'd mentioned."

I lit up a Pimentel No. 2.

"Not in the office. Smoke a panatela."

"The rotting leftovers of an alien banquet."

"It's the way of the world."

"The world. Drums full of food. You never see anyone whistling in the street anymore, you know that? Anyway. What about Mitry?"

20

"He's worried, that much was obvious. Kept saying, I don't like it, I don't like it one bit—after making me swear I wasn't kidding. He said he never reads the crime pages. I asked him why he was worried and he just said, It's the second one, the second one. I don't trust the guy, Mandrake."

"But he's our client."

"Unfortunately. He said he'll be in Angra all week."

I lit up the panatela. Wexler and I sat and watched the smoke. After a while, I said, "Ada thinks she's a horse."

"She's as beautiful as a horse."

"You're in love with her, you perfidious kike."

"I don't know. But no matter how you look at it, she's too good for you."

"Her mother agrees with you entirely."

We sat and thought about Ada. I went to the window. The traffic on Avenida Rio Branco was beginning to get bottled up.

"A masseuse named Carlota, alias Danusa, goes to her friend's apartment, one Gisela, actually Elisa, to give our client a massage, so to speak."

"A whip, a black mask, ropes—de Sade and Masoch all rolled into one."

"Now they're dead. You think Mitry's a jinx?"

"Or a killer?"

"If Mitry was the killer he wouldn't need the mask and everything. The role of woman-strangler would be enough."

"Symbols. Symbols."

"Can you imagine Giles de Rais in a black mask?"

"He went one better—a French field marshal's uniform, and it wasn't just a costume. The sadist as patriot. Pals with Joan of Arc. But a face like Jack the Ripper's, ordinary, one of those meek little guys you see in the elevator staring at the ceiling while he waits for the door to open."

"What makes a guy strangle a virtual stranger?"

"Those girls were not strangers. Some sort of metaphysical rapport existed between them and the killer, as someone will no doubt say on the late-night roundtable on TV."

21

"How about calling Raul? He's in Homicide. Don't forget that cassette."

"It's a moment of stupefying ecstasy when the sadist reaches the zenith of feeling. Or maybe the nadir of affectivity? The apogee, the perigee, the inverted vertexes of passion. What do you say? Sadism is a micropolitical perversion."

"I say we should call Raul," said Wexler.

I called.

"Don't tell me, you're involved in this too," said Raul.

"It's a client."

"Look, Mandrake, I want to talk to you. We're handling this case now."

"So talk."

"Not on the phone. I want to see your face."

"It's as handsome as ever."

"Touch up your blush-on and let's get together."

"Raul's on the case," I told Wexler.

"Him I can believe in."

"When I was a kid I believed in Santa Claus and the Zwig Migdal, the Polish white slave traders who brought over the girls my grandfather used to screw on Conde Lage."

"Enough chitchat. Go see Raul."

"Is that any way for a Jew to talk? Chitchat, sucking air. Tsk, tsk, tsk."

3

"SHE TOLD me she couldn't live alone. What do you have to offer me? Not material things, understand. What I want is love, she said, friendship, company. Well, I was willing to offer her all the friendship in the world. So we had a few more drinks, and then she slipped up and began this business of I'm poor, you understand, all my father left me was debts. Friendship nothing. Just one more pan-handler."

"A dangerous delight."

"That's exactly what she was, sexy mouth and all. She was just out to find a willing man—willing to take orders, sign checks, turn the lights off, pay the real estate taxes, check to see the doors are locked before bed, willing to make arrangements for life insurance and the family plot at São João Batista. I fell for that once, I admit it, but never again, not this cop."

Raul and I were sitting at a sidewalk table at Amarelinho's drinking beer. Nearby, with a handful of spectators clustered around, was one of those performers who swallow fire, though street acts like this were more common on weekends, when the suckers came out to stroll. In addition to eating fire, this performer, a husky black missing most of his teeth, was a contortionist, juggler, and clown. He was wearing a pair of baggy pants and suspenders; his thick muscular chest was bare. In between acts he told jokes and imitated a gorilla scratching himself and bounding through the jungle. The idea was to joke the ragtag white spectators into feeling important: There was, after all, someone in the world beneath them—even if it was a toothless black guy imitating a half-wit monkey.

"So it's back to the single life?"

"To tell you the truth, I'm not even sure I could get it up anymore," said Raul.

We were slightly inebriated.

"That's a good idea—quit drinking, quit smoking, eat Sunday dinner with the family, be buried with the club flag wrapped around your coffin. Watch lots of television."

The fire eater climbed onto a box, flung his legs over his head, and sat doubled up with his chin resting on his pubic area.

"She was a contortionist too," said the black artiste, "and she was in this exact position, except that she was stark naked and the door was open."

"Oh, to sleep the sleep of the chaste," Raul went on, blowing smoke rings.

"That's no way to smoke a panatela," I said. "Anyway. What about the girls?"

"They worked together in a shopping center in Madureira. Only Carlota was married. Then one of them came up with the bright idea to leave that lousy life behind and make some easy money. Used to be you had to have a madam to arrange johns; now you just put an ad in the paper."

"So this guy from the interior of Minas comes wandering down the corridor"—his legs still draped around his neck, the black guy was rolling his *r*'s and making silly faces—"and when he sees the woman in this position, he runs out screaming, Help, help, there's a man in there with wild hair and a frizzy beard, and somebody's slashed his throat from top to bottom."

"I think Carlota's a prettier name than Danusa," I said.

"She must have thought Danusa was more of a turn-on. I'll tell you a secret. It wasn't just the two of them. There's a third."

(The "other one" mentioned by Gilberto?)

"This story is getting interesting."

"Interesting? You're dying of curiosity, admit it."

24

"I am."

"Name is Oswalda. I'm looking for her."

"Shouldn't be hard to find a woman named Oswalda."

"She's got an alias: Cila. And here's a picture." Raul showed me a tiny photograph.

"Can't see much."

"It's all I have. Got it from Personnel at the shopping center."

The contortionist was breathing fire and juggling torches. He touched the fire to his skin and made monkey faces.

"It was Cila's plan to set themselves up in business; she put the idea in their heads. At least that's what a girl who worked with them said. The way she tells it, Cila's the real domineering, calculating type."

"I read in the paper that the husband's a suspect."

"The paper? Aren't you always saying you never read the paper?"

The husband-as-suspect was merely a stalking-horse ("stalking-horse, that's quite an old-timer you've dug up there") on the part of the police. Gilberto couldn't have killed Carlota, because at the time of the murder he was at work, according to testimony given by what were considered to be unimpeachable witnesses. Gilberto had vanished, and Raul regretted not having picked him up right away, innocent or not. There was one more detail, which Raul could not, as yet, divulge. The two murders were connected. Human behavior is illogical, and crime is human. So. For Raul, logic was a science whose objective was to expose the principles that lie behind reasoning, principles that can be applied to test the validity of any conclusion drawn from suppositions. A trap.

"What about the doorman?"

"The doorman? He doesn't know anything. Didn't even see her leave."

The performance was still in progress. "A woman went to the priest and confessed that she'd committed adultery with her neighbor. Against your free will? asked the priest. No, she said, against the garden wall."

Raul and I went to college together. He had attended Jesuit high schools. As for me—I don't like to talk about my life to anyone.

I dropped a quarter in the contortionist's paper sack.

"A guy named Epifânio cut his wife up into little pieces, put the pieces in a suitcase, and left the house. But he couldn't manage to leave the suitcase anywhere. He had had no logical reason to kill his wife, but he had killed her. And he had every logical reason in the world to leave the suitcase in any one of the many places he found himself, but he didn't, he took a bus to São Paulo and came home by the same route, with the suitcase, and the wife inside the suitcase. Now do you understand what I mean?" asked Raul.

In college we had both gone out with the same woman, Ligia. Ligia thought I had fainted one day in the morgue. Raul knew it hadn't been a fainting spell but an attack of nausea, yet he pretended to accept Ligia's conclusion. Sette Neto had asked us to describe the internal and external lesions of a strangulation—a young girl stretched out on the aluminum autopsy table. He ran his finger along some red marks on the girl's face and asked if anyone knew what they were. Lacassagne's scarlatiniform rash, answered Raul. Sette Neto didn't like his students to answer his questions. He yanked up the girl's eyelid and asked, And this? Exophthalmos, with congestion of the conjunctiva, and mydriasis, Raul responded. If we had been medical students, maybe Sette Neto could have forgiven the audacity of the response, but law students in a medical law class shouldn't know such things. Irritated, Sette Neto stuck his finger in the dead girl's ear. Otorrhagia resulting from the rupture of the tympanic membrane, said Raul, adding that the cadaver might perhaps also present fracture of the hyoid, and fractures of the thyroid, cricoid, and arytenoid, depending on the victim's laryngeal development, which at eighteen years of age might not have reached the necessary degree of ossification. Epicranial ecchymosis and congestion of the subpleural, subpericardial, and petechiae membranes might

26

also possibly be found. Sette Neto listened to all this, more pale and more furious by the minute, and then burst into the famous paroxysm of rage that made Raul a hero. (Meanwhile, I was vomiting in the washroom.) Sette Neto suddenly began pummeling the cadaver's chest, pulling out his hair, and hers—an unforgettable spectacle. The tyrant who'd spent the whole year coolly torturing his victims had been transformed, in front of everyone, into a raving lunatic, a madman screaming incoherently. Raul and Ligia went for a beer on the corner of Mem de Sá and Lavradio. Later they married. Later still, Ligia discovered that she loved me, or that she was still in love with me. Ah, life.

The contortionist put on a faded gray shirt. A dark woman, with a face like an Indian's, was standing beside him. He picked up the money and put the tools of his trade —extinguished torches, ropes, a can of kerosene—into a bag. Now he looked sullen and threatening. He noticed that we were watching him, seemed to remember the twenty-five cents, and made a friendly gesture, thumbs up.

I pointed to a glass of beer. "Come over and have a draft with us. Your wife, too."

His name was Almir and she was Doralice. They were unemployed circus performers. Doralice had done an act with trained dogs, but the animals died of distemper. The Gran Maravilha Circus had closed. "People just stay home and watch television." They each drank two beers, ate some french fries, and excused themselves, explaining that they lived some distance away and had two children at home waiting for them.

"These prostitutes who work on their own—they can disappear without leaving a trace. Move away, change their names, dye their hair, go to Bahia, any godforsaken place. Have you heard the one about the Japanese guy and the photographer?"

"Have you heard the one about the woman hunchback?"

"Who's this client of yours?"

27

"I don't trust you. I don't trust any damn cop, much less a limp dick."

"Obstruction of justice."

"He's just a nervous john, scared to death his name will appear in the papers."

"You might as well level with me now, or later on I won't lift a finger to protect your client."

"His name is Roberto Mitry. He's worried because he left a cassette in Elisa's apartment, the first one who was killed."

"A cassette? I was in her apartment on Beira Mar and I didn't see any cassette."

It was getting dark. The heavy traffic on Rio Branco was crawling. Horns honking. The facades of the City Council Building, the Municipal Theater, and the National Library were brightly lit.

"Do you remember the eagle that used to live up there on the cornice of the National Library?" I asked. "A harpy eagle, *Harpia harpyja,* one of the largest of the Falconidae, with a white crest. That bird must have had a wing span of over two meters. He cut through the air at 280 kilometers an hour. Snatched doves in midair. I hope he got the one that shit on my head once—I was sitting right here. Could be he never had the time, the way those pigeon fanatics rushed in, pious souls demanding action. The city took action, the eagle took off. And I bet he was the last, the last in Brazil, last in the world. But pigeons and doves, those fierce fowl that artists in their ignorance chose to symbolize peace, they'll never disappear."

"I think roaches are worse," said Raul.

"Be realistic," said Wexler when I got back to the office at five P.M. "We don't have to play detective on every case that comes through the office. That's just a personal obsession of yours. We're lawyers. Our objective is not heuristic—the truth is irrelevant. What matters is defending the client. But you, you want to know everything—who's guilty, who's innocent—and most of the time it ends badly. Remember the cold-storage case? Or the woman, crazy or not crazy, who was locked away by her relatives? We still don't know—in spite of the mess you got yourself in—whether she was crazy or not. Remember? Be realistic."

"Realistic?" To me, that word was merely a justification for convenience, for the small undignified acts and omissions we're responsible for daily.

"Remember King David?" asked Wexler.

"King David defeated the Philistines, the Moabites, and made Jerusalem the capital of the Jews. I studied with Father Lepinski, remember? He used to say David was no better than a genocidal killer, an adulterer, and an imperialist."

"Lepinski? You yourself said he was mad. Listen: King David sinned and the Lord decided that as punishment his son would die in his place. On learning this, David fell prostrate on the ground praying and begging the Lord to save the child. The palace elders tried to persuade him to get up and come eat with them, but he refused. On the seventh day of David's fasting and praying, the boy died. The servants were afraid to tell him, they were terrified of his response; if the king was so desperate while the child was still alive, what would happen when he learned of his death? David, meanwhile, noticing the servants' sullen murmuring, realized what it meant. So he got up off the floor, bathed himself, and sat down at the table to eat. He knew there was absolutely nothing more he could do. Do you get the point?"

"You Jews are a strange people. And so's your God."

At that moment, Sônia came in to announce that we had a visitor.

The visitor strode into the room with the élan of someone who owns her own body, dressed in a well-cut custommade linen suit, clearly evaluating me and the furniture like someone looking over items for sale at an auction. She handed me an envelope. "The bearer of this letter," I read, "is the daughter of an old friend of mine, Vasco Japiassu. A fine fellow (descended from the Baron of Aroeira, who made history during the Regency), a man of tradition and character. I ask that you extend toward Lilibeth your kindness and patience. Your friend and colleague, Medeiros."

"Dr. Medeiros said you're a man of action, and I'm in no mood to waste time going around in circles." She paused. I waited. "Nothing's supposed to shock a lawyer, right?"

"Lawyer, policeman, priest, doctor. Sin, crime, disease."

Lilibeth stared at me, seeming to meditate on what I had said.

"It's best to get right to the point, then."

"It is."

"What would it involve for me to prosecute my husband for adultery?"

"Adultery is a crime for which prosecution depends on a private individual, rather than public authorities, to instigate legal proceedings. The offended party has by right a period of thirty days from learning of the act in which to file suit. Apprehension by the police must take place in flagrante." (Be patient, etc.)

"In flagrante?"

"Under the law in flagrante delicto means there is evidence that the person has just committed the crime. It comes from the Latin *flagrans, flagrantis:* while the crime is blazing, as it were. In terms of flames, of course, adultery in flagrante is second best only to arson."

"You mean the two of them would have to be caught when they were . . . ? Mmm . . . That's impossible."

"It's sufficient if they are discovered alone together in a bedroom, behind closed doors. But you really should think twice before instigating a suit."

"I already have."

That the crime of adultery existed at all in Brazilian law seemed superfluous, an anachronism; it should have been excised a long time ago. Someone had told me that it was to be abolished in the process of elaborating the new penal code. I almost informed my visitor of this, but Medeiros's letter of introduction stopped me. (Patience, etc.)

30

"Would you mind explaining your motives? Statistically speaking, the objective of this type of action is generally to guarantee custody of the children or to avoid responsibility for child support."

"I don't have children."

"The plaintiff, in order to ensure that the suit is not declared null and void, as well as to promote the course of the proceedings, must be present at all deliberations. A real agony, terribly unpleasant. Try to come to an agreement."

My least favorite thing in the world was explaining the law to a client.

"I don't want to come to an agreement. Are the two of them guilty, or just my husband?"

"Your husband and the woman, both are considered agents of the crime."

"It's not a woman."

I waited.

"Don't you find that unusual?" Lilibeth smiled. "To tell you the truth, if it weren't so grotesque to discover your husband in bed with another man, it would be an interesting case, don't you think?"

"Extremely," I said gravely. "Were we to go on with this, I believe it would be the first such case in Brazilian jurisprudence. Extremely enticing from the hermeneutic perspective. Adultery in flagrante, prosecuted by the wife, is rare enough in itself, even more so when the corespondent is another man. Quite extraordinary."

"But would it mean sending my husband to jail?"

"Well, no, he certainly wouldn't serve time. The law prescribes a penalty of fifteen days' to six months' confinement. If convicted, he would undoubtedly receive a suspended sentence and probation."

"It's a man's world. And this is the twentieth century."

"Any woman would receive these same allowances."

An uncomfortable silence.

"Since it's not a question of custody or disposition of possessions, but rather a desire—understandable—for retaliation on the part of an offended party, I'd suggest you forget your punitive intentions. Revenge for certain offenses brings the victim more opprobrium than vengeance. Why not simply separate—nowadays at least divorce is an option, even though full of obstacles—and be free to forget all this?"

"You're not really being much help. I was hoping you'd be able to find a solution to my problem."

I understood that the woman wanted revenge. But as a lawyer, I had to advise what I thought would be best for the client. Summoning all my patience (ah, Dr. Medeiros), I tried again to persuade her to give up the idea of a suit.

"Are you married?" asked Lilibeth.

"Well . . ."

"I understand perfectly. When a man answers that question that way, it means he has some sort of non-binding arrangement."

I too understood perfectly. Next they say I'm a womanizer. I keep my mouth shut and women provoke me. The looks Lilibeth was giving me. Damn, did I come off that available? I assumed a professorial air: "The penal process is a piece of theater, consisting of various interlinking acts, the German jurist's *verfahren*. It's also a novel describing the existent relations between the judge and the other parties. *Rechtsbeziehungen*. The Romans used the term *iudicium—iudicium est actus trium personarum: iudicis, actoris et rei*. The act with three people or, better, characters: the judge, the plaintiff, and the defendant. The protagonist, the antagonist, and the tritagonist."

"None of your fancy words impress me, I hope you realize."

"I do now."

"Do you think you could spare the time to listen to the story of my marriage?"

"Of course."

"It's a very interesting story."

"I'm all ears."

"I'll start with my wedding day. Everyone was there, that is, all the important people, executives, politicians, everyone from *society*. All the women looking fabulous. I was in no condition to notice, but my mother said she'd never attended a wedding that brought together so many elegant women. Now when I look at the pictures, I don't really have that impression—all those women wearing Borsalinos, *canotiers*, capelines, *regardé moi*, bretons, pillboxes, berets, turbans, feather headdresses, aigrettes, and other ridiculous headgear, and the dresses look like they're made out of curtains or upholstery fabric. I have to admit that I'm the one who looked beautiful, but all brides are beautiful; it's the groom who usually looks like a dope. But Val—his name is Valdomiro, but everyone calls him Val; he detests being called Valdomiro—Val doesn't look half bad in the photos, but then he wasn't your normal bridegroom, either. It's wild the presents we got, every single thing you can imagine. We almost had to rent storage space for the leftovers. In the end we sent half of it, a whole truckful, to my father's country place in Vassouras, and the other half, smaller but more expensive, we had delivered to our house, in Gávea. Notices of the wedding appeared in all the papers, not just in the social columns either, and on all the TV channels. When I saw the papers I couldn't resist a silly twinge of vanity, realizing there wasn't a woman in Brazil at that moment who didn't envy me. Just to give you an idea: Val got pretty loaded at the reception and didn't want to leave. People, friends, warned him to stop drinking; they told him all the old off-color jokes about wedding nights. We had a suite reserved at the Copacabana Palace and the following day we were leaving for New York. It was really late by the time we got to the hotel. Val fell into bed immediately and slept straight through, I couldn't wake him for anything. In the morning we went to the beach, read the notices in the papers, and went back to the hotel. I wanted to have lunch in the room, but Val insisted on going downstairs to the restaurant. He drank heavily at lunch, and the thing is he wasn't the type to drink like that, just the opposite really, he was always worrying about his health, his physique, avoiding all excesses, but

33

there he was drinking like a seasoned alcoholic, and when I objected he started swearing at me. He said, We've only been married a few hours and already you're starting to boss me around—those weren't the words he used, but it was something like that. Just to give you an idea. I should have realized right then it wasn't going to work, I should have gone back to my father's that very day, but who would have the courage to do that? Would you—after a blow-out wedding like that? So I went to New York. We stayed in an ultra-swanky suite at the Regency on Park Avenue. You know who else was staying there? Elizabeth Taylor. One day we rode the elevator down with her. She's got an awful double chin, and she's short and kind of chubby, but what eyes! Her eyes are incredible, violet— can you believe it?—she looks like a cat. Val hardly touched me while we were in New York. We went to all the musicals, we went to the opera and the ballet at Lincoln Center, took the boat trip around Manhattan, visited all, or almost all, the museums, ate at the typical places in the Village, SoHo, Little Italy, Chinatown, the whole tourist circuit. One day, after we'd been there about a week, Val took me to see one of those movies Americans call Adults Only or X-rated. I'd never seen any movies like that, and that first one, well, it was pretty intense, but it wasn't terrible. I mean, it didn't shock me really, I even got sort of excited. But the movies we saw after that were all with homosexuals, and, well, two men doing that sort of thing—I mean, that's a little different. Maybe it sounds silly, but two men doing it just as if they're a man and a woman, I'm telling you, that's hard for me to take. It was after we saw one of those movies—listen, I'm not going to leave anything out, and I never told this to anyone—that Val and I had intercourse, just that once during the entire trip. Just to give you an idea. But I was blind and didn't suspect anything, or didn't want to. All the presents were still in their boxes, or almost all of them.

"When we got back to Rio I asked Val why he had married me, and we had a terrible fight. I wanted, I want, to have children. Val hated children, at least that's what he

34

said then, that it would be better to get a dog, that I was turning into a shrew already, that all wives were bourgeois. Can you beat that?—a parasite who never worked a day in his life talking about the bourgeoisie. To sum it up, and there's really not much more to tell, that was my life with Val. Oh, I forgot to say that we had gone to bed together—once—before we got married. And now the culmination, the crowning moment of the entire story. I was out playing tennis at the country club, but it started to rain, so I came back home, and there was Val in bed messing around with a guy we knew. Exactly like in the movie. I love the smell of your cheroot. What kind is it?"

"Panatela. Short, dark."

"So what do you think of my life?"

"I've heard worse."

"I doubt that a less-sheltered woman would make the same mistake."

"Maybe."

"Maybe, what?"

"Maybe. Could be. Or not. Sometimes. Et cetera."

"You don't like me, do you?"

"If you really thought I didn't like you, you wouldn't ask."

"The person most shocked by what happened was my father. My mother, too, but not as much. But I'll tell you something that's going to surprise you. Val's a—how shall I say?—good person. If you met him, you'd like him. He's really fun, he's got a fantastic sense of humor, he's intelligent and cultured, knows everything about art, reads a lot. And he's always helping people without expecting anything back. I think it was my fault. We should have been just friends—he'd be a fantastic friend—but I wanted to make him into a husband because it's the thing now to get married, everyone's getting married, have you noticed? Val didn't want to; he agreed only on the condition that it would be an intimate ceremony with a half-dozen friends, but then my father ended up putting on that million-dollar production. To tell you the truth, I didn't mind. As long as I was getting married, why not do

35

it by the book, in church, with a wedding dress, trousseau, reception, the works. Every bride wants a church wedding with a white dress and a veil. Am I boring you?"

"More or less."

"You are the most enigmatic person I've ever met. Do you know why I asked the brand of your cheroot? So I could give you a box as a gift. Now I don't feel like it anymore. I like people who are transparent. I'm an open book, you're an introvert. Am I or am I not boring you?"

"More or less."

"You know why I'm telling you all this, all about my marriage? It's because I needed to talk to someone, anyone who would listen, and I've got to admit you're a good listener, at least. I believe that each of us creates our own destiny, so I'm not going to blame Val anymore for what happened. And by the way, you were the first person ever to suggest I should give up my ridiculous scheme, adultery in flagrante, I don't know where my head's been at lately. What kind of cigar again?"

"Panatela."

"There was something else."

"Short. Dark."

"You wouldn't believe my mother. She's always happy and always upset, but don't ask why, because I don't have the slightest idea. Neither does she. My father does everything she wants, and all she does is what she herself wants."

"What does a pillbox hat look like?"

We talked another half-hour, until Lilibeth stood up and extended me her hand. "It's panatela, right? Short, dark."

"Or Pimentel Number Two."

After she left, I asked Sônia to get Raul from Homicide on the line.

I waited for the call to go through. It was a good idea not to resist being seduced by a beautiful woman. Ada, muscular grace; Lilibeth, harmonious balance. I also thought about Berta Bronstein and Eva Cavalcanti Meier.

4

BETSY BEAN was a Siamese cat with crossed blue eyes. She had been born in the house of a Japanese named Mitsuko, where she became accustomed to eating raw sardines. When she came to live with me she learned to eat eggs, meat, vegetables, and beans with rice, Cuban style. As she got older, in addition to turning cantankerous, she had started to demand a diet consisting exclusively of fresh sardines, even going so far as to refuse the prefrozen variety, protesting insistently and vehemently the instant they were put on her plate. Because of the burden of guilt I was carrying for having taken Betsy, still pubescent, to be spayed, I made the daily trip, or sent the maid, to the outdoor market or the fish vendor downtown in search of fresh sardines. Now, barely dawn, Betsy was rudely demanding that the aluminum tray of sand located in the utility area, which served as her bathroom, be changed. When she was young, Betsy had rarely expressed herself; the only sound she made, really, was when she sharpened her claws on the carpet or upholstery. It would have required a tail-pulling or worse to get her to emit even a small meow. But now she would wail heartrendingly for no apparent reason, stopping only after I'd pick her up and shower her with kisses and attention. She had come to detest solitude, one of the great pleasures of young, healthy cats. Whenever I got home from the office, she would follow me around the house, undignified as a dog, begging for affection. And to think she had been capable —not that long ago, either—of coexisting with a lizard. (One day, during the time I was living with Berta Bronstein, I had been walking along the beach in Leblon when I saw a guy with a lizard more than a meter long, black with yellow spots shining in the sun, a nylon cord around his neck. It was love at first sight. I asked what the lizard ate. "Eggs," said the man. "He had eight of them already today before coming out to stroll." The lizard flicked its tongue momentarily, as if he still had the taste of egg in his mouth. "And to think there are people who kill animals like this to make watchbands," I said. "Not this one," said the man with a certain pride in his voice. "This one's big enough for at least a pair of shoes, plus maybe a wallet." I bent down and stroked the animal; his skin was loose, like baggy clothing, and the body inside felt as if it consisted of one extremely hard bone. "Two thousand cruzeiros," said the man. I couldn't resist. The first thing Berta said when she saw him was "I can't believe this." Later she added, "Besides which, he's got a double-reversible sex organ and a transversal cloacal slit." Ah, women. Betsy's reaction, on the other hand, had been to stop in front of the lizard in the middle of the living room, squatting, like cats do when they're enjoying themselves and resting at the same time, but she did it respectfully. Diamond Jim, as we dubbed him, was no mouse, but he certainly was a fascinating and welcome mystery. For over a month cat and lizard played and ate eggs together contentedly, until finally Diamond Jim—"It's either him or me"—was sent to a friend's vacation house in the country. Ah, women.)

"You're getting old," I said. Betsy declined to answer, but leapt agilely to the windowsill to show she wasn't as old as all that.

I had already changed the sand in her tray. Now I chopped three previously cleaned fresh sardines and put them on Betsy's freshly washed plate; then I looked for a book to read. I liked to read in bed in the morning before going to the office. That day I happened to be flipping through one of the books from my childhood, in which courage was the greatest of virtues, the courage of the romantic individualist hero—not Hegelian civic bravery,

38

but the irrational, violent, often unjust but never unprincipled bravery of my adolescent dreams. Courage is not the same thing as lack of fear. I strained to remember where I'd read that. Several books already lay open on the floor. I liked books but had no particular admiration for writers, just as I had no admiration for vintners or cigar manufacturers. A popular and distinguished novelist had once been a client of mine.

The phone rang. Wexler.

"A guy named Gilberto was here, the one who was married to Carlota. He wanted to talk to you."

"Must be an early bird. Any message?"

"He seemed scared. Said he knew where to find Cila. Try to get in here reasonably soon, okay?"

"As soon as I finish reading *Protocols of the Learned Elders of Siam*. Trying to get rid of a hangover."

"I wouldn't be surprised if you were doing just that." Wexler was in a bad mood.

After our first meeting, Gilberto had gone to São Paulo, where he worked a few days at odd jobs. He stood on the Viaduto do Chá holding up a sign—commercial advertising.

"What did the sign say?" I asked him.

"I don't know."

"A good way to hide from the police," said Wexler.

"Did you clear my name?"

"We need to have power of attorney."

While Sônia was typing the paperwork, Gilberto told his story. On returning to Rio, he had found a position as handyman in a residential building in Ipanema. At night he slept in the engine room of the elevator. At first it was awful; rich people come and go as they please, so the elevator went up and down all night long, making a constant racket. But in the end he got used to it. One day, on his day off, walking down a street in Ipanema, he saw Cila in a store window. She appeared for just a moment to take a piece of merchandise out of the display. Gilberto had started toward the door to talk with her, but then became afraid she might notify the police.

"She's mean enough."

"What would you have said to her?"

"I crossed the street and stood on the other side. I wanted to make sure it was her." But Cila didn't appear in the window again. Gilberto waited for a while, then gave up and left.

After Gilberto scrawled his name on the power of attorney form, I gave him some money and told him to stay on the job and show his face as little as possible.

The shop where Gilberto had seen Cila was on Rua Vinícius de Moraes, in a string of very pricey boutiques. The name Messina was painted on the glass door in gold letters.

"Good morning," I said, walking in. I smiled obsequiously, putting on an innocent face. The boutique was overflowing with merchandise inhabitants of the swankier neighborhoods of Rio, like the Zona Sul, considered to be "in good taste," clothing with foreign labels, decorative objects of crystal and bronze, handbags and shoes. Two young women, resolutely in fashion, stood in the corner chatting.

"I'm looking for a dress for my wife."

"Do you know her number?"

"Number?"

"What size she wears."

"She's a little on the chunky side."

The two women exchanged glances. Chunky women did not shop at Messina.

"The largest we have is forty-four."

"I think that's it. Either forty-four or eighty-eight."

They laughed. Then one said, "Come with me. I'll pick out a few things for you to look at."

I followed her into a corner. "Is Messina the name of the owner?"

"No, it's nothing, not a name, not anything. You know, like Mesbla, or Fanta."

40

"It's not a flower?"

"I told you, it's not anything."

"Then there is no Mrs. Messina."

"The owner's name is Laura. Laura Lins."

Laura Lins' employee showed me various styles. I looked them over and said I thought it would be better to come back with my wife and let her decide for herself. While I was talking with the salesgirl I had the sensation that something important was escaping me, something I couldn't put my finger on. Cila. Messina. There was something there.

As soon as I got home I called Wexler.

"S-c-y-l-l-a. Don't you see? Cila. It finally dawned on me. Scylla, the sea monster in the Strait of Messina—where the sailors had to steer a delicate course between her and the dreaded whirlpool Charybdis."

"So?"

"So why would a woman in hiding, named Cila, call her boutique Messina?"

"Not everyone's read Homer, you know," suggested Wexler. "Especially not her. Maybe somebody else came up with the name. Besides, don't forget she's changed identities. She's Laura Lins now, right?"

"Right."

We talked a little longer. I invited Wexler to have dinner with me, but he had an appointment.

I've always surrounded myself with women. When I met Berta Bronstein I maintained intimate relations with various others. Two (or three?) were married, and I saw them less frequently than the single ones. I'd go to bed with one per day. But after Berta my gynecomania began to abate, finally settling on the person of Ada. Now, arranging the books on my bookshelf and coming across a bunch that belonged to Berta—Millet, Friedan, Green, Dworkin, Steiner, Horter, Rich, authors she had insisted I read—I longed for that continuous feminine company. Ada and I had decided not to live together. Today was the day she cleaned her apartment and went to bed early. I

41

set Betsy on my lap, even though ethologic considerations were, at the moment, not foremost in my mind. She had several times let out an unfamiliar meow, the significance of which, under other circumstances, I would have felt duty-bound to investigate. But, putting her on the floor, I realized I was irritated with her, and with myself, for the way she followed me around, rubbing my legs, nibbling affectionately at my heels. I thought of Ada's solid, well-muscled legs, the shape of her body from behind. I took a shower and tried to read. "An autumn day, still, dark, and gloomy, Low, oppressive clouds." I closed the book. An epigraph: "He who has one moment to live has nothing more to conceal."

I called Raul. "What are you up to?"

"Why?"

"Come on over. I'll let you tell all your old jokes."

Raul arrived with a bottle of Periquita under his arm.

"Did you know there are areas of Brazil where Periquita is slang for cunt? That's why I chose it."

"J. M. Fonseca. Not a bad wine."

"The names those Portuguese come up with," said Raul. "Have you heard the one about the guy from Lisbon who went to the doctor, took out his cock, and asked to be examined?"

We opened the Periquita.

"Certain wines can be slugged down in long draws, without food, just a cool, inebriating drink. This one, meanwhile, would taste great with a nice platter of tripe *à la Porto*."

We drank, clicking our tongues and indulging in other non-verbal commentary.

"Did you find the cassette?" I asked.

"No," said Raul.

I grabbed an ice-cold bottle of Acácio out of the refrigerator. Raul looked at me with what seemed like affection. He was beginning to get tipsy, which made him light-hearted and generous. When I drink, I get sullen and aggressive.

"I'll tell you a secret," said Raul. "The guy made a P on

the women's faces. A thin, clean-cut *P*, in one continuous line."

"It was me. I strangled them and carved a *P* on their foreheads."

"They were choked, not strangled. In strangling the neck is constricted mechanically by means of a rope, whereas in choking it's done with the hands. And the *P* wasn't carved on their foreheads, but on their cheeks."

"Their cheeks."

We began laughing at the word cheeks, loud guffaws that ceased abruptly.

"What wine is this we're drinking?"

"I told you, Acácio."

"I'm bushed."

After Raul left, I lit up a Havana medio. A videocassette. Anything at all could be on a videocassette.

I woke to the sound of Josephina breaking dishes in the kitchen. Josephina was a young, thick-set woman, married to a chronically unemployed jealous type who hung around the house tidying things up and watching television and who, out of jealousy, beat her up occasionally. I would have liked for her to have been fitted with a pair of dentures at my expense, but feared it would upset her conjugal bliss.

I picked up the phone and dialed.

"Is Mr. Mitry there?"

"Who's calling?"

"Dr. Mandrake."

"Dr. . . . who?"

"Mandrake."

"Just a moment, please." The plinking of a music box in the background.

"Mr. Mitry isn't in."

"Could you give him a message?"

"Yes, what is it?"

"Tell Mr. Mitry that the police have the videocassette."

"What's that?"

"I'll dictate: The police have the videocassette."

"The police have the videocassette."

"Right. Thanks."

At the office, when I told Wexler about the call, he asked what I expected to come of it.

"I don't know. He told us he's in danger, but he doesn't have any enemies. I'd like to see if he'll open up."

"Berta Bronstein called."

"For me?"

"No, me. Did you know she's competing in the National Women's Chess Championship?"

I knew. And I'd decided I would go to the match that afternoon. When we lived together—Berta and I—in addition to playing chess we went to the movies a lot. The last movie we saw before we broke up was an old Vincent Price flick, *House of Usher,* maybe in the hope that the Price-Poe combination could save our relationship. Berta was tall, thin, and pale, with blue eyes and black hair. At home, after the movie, she attempted her Vincent Price imitation, modulating her voice and widening her big, expressive eyes. But she couldn't quite manage it; she was too unhappy.

The first match—Berta playing black against a thin, diminutive woman wearing rimless glasses—took place in a great hall full of spectators. Berta was playing with the same level of concentration that had exasperated me so often in the days I played reckless, headstrong chess— never, however, risking the queen. Which was what Berta was doing at that very moment: losing the queen, apparently distracted, causing her adversary to tremble with excitement as she moved her piece. But it was the Würzberg ambush. I watched Berta's triumph and then moved toward her, shouldering aside some of her more enthusiastic fans.

"Congratulations."

44

Berta started, surprised, fighting the pleasure she felt to see me. She had suffered a great deal and believed some retribution was called for.

"I challenge you to a match," I said. "I'll be black, I'll give you a two-pawn advantage, and I'll play with my right hand tied behind my back."

"You've got absolutely no class, do you know that?"

"Let's go for a cup of coffee," I said.

"What is it with you? Skinny, and green around the gills."

"Fatigue." Suddenly I felt dispirited.

"Booze," said Berta.

"I'm drinking a lot less, actually. And I've still got that unicorn you gave me." I opened my shirt and showed her the gold pendant. She pretended not to care.

We drank our coffee in silence.

"Lots of girlfriends?"

"No, nothing like that."

"How can it be? The great fornicator—abandoned by women?"

"The pure and honest truth."

"Thanks for the coffee. Bye."

I asked for another. I'm going to throw away all her letters, I thought. One was more than twenty pages long, and every paragraph started with I love you. Berta. Her hands were cold the first time we slept together. And she hadn't been able to stop talking in a high, reedy voice, like a frightened sheltered child. She had had a very strict upbringing, as a Yiddish *meydele*.

Mitry got to the office shortly before the time we'd set by phone. It was obvious that he was nervous.

"So. The police have the videocassette?"

"That's right," I said.

"I need it back. Immediately."

"We're working on it."

"I want it now, right now, do you hear me? That's what I'm paying you for."

45

"You haven't paid me anything yet."

Mitry stuck his hand in his pocket and pulled out his checkbook. "Well, how much is it? Come on. I'm losing my patience."

"I'm debating."

"You're debating?" His voice was sharp.

"I'm debating whether I should tell you to go to hell or tell you to stick your checkbook up your ass."

Mitry looked at me, astonished. He put his checkbook back into his pocket. "Please try to understand my position. I'm from an important family. When my grandmother, Laurinda Lima Prado, died earlier this year, you should have seen the cemetery."

"Tell me about it."

"What?"

"What was it like, the cemetery?"

"Ah! Well, all the important government people were there, business people, intellectuals. And all the far-flung branches of the family tree—relatives from São Paulo, Rio. The French contingent."

"The hemophiliacs."

"Them, too." Mitry smiled. He didn't want to argue with me. He wanted the videocassette. Resuming his attitude of studied boredom, he went on: "My father was a French count. He drowned in Angra. Grandmother Laurinda was a muse and a patron of the Week of 'Twenty-two. An extraordinary woman."

"The guy who killed the women wrote a *P* on their cheeks."

"A *P*? Why not a *W*?" Another smile.

"A *P*. Perhaps with the same significance."

"I don't want to pressure you, but I'd like a prognosis regarding the cassette. With money, everything is possible in this country of ours, wouldn't you say?"

"Not always."

Mitry looked at me suspiciously.

"Do you have the cassette already?" This was a very important question, as I would come to realize later, much later.

"No."

"It's of no interest to you." Mitry's voice was tense. His jaw moved up and down restlessly. Little drops of sweat appeared on his forehead.

"I don't have it. As soon as I do, I'll call you."

After I had recounted the interview with Mitry, my partner had launched into some mysterious research at the courthouse. Finally he explained what it was all about.

"I checked out Laurinda Lima Prado's will. Second Jurisdiction."

"We're lawyers, not detectives," I said, but Wexler paid no attention to the joke.

"She died without a dime. How about that? Without a dime. Her father, the distinguished Barros Lima, left her nothing but debts."

"You're a genius. But what of it?"

"Grandma Laurinda married a millionaire from São Paulo named Priscilio Prado, who went broke and shot himself in the head."

I lit up a Havana supremo.

Wexler drew a couple of neat squares on a sheet of paper.

"Here we have Barros Lima, married to Vicentina. They have two daughters, Laurinda and Maria do Socorro. Laurinda presided over the most elegant salons in Rio and São Paulo. There wasn't a writer, musician, painter, famous politician, wealthy industrialist, or agriculturalist who didn't frequent, or wish to frequent, the home of Dona Laurinda, the grand patron of Carlos Gomes' operas, literary journals, vanguardist movements. She helped to bring Serge Lifar to Brazil, the Russian Ballet, maestro Toscanini."

"Who told you all this?"

"Dona Miloca. Remember Dona Miloca?"

"No."

"One morning the city of São Paulo was appalled to learn that Priscilio Prado had shot himself in the head. They say Dona Laurinda used to take her protégés to bed while her husband played poker at the Motor Club. They

47

had three children." Three more neat squares on the paper. "This is Fernando Lima Prado, who married a woman whose name I didn't make note of. This is Maria Augusta Lima Prado, who married a French count, or perhaps a false French count, named Bernard Mitry, who thought she was rich." Two more squares. "Fernando and wife had an only son. Thales Lima Prado, cousin of our Mitry, who is the son of Maria Augusta and Bernard."

"End of story."

"No. Here's the best part. Roberto Mitry's father, the false count, abandoned his wife and small son and went back to France. Fernando, Thales' father, committed suicide. In other words, both father and grandfather did the same thing."

"Where are you headed with all this?"

"Mitry did not inherit his money. He tries to make it look like he was born rich. Why? People usually prefer to take pride in the opposite. All of a sudden a light went on in my head. I've got a theory on this. It was Mitry who strangled the women. Cila escaped, but she knows everything."

"And why did Mitry come looking for us, starting the whole game?"

"He wants the videocassette. He knows we know the gang in Homicide; therefore it should be easy for us to buy the tape and wipe his name off the map."

"What do you suppose is on the cassette?"

"I don't know."

"And why did he kill Carlota?"

"The only reason he hasn't killed Cila yet is he doesn't know where she is. The three were friends. There's a connection there, we just have to discover it."

I sat for a while smoking, thinking about what Wexler had said. Something didn't fit quite right, though I couldn't figure what it was. But I had nothing to lose by following up on my partner's tip.

A good lawyer, Wexler would say, has to have a good head and a good pair of legs.

We hailed a cab in Cinelândia and headed for Ipanema, the corner of Vinícius de Moraes and Visconde de Pirajá.

There was only one salesgirl in the store.

"Good afternoon. Remember me?"

The girl looked doubtful. Pointing to Wexler, I said, "This is Dr. Vrosmer, my colleague in the Treasury Department. We've come to take a look at the books."

"The books?" Bureaucracy wasn't her department.

"That's right, the books."

"The owner isn't here."

"When is she expected?"

"I don't know. She hasn't been in for three days."

I got only one more shred of information out of her: Ms. Lins lived somewhere on Rua General Urquiza, in Leblon.

"What's my name again?" asked Wexler, back out on the street.

"Vrosmer. Grosmer, Krosmer, a name that's hard to remember and hard to verify. Cila, from her cave on the Strait of Messina, will not be able to ascertain whether or not we are truly from Treasury, Dr. Prosmer."

When I got home, I called Felipão, a private detective who lived in Fátima. "Her name is Cila, or Oswalda. She was a hooker, fake masseuse, now owns a boutique called Messina on Vinícius de Moraes. Current alias is Laura Lins. Bleaches her hair. Lives on General Urquiza, in Leblon. I want you to get me the complete address."

"No problem," said Felipão.

I was standing at the window in my office looking out at Praça Floriano when Felipão called. It was early, and the people who frequented the square hadn't yet emerged from their dens—kids who sold peanuts, shoeshine boys, thugs, the guy who ate glass, the toothless black acrobat, the old magician dressed in black.

"I located the lady in question. General Urquiza forty-two. The block closest to the beach. New building. Laura Lins. Not home, though. The doorman thinks she's away, but the maid says when she left for a day off Saturday afternoon her employer didn't say anything about a trip. The door between the maid's quarters and the rest of the apartment is locked, and whenever Dona Laura goes away she leaves it open for the maid to feed the fish. The aquarium's in the living room. That's the scoop. Anything else?"

"What's the maid's name?"

"Maria de Fátima. Fafá. From Paraíba. I told her I was working for a lawyer and gave her your name."

"Well done, Felipão. Send me the bill."

I jumped in a taxi, straightened my tie, and lit up a Havana medio. Laura Lins—quite a musical name she'd invented. I imagined what she'd look like—smooth skin over firm, warm flesh—and felt the beginning of an erection. Worse than a sickness.

Behind an unbreakable glass door, the doorman at the building on General Urquiza raised his receiver, gestured for me to pick up the telephone there outside, and asked which of the residents I wanted to speak with. Through the glass I could see a sofa with two cushions, an enormous, colorful wall-hanging, and a table with the apparatus for the intercom.

"Ms. Laura Lins."

"She's out of town."

"Then I'd like to talk with the maid. I'm an attorney."

"Just a moment." The doorman cut me off. He pushed some buttons on the panel in front of him and spoke into the phone. Plugged me back in again and told me to wait at the service door, around the side, near the entrance to the garage. At the garage door there was another doorman, as unsociable as the first. "She's on her way down," he said. The garage door opened vertically, swinging up to allow a limousine to emerge; a middle-aged man was reading a newspaper in the back seat. A guard stared at me suspiciously from inside the garage, then pressed a button to close the door. Soon afterward Fafá appeared, stepping out of a smaller door built into the large one. She was short, dark, young, and looked worried.

"You wanted to talk to me?"

50

"I'm not sure if my assistant spoke with you, but some revenue inspectors have levied a fine on Dona Laura's store and I need to speak with her to know what to do. We're talking about substantial fines, here, understand?" Fafá, who clearly hadn't understood anything I'd said, nodded affirmatively. "Do you know where she is?"

"No, I have no idea. I'm real worried, the fish must have died already." She glanced from one side to the other, and lowered her voice. "Last night I had a dream."

"A dream?"

"Dona Laura always locks the door at night, but as soon as she wakes up she lets me in. Whenever she goes away, she lets me know. She leaves a list of things for me to do —feed the fish, water the plants, open the windows so they can breathe, make sure all the doors are locked up tight, don't talk to strangers." At that, she stopped talking.

"I'm not a stranger. I'm her lawyer. What was the dream?" I asked affably.

"I dreamed that Dona Laura was in her room, she was dead. I guess that's silly."

"I don't know. Dreams often have a lot of truth to them. Maybe we should talk to one of her friends."

"She doesn't have any friends, or relatives. She's alone in the world."

"Okay, you go back upstairs and wait. I think I'd better contact the police."

Leaving the frightened girl, I went and called Wexler from a pay phone next to the Marina Hotel, around the corner on Rua Bartolomeu Mitre. Wexler had crossed paths with the district chief of police in college.

"Locate Licurgo and tell him I'm on my way to pay him a visit," I asked Wexler.

The station was on Afrânio de Melo Franco, so I walked. Licurgo was waiting for me. Wexler commanded a fair amount of respect from policemen, court clerks, prosecutors, and judges.

"And what makes you think your client is dead?"

"There are fish in the aquarium and she wouldn't let them starve to death."

"And you think that's sufficient reason for us to break down the door to her apartment?"

"I do."

"A cop is a mixture of scientist, psychologist, and artist," said Licurgo, giving me a long look that meant Don't try to put one over on me, I'm all three. And more.

"I believe it," I said, hiding my irritation. The only cop I argued with was Raul. Any guy, to be a cop, had to be a little, if not a lot, out of his mind. I also didn't argue with dentists or public functionaries behind grates, but that was for other reasons.

"You came here with a conjecture. What is it?"

"An artistic premonition," I said.

"You're not playing with me, are you?" Licurgo paused. "That would be a mistake."

"Of course it would. Just as it would be a mistake if we didn't break down the door to that apartment."

Licurgo studied me again. Then stood up unexpectedly. "Let's go."

We were accompanied to the front door of Laura Lins' apartment by a detective carrying a pair of pliers, as well as by the now-respectful doorman.

"This'll be a snap." The detective fitted the mandibles of his pliers around the cylinder of the lock and yanked. "Now just give a tug on the bolt and presto. They spend a fortune on these apartments and put in a piece of junk for a lock. Then they're amazed when somebody breaks in."

"You wait downstairs," Licurgo ordered the doorman.

We walked through the doorway into a vestibule. A spotlight shone down from the ceiling on a painting facing the door. I detected a slight odor, like the superficial layer of a denser and more enveloping fragrance. Daylight filtered into the living room through smoked glass in aluminum frames. The room had been decorated by a professional. Furniture, paintings, lamps, and carpets created the type of luxurious modern ambiance that would be obsolete as soon as something new was in vogue. "Playtime for parvenus in an underdeveloped country," I said. "What?" asked Licurgo, in a low voice. "The decor," I whispered back. Colorful dead fish floated in an aquarium nearly two meters wide; one lone black-striped survivor, larger than the others, swam blithely behind the glass. The aquarium was near the window in the L-shaped living room. An open doorway showed a slice of pantry, bright-colored tiles; we passed through the other door and into a small sitting room with a sofa, two armchairs, an enormous television (on, no sound) and a coffee table with magazines—*Amiga, Status, Donald Duck.* Two doorways, one to a bedroom and bathroom and the other a hallway. The bedroom contained only a double bed and appeared not to be in regular use. Licurgo and the detective were tiptoeing around cautiously, as if delicate clues lay on the floor and might be destroyed by their footsteps. I unconsciously adopted the same way of walking. Licurgo and the detective exchanged looks silently. From the sitting room we entered a hallway filled with reproductions of erotic Japanese paintings, at the end of which was a door. By now the odor was overwhelming, and then we saw the cause. The bloated body of a woman was fallen across the bed; her swollen face looked like a grotesque doll's, its tongue sticking out in a horrible grimace. For some time we contemplated the body. The bedclothes were strewn about. A bedside lamp had fallen onto the floor. The doors of a large built-in closet, which took up one whole wall, were open, revealing a profusion of clothes, shoes, belts, handbags, and scarves—a wild combination of colors and shapes on hangers and fixtures. The closet gave off the pleasing smell of fine clothing, leather, the smell of clean new things, as opposed to the nauseating odor coming from the bed. "She would've had to live an awful long time to wear all this stuff," said the detective. "If my wife saw this closet, she'd die of envy." I felt like throwing up. "Don't touch anything," said Licurgo. "I'm going to want a very thorough going-over." Licurgo tugged my arm and we left the room, followed by the detective, who was instructed to make the call to Forensics from the desk downstairs, since there might be fingerprints on the telephone in the apartment. I sat down on the couch with Licurgo. "You're not hiding anything from me, are you?" asked the chief.

"Would it be all right if I got a pan from the kitchen?" I asked.

"What the hell do you want a pan for?"

"To take the dead fish out of the aquarium."

"No, I don't want you messing with anything."

"Look, Licurgo, I was the one who discovered the crime."

"So what? All that does is create problems for me."

"You see that black fish? He's hung on all this time, who knows if he'll even last a couple more minutes. Just let me get rid of the dead ones and give him a little food."

"The dead fish stay where they are. They'll have to be examined."

"What for? They're not murder victims."

"You're beginning to annoy me."

"All I want to do is save one poor fish."

In the kitchen Licurgo found a container with the label "Hipromin—Staple Flake Food for Tropical Fish," and he littered the surface of the tank with the slightly grainy powder that was inside. The fish ate, making quick sallies, gulping greedily at the food.

"A woman dead in the back room and here we are worried about some damn fish. And fish bring bad luck, to boot."

Licurgo looked at the pan full of dead fish.

"Everything brings bad luck," I said. "Let's get out of here. I can't take the smell."

Downstairs, Licurgo interrogated the doorman.

"Did Dona Laura have many visitors?"

"Just two people, really. A man and a woman. Sometimes they didn't show up for weeks."

"They came together?"

"Not that I remember."

The doorman couldn't manage to describe the visitors.

54

The man wasn't old but he wasn't really young, either. Medium height, I guess. Build? Not really thin or fat.

"What about the woman?"

The same thing. Neither this nor that.

"People don't know how to see," said Licurgo, unconcerned with the doorman, who was listening. "They just don't observe the world around them, they're complete zombies. There are no two people alike, no two noses alike in the world, but do you think witnesses understand that? It's tough being a cop."

The men from Forensics were a long time coming. When Licurgo and the doorman took them upstairs, I discovered I had been locked in the glass booth. My first reaction was to pound on the elevator button, but then I examined where I was. Behind a marble wall I found a series of cubbyholes marked with apartment numbers. In box C-01 was a letter, which I slipped in my pocket.

When the doorman returned I said, "You left me locked up in here."

"Sorry," he said dryly. "I didn't realize it till I got upstairs."

As soon as I got to the office, I went into Wexler's office, closed the door behind me, and opened the letter.

5

LAURA MY LOVE,

I don't agree that our relationship is cooling off as you say it
is. This has been an impossible week, you have to understand.
Bebel has been sick and when Bebel gets sick she's so clutchy
she won't let me out of her sight, and you know her father is
exactly no help at all, he has only two things on his mind:
politics and money. I love you, I love you like I did the very first
day, with the same devotion. I miss your body, I want to kiss
you, I want to hear your voice, I want to know how things are
at the boutique, I want to be near you, I want to cook you that
Shrimp Bobó you like so much, I want to lie beside you, close to
you, and whisper in your ear how I love you. There's something
wrong with your telephone again. I called yesterday and today
all day too but no answer. As soon as Bebel's feeling better I'll
be there with all the caresses in the world. We'll dance all night
at L. What do you say?

Your Rosinha

The name and address on the envelope: Rosa Leitão,
Avenida Sernambetiba.

Wexler listened without saying a word. Then: "The bi-
sexuality of prostitutes. Okay, it was mailed at the post
office in Barra da Tijuca. The handwriting suggests a reasonably educated person. The style is the idiotic, sugary
kind typical of love letters."

I thought of my first girlfriend, an upstairs neighbor
when we lived on Rua Evaristo da Veiga, almost on the
corner of Treze de Maio (I used to lean over the terrace
rail and spit on the heads of the people going by all decked

56

out on their way to the Municipal Theater), a tall dark girl, with thick curly hair like a mass of frizzled black vines trailing down to her shoulders; she looked like a beautiful leafy tree. We were thirteen. I lay awake nights thinking about her. I started early loving women.

"You want me to call Raul and fill him in?"

"Please. I've got to go make a deposition."

Licurgo wasn't in his office. The clerk took down my statement.

"That the deponent was contacted by Oswalda de Souza, then going by the name Laura Lins, to act on her behalf regarding a court action involving the victim's commercial activities, as she claimed to have been wrongly fined by inspectors from the State Treasury Department; that the deponent, meanwhile, having found no evidence of a fiscal action registered against his client, with whom he had made an appointment, suspected that something out of the ordinary had occurred and communicated this to the police; that, accompanied by Police Chief Licurgo and a detective whose name he does not recall, the deponent entered the victim's apartment and found body of same; that he has no knowledge of any information which might aid in explaining her demise; and had nothing else to say, nor was asked."

Toward the end of the day Wexler invited me to have dinner with him.

"They're having a dance across the street there, in the square."

"Sorry, my card is full up. Besides, I make a point never to dance with balding lawyers."

We had dinner at the Cosmopolita on Visconde de Maranguape. Even before deciding what to eat, we asked for a bottle of Terras Altas.

"I'm up to my ears in work," said Wexler. "This week alone four new clients walked in off the street, and you don't want to hear about it. Do you think that's fair?"

"No."

"You're obsessed, you're like a crazy man. All you think about is this case with the masseuses. Or is it a woman? Lilibeth?"

We sat in silence. The wine began to take effect.

"Okay. Do what you want," said Wexler.

A couple entered the restaurant and the woman sat down facing me. She slipped a hand to the back of her neck, lifting free the hair at her collar, a sensual gesture that seemed to release the heat radiating from inside her body. She was beautiful, though before long I lost interest.

It was not yet eight A.M., and Raul, without ceremony, sat down on the edge of the bed—Josephina had let him in—where I was still reclining, a book in my hands.

"I just don't trust people with dogs. Have you noticed the way they treat them—submissive, slobbering animals—ordering them around all the time and teaching them sadistic tricks? Makes me want to vomit."

"And you came all the way over here to sit at my bedside and deliver an anti-canine diatribe?"

"No. Rosa has vanished."

"Rosa who?"

"Laura Lins' girlfriend. As soon as Wexler called me I got right on it, but she disappeared several days ago. We're investigating—on the hush-hush. She left all her jewelry at home, with the exception of the solid gold Cartier she never takes off her wrist. The Mercedes sports car is in the garage. The commissioner's claimed this one as his baby. He called me in to ask me what I was doing at Dr. Leitão's apartment."

"You went over there?"

"Sure. Avenida Sernambetiba. Not only wouldn't he see me, but he called the chief of security, who's a friend of his. I told the commissioner and his boys that there's a possibility Rosa's disappearance is connected to Cila's murder. They told me to stay out of it; for now, they said, but it sounded to me an awful lot like for good. Guess I've been sidelined. But they'll learn not to fuck with me. Remember the letter you pocketed—we'll dance all night at L.? You know what L. is?"

"No—what?" I said, getting up and heading to the bathroom to brush my teeth. Raul followed me.

"One Brazilian pees, they all pee," said Raul. We urinated simultaneously, avoiding looking at each other's penis.

"L. is for Lesbos, the gay nightclub."

"Did you check out whether Mitry's the guy who frequented Cila's apartment?"

"It's not him. I showed the doorman his picture. He was dead sure. Another tidbit: Mitry's got a little trip lined up, to Europe and the U.S. We've got an informant in Mitry Commercial Enterprises. But getting back to Lesbos—I've got to take you up there. You'd expect it to be red brocade, complete with mirrors, revolving spotlights, and strobes, right? Not even close. The place is downright suave—all beige and yellow with people slow-dancing, like in the old days, soul-kissing to baroque adagios. I've got to admit, it was kind of nice."

I thought of Ada, her favorite sexual fantasy: to kiss another woman on the mouth, on the breasts.

"And do they know at Lesbos that Rosa's the wife of Gonzaga Leitão, president of the Brazilian Association of Commerce and Exportation, congressional representative, et cetera, et cetera?"

"Sure, but that's no problem. Lesbos is a private club, very high society."

"Classical adagios."

"Albinoni. Tum, tararum, tum tum. I'm telling you, it makes you want to put your arms around one of them and just sway back and forth. They say lesbians are terrific, you know. Come to think of it, you're the one who's had five thousand women, you should be able to set me straight on that."

"Were there any men there?"

"A few. Very smooth aristocratic types."

"And you there, looking like a cop. Didn't that cause a stir?"

"I was dressed as a waiter. Iron Nose, the owner of the place, owes me a few favors."

That was the first time I heard of José Zakkai, or Iron Nose, as he was called.

Raul had paid him a visit downtown in one of the offices he occupied, where Iron Nose received him from behind an enormous desk. "I see you're moving up in life, eh, Nose?" Raul had said. The other responded: "It all comes down to knowing how much dough to throw in the pot. As Plato, my favorite philosopher, says, there's a sucker born every minute. Cradles of shit, cradles of gold, there's jerks rocked to sleep in 'em both."

"He knows every swindle in the book, high-life and low-life. I asked him if he could fill me in on Mitry. He said he'd think about it, as if he knew something. That's Iron Nose."

"Two dead prostitutes. Also, an ex-prostitute, owner of a boutique. A fourth woman vanished. Nothing that's going to catch the world's interest for too long," I said, picking up the phone. "Graham Bell may not have been as important a genius as the woman who invented goulash, but there's no way to deny that the telephone's— Hello, Mrs. Rosa Leitão, please? No? Who am I speaking with? Her daughter? This is attorney L. Wexler, yes, Wexler, just like the cinematographer. Exactly. I have a very important matter to discuss with her. Yes, please ask her to call me."

"I prefer beef stew," said Raul.

"Bright girl. *Who's Afraid of Virginia Woolf?* Black and white is harder. That's an ancient flick."

I was a silent and withdrawn—though happy and confident—child and adolescent who liked to curl up alone in a corner and read. When I announced I was going to law school, friends and relatives alike thought my decision absurd; no one could imagine me delivering objections and rebuttals in front of a jury or even arguing a simple settlement exadversum. In college I did extremely well in some subjects, such as Introduction to Jurisprudence, Forensic Jurisprudence, Criminal Law, and Criminal Procedure; and I finished second in my class. Those days, in contact for the first time with the philosophers of law and the great masters of criminal law, I believed I wanted to study them my whole life.

Just as I had defied the expectations of others and became first a good student and then a good lawyer, no one expected I would become such an avid seducer of women. How could this possibly happen to a boy who had listened enraptured to the inspiring words of Professor Father Lepinski expounding against the sin of the libido? This priest (who was also a vegetarian, like the followers of Mani, "The Ambassador of Light") preached chastity and asceticism with all its oppressive abstinences. "It is good for a man not to touch a woman," Lepinski cited from St. Paul's Epistle to the Corinthians. Marriage was acceptable (even to St. Paul), since it was "a way to avoid lechery." "But, but, but"—and this objection was pronounced with a Polish accent and increasing intensity, like the lashes of a whip constantly anticipating a terrible revelation—"but even in marriage, the sexual act is tainted with sin." (St. Augustine, who would think it?) It was woman who led man to sin, explained Lepinski. Hadn't it been that way since Eve, the temptress, the aggressive and sensual root of all Evil? "Every woman should blush to contemplate the fact that she is a woman," inveighed the priest with scorn, quoting his favorite theologian, Clement of Alexandria. Concupiscence destroyed Sodom, Gomorrah, Egypt, Greece, Rome, and the United States. But, as far as I could see, in spite of the world's efforts to the contrary, people were changing, and yet they were not changing more only because they were repressed; those who were changing lived in fear of being called disloyal, incoherent/inconsistent, treacherous. Of this I was sure, and I wasn't going to let anyone tell me what to be or do. I was no longer interested in law (another change), nor was my greatest pleasure taking a woman to bed. How long would this last? I knew it wasn't that I'd become a

61

morally better person than I'd been during the period when I was copulating, alternately, with eight different women. The fact was, I still liked women—perhaps even more—but I had changed.

I found Wexler standing at the window in his office. It had rained the night before; everything appeared luminous in the crisp air: the trees in Flamengo Park, the dark sea-blue of the bay, the fountain suddenly surrounded by open space after the demolition of Monroe Palace, where the Senate had convened when Rio was the nation's capital. I contemplated the view to my left, a mass of buildings lining both sides of Avenida Rio Branco, an endless concrete canyon.

"How are things going?" I asked.

There were a million things to be done, clients to attend to, appeals and briefs to be written, appearances in court.

As if I had read in Wexler's face what was going through his head, I said, "You've been a good friend to me, a brother. You carry the whole weight of the office on your shoulders, like the good, honest, indefatigable Jew you are."

"Ummm," was Wexler's answer.

"You're my best friend."

"You don't have friends, plural. I'm the only one."

"Figenbaum was my friend."

"Figenbaum is dead."

"A group of people were shipwrecked and decided to put saltwater on their cracked lips, hoping to reduce the fever that was wasting them, but it only made them thirstier and eventually they were compelled to find relief by drinking their own urine."

"Is that so?" Wexler didn't seem terribly interested in my dream.

"A lottery had been instituted to sort out who would have to do the killing and who would have to die and be eaten by the others. I put my name in. And you know which I was picked for?"

At that moment we heard a throat being cleared behind us.

"The door was open," said the young woman standing in the middle of the room. She was short, with thick legs and a round face, like a large intelligent baby. Her pocketbook was so big it looked like a suitcase.

"The door was open," she said again.

"Are you looking for someone?" asked Wexler.

"My name is Bebel Leitão. Maria Isabel Marques da Costa Leitão." She was nervous and spoke in an almost inaudible voice. "I'm Rosa Leitão's daughter. A Dr. Wexler called the house and left a message for my mother."

"Please, have a seat," I said, forewarning my partner with a look. "This is Dr. Wexler."

Her fingers trembling, Bebel Leitão took a pack of cigarettes out of her purse. She continued to dig around in her bag with one hand while the other brushed away the hair that kept falling across her face. "Does anyone have a match?" She looked forlorn.

Wexler lit her cigarette. She inhaled deeply.

"Would it bother you if I smoked a cigar?"

"Bother me? Why should it bother me?"

I lit a small dark panatela. No luck anymore finding Pimentel No. 2, which was the only one I liked to smoke on an empty stomach.

We waited.

Bebel snuffled and cleared her throat, lighting a second cigarette from the first. She was on the verge of tears. Wexler took her by the arm and led her to the window.

"Have you ever seen a prettier day? Only in Rio. See that fountain at the back of the park? It came from France, the whole thing, over a century ago."

Bebel snuffled, unimpressed.

"The man from the police said that lots of people disappear every day and are never heard from again. What did you want with my mother?"

"Well, a woman was murdered, a client of ours, and it could be your mother knows something about it," I said.

We waited.

Far off, out the window, the cable car slowly climbed the side of Urca, heading for Sugarloaf Mountain. Outside

63

the Odeon Theater a line was forming for the next show-ing of *Orgy of the Perverts*—"a genuinely pornographic film."

"I think I know where she is," said Bebel finally. "I found the letters that woman wrote her. I tore them up and threw them in the garbage."

The cable car disappeared into the wheelhouse on top of Urca, the halfway mark.

"That woman had a country place in Itaipava. I'll bet that's where my mother is. Hiding out. She's not the per-son she pretends to be. Hiding from Daddy, from me."

"Where in Itaipava?"

"Arcas Highway. I don't know the number; I've never been there. I don't even know what the house looks like, but she refers to it in one of the letters."

I knew the area. Arcas Highway stretched on for miles; it would be tough to locate the house without a number. The letters Bebel had destroyed talked about skinny-dip-ping in the pool, torrid embraces in front of the fireplace, but she had been too embarrassed to tell us that; she merely referred to the existence of the pool and the fire-place. All the houses in that neighborhood, or almost all of them, had a pool and a fireplace and other creature comforts.

"Have either of you read *Portrait of a Marriage?*"

"No, we're members of B.A., Bachelors Anonymous."

Bebel gave Wexler a look that made it clear his joke had had the opposite effect from what he had intended.

"One of you could take me, ummm . . . I mean go there with me."

"How old are you?" I asked. Wexler looked at me suspi-ciously: Just what does Mandrake mean by that question? The prurient partner. All I wanted to know was whether Bebel had a driver's license.

"Of course I do. Want to see? Eighteen, and I've been driving since fourteen."

"You're going to waste a whole day on this?" Wexler's voice took on the mixture of silliness and indulgence adults use when talking with children. "We"—a glance in my direction—"have a lot to do here. A lot of work."

"What?" Bebel seemed not to understand what Wexler was saying.

"Clients," I said. "My partner was just saying to me, when you walked in, that our clients need more attention."

"And I'm not official business?" asked Bebel.

"No. And since your mother doesn't want to see anyone, as you yourself suggested, then why not just leave her in peace?" said Wexler.

"There are dozens of houses on Arcas Highway," said I.

Bebel's lower lip shifted forward even more prominently. She snuffled but didn't cry.

"I'll pay, I'll hire you." It was practically a whisper.

"She'll pay, Wexler." We chuckled discreetly.

"Ai, ai," murmured Wexler, shaking his head the way Jews do when they've resigned themselves to some new misfortune.

Bebel's car was in the Menezes Cortes parking garage. We walked the odd-number side of Rio Branco to Rua São José. When we came to McDonald's, Bebel announced that she was hungry. Then, after a cheeseburger and a Coke: "Do we have time for an order of french fries?"

She ate them as we walked. Her car, a little Fiat, was on the fourth floor of the empty garage. Apparently frightened, Bebel leaned closer to me, her arm and side grazing mine.

I had to admit right off, Bebel was a good driver. Women are better drivers than men, anyway. When we got to Avenida Brasil, she put a disco tape on the cassette player. "I'm out of cigarettes," she said. We stopped at a bar, I hopped out and bought her two packs of Hollywoods. "I'm smoking an awful lot. Do you think I'll get cancer?"

"Probably."

"But it takes a while, right?"

"Maybe."

"I don't care. I don't want to live past thirty. Old people are awful, I want to die young."

I'd heard that one before, over and over. "People who

talk that way, when they get to seventy are still clinging to life like leeches. You're such a careful driver, you probably won't get killed in an accident, so I'd say it's a pretty sure bet you'll die of a lovely cancer."

"I'll kill myself first."

"I know a suicidal face when I see one. They're skinnier than you."

"I'm on a diet," said Bebel with a straight face.

"Cheeseburger, Coca-Cola, and french fries?"

"That was just today," she said, without much conviction.

I watched her heavy tan thighs and smooth knees as they moved with the shifting of the gears. I felt an urge to embrace her and pictured her breasts and the part of her belly around the navel. The beginning of an erection, soon controlled. Worse than a sickness.

"Do you believe in the evil eye?" asked Bebel. Every year on December thirty-first she and her mother tossed flowers into the ocean in front of the house as an offering to Iemanjá, the goddess of the sea. Twice a year they went to a macumba priest for the ritual "closing of the body," to protect them from harm. Bebel wore a gold and ivory *figa*, a good luck charm, around her neck. "Pretty, isn't it?" The *figa* was nestled between her swelling, luxurious breasts. "The one day I went out without it, I broke my leg, can you believe it?"

"I believe it."

"I was on my bike, stopped at an intersection, and this guy on the sidewalk kept staring at me. I had shorts on, but he wasn't looking at my legs or my bum, you know, like men do, but right in my eyes, as if he was trying to tear them out. It was really scary, he gave me the creeps. I closed my eyes and started pedaling. I just wanted to get out of there fast, away from that guy. I got hit by a car and broke my leg."

"Couldn't you just turn your head and not look at him? Did you have to close your eyes?"

"No, I really had to."

Bebel's eyes were brown, bright, and shining. Eighteen years old, I mused.

"I liked the way you associated one Wexler with the other."

"I'm addicted to movies. Especially the cinematography."

"Who did *Citizen Kane?*"

"Too easy."

"So tell me."

"Gregg Toland."

"How about *The Heart Is a Lonely Hunter?*"

Bebel lit a cigarette with the lighter from the dash. Loaded up another cassette.

"Give me a hint."

"Body and Soul."

"Give me the first letter."

"H."

"H. . . . H. . . ."

"You know everything, huh."

"Give me another movie, one of his movies."

"Rose Tattoo."

"James Wong Howe. Whew, I don't know why it took me so long."

We started our investigative work even before we got to Arcas Highway. First at the little supermarket in the middle of the village. Then a drugstore, a gas station, bicycle shop, corner grocery, bar, and a man who rented horses. No one gave us any useful information. There were lots of houses with pools and middle-aged women who dressed (and acted) like breezy, independent teenagers.

"When I first came here there were just three little farms on this road—barely passable, it was in such bad shape. Now look at the houses," said the man in the local bakery.

"Must be good for business, though,"

"Only in the summertime. This time of year it's not so hot. They bring everything from the city."

"What next?" said Bebel.

The first house on the street was closed, the owners in Rio; but merely waiting for the caretaker to open up, listen

67

to our questions, and answer took an incredible amount of time. The same thing with most of the other houses. By the time we reached the halfway point it was dark; night had fallen suddenly, as if day were a light switched off by a circuit breaker. We stood at the gate of a large house on a rise, maybe a hundred meters from the road. No doorbell. Bebel shouted a few times but got no response. A light was shining inside the house, but that didn't necessarily mean there was anyone home, since it was common for people to leave a light on to scare off potential thieves. There had been a rash of burglaries lately in the summer resort areas. Out back we could see a smaller house, quite brightly lit, probably the caretaker's. We decided to open the gate and walk on in, yelling "Anybody home?" the way they do in the country.

The dog attacked me without a warning bark, appearing all of a sudden out of the darkness—"silent as a ghost," Bebel said later—and did not manage to wound me seriously only because the caretaker, having switched on the outside lights just in the nick of time, saw that we weren't prowlers and called him off. It was not much more than a scratch, but even so I was worried about getting rabies (I have a hypochondriac side), and demanded to see the dog's certificate of vaccination. When it was all over—the caretaker ministered to my arm with merthiolate and bandages—it was almost nine P.M. and we didn't have much energy for continuing our search. Bebel suggested we spend the night in a hotel in Petrópolis and go on with the investigation the following morning.

The idea struck me as absurd. I told her we were close enough to Rio to go home and come back the next day. Bebel argued that if we returned to Rio for the night it was unlikely we'd ever continue our search in Itaipava. It was a protracted conversation. Finally, Bebel confessed that she had left home and had no intention of going back; if we went to Rio she would have nowhere to stay. None of these arguments convinced me, but without having any idea why, I ended up agreeing with her.

"A double?" asked the man in the hotel, smelling a tip when he saw no luggage. A fat, wily rodent of a man, with minuscule, malicious eyes; in my profession I was plenty familiar with the type. I tossed my Bar Association I.D. onto the counter. He waved it away as if he wasn't interested. "Two singles," I said. The desk clerk turned his back to us—You don't want a double, that's your problem —and shoved two keys in my direction.

They were adjoining rooms. I tipped the kid who had insisted on carrying Bebel's handbag, and he disappeared. We avoided looking at each other. I handed her the bag.

"Lock your door and turn the bolt," I said.

"I'm not sleepy," said Bebel, poised at the door to her room.

"Lie down and sleep will come."

I waited until I heard the bolt slide and only then went into my own room. The bite on my arm was throbbing. Maybe I should see a doctor. I washed my face and rinsed my mouth with cold water (no toothbrush). It occurred to me that we hadn't eaten dinner. I lay down. Too hungry to sleep. Someone knocking on the door.

"Who's there?"

"It's me."

I opened the door. "What do you want?"

"I want to talk to you."

"We'll talk in the morning."

"I'm not sleepy."

"Like I said, lie down and sleep will come."

Bebel stared at the floor.

"Let me in." She pushed open the door and entered. (I remembered the girl who was put away in an asylum for staring at the wall.) I turned on the light and saw that Bebel was wearing a slinky floor-length silk nightgown. Shimmering mother-of-pearl.

"I left my cigarettes in my room."

"Good idea, go back there and smoke. I'm dead tired."

"Do you have a girlfriend?" Bebel looked me straight in the eye.

"Yes. Her name is Ada."

"What does she look like?"

"She's got big eyes and her ribs stick out."

"You really like her?"

(All she does is stare at the wall all day long and she's not eating right, the parents told the doctor. An energetic, hard-working family. She stares at the wall? If it had been the TV nobody would have cared, but the wall! I'm afraid it's serious, said the doctor. Shock treatments began the day after she was hospitalized.)

Bebel was standing right up close to me now, a provocation: "You think it would be wrong?"

"Well, at least you've got a driver's license," I joked. Nervous.

"Then it's okay. Right?"

I didn't answer. I already knew what was going to happen. My heart beat faster.

"Lie down over here," said Bebel, pulling me to the edge of the bed.

"No, my arm hurts."

"I know very well your arm's just fine," said Bebel.

"Instantaneous intimacy. Nescafé."

"It's not instantaneous. We've known each other for quite a while already. At least that's the way I feel."

"Orange juice concentrate."

"You're delirious," said Bebel, pulling my head down to meet her breasts. She was no longer the frightened little girl. Bebel was claiming her latent, but absolute, sexual superiority, mixed with maternal instinct, I thought, my nose pressed against the fabric that covered those young breasts. My mouth was beginning to water.

"Did you take a shower?"

"Uh-huh."

"Where did the nightgown come from?"

"My bag. You like it?"

"You knew this was going to happen?"

"Not this exactly."

70

Bebel's nipples were erect, and she kissed me with her tongue thrust out of her mouth as if she was having her throat examined. Tongue rigid. But that didn't lessen my desire.

"What do you like to do in bed?"

"You teach me. Want me to take off my nightgown?"

"We've got time. I like to talk . . ."

"So talk."

". . . to couple physical and verbal stimuli."

"So couple."

We spent a lighthearted and rhetorical evening together. But by morning, which dawned cold and damp (typical of Petrópolis), the charm had worn off. I felt like going my way, being alone. It's always foolish to act on transitory lascivious impulses. If only women could take things more lightly. But, stupid me, I'd been taking life too seriously, also. And when Bebel asked if I liked her, I gave the conventional yes answer. And then made a speech on the marvels of sex with love. It was a familiar situation—waking up beside a woman I barely knew and launching into the day's routine, making new plans to meet or inventing excuses not to. I felt lousy.

"Are you in the mood?" (Love purifies sex.)

"In the mood for what?"

"You know." Still in bed, still without coffee.

"Say it."

"It turns you on, doesn't it? Talking about it."

"Uh-huh. So talk."

"Are you in the mood to . . ."

"Uh-huh. Elaborate, with more feeling."

"Are you in the mood to fuck me?"

"What else?"

"To stick your big prick in my cunt?"

"Ah, the festive, felicitous pomposity of obscene language."

"Why pomposity?"

"The extravagant fanfare, the glorious ostentation of desire. Potency engenders great pride."

I thought of Father Lepinski.

71

"Was that priest sick in the head?" asked Bebel, after listening to the story.

We left in search of Rosa. It was a tedious morning, frustratingly slow. At noon, already getting on each other's nerves, we came to a house with an enormous front lawn, a small pond, and old-fashioned arbors covered with flowering vines. Underneath were stone benches and statues with broken noses. A uniformed maid opened the door and slowly crossed the grass on a flagstone path to the gate.

"Is Dona Rosa in?"

"Yes, she is," said the maid, opening the gate and turning slowly back to the house; Bebel and I followed along behind, jittery and impatient. Finally we entered a wide hall with a staircase leading to the upper floor.

"Bebel, what are you doing here?" From the top landing a thin, suntanned woman looked down at us.

"I came to see you," said Bebel unsteadily. Up close the woman didn't look as young as she had from the top of the stairs. The type that diets by just not eating. Sure, if you stop eating, you get skinny. I recalled various clients less favored by fate. Rosa was wearing shorts; her legs looked younger than her face.

"Who's your friend?" (A sparkle in her eye?)

"He's a lawyer, Mother. Everyone's been looking all over for you, it's been one hell of a confusion."

"That's not true. I called your father. Everything's fine."

"When did you talk to Daddy?"

"Yesterday. Didn't he tell you?"

"No. But, well, I left home and didn't see him after that."

"You left home?"

"I'm going to live by myself."

"Of course you're not serious," said Rosa, closing the subject.

"I'd like to have a few words with you in private," I said. "Will you excuse us, Bebel?"

72

"I can't stay?"

"No. Sorry."

"Why?"

"Didn't he already say no, young lady?"

"Shit!" exclaimed Bebel, stomping out of the room.

"Kids today," said Rosa. "Look, I have to make a few phone calls. Will this be quick, this discussion?"

"More or less. I'm an attorney. I represent, or I should say represented, Laura Lins."

"Laura Lins. Laura Lins. Do I know her?"

"You do."

"I can't recall—"

"Perhaps this will jog your memory." I handed Rosa the letter to Cila I had brought along in my pocket. She read it, impassive.

"So?"

"Laura was murdered. I'm interested in finding the person responsible. I need some information from you."

"Are you from the police?"

"I already told you I'm an attorney. Anything you say will go no further than the two of us."

"I have no desire to continue this conversation." Rosa waved the letter in my face.

"Then you'll have to continue it with the police. Your choice."

In a theatrical gesture, Rosa tore the letter to bits and clenched the pieces in her closed palm. "Laura never mentioned any lawyer. You're obviously an impostor."

"The letter you just destroyed was a photocopy." I sat down in an armchair and took out a panatela. I squeezed the cigar between my fingers, up close to my ear, and murmured, "Hmmm, a little dried out."

"Are you really a lawyer?"

I showed her my Bar Association card.

"Wait here, I'll be right back," said Rosa.

She wasn't long.

"I called a lawyer friend of mine. He told me I can trust you. Would you like something to drink? A cup of coffee?"

"No, thank you. I'd rather hear about Laura."

"Well, first off, her name isn't Laura. Do you mind if I make my phone calls? If I wait till later the people will have gone out."

"Of course."

She picked up her address book, consulted a few pages, and dialed the phone. "So. Her name wasn't Laura."

"I know. Cila, Oswalda."

"Cila was born and raised in the interior of Maranhão. Her father was a tailor, alcoholic, and he hated her. It does happen, you know. Hello? Is Madame Barki there? Rosa Leitão. I'd like to make an appointment for a facial. Her mother helped with the sewing; they were extremely poor. Cila was the prettiest— Yes, on Thursday? Fine. What time? Eleven? Yes, eleven o'clock Thursday." Rosa hung up the phone. "The prettiest girl in town. She was a raging success at all the parties she attended, without the consent of her parents, who punished her severely whenever they found out. In fact, they punished her for any reason—that's what she told me. She could have been lying, of course, to justify what she did on her thirteenth birthday." Rosa dialed again. "This is Rosa Leitão. I'd like an appointment, mmm, today, late afternoon. What do you mean you don't have an opening? My hair is atrocious, a-trrrocious! Is Jambert there? Tell him he just has to fit me in. Mmm. Now, where was I? Ah, she hitched a ride with a truck driver to São Luiz, and from there headed to Rio— Five o'clock? Five o'clock's perrrfect, thanks. You can imagine how the truck drivers felt sorry for the poor orphan whose only living relative lived way down south. And that's how she managed to travel the thousands of miles separating her from the city of her dreams. She knew nothing of Rio, except for a reproduction of a photo of Avenida Rio Branco taken a little after the turn of the century by Malta, the old-time photographer, and she carried the picture around in her wallet, along with a little medal of Our Lady of Carmo." On the phone again: "Angela, dear, I'm coming in to town today —no, no. I was at a friend's. . . . Well, I'm at Jambert's at five. . . . Mmm, okay, you give me a ring if I don't get back

74

to you, and we'll decide then. . . . Okay, bye, sweetie. It was a funny picture. Men in straw hats and dark suits carrying canes, striding down the sidewalk, or idling in the middle of the street. No cars to be seen, groups of people chatting, children all dressed up like grown-ups, and the few women up to their necks in long, somber dresses, carrying umbrellas. In those days women avoided the sun like the plague. They were right, of course; it's ruined my skin. So that was Avenida Rio Branco, which today is utter madness. Anyway, the last truck left our friend in Benfica, on a street full of industrial warehouses, where she wandered until a watchman stopped her and asked if she was lost. Our astute babe-in-the-woods told the watchman she was looking for Our Lady of Carmo, where her uncle was a priest. She ended up being dropped off, by the police no less, at the door of the church, downtown on Rua Primeiro de Março. Cila was fascinated with what little she'd seen of Rio, it was a far cry from Bacabal—yes, that's it, the name of the city where she was born—but she was also frightened, which is why she sat inside the church until nightfall when the priest came and asked her whether she had anywhere to go. Cila told him the orphan story and showed her medal of Our Lady. He took her to the home of some nuns, who allowed her to stay, doing domestic chores in exchange for room and board. As opposed to her success with men, Cila was never the least bit popular with women. Even I felt strong antipathy toward her when we first met. Of course later, when she tried to seduce me, I fell hook, line, and sinker. Anyway, the nuns couldn't stand her. They considered her lazy, slovenly, incorrigible. When she turned fifteen she ran away again, this time from the nuns, and went to work as a live-in baby-sitter for a family in the suburbs. Her boss was a single mother who knew there are only two kinds of men—cynical egoists and egotistical fools. It was during this period that Cila discovered the pleasures of the amorous life, first with her boss and then with a young bank clerk from the neighborhood who put her on the back of his motorcycle and took her to a cheap motel on Highway

Dutra, where, if you'll excuse the expression, she was deflowered. When the boss found out that Cila was no longer a virgin, she was sent packing and went to work in a shopping center in Madureira. During this time, at age seventeen, Cila met a very rich man who provided her with an apartment, clothing, jewelry, and the capital to open the boutique Messina, in Ipanema. That's when we met and became friends. Soon after, Cila quarreled with her sugar daddy. At least that's what she told me. But she was an inveterate liar, in addition to being stingy and acquisitive. Not that it's so inexcusable to be an avid consumer, especially if you come from the bottom of the heap the way she did, but disloyalty and lack of generosity are deplorable."

"Does this house belong to her?"

"Ha! I rented it for her."

"And she went on seeing the man?"

"One day when I arrived at her apartment the doorman let me go up without buzzing her on the intercom as he usually did. I rang the bell and Fafá opened the door, but Cila appeared suddenly, extremely nervous, and stopped me from coming inside. I asked her if there was someone there. She turned white and told me to go away. Please, she said, I'll explain everything later. I want to know who it is, I said. Please—she was whispering and so nervous she began stuttering—I'll explain everything later. Is it him? I asked. Cila nodded her head. She looked so awkward and unhappy and—since I'm not cruel like the majority of people—I felt sorry for her and left. Though I must admit that before leaving I called her a cheap tramp, a common whore, but that's what she was. It wasn't the least bit unjust. A common whore."

"So it was her protector who was there that day?"

"Had to be."

"Do you think he's the one who killed her?"

"Who knows? I never saw him. I don't have the slightest idea what went on between the two of them. So how about the letter? Now will you hand over the original?"

"You tore it up. There was no photocopy."

Bebel walked into the room. She was still piqued and made a point of showing it. "So. Is your little conversation over?"

"It is," I said.

"Now can I talk to my mother?"

I sat down on a bench on the veranda. The sun had dissipated the mountain fog. The trees and other vegetation surrounding the house were intensely bright. I could hear voices, without understanding what they were saying: mother and daughter arguing inside the house. The sky was blue and clear. The argument continued.

Ada wanted to get married and raise a family, but I didn't want to leave anything behind in this world. The one who should have had offspring was Betsy, but I had prevented that. What the world needed was more cats and fewer people.

As soon as we got back to Rio I called Wexler.

"Where are you?"

"I'm watching a videocassette. But not that one."

"Are you coming to the office today?"

"Is there something urgent?"

Wexler could have said yes, but he was the most generous person in the world.

"Can I go on?"

"Of course."

"Everyone told me it would be crazy to get married at my age and that the guy was a gold digger. He worked as a sales rep for a drug company and I really liked him a lot. But everything I liked, he hated. What do you think about the Indians?"

"What Indians?"

"Our Indians. Are you for or against?"

"How can anyone be against the Indians?"

"He was, my fiancé was. He made me take a bumper sticker off my car. All it said was INDIAN LANDS IN INDIAN HANDS, and he convinced me the Indians were as predatory as the white man. He said the ancestors of the American Indians completely destroyed the Pleistocene megafauna—giant bisons, antelopes, giant rodents, elephants, maybe a hundred million animals, and caused the extinction of dozens of species in the New World in just over two hundred years. I was horrified. He'd read all this in some book. I still don't know if it's true or not. People should be careful with books. Fortunately I realized that my boyfriend just wanted to boss me around, head and body, like all men. That's what men want, to make women submissive. A relationship based more on power than pleasure."

"I read that once in a book."

"I decided I wasn't going to marry that guy or any other. My parents sent me to finishing school in Switzerland. There was a girl there who used to lock herself in the bathroom with pornographic books and masturbate. That really made an impression on me. The other day I ran into her, she's married already. I asked her how she liked married life and she said masturbating in a Swiss bathroom was better. But then no one made her get married, right? All my friends who've married have separated within a period of six to twelve months."

"What did you learn in finishing school?"

"French, German, horseback riding, photography, ceramics, art history. Lots of things."

"And what have you done, or plan to do, with all that knowledge?"

"To tell you the truth I already forgot everything that was worth remembering. The rest just helps you live."

"Daddy buys the horses."

"Just one. It's not so expensive to stable a horse. I mean, I don't know how much, really, but it can't be all that expensive. Daddy also buys me books, cameras, gives me a monthly allowance. I'm a parasite. There, are you satisfied?"

78

"More or less."

"I'm a parasite sitting in a motel fucking and watching porno flicks with my mother's lawyer. During intermission we toss obscenities back and forth."

"I'm not your mother's lawyer."

"Whatever you are. You're trying to humiliate me, aren't you? Well, you've succeeded."

"Fucking you?"

"That too. And calling me a parasite. What do you want? You want me to spit on my father's money, cover my head with ashes, vote for the communists?"

"How about just getting a job?"

"A job—shit! Doing what?"

"Stableboy. Brickmaker."

"Look who's throwing stones. What you do is pretty damn useless, too."

"Truer words have ne'er been spoken. I'm going to turn off this piece of crap."

"You're the one who wanted to watch it."

We looked at each other in the ceiling mirror.

"My body looks good from this angle, don't you think?"

"Looks good from any angle."

"You don't think my legs are too fat?"

"I like them that way."

"My breasts aren't very big."

"They're very beautiful."

"Hold them."

I watched my hands holding Bebel's breasts. Bebel watched her hand holding my penis.

I loved Ada. But that didn't prevent me from being interested in other women. (Ah, men.) I think I'm having a relapse, I thought, arriving at Lilibeth's. Satiety: a degree or extent that fully satisfies, gratification of physical and moral needs to sufficiency. An oft-used word in old-time lawyers' speech—it is proven to satiety . . . to be satiated, to want nothing more. But I did. That's why I was there at Lilibeth's (while Wexler carried the weight of the office on his shoulders) on a rainy and provocative evening. We were drinking coffee and eating cookies, reclining on a pile of large, colorful cushions.

"So, what have you been up to?" she asked.

"I spent the afternoon in a motel."

"Rationalizing a potentially mediocre performance?"

"Maybe."

Lilibeth had big feet; the soles, dark from dirt, shone as if polished with flannel; the big toes were disproportionately larger than the others; toenails painted white. Her body was shrouded in a long, tentlike dress.

"I'm getting fat," said Lilibeth.

"Everybody's getting fat and worrying about it. Affluence is fattening. One of the onuses—perhaps the only one—of wealth: lard."

"It's simple. If you don't want anyone to notice you're fat, just wear baggier clothes and meanwhile only open your mouth when you have something silly to say. I'll lose it all in a month."

As Lilibeth adjusted her dress, I got a quick look at her thin legs. An uncomfortable and expectant silence fell between us. She fiddled with the dress again, giving me a smile that I understood as modest and encouraging at the same time: Take the initiative and I'll do my part. One of her legs was now flexed, drawing attention to the knee: fragile, reliable, clean, intimate. We were still expectant, uncertain. Lilibeth hugged her leg closer and rested her chin on the knee. I leaned over and barely skimmed my lips across her knee. I could feel her breath on my face; my gaze followed her leg down to the foot, pausing at the ankle, where an artery throbbed, the skin bulging with each pulse. I lay down on my back on the cushion, pulling Lilibeth's obedient body along with me. Then I sat up to admire the body stretched out at my side. Finally, without urgency, I touched Lilibeth's toes one by one, feeling the dryness of the bones, caressing her calf with my fingers and the palm of my hand. Lilibeth's legs moved farther apart. Quickly, easily, I unveiled her pubis and belly. She raised herself up on her elbows and skillfully slipped the dress over her head. The nylon carpet was itchy, so we went into her room, to the wide bed covered with soft perfumed sheets, ready and waiting to receive us. Ah, women.

On arriving at the office, I worked arduously drafting the final summation for a difficult counterfeit case and two initial petitions. The first was a case of embezzlement in which the accused, a highly placed public functionary, swore innocence but had no credible way to explain the origin of his numerous possessions. The second concerned the irregular issuance of a warrant. There had been no official authorization for the warrant, the merchandise in question was nowhere to be found in the warehouse, and the client had issued more than one invoice for the same nonexistent merchandise. Fraud and counterfeiting were equally thorny issues, and I spent the afternoon studying the law and the precedents.

I left the office at eight P.M. and met Ada in the Grandeza Restaurant on Rua Primeiro de Março. We ordered roast goat with broccoli and a bottle of Dão Meia Encosta. Before we sampled the wine I took out a pen and wrote on Ada's plate: I love you.

She erased the words with her napkin. "You're like a little kid."

"I don't deserve you."

"This type of conversation makes me nervous. Have you been up to something dumb? No, don't tell me, I don't want to know."

This woman with the open and generous face was the woman of my life. Why did I see other women if they meant nothing to me? Or did they?

I love you, I wrote on the palm of my hand and showed her. "Let's get out of here so I can hold you."

"Not until we eat. I'm dying of hunger."

When we reached the apartment I saw that the door had been forced open. "Don't go in," said Ada, frightened.

Betsy meowed from somewhere inside.

I pushed open the door. Even from the hall I could see that the living room had been turned upside down. The lamp on one of the end tables was on. Betsy was nowhere to be seen. She had stopped meowing.

"There's no one here," I said.

I walked in, Ada followed.

"Betsy!"

I stood there, motionless, unsure what to do. Then, automatically, moved to the counter and picked up the telephone.

"Put that fucking thing down!"

There were two of them, wearing windbreakers. One was tall, brawny, and clean-shaven. The other had a reddish beard, a mole on his nose, and a Browning .45 in his hand. He was the one who did the talking.

"No noise."

I looked around for Betsy.

"Where's the tape?" The big guy tied my hands behind my back, while the other one kept his gun leveled at me. "I said, Where's the tape?" The guy with the beard stuck the pistol in his belt and a knife appeared in his hand.

"Tape?" I asked, looking at Ada. She was very pale, paralyzed.

The big guy kicked me in the shin. One of the worst pains there is, but it passes quickly. "The videocassette," he said calmly.

The bearded one was irritated. "Cassette, tape, where is it? Speak up." I could smell his breath, sour, tense.

"There's no cassette here, none at all. Haven't you already searched the place?"

The big guy gave me another kick.

"Son of a bitch," I said. I didn't feel a thing until the bearded guy's hand had withdrawn the knife. It didn't hurt a lot, the kick had been much worse. I felt blood saturating my shirt. I have to stay on my feet, I thought, or they'll kick me in the face, but the blood was already dripping on the living-room rug. I felt the bearded guy's hand on my face, I smelled perfumed soap. It was like a dream. I tried to get up, to pull free of the hand holding me by the chin. It was like a dream. The woman next door sat down at the piano and began her monotonous daily exercises. Ada moaned. "Enough, the man's dead." An odd accent, coming from the big one. The gold chain was yanked violently from around my neck. The piano seemed to get louder. Ada was there next to me. "I called Miguel Couto," she said, and lay down beside me. I closed my eyes, I would never wake up again. It was so good to sleep.

6

I SLEPT and woke a number of times. Finally, when I opened my eyes, Ada was there beside the bed.

She started to smile, then clapped a hand to her mouth. "I lost a tooth." Ada buried her face in her hands and began to cry.

"Sit down here next to me," I said.

She sat on the side of the bed opposite the intravenous bottle, still hiding her face in her hands. "Who were they?" she asked.

"I don't know."

"Remember when we used to pretend you were raping me?"

"Oh, baby, don't cry. Try to forget it."

The nurse came in and saw my face. "Are you in pain?"

"A little," I lied, wiping my eyes. He set down his metal tray of medical utensils and began to prepare an injection. When it was ready, he stood there holding the needle for a while and then finally put it back on the tray. No analgesic would cure my pain. He knew. And left the room.

Wexler walked in, pulling a light panatela out of his pocket.

"You're allowed, aren't you?"

I took a few puffs, the bitter taste of smoke on my tongue.

The nurse came back. "What's this? No, no, no." He delicately removed the cigar from my mouth.

"They took out a piece like this of your intestine," said Wexler, demonstrating the size with his fingers.

"I won't even miss it," I said. "What day is it?"

84

"Thursday."

Late in the afternoon a doctor appeared. I was alone in my room.

"Fit for another go-round," he said after examining me.

"What did they do to my girlfriend?"

"Well, they knocked her around a little. Nothing much, we sewed her up good as new. A couple stitches."

I must strike my clients as callous, too, I thought, trying to overcome the aversion I felt toward the doctor.

"Looks to me like they used the knife handle. In the vagina and the anus." He spoke so naturally; only doctors know how to talk about such things.

He left the room without my noticing. I pushed the button calling the nurse.

"Where's Ada?"

"She went out to buy you some fruit."

A minute later Ada was back. She's walking differently, I thought.

"Will you sleep here with me tonight?"

"She's been sleeping here the whole time," said the nurse. "As soon as they released her, she moved in here."

"Feel like watching TV?" asked Ada.

"I detest television. I've got to talk to Wexler."

Ada picked up the phone on the bedside table. "Let me dial it for you."

I asked Wexler to locate Hermes. A knife. The haft of a knife. I closed my eyes and saw a knife glinting.

When he was a sergeant in the Brazilian Army, Hermes de Almeida had been prosecuted in the Military Tribunal for having killed his immediate superior, Captain Artur Antunes. Both men were serving in an elite unit of the Secret Service called NUSS, Nucleus of Special Services. They were specialists in *Persev*, the code word designating a set of techniques and tactics of knife handling. I had proved that my client, attacked by the captain, had been obliged to exercise his legitimate right to self-defense. Once absolved, Hermes left the Army.

"I had a hard time finding you," I said.

"I'm on the road a lot," said Hermes.

Hermes was a laconic man of medium stature and deliberate movements. The skin on his inscrutable face was polished and hard as agate, and uniformly pale as a doll's. While we spoke, his body remained immobile as a statue, only his right little finger giving signs of life. A nervous tic that Hermes was unable to control. We were alone. Ada had retired to the bedroom.

"I want you to teach me the secrets of *Persev*."

"It's a difficult art," said Hermes.

I opened my shirt and showed him my abdomen. He examined the scar with indifference.

"I'd like to return the favor."

"Buy a gun," said Hermes neutrally.

"No, I want to use a knife. It's become an obsession. For days I've thought of nothing else."

"The person who did this is an incompetent." Hermes' laugh was cold, hollow, close-mouthed. Who was he laughing at? Me or the ineptitude of my aggressor?

"He almost managed to kill me."

"A specialist goes for the arteries." Hermes ran his finger lightly along my carotid. Goose bumps. The carotid, he explained, was always easy to reach; an incision three centimeters deep would cause the individual to lose consciousness in seconds. His favorite artery was the subclavian. The puncture needed to be six centimeters deep, however, and thus it was not an advisable target in combat with a difficult adversary, since success depended on a grip of reduced dexterity. When executed correctly, however, the blood burst out in an unstoppable jet, strong as a fire hose; consciousness was lost in two seconds and death followed in the third.

"Remember the samurai Yojimbo, the way the blood spurted up in the air like an oil strike? Was that the subclavian?" I asked.

But Hermes was not a moviegoer and continued the lesson. The ideal target was the heart. Loss of consciousness was instantaneous, and if the steel penetrated the appropriate eight centimeters, death occurred in two seconds. The guy who had wounded me knew how to handle his weapon but must not have had an adequate understanding of anatomy. The intestine was not a vital point. "Might kill you, then again might not." Among the secondary targets the stomach was better, although penetration would have to be twelve or thirteen centimeters. "He could have slashed your brachial artery, here on the inside of the arm at about elbow height, or the radial, at your pulse. You'd die in two minutes."

"Teach me."

"Buy a gun and shoot for the guy's third shirt button. The third button. It's more certain than the head."

"I got you out of jail. You never paid me back. You owe me."

Silence. Hermes' opaque face.

I waited.

"I made a mistake. You should never leave a debt hanging," said Hermes.

7

WE WALKED up to the door of an old two-story building, with wrought-iron balconies and Portuguese-style masonry arches, on Avenida Gomes Freire.

Hermes rang the bell. The door opened. Someone yelled something from the top of the wooden staircase. Parallel to the guardrail hung a thin cord, which was fastened to the bolt of the old-fashioned lock. Hermes and I climbed the stairs, observed by the guy on the landing—stocky, middle-aged, flushed, wearing a stained gray apron. He greeted us and led us to a room that contained a bench with a lathe and a table scattered with various tools. The man pushed the tools aside and spread out a piece of green velvet on which he placed five brand-new, gleaming knives. He pointed them out, one by one.

"Bowie. Ka-bar. Loveless. Randall. Mark Three. These babies are rare jewels, nobody else's got them. The Bowie's blade is genuine Sheffield, tempered at seventeen hundred and forty degrees Fahrenheit. Double tempered. Hand sharpened on a grindstone. There's none better anywhere in the world."

"I don't like the big handle on it." Hermes picked up the Bowie.

"It's the English style."

"But it's an American knife. They turned it into a decoration."

"How about the Mark Three? Used by paratroopers and British commandos," said the man.

"Skip the lessons, Lemos," said Hermes. "The commandos used the F-S, Fairbairn-Sykes." He looked at me. "I don't like the cylindrical handle on the Mark. The Loveless is good, but for combat—attack or defense—the Randall would be best. It's a model fourteen; see the finger recesses on the haft?"

"I've got a Kukri, but it's not for sale," said Lemos.

"I'll take the Randall," said Hermes.

"I'm working on a deal to buy a Dennehy and a Collins. You interested?"

"Next time I'm in Rio I'll look you up."

Hermes reached out his hand and picked up the knife. A friend of mine raises birds. I once saw him stick his hand in a cage and grasp a bird to transfer him to another cage. That was the way Hermes held the Randall, as if it were alive, capable of escaping from his hand.

"What about the shoulder strap and case?"

Lemos brought out a leather case, a sheath, attached to a shoulder strap. Hermes took off his jacket and slung the strap over his shoulder, hooking the end to his belt so the sheath fell on the left side of his chest, angled toward the right. He slipped the Randall into the sheath and put his jacket on again, leaving it open this time. There was no noticeable bulge.

We left the weapon dealer's place and returned to my apartment. Ada opened the door.

"I want to talk to you alone," said Hermes. Without a word, Ada turned and went back to the bedroom. I followed her.

"Who is that guy?" she asked.

"A friend."

"He looks like a . . ." Ada couldn't finish the thought.

"A *Persev*."

"What's that?"

"Perforate and sever."

"Perforate and sever what?"

"I'll explain it to you later."

"Explain it to me now."

"I can't."

Ada lay down. She looked smaller and more fragile, a frightened old woman.

"Why don't you do some exercises?"

Ada didn't answer.

"Well, are you going to?"

"No."

"Then watch a little TV."

Ada closed her eyes. "I've got a headache," she said weakly. I could see she was on the verge of tears.

"I won't be long."

Hermes was standing in the exact same spot. He hadn't moved a millimeter.

"I've never lived with a woman," he said. He removed the knife from its sheath with a magician's flair. "There are people who hold a knife like this and flail it up and down like a hammer. Don't. Ever. Don't use it like an ice pick either, unless your target is the heart of a guy who's lying on his back. The proper way to grip a knife is with a flat thumb, supporting the upper portion of the haft at the level of the fold of the phalanx with the flange of the index finger. Watch."

Cold and didactic, Hermes explained the sanctioned techniques. Those of Fairbairn, Applegate, Styers, the Nepalese Gurkhas, the Spanish gypsies, Kenjutsu.

"In the Special Services we studied all the techniques, but the one we used was Araujo. I'll teach you the fundamentals. Target selection. The grip. The posture. The *stoccata*. The cut. The *in-quartata*. The *passata sotto*."

It was dawn by the time Hermes had finished. In front of me sat a mess of papers filled with notes and drawings.

Before leaving, Hermes turned to me with his gray-eyed mask and said in a mechanical voice, "Keep it in your hand as much as possible. Get used to it as if it was an extension of your body. Always hold it firmly, the handle locked in place. Don't arch the thumb. Keep the blade lined up with your forearm."

At the door he said, "My debt is paid."

"Paid," I agreed.

"Don't look for me again," said Hermes.

I went into the bedroom and lay down next to Ada. She was tossing and turning, her face tight with fear. I touched her shoulder lightly, waking her.

"I was having a horrible nightmare," she said. I could tell the hand on her shoulder was bothering her. I took it away. A knot in my chest.

"The doctor said you could lead a normal life." I was sorry as soon as I'd said it.

"I don't want to."

"You're fine, now, like me."

"Like you."

"We were bitten by mad dogs—"

"—and we're already all better." Ada began to cry.

"You want me to make you some coffee?" I asked.

"I'm going away. I'm leaving you. I'm going to my mother's."

"All right. Did you buy tickets already?"

"Mmm, yesterday." She was still sobbing.

I felt like crying, too, and it would have been good for both of us if we had cried together that day. But I went into the kitchen, boiled water, made coffee. The way Ada had drawn away from me, shrinking from my hand, had wounded me so deeply that I felt sick—a pain in my chest and shortness of breath. I stayed in the kitchen a long time before finding the will to go back to the bedroom.

We drank our coffee in silence.

"I'm going out for cigars. Do you want anything?"

Ada shook her head.

I sat down on a bench in the Praça Antero de Quental and smoked, watching the children and their nannies in white uniforms. By the time I got back, Ada was gone. I'll go after her. I'm not going to lose the woman I love without a fight, I thought. But even so, it took me a whole week to do anything.

8

THE NIGHT before I followed Ada to Pouso Alto, I was awakened long before dawn by a woman screaming. The piercing cries seemed to be coming from the four-story building across the street, apartments inhabited by rowdy young people, childless couples (sometimes because they were the same sex), or groups of two or three roommates splitting expenses.

In the silence of the night—a silence that is never total, since there's always a motorcycle or a car in the distance, footsteps on the sidewalk, or some insomniac neighbor's television—the woman's screams must have carried quite a distance. And they went on for a long time, disturbing, frightening. It sounded as if she was suffering a great deal, and was stubborn and unyielding, since it was a powerful voice and the screams went on and on.

I dressed and went out into the street. The screaming had stopped, but I approached the door of the building across the street anyway, where I found the doorman sitting in a chair with a transistor radio glued to his ear. When I questioned him he said that "all the racket" must have been "just some husband and wife fighting," there was no way he was going to get involved. Not him or anybody else; the people in neighboring apartments hadn't even bothered to get up and turn on the lights and at least look out the window to see what was going on.

All the way to Pouso Alto I thought about the cruelty of urban life, trying to convince myself that cities in the interior were more humane.

When I arrived—still thinking about the night before—and saw the city, with its ugly houses and cobblestone streets and people on horseback, I decided that the self-centered indifference typical of people in Rio could not possibly exist here. On the other hand, people in such a small city probably watched each other more closely, a reciprocal sort of oppression, as if regard for one's fellow creatures was offset by the violation of intimacy and, finally, of everyone's freedom.

The young girls were chubby and rosy-cheeked from the cold June air, pretty really; nevertheless I detested the city immediately. I arrived at the hotel where Ada had made a reservation for me, lugging an incredibly heavy suitcase (because of the great number of books I'd brought along). The Hotel Primavera was a white building in the style of the square-shaped health spas in the south of Minas. A wrought-iron cage of an elevator slowly carried me up to my room on the sixth and top floor. The window opened onto a hill shaved bare by the burning over of what had been a plantation of coffee trees and was now pasture, or nothing, since there were no cattle to be seen, just the dull green of sparse vegetation.

The room rate included breakfast, lunch, and dinner. Meals were to be taken at the appointed time.

I hadn't told Ada exactly when to expect me. After asking the desk clerk for directions, I set out on foot for the São José School, crossing in the process a good part of the city. People noticed I was an outsider and stared, curious. The girls had large, alluring breasts. Could it be the diet? I wondered, without irony. The region was known for its dairy products.

Classes were over by the time I arrived at the school; the children were just running out the door, boisterous and happy, with neither mothers nor fathers waiting for them. Violence had not yet come to Pouso Alto. I asked a janitor—probably the only one for the whole school—where I might find Ada.

She was in her classroom correcting papers. Never one to walk in without warning, I knocked at the door. Hearing her voice—"Come on in, it's open"—I felt my heart skip a beat.

Ada was sitting behind a desk on a raised platform in

front of a blackboard covered with words and numbers in white chalk. When she looked up and saw who it was, the blood drained from her face. I walked straight for her wooden chair, my steps echoing in the empty room, and took her hand to help her down off the platform. After a breathless embrace, we stood facing each other for a long time with nothing to say. Then we both began to talk at once, almost greedily, about how much we had missed each other. Ada was surprised by my beard; she said I looked older and not as handsome as before.

We went directly from the school to the house; Ada's parents were expecting me for dinner. We had never met.

They lived in a two-story house, Norman-style, with red trim around the windows and a garden out front. Ada's father, Pedro, was decked out in a jacket and tie. A large man, slightly overweight, ruddy-cheeked, with thick white hair, he shook my hand firmly and seemed sincerely pleased to welcome me to their home. He smoked hand-rolled cigarettes, out of preference and also because he believed they were the only ones that weren't bad for your health.

Dona Lazinha, as Ada's mother was called, took quite a while coming down from upstairs. I was surprised when I saw her; she was very well preserved, more like Ada's sister than her mother. Her greeting was cold, almost hostile. I pretended not to notice and treated her with perhaps exaggerated deference, which didn't have the least effect on her manner. At dinner, her conspicuous, studied indifference toward me clearly made her husband uncomfortable.

Several times I noticed the couple trade irritated glances. Later Ada told me that after I left they had had a bitter argument and ended up sleeping in separate bedrooms. Meanwhile, attentive to her mother's reactions, Ada treated me ceremoniously. Dona Lazinha was the typical altruistic mother who sacrificed herself for her family and in exchange expected total submission to the rules and values she arbitrarily established.

Back at the hotel, I sat on the veranda and lit up a

panatela. The manager wandered over and said he'd smelled my cigar. Sounds and smells traveled far in the clean, silent night air. Besides running the hotel, Abreu was a beekeeper, and the honey he produced was absolutely pure, he assured me, as opposed to the "adulterated" stuff generally sold in the area. The way to test honey for purity, he advised, was to dab a little on one palm and then rub the two together several times: if the honey was a hundred percent pure it would be absorbed without a trace, instead of sticking and creating tiny viscous crystals that only came off with soap and water.

At breakfast, Abreu set a small dish of honey on my table. Although no connoisseur of nectar, I was impressed by the quantity of vitamins and minerals it contained as well as the prosaic way nature produced it. On tasting, Abreu's honey seemed little different from the corn syrup version sold in the supermarkets in Rio. I dabbed a little on my palm. Rubbing my hands together, I noted that it did not in fact lose its sticky texture, and I made a point of demonstrating this to Abreu, gluing my palm to his, which made me wince.

Ultimately, there really wasn't a lot to do in Pouso Alto. I had dinner each night at Ada's. Pedro extolled the delights of a tropical climate at that altitude—a year-round temperature rarely below fifty or above eighty-two degrees. And he insisted on exploring with me the possibility of my opening an office in town.

Although admittedly a small-time—but not the smallest —coffee grower, Pedro was blessed with prestige and counted as friends important and influential people who would be glad to help me. Of course I would have to change specialties; crime was rare, and what crime existed was not committed by people rich enough to pay fancy fees, or, if they were, the case would be swept under the rug without trial or sentencing or any work whatsoever for an attorney.

But Pedro's favorite topic was coffee. He predicted his

farm's harvest for the year would be fifteen hundred sacks of coffee beans, fifty percent lower than the previous one. His brother, with forty-five thousand trees, would produce only two hundred and fifty sacks, due to damage from last year's frost. A credit dispute had divided the farmers; salaries were up, and fertilizer was double what it had cost before; the government-fixed price for coffee was totally unreal even without deducting various taxes, cost of sacks, transport, etc.; government loans, which allowed a coffee producer to hold on to his crop in hopes of better prices, had been suspended, obliging the farmer, already deep in debt, to sell on the open market, which was favorable only to the middlemen. A friend of Pedro's who owned 110,000 producing trees was planning to cut down almost half of them just to reduce costs, which would mean unemployment for half the seventy workers he usually needed at harvest. This unjust forfeiture, Pedro insisted, red-faced, would spell the end of the coffee farmer. The country was exporting less and less all the time, and the coffee producers were going broke as a result of ruinous policies instituted by incompetent technocrats; at least thirteen farms in the township had recently been sold; even the dairy herds, which constituted the other economic pillar of the region, were being liquidated for the price of slaughter, and no one seemed the slightest bit concerned. Yet the financial ruin of farmers would almost certainly provoke social convulsions because of the resulting mass unemployment of day laborers.

When Pedro was done talking I said good night, once again without having been able to spend any time alone with Ada, and went back to the hotel, where I tried watching the late news on TV—all the old familiar themes: international conflict, corruption, social tension, space exploration, scientific discoveries, crime, the cost of living, natural disasters, sports, and various mundane subjects.

In some places time passes exceedingly slowly.

I generally spent my evenings reading the books I had brought with me. When I got interested in a subject, my curiosity knew no bounds. Wexler always said I was an obsessive-compulsive. When I was with Berta, it was chess. I managed to get hold of a few rare facsimile editions, such as *Libro de la invención liberal y arte del juego del Ajedrez,* written in the sixteenth century by the great Ruy Lopez de Segura, and the thirteenth-century handbook on chess by Gioachina Greco, also known as El Calabrese. I'd stay up all night facing a set of ivory chessmen that had cost me a fortune, studying the book in which Nimzowitsch explained his system, or analyzing manuals written by Capablanca, Lasker, Tarash, Pachman, Tartakower, or Znoski-Borovski. All those old books and manuals were still around someplace, in a forgotten corner of the bookcase. I had diligently studied the matches described by Alekhine, Botvinnik, and Golombek. But after Berta and I broke up I lost interest in the game. Was I a fickle man? I wondered, glancing at the pile of new books at hand. What did it matter. Consistency wasn't a virtue, it was a vegetal trait that I did not, fortunately, possess. The books in front of me, which at the moment captured my interest, concerned an extraordinary instrument, one of man's most basic tools, the first weapon to be produced scientifically—the knife. There were several classics among them: *O Trattato di Scienza d'Arma,* by the great theoretician Camillo Agrippa, first published in 1604; *Manual del Baratero o Arte de Manejar la Navaja, el Cuchillo y la Tijera de los Jitanos,* author unknown, Madrid, 1849; *La Coutellerie depuis l'Origine jusqu'à nos jours, fabrication ancienne et moderne,* by Camille Page. (Camillo Agrippa, Camille Page, Camilo Fuentes—an awful lot of Camilos for one story, as I would discover later, but that's life, full of cloak-and-dagger coincidences.) I'd brought along some modern works as well: *Weapons & Fighting Arts of the Indonesian Archipelagos,* by the renowned British specialist in Asian martial arts, Donn Draegar. Draegar described a meteoric Indonesian knife with seven sinuosities made of meteoric iron, the handle of which used to be decorated with elegantly sculpted figures of women. It was called the kris, and was considered the most lethal of daggers. I also had books by the four modern masters of the knife fight: *Cold Steel* by John Styers; *Kill or Get Killed* by Rex Applegate, who invented the majority of dirty tactics, such as the backhand attack; and *All-In Fighting* by W. E. Fairbairn, whose technique was said to have caused the most deaths worldwide. Fairbairn, another Englishman, had begun the study of his art and science in the thirties; by the start of World War II, his efficient techniques already well elaborated, he patriotically offered them to the service of his country. They were officially adopted by the British Army, and in the forties British commandos, with the dual assistance of the information in Fairbairn's handbook and the knife he had designed, known as the F-S, killed an incalculable number of people, most of them Germans. (The Hasna, a knife designed by an Arab named Abu Harb, was also used on a large scale, in the Chatila and Sabra massacres in Beirut during the 1980s.) Finally, I had with me a book by Joaquim Araujo, *Vade Mecum do Combate Individual a Faca*, which contained techniques based on the *in-quartata* and *passata sotto* maneuvers, which had been further developed by the instructors of the Brazilian Army in 1945 after the return of the Expeditionary Force from Italy, when the Nucleus of Special Services, NUSS, was created.

Joaquim Araujo had been an anonymous fencing teacher at the Portuguese Gym Club in Rio de Janeiro, and his book, originally written in 1936, had been published by the author himself in a small printing of five hundred copies and distributed among his friends. With the exception of one copy, which ended up on the bookshelf of an Army major named Manoel Alberto Vilela Monteiro, who had served in the Sampaio Regiment, the entire first printing had been lost.

Araujo died in the early forties, leaving no heirs, and Vilela Monteiro, the first commander of NUSS, appropriated and reprinted the manual. According to the preface by Colonel Luiz Carlos Azevedo, the text of the present edition was identical to the original; only the illustrations were new. The techniques and strategies of the vade mecum, the preface also advised me, had been "adapted to the physical stature and temperament of the Brazilian male."

Immersed in the world of slashed arteries and perforated organs, imagining myself a sinister and avenging hero, I could not have been very good company, neither for Ada nor for myself. I walked back and forth on the hotel veranda, looking self-contained and stand-offish so that no strangers would approach me; the only person I enjoyed talking to was Lopes, an eighty-five-year-old Portuguese man I had met by chance on the street. Lopes walked energetically and conversed lucidly, in spite of his lack of teeth. We took long strolls around the city. Lopes did not believe that exercise was responsible for his longevity, but rather his never having felt envy toward anyone. He lived in a roominghouse where he had everything he needed, except a woman in his bed—and he said this last with the sly look of someone who wasn't telling the truth and wanted you to know it.

The second week dragged on even longer than the first. I had discovered—or, really, had been discovered by—an illegal casino, which, with the help of the doormen from the hotels of neighboring spas, attracted gamblers from all over the area. A taxi picked them up, free of charge, and drove them down a dirt road to the renovated great house of an old plantation, where they found various roulette wheels, baccarat tables, blackjack, craps, and other games. In two visits I lost small amounts of money at roulette. It was only the anxious faces of the people who filled the room that interested me.

Returning to my hotel, I would read my sinister books. One thing that fascinated me was the problem of blood: the terrible quantity that gushed out, whether the subclavian artery or the throat was cut, squirting the killer in the eyes and mouth; the necessity to keep mouth closed and eyes open, in order to avoid nausea (blood is sweet

99

and sickening); the unavoidable gurgling sound that might come from the victim's throat. Then there was the probable discharge of feces and urine to contend with. The assassin should always roll up cuffs and sleeves to protect his clothing (it was always easier to wash arms and shoes). If the attack was to be from the front, the neck remained the primary target, though the heart was considered an excellent alternative. In the latter case, the blade would have to penetrate eight centimeters on a strictly horizontal plane, for access, through the ribs, to the organ proper, and the weapon should be immediately withdrawn since the subject would fall immediately, conceivably breaking the blade. An ordinary knife, of untraceable origin, was better left in the victim, because, owing to natural suction and the contraction of the flesh, removal could be time-consuming. Those who wished to make the victim bleed, out of personal pleasure—a professional should be warned, meanwhile, never to permit himself any pleasure that interferes with his technique— or some other circumstantial exigency, should use a needle-knife, a weapon designed to function like a funnel through which blood flowed without coagulating. This knife was actually a tube cut open on an angle, producing extremely sharp edges and a fine point, and was ideal for the neck and kidneys. An ice pick was effective in reaching the medulla, at the base of the cranium, but a chisel or a screwdriver could be used as well.

If I had been able to be alone with Ada, life in that place would not have been so awful. We did have one opportunity, on a drive to São Lourenço, when Dona Lazinha became indisposed and declined to accompany us. Lighthearted, we drove to the neighboring city, where, to be sure, there was nothing more to see than in Pouso Alto, with the possible exception of the Parque das Aguas where we sat hand-in-hand by the lake. I asked Ada to come back to Rio with me, where we would get married and live happily ever after. Ada did not want to live in Rio or in any other large city. We talked for a long time without coming to any conclusion. We sat silently watching

100

geese paddle on the water. On the grass nearby a goose grabbed a frog by the leg and attempted to devour it, but the amphibian body, croaking weakly, would just not fit into the bird's beak. A woman tried to startle the goose into releasing its prey, shouting and waving her umbrella —it was cloudy and beginning to drizzle—but the bird just ran off, followed by another goose who wanted to share in the banquet, and plunged into the lake. It started raining more heavily, and we took shelter under a bandstand and embraced. The few other visitors had left us alone listening to the rain and the honking geese.

The incident with the frog had depressed me. Nature itself is violent, I said captiously. Violence is everywhere. Ada responded that violence required a conscious agent, and the goose hadn't known what it was doing. Violence, she went on, was a human trait, instituted specifically by men, out of their desire to create and agree on myths that in reality were nothing more than rationalizations to exalt their destructive impulses. With a sinking heart, I laughed and said that was two-bit psychology; one shouldn't take such a simplistic view of such complex phenomena. In this very century, I argued, many Parisians, both men and women, tie their pet dogs and cats to trees in the Bois de Boulogne, abandoning them to die of hunger, so that they can go off and enjoy their summer vacations free of restrictions. Perhaps they would similarly abandon sick or aged relatives if the police didn't prevent them. Ancestors of these civilized Frenchmen had practiced the sport of tying a cat to a post, or setting a pig loose in an enclosure, and bashing it on the head until death. Inhabitants of smaller cities in France (and I used France as an example because Ada considered it the "cradle of civilization") would buy men condemned to death in other cities, in order to carry out the sentence themselves, so that they, too, could enjoy at leisure the spectacle of drawing and quartering. That was what people were like, all over the world. Ada looked at me, and me at her, as if we were strangers. She gave me the painful impression that what was in my eyes was pity for her,

101

and maybe it was true that we were drawing apart from each other, that there existed between us an unbridgeable space. Suddenly I blurted out that I wasn't going to sit in an armchair trying to forget, reading the newspaper and paying my taxes on time. I didn't want to forget. It was good to remember and to hate. Struck by my bitterness, Ada didn't know what to say, and her face was sad as we walked back through the park in the rain, chilled.

We drove back to Pouso Alto. There was a message at the hotel from Raul asking me to call. The Narcotics people, Raul told me, had brought in a Bolivian named Camilo Fuentes for questioning. Fuentes was wearing a gold chain with a unicorn. They couldn't hold him long, since he had not been picked up flagrante delicto and there was already a writ of habeas corpus in effect to release him. Raul had Fuentes transferred to Homicide to buy some time.

I ran over to Ada's and explained that I had to go to Rio, a matter of urgency, and that I'd be back the following day. There was no bus at that hour, so I asked to borrow Ada's car.

I paid the hotel bill, threw my clothes and books into the suitcase, and drove out of the city at top speed, oblivious to the rain still pouring down. Halfway to Rio I realized that bringing my things along, books and all, must have meant I wasn't intending to return so soon.

9

HOMICIDE WAS located in a dilapidated building on Avenida Presidente Vargas. From the window in Raul's office you could see the endless line of cars filling the wide avenue that linked the Zona Norte to downtown. The building's walls were dirty and full of holes. Frayed emergency electrical wiring snaked across the floor. The foyer door had broken hinges and looked about ready to fall off. In the corner, on a piece of newspaper, sat a wooden box of ashes, cigarette butts, and dried spittle. The floor Raul worked on was divided by partitions that formed small cubicles where clerks took depositions from defendants and witnesses. The cops wore cheap, informal sport clothes.

"Is he here?" I asked.

"He's in the observation room," said Raul.

There was a one-way mirror through which to watch the person under observation without being seen oneself.

"Is he the one?" asked Raul.

Seated in a chair, talking to the clerk, was a large man with a round face and straight hair.

"He's the one." Pause. "What about my unicorn?" I realized my voice was trembling.

"He's still got it. He's also still got a train ticket from Bauru, in the northwest, to Corumbá. For tomorrow at four P.M."

"You're not going to let that bastard walk, are you?" Seeing Fuentes had unnerved me. Noticing this, Raul led me back to his office, guiding me lightly by the arm as if I were ill.

"Before Christ," began Raul, "let's say during the time of Sophocles—"

"—Sophocles?" I cut in. "What are you talking about? That thug is right here under our noses and you sit there and talk to me about Sophocles?"

"During the time of Sophocles," continued Raul, unperturbed, "or of Plato, if you prefer, there was no theory of criminology per se. The criminal was marked for life, tortured, mutilated, or killed."

"Which is exactly what should be done with that son of a bitch."

"For centuries, even after Christianity had spread to the far corners of the world, this remained unchanged. As a matter of fact, it got worse, when you consider that starting in the twelfth century, with the Inquisition, the criminal was not only put to death but sent to hell. Incarceration as a means of protection and social discipline didn't arise until the seventeenth century. It's a— how shall we say—a classic theory: rehabilitation with penitence. Are you listening to me?"

I was listening—irritated and impatient—but I let Raul go on talking; after all, I wanted his help with what my imagination was in the process of inventing. I saw myself thrusting the Randall into Fuentes' subclavian artery, blood gushing like water from the Praça Paris fountain I sat and watched when I was a kid. Meanwhile, Raul was saying that with the rise of the bourgeoisie the neoclassical school had emerged, that of free choice of evil, and then, in the nineteenth century, the Italian school, with the return of the idea of sin, of voluntary corruption, in which punishment had the objective of reform, rehabilitation. Then came the analytic point of view, multiple causality, crime generated by various factors interacting reciprocally. Since he was a cop— a low-prestige profession—Raul liked to show off his intellect.

"Go to hell, Raul. What I'm interested in is Fuentes. Fuck all your goddamn theories."

"Me, theorize? Theorize about what?"

"Everything. Chess, movies, literature. You're the biggest bullshitter I know."

We sat in silence. I lit up a Pimentel No. 2, the hell with the curtains. There weren't any curtains to stink up in that goddamn police station anyway.

"Fuentes was picked up in the hall of a building on Rua Barata Ribeiro where Narcotics busted a guy with fifty kilos of pure cocaine. Fifty kilos, that's big money. Fuentes maintains he was just looking for an apartment, and there did happen to be an apartment to rent in the building. But Narcotics suspects he's connected to the dealer they busted the same day, in the same place, with the stuff. That train ticket to Corumbá is a tip-off, they say. The majority of the Bolivian coke earmarked for markets in Brazil, the U.S., and parts of Europe, mainly Italy and France, comes through Santa Cruz de la Sierra, via Puerto Suárez, and enters the country at Corumbá. And that's where Fuentes is headed tomorrow."

"So?"

"Narcotics wants Fuentes out. They only let us borrow him momentarily because they figured it would help throw him off the track. We tell him he's a suspect in a murder case and then let him go, saying it was a mistake. The Feds already have things set up in Corumbá, and they don't want to scare off the ringleaders, which is exactly what would happen if Fuentes was locked up. Fuentes is small fry, he doesn't count."

"To me he does."

"Besides, we don't have grounds to keep him anyway; he wasn't picked up red-handed, and any two-bit lawyer would have him on the street in no time. In point of fact, his lawyer is Romeiro Galvão. Even if you were to bring charges right now, for burglary, attempted murder and rape, we'd have to ask the judge for preventative custody, and I doubt he'd grant it."

"So what you're telling me is that you're about to let the bastard go?"

"Narcotics guarantees that the Feds will nab him in Corumbá. Along with his contacts."

I was overwhelmed by a feeling of impotence. There was nothing I could do. Or was there?

I went straight to the office and told Wexler what had happened.

"I'm going to São Paulo, and from there to Bauru to pick up the train to Corumbá. I'm going to follow him. With this beard he won't even recognize me."

"You're out of your mind," said Wexler.

"Maybe."

"Does Raul know about this?"

"You bet. He even gave me the name of a cop friend of his in Corumbá. Do me a favor: Drive Ada's car back to Pouso Alto and tell her what's going on."

"You've gone mad, stark raving mad."

"Maybe. Raul said the same thing."

Wexler repeated a few more times that I was crazy. I really, truly was.

Let the Feds do their job, Raul had said. They're going to nab Fuentes, and they've already got something going in Corumbá. Don't butt in.

I took a shuttle flight to São Paulo and checked into the Ca D'Oro, downtown. From the hotel I called Bauru and reserved a sleeper on the train for Corumbá; the ticket agent said they'd hold my reservation until three-thirty. The connection from São Paulo was due to arrive in Bauru at three.

I arrived at the station at eight A.M. sharp. The line for the train to Bauru started at the top of one of the stairs leading to the lower platform and extended all the way across the passageway to the opposite side. The line was full of Bolivians who had come to São Paulo to shop and now were beginning the long trip home. Camilo Fuentes stuck out in the crowd because of his size. Looking calm and alert, he observed what was going on around him. Even at a distance, I was afraid a man traveling alone might attract his attention, so I struck up a conversation with a middle-aged Brazilian couple who owned a small ranch in Campinas. As we talked, I tried to spot a federal agent in the crowd. There was no one who looked like a cop. When the train pulled in, people pressed forward and I lost sight of Fuentes. The cars were crowded, standing room only. There were several stops before Bauru. Since we'd left a half-hour late, I kept consulting my watch, fearful of losing my reservation. We arrived only five minutes late. There was a long line at the ticket counter waiting for possible cancellations. I picked up my ticket, boarded the train, and located my berth, number eight, noting with satisfaction that Fuentes was already in berth four, stretched out with the door open, apparently unconcerned. My accommodations consisted of bunk beds, both covered with brown vinyl; the lower one, which was wider, was folded, transforming it into a sofa. On the far wall hung a small fan with blue blades, fluorescent lamps on either side of a mirror, an aluminum sink, and two towel racks, each with a faded red hand towel.

When the train passed Guarantã, I made my way to the dining car. It looked ancient, and had dirty beige curtains and tables for two or four with plastic checkered tablecloths. I ordered a steak. The waiter, a short, potbellied man with wavy hair and a dishonest face, wearing a National Rail Network uniform, explained dryly that they only "handled tenderloin." I patiently requested a tenderloin that was "saddled up," that is, with two fried eggs on top, and the waiter, pretending not to understand, asked if that was the same thing as a "mounted tenderloin." "Right," I said, "mounted." There was a can of warm beer and two "snak-paks" of crackers and nuts on the table, which the waiter removed.

The tenderloin was fine, but the egg whites were a little runny. I ate slowly, listening to the clacking of the train, waiting for Camilo Fuentes. A man that size wouldn't take too long to get hungry. From where I sat I had a view of the entire dining car. Four guys, ranging in age from seventeen on up, sat at one of the tables, three listening intently to what the oldest one, who seemed to be the leader, was saying—probably a joke, since they all laughed when he stopped talking. They looked like smugglers, the kind with a car dealer or a fabric store as a front, cautious types who had momentarily let down their guard, after having furtively studied the bearded guy who had walked in, concluding that I was inoffensive. They were drinking beer. Before long two women arrived. One must have been around fifty and the other a little over twenty. The younger one was wearing a bright-colored print blouse with little stars on it, a modest amount of jewelry, and had puffy eyelids covered with green shadow, as if she had slept too long. She had a baby face and perfect teeth, which she constantly showed off with a grin she must have thought was pretty but that made her look slightly retarded. The older woman shot a hostile glance at the smugglers. Her thin face, with delicate lips and deep furrows on either side of the mouth, was intelligent and unfriendly; her hair was short and stiff with hair spray; and she had a birthmark on her earlobe, like a dark drop of blood about to drip down her neck. She drank beer with a vengeance.

The train passed a muddy-colored river that twisted and turned, studded with large rocks; we were close to a village called Piraporanga, and it was then that Camilo Fuentes entered the dining car. He was so enormous that it looked as if there wouldn't be room for him to walk between the tables. He saw the women, with their backs toward him, and swaggered in their direction, examining me and the four smugglers from behind his mirror sunglasses that made him look like a sightless automaton. His difficulty squeezing between tables was just a ruse allowing him to check out the whole scene from behind his Ray-ban eyes. Arriving at the women's table, he made the older one change seats—he didn't want to sit with his back to the table of four. He brushed his arm across the younger woman's seat back and grabbed her by the shoulder. The woman was at first caught off guard, then seemed to take a liking to Fuentes and began to banter with him, though I couldn't hear what they were saying.

While making conversation, Fuentes effortlessly crushed an empty beer can with one hand, casually doubling it over as if it were a wad of paper. His shirt was wide open, and the gold unicorn that Berta had given me glinted on his broad chest. When I saw the pendant my hands started shaking. I knew I had to steady myself; in any case, I couldn't stay in the dining car much longer (I had already downed two espressos) without attracting attention, so I asked for the bill and left. As I passed Fuentes' table, I smiled at the older of the two women, careful not to let him notice. She didn't smile back, but her eyes met mine.

When I got back to my cabin I opened the window, turned on the fan, and lay down on the bunk bed with the Randall in my hand. My penis was aching; I took it out of my pants. It must be horrible to have your cock cut off, I thought, running the edge of the Randall ever so lightly across the shaft. A piercing shiver. I stuck my head out the window and looked down the body of the car, trying to locate Fuentes' cabin. Eventually his massive arm appeared on the window ledge; he must be alone. I returned to the dining car. The older woman was still at her table drinking beer.

"May I join you?"

"Sure. I thought you'd come back."

I signaled to the waiter for another beer.

"So?" she said with raised eyebrows.

"We're going to be on this train for thirty hours," I said, annoyed with the woman's conjecturing look. It irritated me. After all, she was just a tramp, and an old one at that.

"That much I knew," she said.

The beer arrived. I filled both our glasses. She drank. Her arms were solid, pretty.

"What are you doing here, lost in this big world?"

"I'm from São Paulo. Cattle dealer."

The woman laughed. Her teeth were stained with nicotine. "Come off it!"

"What do you mean come off it?"

"What breed is that?" She pointed to a steer grazing in the distance.

"Zebu. What's your name?"

"Mercedes. Talk to me about cattle."

"If I told you everything I knew, the trip would be over and I'd still be talking. I buy cattle here in Mato Grosso and take them to the interior of São Paulo, where I fatten them up awhile before slaughter."

"Zebu?"

"Among others. It's the most common type in Brazil." Was she onto me? "They came from Asia originally, did you know?" I added quickly, and rushed ahead with my smoke screen: "In Minas I buy Guzerá and Gir, in Goiás Nelore and Indubrasil." That just about exhausted what I knew on the subject.

"Don't you people have any cattle in São Paulo?"

"Sure. But not enough to keep up with demand."

"So we raise the cattle and you Paulistas eat them, is that it?"

"More or less. You're from Mato Grosso?"

"I am. How many head of cattle are there in Brazil?"

"Nobody knows that. Where in Mato Grosso?"

"Corumbá."

"That's where I'm headed. I catch a plane there for Nhecolândia."

A freight train full of spindly cattle packed in like sardines went by in the opposite direction.

"There they go, on their way to join the french fries," said Mercedes.

"And you, what do you do?"

"Guess."

"Housewife."

"You're either very stupid or very smart."

"Very smart." I began to feel a certain attraction to this woman.

"Shall we have another beer?"

"Sure. Who was that big bruiser that was sitting with you before?"

"A Bolivian. Speaks perfect Portuguese, though. He sat down and immediately started fast-talking Zélia. Men can't get enough of her. At least his type, the kind that like submissive women. She's in his cabin with him now."

110

"And what does this Bolivian do, besides conquering defenseless women?"

"He says he's on his way to an important meeting in Quijarro. No one's ever had an important meeting in Quijarro. It's a shit-hole of a city." Mercedes added that all there was in Quijarro was an outdoor market and, directly across from it, a railroad station, which was always full of Bolivians loaded down with goods purchased in São Paulo and teenage Brazilians with knapsacks on their backs waiting for the Death Train to take them the twenty grueling hours to Santa Cruz de la Sierra, because these "middle-class kids, who shit and piss all over themselves expecting redemption from their life as parasites, believed that was where coke fell from the sky." Mercedes characterized the Death Train as no more than a bunch of boxcars full of poor Bolivians carrying all kinds of junk "to the boondocks of life." She delivered her tirade in a husky voice, wiping away the sheen of beer sweat with palm or forefinger.

"Getting back to the Bolivian. You didn't tell me what he does."

"He didn't say." Lit by the gilded afternoon sun, Mercedes' face resembled the image on a gold coin. Ah, women.

10

CAMILO FUENTES firmly believed that to survive the hostile world he lived in it was necessary to be ready to kill. His father had died on the frontier; faced with an enemy, he had hesitated. Camilo was only seven years old at the time, but his Uncle Miguel later told him all about it. The man who killed his father was Brazilian, as were the usurpers of a large part of Bolivian territory—a territory so large, in fact, that it had become an entire state in the Republic of Brazil, the imperialist neighbor who, with the collusion of corrupt Bolivian regimes, had been plundering the natural wealth of Bolivia for centuries. Living in a border town, Camilo had grown up enduring the arrogance of the rich neighbors on the other side of the frontier for whom he performed humiliating tasks in exchange for paltry wages. For these and other, more obscure, reasons, he hated Brazilians.

Zélia's too dumb to be dangerous, thought Camilo, ordering her down on the floor on all fours. Then he entered her from behind like a dog, calling her Brazilian bitch, spanking her and making her wail and beg for more, her voice drowned out by the noise of the train.

It was extremely hot in the berth, and Zélia remained on the floor afterward enjoying the torpor of her aching body. Having already lost interest, Fuentes stretched himself out on the bunk and evaluated the possible risks of the trip. Danger existed everywhere, and being constantly on the alert was part of his daily routine. The smugglers were harmless as long as you left them alone, which was exactly what he intended to do. He would have to keep his eye on Mercedes. She drank without getting drunk, a sign of someone who senses she's not among friends. There was another suspicious person on the train, a bearded guy who had kept stealing looks at him in the dining car and then averting his eyes like an indecisive queer suddenly afraid to make contact; but his hostile expression and clenched teeth said he was no homosexual. That guy was another one who would have to be watched. (Fortunately, Fuentes had not recognized me.)

"I'm thirsty," said Zélia.

"Go buy some beer," said Fuentes, handing her some money. His Portuguese was flawless, though the slightest accent was perceptible.

"Like this?" asked Zélia, opening her legs to give him a perfect shot of the thick pubic hair extending from her crack to her coccyx.

"No woman of mine goes naked in front of other men," declared Fuentes. He squatted over her outstretched body and watched, admiring, as his cock rapidly stiffened and swelled to enormous proportions. A real man, he thought proudly, perched on top of her, penetrating her violently; he'd make that slut come a thousand times. Fuentes thrashed wildly, sweat streaming down his face into Zélia's, obscuring her vision, a burning liquid lens that disfigured the shape of the man arched over her. Arrogant, conscious of every movement, Fuentes listened to their slick bodies slap against each other. He was pure Indian, capable of fucking any woman for hours on end. Zélia was on the verge of fainting from exhaustion and pleasure. Other men had invariably lost interest in her much faster; not one had lasted this long in bed. She had always dreamed of someone like Fuentes. Zélia pretended to come once more, this time experiencing a different kind of pleasure, that of satisfying and attending to the man. "I'm your slave," she said, which seemed to give Fuentes even more energy. His arms encircled her as if he were about to crack her ribs; his body slammed against her in violent spasms which hurt all the way down to her bones, especially the ones in the pubis.

113

When they had finished, Fuentes rolled off, lay down on his bunk and said, "Now go buy some beer."

Zélia threw on her dress. Before leaving, noticing the scowl on Fuentes' face, she asked wasn't he happy, had she done something wrong?

"Go buy some beer," he said.

Fuentes was worried. He was on his way to Quijarro to meet Rafael, a man he detested. Rafael got a kick out of calling him Chinaman, which infuriated him, though he tried not to show it. Besides, all Brazilians were despicable cowards. But Mateus gave the orders and he had to obey them—at least for now. The day was coming when no Brazilian would be able to order him around.

Mercedes and I woke up sweating, just as day was beginning to break. My body ached all over from the night spent squeezed into the narrow bunk. The train passed through a hamlet called Aguas Claras and over a clear, tranquil river that ran through a valley thick with trees. "The Green River," said Mercedes. We breathed in the clean, fresh-smelling air from the dense, leafy shade along the river bank.

"I think I'd better go see how Zélia's doing."

"See if you can find out some more about the Bolivian."

"You better not mess with him. You saw what he did to that beer can, didn't you?" I detected an ironic gleam in her eye; but she really didn't seem surprised at my interest in Fuentes. In any case, I lacked the imagination, at that moment, to interpret Mercedes' behavior correctly.

The train made a stop in Campo Grande to take on water. From my window, I could see Fuentes on the platform sucking oranges: solid, calm, alert.

Around noon I made my way to the dining car. Zélia and Mercedes arrived soon after. Zélia's arms were covered with red marks, which she gazed at proudly and exhibited as if they were precious jewels. Looking sullen, Mercedes chose where they would sit. Fuentes was expected, I concluded, since a seat was left empty next to Zélia. When he

114

arrived, Fuentes seemed less suspicious than the day before. His attitude toward Zélia reminded me of the protective way pimps treat their girls.

"Excuse me, sir, may I?"

A skinny young man with a sparse beard had approached my table and, without waiting for a response, sat down, leaned forward with his weight on his elbows, and stared at me from behind thick glasses.

"You are a sinner. I know that you're a sinner, and I can see it in your face. Many paths that seem right to man's limited vision are, in truth, the paths of death."

"All paths are the paths of death," I said. The presence of this proselytizer would allow me some extra time in the dining car without attracting Fuentes' attention.

"No, no, you're headed in the wrong direction. The path to Heaven is open to you even now, and Jesus paid the price, dying on the cross in your place." While the preacher droned on, Fuentes crushed another beer can and Zélia beamed. The man has no imagination, I thought, exchanging a scornful look with Mercedes. "If you confess to the Lord Jesus and believe, deep in your heart, that God raised His Son from the dead, you will be saved. Salvation is free. And do you know why?"

The preacher had two front teeth missing, which gave him some credibility in my eyes. People with teeth missing affect me. Moreover, he was extremely pale and looked like a potential host to all known and unknown tropical parasites.

"The Just One has paid the price of the unjust," said the youth, pounding his fist on the table.

"That means that God loves the sinner," I said, trying to keep up my end of the conversation. The preacher bit his colorless lips.

"But not the sin," he said, wild-eyed, "not the sin! Every one of us sins and every one of us is in need of the Glory of God. Believe in Jesus Christ and you will be saved, you and all your household. Repeat after me"—he was talking without nuance now, like someone who had memorized the words, repeating them over and over, eyes closed, con-

115

trite—"repeat after me: Lord, I am a sinner, I know I deserve the fiery wrath of hell, but I believe that Jesus died for me and I accept him now as my only Saviour. Amen."

"Amen," I said, without being able to contain a smile.

"Don't make fun, you numskull. I'm teaching you how to get out of Mato Grosso and find the way to Heaven."

Fuentes shot a quick, uneasy look in my direction. Was the Bolivian suspicious for some reason? Soon he was back to joking with Zélia, distracted, and didn't look at me again. I'm seeing ghosts, I thought. I asked for the bill, paid, took leave of the preacher, and left without looking at Fuentes & Co. Halfway down the corridor I could still hear the preacher: "You think this is hot? It's a lot hotter in Hell than in Mato Grosso!"

The train was two hours behind schedule. We could look forward to ten more hours of that infinite green plain intersected only occasionally by the flight of a white heron or mottled by a herd of cattle that looked like toys. I sat at the window determined to spot an alligator, the prime inhabitant of these lowlands. I had read somewhere that according to official estimates nearly one million alligators had been poached in the region in the past year alone. Shoes, pocketbooks, watchbands for elegant consumers the world over. But death—an alligator's or a person's— didn't seem a bit transcendent, at least not to me, there in the middle of the wild. I was going to kill Fuentes, and I realized bitterly that the death of my enemy would give me the same satisfaction as crushing a cockroach under my foot. At that moment I felt a sudden longing for Eva, the spoiled daughter of a corrupt senator, and then I was flooded by an even greater longing for Ada, a desire to disappear with her into that immense ocean of vegetation, a desire to turn my back on friends, guilty and innocent, on the multitude of streets, on *ardores urbanos*. Goodbye newspaper reports, courtrooms, clients, cops and robbers, ephemera, and final accusations. I closed my eyes and dreamed of Ada.

Knocking at the door. Mercedes came in and sat down beside me on the bunk.

"The marsh is beautiful," I said.

"What do you mean?"

"Maybe because it has no end."

"That's exactly why it depresses me, because it goes on forever. Kiss me."

I kissed her cheek.

"On the mouth. Or are you sick of me already?"

I kissed her on the mouth, breathing in the smell of beer and cigarettes.

"Do you know his name?" Mercedes asked.

"Yes. Camilo Fuentes."

"He told us it was Pepe Losada."

"Then he's got more than one."

"He's planning to stay at the Grand Hotel. So are we. We're flat broke, and he said he'd pay, he promised Zélia. I'd rather shack up with the devil than stay in any of the boardinghouses in Corumbá, thirty people to a bathroom."

Mercedes got undressed, washed her hands and face, and dried with one of the little red hand towels. "Pepe—or Camilo, or whoever he is—bragged his way all through lunch. He said his cousin's a general, and that he's a personal friend of the governor of Mato Grosso and the chief of police of God knows where. Probably all lies, just like his claiming to own an import firm and a lot of land in São Paulo. He also said a friend of his is waiting for him in Corumbá, at the Hotel Santa Mônica. But let's forget about that creep for a while, okay? Aren't you hot?"

I took off my clothes and propped the pillows on the bunk so we could lie down and look out at the countryside.

"Feel like fucking?" asked Mercedes.

"It's not foremost in my mind, at least not now."

"Fucking isn't everything," said Mercedes.

"No," I said.

"But it's good."

"It is good."

"Are you really a cattle dealer?"

"No. I'm a lawyer. Criminal practice. In Rio."

"Must be plenty of clients there, huh? What is it—every minute or every second somebody's killed?"

"It's not like that really."

117

"I knew you weren't a cattle dealer. A cattle dealer's never unhappy."

"Who said I'm unhappy."

"Do you like me?"

"Yeah. But I'm not going to teach you how to get out of Mato Grosso and find the way to Heaven."

11

THE TRAIN arrived in Corumbá at ten-fifteen P.M. The station consisted of a long platform flanked by rough stone walls, gray in the cold blue light. Bolivian families hurried to unload suitcases, shopping bags, packages, boxes, and bundles. Their trip didn't end here; they would spend several more days on uncomfortable trains before reaching the Cordillera Real. But they seemed happy to have got at least as far as Corumbá—adults talking loudly, children running up and down the platform. Those who would be continuing by freight train would have to cross over into Quijarro, in Bolivia, and wait until the following afternoon; those going by passenger train would wait at the Corumbá station until morning.

I took a cab to the Grand Hotel, which turned out to be on the corner near the main square. The hotel harked back to the forties, with its ornate black marble art deco lobby. The girl at the desk gave me a suite on the third floor.

Camilo Fuentes arrived just after I did, accompanied by Mercedes and Zélia. The two women checked into a room together, and Fuentes took a suite, on the second floor. Before settling in, Fuentes examined his accommodations carefully: the lock; the anteroom with two ancient armchairs and a sofa, all covered with gray vinyl; the large bathroom, well ventilated by a wide jalousie window, with bathtub, sink, bidet, toilet, and shower. Nothing escaped his scrutiny. The bedroom had two single beds (no dust underneath), a dressing table with seat and mirror, a wardrobe, and a tall free-standing fan. One window was opposite the dressing table, another beside one of the beds, and there was a narrow veranda. It was a corner suite; the veranda doors and the window opposite the table looked out onto the square, and the other window overlooked a street. There was no possibility of access through the windows, neither from the street nor the neighboring rooms. The adjacent buildings were lower and thus did not permit a view into the suite. But from the far side of the square, using binoculars, someone could conceivably see into the room via the veranda doors. Fuentes shut them, making a mental note to leave them that way, and opened the windows instead. All the rooms smelled strongly of fresh paint. Fuentes turned on the fan, took off his clothes, moved the anteroom sofa into position blocking the door, lay down, and went to sleep, programming himself to awaken in two hours, which, in fact, he did.

I took a bath, changed clothes, and, the Randall across my chest, went out to see the city.

"Where's the Hotel Santa Mônica?" I asked the girl at the desk.

"On Rua Antonio Maria. Go down the street out front and you can't miss it."

"Do you need a passport to cross over into Bolivia?"

"I don't think so. A little money should take care of it."

The only restaurant still open was getting ready to close, but they agreed to serve me. I asked for grilled pintado and boiled potatoes.

"Do you have any Portuguese wine?"

"I'll check," said the waiter.

The restaurant was a shed with an extremely high ceiling. Scattered around the room were dozens of softly buzzing fans.

The waiter came back with a bottle of Porca de Murça. "Is this okay?"

"Certainly."

"You want me to put it on ice for a while?"

"Of course not. Open it, please."

Red wine with grilled fish was a new gastronomical experience, but it was actually very pleasing to the palate. A violent storm blew up during dinner; cold gusts of wind blasted the dining room and rain drummed on the roof. For a few moments I felt sheltered and happy and forgot the hate hardening my heart. By the time the storm had passed, I was ready to head back to my hotel. On the way, I decided to stop at the Santa Mônica, an ugly building of concrete and blue ceramic tile, with internal walls of brick that had been glazed and painted swimming-pool green with yellow trim. I told the desk clerk I was looking for a Dr. Arantes, who would be arriving from Bauru. After checking the register, he informed me that no one by the name of Arantes had checked in. Feigning interest in a poster of fishermen that advertised a three-day excursion into the marsh, I said I would stop back the next day. It was no longer raining, and in spite of the late hour there were still people on the street. Merchants and their families sat talking in front of the shops they lived above or behind. It used to be like this in Rio, I thought, wishing I had known the city in those days.

Soon after returning to my room at the Grand, there was a knock at the door. Mercedes.

"The Bolivian's downstairs in two-o-six. His friend at the Santa Mônica is called Rafael, but the meeting's going to be in Quijarro, tomorrow morning at eleven."

"You're a love."

"Pay me in kind."

"How do I get to Quijarro?"

"There are several buses, they all stop in front of the bus station. Or you could take a Bolivian taxi. Is it okay if I sleep here?"

"I have to get up early."

"I'll wake you."

"It's a narrow bed."

"I like narrow beds."

"All right."

"Why the sigh?"

121

"I don't know."

"Sick of me already?"

"No."

"Thinking about someone else?"

"Maybe."

"Let's take a shower."

We showered together and went to bed. Mercedes ran her hand lightly over my body. I lay still with my eyes closed.

"You like?"

"I like."

"A lot?"

"A lot."

It certainly didn't seem as if Mercedes' head was as full of problems and schemes as mine.

I woke at five, grabbed the Randall, and went into the bathroom. Sitting on the toilet, as I emptied my intestines I played with the knife, imagining Fuentes' death. His being lefty, which I'd noticed when he was crushing beer cans on the train, would make my job easier. Confident of his strength, Fuentes would extend his left hand to hit me (of course, it might happen that he would have a weapon, but, either way, I saw the way he would move), his left foot pushing forward and turning as his wide body leaned slightly closer, making the most vital side of his thorax more vulnerable. I would skillfully execute a *passata sotto*, right foot moving forward and bending my knees slightly, especially the left, without, however, touching the floor. This complex movement, with the torso still doubled over, would enable me to avoid Fuentes' attack and lunge violently at his heart. Taken unawares, the Bolivian would fall, dead, to the floor, even before recognizing his assassin. I dreamed this scenario several times, with variations, wide awake, until it no longer gave me any pleasure. Then I got up and took a shower.

Just as I finished dressing, Mercedes woke.

"What time is it?"

"Six o'clock."
"You're leaving already?"
"Yes."
"Do you know how to get there?"
"Yes."
"Will I see you later?"
"Yes."

Early as it was, the sun was already fierce, but the temperature was pleasant. I crossed the square, stopping in front of the statue of General Antonio M. Coelho, a local hero in the war with Paraguay. The tall trees in the square were brilliant with red flowers. The street outside the bus station was already open for business: a jumble of storefronts selling flour, toilet paper, small appliances, toys. Lots of Bolivians, loaded down with bags and parcels, were already waiting for the bus. There was a bit of a crush when it arrived, with lots of people pushing to get their bundles in the outside baggage compartment. Then, as each passenger got on the bus, his or her parcels were examined by the driver and his assistant.

"Es trigo," said the driver, irritated, in Spanish. *"Abajo."*

A woman with an enormous sack of carrots explained to me that each person was only permitted a maximum of ten kilos of flour; more would be confiscated at the border by Brazilian Customs. She asked me to pass off her extra ten kilos as mine and, before I could answer, shoved a receipt into my hand: Casa Carioca, Rua Manoel Cavassa 212, ten kilos flour. The price was illegible. Flour was still slightly subsidized by the Brazilian government, so it continued to be smuggled regularly into Bolivia.

The filthy, dilapidated bus bore the name Tigre del Chaco Public Transport Company. Its route was short: Corumbá to Puerto Suárez, via Resguardo and Quijarro. In Arroio da Conceição, on the border, the driver ordered everyone off the bus. Two Brazilian functionaries collected customs slips and boarded the bus to inspect the baggage we had been instructed to leave behind in our seats. Then they carefully examined the bundles in the outside compartment.

A hundred meters farther, in the Bolivian half of Arroyo Concepción, the bus stopped again. Everyone filed off under the indifferent gaze of soldiers armed with rifles.

"They're looking for guns, but they know they won't find any," the woman whose flour I was smuggling said in pidgin Portuguese. We were standing in the middle of the group, alongside the bus, waiting for the soldiers to finish their inspection.

I got off in Quijarro, in front of the train station, an immense stone building covered with sheets of zinc. White clouds, motionless and opaque as blocks of plaster, floated in a blue sky. Quite a number of people were waiting for the Death Train, due to arrive at one o'clock, some of whom had spent the night in the station surrounded by every variety of goods and packages: mattresses, appliances, stoves, as well as all sorts of bags and cartons that bulged with unidentifiable merchandise. Eight-year-old kids were hawking rice pudding, slices of melon, meat turnovers.

Facing the station from across the street was the Bar e Restaurante El Paso, a squat stone building with tables scattered over a large dining area and a counter stacked with cigarettes, cassette tapes, batteries, packages of macaroni, cans of soup. Beside the counter was a doorway with a half-open greasy curtain through which I glimpsed a small room: two young women sitting at a table with a small child. One of them got up and came to ask me in Spanish what I wanted. A beer, I said, and greedily gulped down the Pilsener Tropical Extra she brought me.

I waited.

A chicken meandered in and pecked away at a big piece of bread that lay on the floor, its head jerking up and down as it attempted to yank off a chunk small enough to eat. I thought of Ada. Actually, first I thought of the goose in São Lourenço Park trying to eat a frog. Two hefty girls arrived, moving sluggishly and sweating profusely: Brazilians who were clearly sorry they'd come and anxious to go home. Time passed. It got hotter and the number of flies multiplied. Three Bolivians, two Indians, and a white guy walked in. Then a German couple, clearly suffering from the heat. Distracted by the German woman, who was chubby as a pedigreed suckling pig but, even so, attractive, I hardly noticed Camilo Fuentes arrive, accompanied by a smaller man with purplish lips, a red beard, and a mole on his nose—the Perfumed Hand who had stabbed me and raped Ada with the knife handle. They sat down and ordered beer. Even though it was impossible to eavesdrop on their conversation from where I was sitting with my back to them, it seemed to me they treated each other like adversaries; even at a whisper, the hostility between them was apparent. They talked for some time. The Perfumed Hand, whom I now knew to be called Rafael, was first to get up.

"Tomorrow, one o'clock, at Dancing Days. Don't be late," said Rafael.

Back in Corumbá, no one at the desk in the Grand Hotel knew of a place called Dancing Days.

I called Arquelau, Raul's friend the detective. He told me it was his day off and said I could stop by his house if I wanted.

There was an outdoor market on Arquelau's street. Booths along both curbs offered fruit, vegetables, grains, clothing, meat, and fish. People selling records had set up a sound system on the sidewalk and were blasting the latest hits at top volume. An enormous fish in one of the booths caught my attention.

"*Jau,*" said the merchant, in answer to my question, "eighty centimeters. I caught it myself, in the Paraguay River."

I arrived at Arquelau's with the giant fish under my arm. He was waiting at the door.

"Any trouble finding the place?"

"No."

We went inside: an old-fashioned room with china closet, colonial-style dining-room table, matching chairs with leather seats. A television, a sofa, and two armchairs.

"For you," I said, handing Arquelau the fish.

"Thanks very much," he said stiffly. "This fish can be eaten both fresh and salted, you know. Salted, it's a bit like *bacalhau*." He stood there with the fish in his arms as if he didn't know what to do with it.

"Tasty?"

"Some people prefer *jiripoca*, or piranha," said Arquelau diplomatically.

"Piranha?" I felt obliged to act startled—the city rat being initiated into the myths of the jungle.

"Cook it slowly for half an hour and it melts in your mouth. *Jurupensem* is good too. Have you tried that?" The two of us were standing in the living room, Arquelau still holding the fish. "*Jurupensem*, pintado, *surubin*— there are a lot of different names for it."

"Yes, of course, delicious."

"And *barbudo*. Have you tried *barbudo*?"

"*Barbudo*? Sure." Christ! The guy just stood there holding that enormous fish; it was beginning to get on my nerves.

"Did you eat the head? The way they fry it?"

"I think so."

Arquelau looked down at the fish with a vague expression. "There's more fish in these rivers than stars in the sky." Then he excused himself and disappeared through a door with my gift. Soon he was back, reeking of toilet water and asking me to have a seat. We talked about Raul.

"When I was in Rio I stayed with him. He was living with that girl. Elvira?"

"Marta. Or maybe Clotilde?"

"A girl with big thighs."

"They're separated."

"I separated from my first wife too."

I waited.

"But I remarried. Here in Corumbá you've got to get married."

"Here and everywhere."

Silence.

Arquelau sighed. He fiddled with a hat that had been sitting on the table. "Straw from the carandá palm."

Another silence.

"Did you want something from me?"

"Do you know a guy named Camilo Fuentes? A Bolivian?"

"No."

"What about a guy with a beard, called Rafael?"

"There's lots of guys with beards."

Dancing Days he knew. A bar and restaurant on the corner of Avenida Bolívar and Calle Velasco, in Puerto Suárez. Bolívar was the main drag in town, loaded with import stores.

"I don't know what you're after, but you'd better be careful."

Arquelau had a brother named Arquêmico. His father had been a professor of Greek, back in the days they taught Greek. His sister's name was Arquidêmica.

At the Grand Hotel, I found Mercedes in my room.

"I washed your dirty clothes and hung them up to dry in the bathroom," said Mercedes. Underpants, shirts, and socks dangled from the shower rod.

"I had to really hunt to find the stuff. Do you always put your dirty laundry back in the suitcase?"

"You look awfully pretty today."

"Pretty? Me?" Mercedes walked into the bathroom to look in the mirror. I followed.

"Pretty, nothing."

"Of course you are."

"How was Quijarro?"

"Fuentes met the other guy I'm looking for. Rafael. They're getting together again tomorrow, in Puerto Suárez."

127

"Do I look better with my hair loose, or up, like this?"

"Loose, no hair spray."

"I don't use hair spray anymore."

"That's the way I like it."

"Do you like me, really?"

"Many years before Christ there was a poet in Greece who used to say, 'Mine is a high art—I severely wound those who wound me.' Mine is an even higher art—I love those who love me."

"You're crazy sometimes, you know? I don't even know what you're talking about."

I lit up a panatela. We lay down on the bed. "I read a story once, about a man who's condemned to death. He's up on the gallows about to be hung and when the executioner slips the rope around his neck, the man asks if he can have one more minute of life. Why do you want one more minute of life? asks the executioner. And the condemned man says, I want one more minute to think about Belle Elize."

We began playing with each other, mutual enjoyment à la hands and mouth, provoking and stimulating desire of the flesh, with the urgency of people on the run.

"Would you do that, too, ask for one more minute of life to think about a woman?"

"The guy was a sailor. *Belle Elize* was the schooner in which he'd sailed all over the world."

12

WHEN THE SUN appeared over the red flowering trees in the square, I was already awake. I got up and showered. Just as I was about to leave, Mercedes woke.

"Do all Rio lawyers carry a knife?"

"What knife?" I had been careful to keep the Randall hidden from Mercedes, so her question caught me off guard.

"Oh, the one in a leather case with a shoulder strap."

"It's for peeling oranges."

"Come over here. Lie on top of me."

"I don't have time."

"Just for a minute."

"Like this?"

"Full length, yeah. I love to feel the weight of you."

"I've got to go."

"Be careful." Mercedes grabbed my arm. "If you find some things out about me, don't be mad, okay?"

"What things?"

"Anything."

"For example?"

"I can't tell you now. You'll find out."

"I detest mysteries. Out with it."

"I can't. Damn. Life is complicated."

"If you don't want to tell me, don't tell me."

"I can't."

"You don't have to."

Across from the hotel I got a Bolivian cab. En route, the driver stopped to pick up another passenger, a woman, who sat up front with him. The two of them chatted in

Quechua, but every once in a while she came out with a badly pronounced epithet in Portuguese. Life in a border town.

"This is Calle Bolívar, here," the driver said in Spanish, as we pulled into Puerto Suárez. We had crossed the border with no difficulty, merely a superficial inspection of the trunk.

All the houses in Puerto Suárez had the portrait of a man in uniform painted on them, and "Welcome, General!" in faded green lettering. Workers were beginning to cover the general with whitewash. Calle Bolívar, lined with import stores, one beside the other, was sandy and sun-scorched. I let the driver pass Dancing Days and got out a short distance up the street at a small park. It must have been over a hundred degrees. The streets were empty, with the exception of two cars raising dust as they passed and a girl on a bicycle wearing a pink skirt with geometric designs and a short tight blouse that left her midriff bare. Indifferent to the heat, she seemed to glide above the ground propelled by a cool breeze; as she passed, her soft jet-black eyes gazed at me and she smiled. It seemed like a good sign, and I walked into Dancing Days confident that everything would turn out all right.

Fuentes was already there, along with Rafael and another man, around forty, very tan, with curly gray hair. Fuentes noticed my arrival and said something to the gray-haired guy, who looked in my direction. They were suspicious. What stupidity to barge into the middle of everything, I thought, realizing that I had been rash to come to Dancing Days. I asked for a beer. As soon as I finished it I left, trying to act as natural as possible and without looking in the direction of Fuentes' table. Out in the street, I hailed another cab and asked the driver to park about fifty yards from the restaurant. I was interested in the gray-haired guy; I already knew where to find the other two. Slipping my hand inside my shirt, I fondled the haft of the Randall.

"A woman?" asked the young, long-haired driver, smiling.

"No. A man."

The cabbie raised his eyebrows in the rearview mirror, trying to figure me. It wasn't long before the man I was waiting for calmly walked out of the restaurant, stopping in the doorway to light a cigarette, and got into the car waiting for him at the curb.

"That's the guy. Let's follow him."

According to the signs, we were headed for the Puerto Suárez airport.

At the airport, the gray-haired man walked straight to the counter, picked up a phone, and talked for some time. Still nonchalant, he sat down and dozed briefly, waiting for the plane, a Lear jet, which arrived and stood on the tarmac, engines running, waiting for him to board. He did, and the plane slid down the runway, lifted off, and disappeared.

At the counter, the airport employee said he didn't know the passenger's name. All he knew was the plane's destination: São Paulo, Brazil.

Nothing to do but hire another Bolivian taxi and return to Corumbá. By the time I got there I was hungry and decided to go back to the restaurant where I'd had dinner my first night in town. I ordered pintado again and the same Portuguese red wine. They were out of the Porca de Murça, so the waiter brought me a bottle of Terras Altas, which I accepted. I was sipping wine, waiting for the fish, when the proprietor, a stout Portuguese named Alberto, stopped by my table. I invited him to sit down with me. Alberto had left Portugal with his parents when he was six years old and emigrated to Belém do Pará, on the Amazon in Brazil. I asked him why he had left Belém and moved to Corumbá.

"Have you ever loved anyone?" he asked.

"Everybody's loved someone at least once," I said.

"Everybody no, not everybody. And love only happens to a person once," said Alberto. "I followed a woman here, a goddess, a saint. She walked into my family's restaurant one day, in Belém. I fell hopelessly in love with her the moment I saw her; she was still just a girl, fifteen years old. I was the one waiting on her table but she didn't look

131

at me, not even for one miserable instant. I asked the woman with her—later I found out it was her aunt—where they were from. Corumbá, the woman said. Then they were gone. I just could not get that girl out of my head, and I'm not the least bit embarrassed to tell you I cried myself to sleep nights, I suffered so. I lost a lot of weight and began spitting up blood."

Alberto raised his glass as if to toast the fact that he had gone so far for love as to spit up blood. "I was so out of my mind that I abandoned my old mother—God rest her soul in heaven, and my father's—and came to Corumbá after the girl."

The bottle was empty. I asked the waiter for another.

"When I got here I searched for her everywhere. I opened this restaurant, worked hard, saved money, prospered, and still my heart bled like a beggar's, like a poor man without so much as a crust of bread. One day, one unforgettable day, as I was walking past a church I looked in and saw that a wedding was taking place. The bride, all dressed in white, with a garland of orange buds and a long lace train carried by two small children, was walking like a princess down the aisle of the church. When I saw her face I felt something terrible, it was as if I had been struck by lightning. It was her, the woman of my dreams. I left the church a blind man, a dead man, stumbled to the river, and threw myself in, hoping to drown or be devoured by the hideous piranhas."

At this point in his narrative, Alberto was wearing such a poignant look that I stopped my first forkful of pintado in midair. Surely it would be rude to eat in the face of so much suffering.

"But this is a happy story," said Alberto, brightening. "I was born on the banks of the Elvas and swam quite well, so I didn't drown, and the piranhas took no interest in eating my miserable hide."

Love, Alberto knew, meant devotion, respect, but also patience. What goes around comes around. Six months after the wedding, the girl's husband went fishing in the marsh, fell in, and unable to swim, was drowned. Alberto waited a year before beginning to court her.

"This deserves another Terras Altas," I said.

None left. We substituted a bottle of Granleve. Too good to be true, for Corumbá. I left the restaurant drunk, which made me happy. Besides, I liked love stories like Alberto's, with happy endings.

13

RAFAEL HAD ARRIVED with instructions from Rio, but Fuentes didn't give much credit to what his partner in the mission said. After having been busted in Rio, Fuentes was in no mood to risk his hide again without a very convincing reason. If the orders really came from the top, from the Main Office, then he'd do the job. If not, it would be better to lie low. The cops had let him go, but they knew his name and were clearly suspicious.

"What do you want, a personal audience with the Main Office?" asked Rafael sarcastically. Fuentes knew that was impossible; no one had ever seen or spoken to whoever it was that gave the orders. Sometimes he doubted that the Main Office existed at all.

"Mateus is in Campo Grande, right? I want the orders straight from him," Fuentes had answered.

This conversation had taken place in Quijarro. The following day, when Rafael called him, Mateus was cold—only one day to make his contacts in Campo Grande, and now he had to go all the way to Puerto Suárez to convince a pigheaded hit man that his orders were for real. The Fuentes-Rafael duo had already proved incompetent—disastrous really—at executing a simple hit on a harmless lawyer. (That's what they thought of me: a harmless lawyer.) And he, Mateus, had been against giving them this new assignment in the first place.

Things went badly at Dancing Days. Mateus didn't like it that Fuentes had been picked up in Rio, and it worried him that the Main Office hadn't been informed. They really needed more people on the administrative end; traffic was getting heavier by the day, especially international operations. Mateus became sourer still when Fuentes mentioned that he thought the bearded guy who had just walked in the restaurant was following him. Even though Fuentes had not identified me as the "harmless lawyer," Mateus, an executive used to making spot decisions, resolved at that moment to contravene instructions from the Main Office and cancel the project they had been about to undertake. He explained to his operatives that unexpected events had forced him to come to this decision. They would be paid the fee stipulated in their preliminary contract.

"But you have another job to do," he told Fuentes. "Take care of that guy over there. I want him out of the way as soon as possible."

Once he had given Fuentes these instructions, Mateus didn't look at me again. It made no difference to him who I was. He knew that, because of the botched job in Rio, Fuentes would not screw up again so soon. Besides, the error—he knew now—had been Rafael's.

Mateus left first. He did not expect me to follow him, though he hadn't discounted the possibility either. He was confident that Fuentes would do the job—so confident that he dozed at the airport waiting for his plane.

Fuentes and Rafael left Dancing Days together shortly after Mateus. No sign of the bearded guy. Either he had followed Mateus or gone back to the hotel, thought Fuentes.

"Need any help, Chinaman?" asked Rafael with a sneer.

Fuentes' face darkened. No, he didn't need help knocking off some shitty Brazilian. He was actually happy to be able to carry out this assignment on his own. Without a word of goodbye, he ducked into a taxi and headed for Corumbá.

On arriving at the Grand Hotel, Fuentes stopped in his room to grab a small bag of tools. Then he went up to the third floor and stopped at the door to my room. He carefully examined the lock and was pleasantly surprised: It was not engaged.

He slipped inside silently. A quick glance through the

135

open door was enough to inspect the bathroom. In the bedroom another surprise: Mercedes, Zélia's friend, lay stretched out in bed. She was apparently a light sleeper, because she awoke as soon as Fuentes walked into the room, though he had not made a sound. Fuentes noted that she had awakened instantaneously and, immediately alert, shot a glance at the pocketbook on the dressing table.

"What's up, Pepe?" she said, smiling, but her eyes and body were tense. Fuentes walked over to the dresser and picked up the purse.

"What are you doing here?" asked Mercedes, with the same smile.

"I could ask you the same question."

"That guy from São Paulo asked me up to his room," said Mercedes. "He should be back any minute."

Without taking his eyes off her, Fuentes opened the purse and began examining the contents.

"Give me a cigarette, will you?" she said. She was no longer able to smile. The muscles in her jaw were visible for a few seconds.

"Pretty, real pretty," said Fuentes, withdrawing a snub-nosed .38 from her purse. He also removed her identification and thumbed through it quickly with increasing interest. "You fucking bitch."

Mercedes made a dash for the door, but Fuentes knocked her to the ground with a violent whack on the side of the head. Then he kneeled over her, straddling her stomach, and punched her in the face, hard, again and again. Mercedes knew she was pinned; she lunged with both arms, flinging her hands at his face in an attempt to gouge his eyes with her nails. She missed with the left, but the fingernails of her right hand made contact with his eyeball. Wounded and enraged, Fuentes abandoned the little game he'd been playing with his victim before killing her. He took Mercedes' wrist in one hand, elbow in the other, broke the bone of the offending right arm in half, and then began beating her unprotected face with closed fists and elbows until he had turned it to a bloody pulp. Then, just to make sure that the Brazilian bitch was dead, he slowly turned her head until he felt the neck snap. Cursing, he went to the bathroom to wash up. A piece of fingernail was embedded in his left eye; he pulled it out with a trembling hand. Blind in one eye, and furious, he returned to the bedroom and kicked Mercedes' body with all his strength.

When I asked for the key to my room the desk clerk smiled and gave me a conspiratorial look and said, "She's already upstairs."

I climbed the stairs slowly, still woozy from the wine at lunch. The door to my room was open. I felt the skin on the back of my neck bristle with premonitory goose bumps. As soon as I saw Mercedes, the effect of the alcohol disappeared completely. My first reaction was to try to revive her, but it was obvious soon enough that she was dead.

The Randall in hand, I ran downstairs to Fuentes' room. The door was closed. After knocking several times, I returned my knife to its sheath and went back down to the lobby. The girl at the desk informed me that Fuentes had checked out an hour before.

"Mercedes is dead, in my room," I told her. "Call the police." I hurried toward the river. Any deserted place would do. Then, careful that no one was watching, I drew the knife from its case, poised to throw it into the water. The waning light of sunset reflected off the blade, an intense rosy gleam. Somehow this made me change my mind, and I slid the knife back into the sheath.

Arquelau's place was nearby, but he wasn't home. Probably at the Grand already, I thought. My shirt was drenched with sweat, but I couldn't take off my jacket because of the Randall. An ambulance and a police car were parked outside the hotel, surrounded by a large number of spectators. In the lobby groups of guests stood talking in low voices. I found Arquelau in my room, along with two other men who stared at me with great interest

137

and then, when they saw he knew me, went back to rummaging through my things. Arquelau gestured for me to follow him into the hall.

"It wasn't me."

"We know that. Whoever killed her is wounded, possibly in the face. There's skin under her fingernails. Do you know who did it? What was she doing in your room?"

"Raul told me I could trust you."

"So?"

"Look for a man named Camilo Fuentes."

"Who was she?" asked Oliveira, the chief investigator, approaching us.

"I met her on the train, on the way here from Bauru."

"Is that where you're from?"

"No, Rio. I changed trains in Bauru."

"What's your business in Corumbá?"

"I came to go fishing. In the Paraguay River."

"He's a friend of a friend of mine, a cop from Rio," said Arquelau.

"You're going to have to stick around awhile, at least a day or so, and give a statement."

"I'm checking out and moving to the Santa Mônica."

Rafael Marinho had left the Santa Mônica that morning. In the hotel register it said he was a salesman and lived at 354 Avenida Nossa Senhora de Copacabana, apartment 401, in Rio. A phony address, no doubt, but I made note of it anyway.

My room in the Santa Mônica was air conditioned. I locked myself in and waited for something to happen. But no one came knocking at the door. The phone didn't even ring.

I woke at seven A.M., took a shower, and went down to breakfast in a room with Formica tables covered with blue plastic tablecloths. A man with thin hair falling over his forehead placed papaya, bread, and butter on the table and filled my coffee cup. The other people breakfasting looked like members of a tour group. When two elderly women in Bermuda shorts walked in, a third, seated at

138

one of the tables, welcomed them with the greeting "Morning, you two beautiful dolls." From across the room two Europeans, one with the face of a spoiled child, observed the rest of their group with undisguised disdain. There was not a pretty woman in the lot. They all looked strikingly alike in their lavish, happy-go-lucky vulgarity (probably from some small wealthy city in the interior of São Paulo). How had two bored, slightly effeminate Europeans ended up in a group like this?

As early as it was, the temperature was comfortable. On my way to Arquelau's I passed the tour group noisily taking their place on a bus in front of the hotel. The red blooms on the trees seemed even more brilliant that morning. I thought of Mercedes, the red birthmark on her ear, the smell of cigarettes on her breath.

Arquelau opened the door in his pajamas.

"It's not too early, is it?"

"No, come on in."

In the living room, on the table, a large number of books were spread out.

"I teach Portuguese at a night school," said Arquelau, as if to justify the books, which he began to gather up—taking special care with the oldest, the one he had been poring over when I arrived, in an attempt to trace the etymology of the word Brazil. He would have enjoyed discussing the various theories, but the troubled man who had just dropped in was clearly not the right person for a conversation about word etymology.

"Mercedes is going to be buried today at five o'clock," said Arquelau. "This book is by Assis Cintra, he died about fifty years ago. Just look at this fascinating entry, from Percival, in the year 1220: *comprydas meyas teintas en brasil.* The Portuguese language was just in its infancy, having been born in the eleventh century. It took poets and people scarcely seven centuries to create this tongue we take for granted."

"Is the cemetery far?"

"I know you're hiding things from me, but I'm not interested in what they are."

"Thanks."

"Stop by the station and ask for a clerk named Alfredo," said Arquelau, returning to his books.

I arrived at the station at eleven. Alfredo was a fat man, of Syrian or Lebanese background, with a hooked nose. He pounded a noisy old typewriter as I made my statement to the effect that I had come to Corumbá on vacation to fish; that I met Mercedes on the train; that she had picked up the key to my room at the desk, as she had several other times before; that I had gone for a ride to Puerto Suárez and then eaten lunch at the Elvas Restaurant; that, on returning at about five P.M., I had found Mercedes' body on the floor of my room.

Mercedes' mother wore black. Her chin was covered with silky white down, and her face was etched with deep crisscrossing lines, like a wall covered with fraying and irregular plastic tiles. She told me her name was Paulina. Only she and I and Zélia were present for Mercedes' burial in Corumbá's tiny cemetery. Two men wearing suits and ties stood at a distance talking.

"I knew this would happen someday," said Paulina dryly, bitterly.

"Was it Pepe?" asked Zélia.

"Pepe, Pepe! If it wasn't him it would have been someone else," said Paulina.

"It was. His name is Camilo," I said.

"The police cut her all up, how could they do a thing like that to her?" said Paulina.

"In cases like this it's the law," I said. "They have to do an autopsy and prepare a report."

"It was Pepe?"

"Camilo," I said.

"He burst in on me with his eye bloody and started going through her suitcase, yelling and cursing, but then the maid came to do the room and he left. Was it him?"

"Yes."

The gravediggers lowered the coffin. Off to the side of the grave was a small basket of old rose petals that had

140

already lost their aroma, leftovers from someone else's demise. Paulina scooped up a handful of petals and threw them down onto the coffin. Zélia and I did the same.

"I hope she's gone to heaven," said Zélia.

"I doubt it," said Paulina.

At the gates of the cemetery we separated. Soon after, I noticed that Zélia was trailing along behind me.

"Are you following me?"

"I hate that old hag, I never want to see her again," said Zélia.

We walked on. Zélia stayed at my side.

"Where are you going?" she asked.

"To VASP airlines, to buy a ticket back to Rio."

We didn't say another word until the ticket agency. Once in a while Zélia had to practically run to keep up with me. The day was heating up; we were sweating.

I managed to get a ticket for the following afternoon.

"Aren't you even going to invite me for a drink or something?"

We went to a bar on the corner of the park opposite the Grand Hotel. White wood tables in the open air under colorful awnings.

"I've never been lucky in life," said Zélia, sipping her soda. "How about you?"

"I don't know."

"You don't know if you're lucky or not?"

"I'm not unlucky."

"All I've had is bad luck. Pepe and I were going to get married."

"Camilo. He told you he was going to marry you?"

"Yeah."

Two men sat down at a nearby table, the same two that I'd seen in the cemetery. They looked like municipal functionaries.

"Probably just a line."

"He's not the first man who's wanted to marry me, you know."

The two functionaries sat silently and drank their mineral water.

141

"We even decided where we were going to live—São Paulo. That's where his business is."

"What does he do?"

"I don't know."

"Didn't he tell you anything about his work?"

"Just that he couldn't fool around on the job."

"What about Mercedes?"

"What do you mean, What about Mercedes?"

"Where did you meet her?"

"Here. She's from here. But she travels a lot."

Zélia explained that Mercedes had called and asked her to meet her in Bauru.

"When I got to Bauru she said, Now we're going to Corumbá."

"Did you always do everything she told you to?"

"She didn't tell me, she asked me."

"What did Mercedes do, for work?"

"She didn't. At least I don't think so."

I left Zélia and walked through the park. I sat down on a bench. The two men sat down next to me. One of them took a handkerchief out of his pocket and mopped the sweat from his forehead. Then he said: "I'm Inspector Viana, federal investigator. This is Inspector Cordeiro de Melo."

I waited.

"We'd like some information about Camilo Fuentes."

"I don't know what you're talking about."

Cordeiro de Melo smiled. He had large yellow teeth. "We know all about you. You came from Rio, passing yourself off as a cattle dealer, but you were actually following Camilo Fuentes. And you managed to stay on his heels as far as Puerto Suárez."

"And what about you? What have you been doing all this time? The guy kills a woman and you let him get away."

"You screwed everything up," said Viana patiently. "Fuentes saw you in Dancing Days, went to the hotel, and found Mercedes."

Mercedes. Mercedes. Mercedes. Ah, women.

"I guess Mercedes kept you well informed," I added, disturbed to verify the truth that had been dawning on me.

"Mercedes and our people from Rio. You fucked up, and Mercedes is the one who caught it. She was one of our most experienced operatives," said Cordeiro de Melo.

"Do you have any idea how many miles of border exist between Brazil and Bolivia? More than three thousand," said Viana. "We manage to discover that an enormous portion of the coke entering Brazil comes in through Puerto Suárez and that the ringleaders meet here in Corumbá to oversee the operation. And what happens? You come down from Rio and screw it all up. One of our best agents is dead, the birds have flown the coop, and the coke is someplace else by now waiting for another opening."

"I wanted to get Fuentes," I said gloomily.

"They'll get him for you now. They know we identified him. Fuentes is a dead man."

14

FUENTES DIDN'T know how to contact the people he worked for. He knew only Mateus, who conveyed the orders, and Rafael, who worked with him on some of the missions. And he knew neither of their addresses.

He had not managed to "take care of" me, as Mateus had instructed, which upset him a great deal. After killing Mercedes, he thought it best to disappear as rapidly as possible. Fuentes no longer had any doubt that the cops in Rio had let him go in order to follow him to Corumbá. He figured I was a cop, too, working with Mercedes; he had seen us together on various occasions, on the train and in the hotel. From his point of view, Mercedes had died because she had committed the error of letting herself be distracted, sleeping in my room; certainly she was my lover. No sex on the job, that was his motto. He, too, had behaved carelessly, had been inattentive; unaware that Zélia was the bait dangled in front of him by Mercedes, he had almost got himself fucked. He would have liked to talk with Mateus, to tell him what had happened, and explain the reason for not having executed his mission. He didn't want his professional reputation to suffer. Fuentes was sure Mateus would understand; Mateus liked him; Mateus respected serious people like him.

Fuentes lived on Avenida São João, in São Paulo. Near his building, on the opposite side of the street, was a newsstand that belonged to a friend of his. After asking what happened to his eye, which was covered with a gauze pad and adhesive tape, Benito, the newsman, told Fuentes that a couple of guys had been around looking for him. It

144

was unlikely to be Mateus' people; they usually left a type-written message under his door when they didn't catch him at home. It could've been the cops, but how would they have found out his real address? Unable to come up with an answer, Fuentes decided to stay away from his apartment for a while. He couldn't leave town, since his apartment was the only point of contact with Mateus. He would have to hide out in São Paulo itself, or maybe go to Rio—both were metropolitan areas of over ten million inhabitants where it was easy for a person to drop out of sight and survive. He threw some clothes into a small bag and gave Benito some money, asking him to pay the gas, electric, and telephone bills, which were in the name of the former tenant. Benito was also to pick up any messages from Mateus and to meet Fuentes in the lobby of the Marabá Cinema on Avenida Ipiranga on the fifteenth, two weeks later, at eight P.M. Then he went to the bus station and got on the first bus with an empty seat to Rio.

Fuentes spent the seven-hour bus trip totting up the balance sheet of his life. He lived in a country he hated, in the midst of people who despised him and were his enemies. Why? There had to be a reason. He liked his job, of course (especially when it was Brazilians he had to kill), but that wasn't all of it. (Perhaps I'm being unfair here; Fuentes' motives were actually more complex than I first supposed when I began trying to understand him.) He knew that killing was a sordid thing to do. But hadn't they killed his father? That's what life was, a life-and-death struggle between people. Between animals. Countries. Forces of nature. Two years before, when he got into a brawl in a restaurant in the neighborhood called Boca do Lixo, frequented by whores and pimps and weary businessmen, he hadn't expected that his life as a small-time marginal would change so drastically. Two couples who were drinking whiskey at one of the tables had laughed at him, at his clothes, which were old and shabby and much too tight. These four were young and well dressed—the women attractive, the men with the kind of physiques developed at muscle-building gyms. Men of that type,

Fuentes knew, were often not very strong; strength was based on more than simple muscle articulation. They had laughed at him: "I guess the stiff was a size or two smaller than you, huh?" and one had stuck his foot out in the aisle to trip him as he walked by. Because he was a Bolivian, an Indian; because he was poor and badly dressed; because Brazilians were disgusting dogs. Fuentes stopped beside their table. One of the girls let out a whoop of laughter, half enjoyment, half fear, sensing that the situation was not as comfortable as her friends imagined. The two men stared back at him, sneering, arrogant. In a rapid movement, Fuentes extended his hand, grabbed one of them by the hair, pulled his head forward and gave him a tremendous blow on the nose. The sound of breaking bones was audible before the man fell to the floor, dragging his chair with him. The other one, startled by Fuentes' quickness, leapt to his feet with his fists poised in front of him, like a boxer with his guard up. One punch in the stomach was enough to knock him to the floor senseless. In spite of his fury, Fuentes' face remained impassive throughout the short fight. It didn't take long for the police to arrive and take him in, but a witness to the incident interceded in his favor and managed to get him off. His protector had been Mateus. The two of them talked several times after that and discovered they had the same ideas. Mateus was always saying they had the same ideas: The world was full of creeps, exploiting parasites, sybarites, thieves protected by corrupt authorities. One day Mateus told Fuentes that a friend was willing to pay well to have one of these creeps eliminated. Would he accept the assignment? It would be an easy job, the target was a São Paulo lawyer named Barreto who had an office on Rua Brigadeiro Luiz Antônio. Mateus said he would leave the details to Fuentes' discretion, "but don't forget, the best plan is always the one that allows for the easiest escape." Mateus would supply whatever weapon Fuentes deemed necessary. The Bolivian knew he was being tested. He even liked the idea, because it would give him a chance to demonstrate his ability.

146

Forgoing any advice or assistance from Mateus, he said he would take care of it on his own.

Barreto was delivered to his office every morning at ten o'clock by his wife; he went to lunch around one and from the restaurant proceeded directly to the courthouse, after which he returned to the office. His day ended at seven, when his wife picked him up and they went home to Itaim. He was a slender man, with glasses and a goatee, who walked with tiny, unsteady steps—hardly the adversary Fuentes had imagined. (But looks don't mean shit, he thought.) Barreto's office was located in a small, quiet building with two self-service elevators. Fuentes concluded that the best time and place for the job would be at the end of the day, in the hall on the sixth floor near the office, as Barreto waited for the elevator. He hit on the idea of the weapon by chance when he saw a boy in the Praça da República playing with a yoyo. Yoyos had been in fashion when he was a kid and were just now making a comeback. The boy wasn't very good with it, though; in fact, he didn't even look all that interested in the thing. So it didn't take much to convince the kid to sell him the yoyo for a few coins. He changed the string to a thicker one made of nylon. At six forty-five, with the yoyo in his pocket, Fuentes went up to the sixth floor of Barreto's building and waited in the hall. Having pushed the elevator button as soon as he heard footsteps, Fuentes was standing there playing with the yoyo when Barreto appeared. As he waited for the elevator, the lawyer watched Fuentes clumsily attempt a fancy maneuver. The elevator doors opened, and Fuentes gestured for him to go first. As soon as Barreto turned and stepped in front of him, Fuentes wrapped the cord around his victim's neck, crossed the two ends, and, setting his back against Barreto's, leaned forward and pulled hard on the cord, hefting the lawyer up onto his back as if he were a sack of potatoes. Barreto let out a small hoarse grunt. That was all. Fuentes held the body in place a few more moments ("about the weight of a plump turkey"), even though he was sure the man was already dead. Then he carried Bar-

147

reto down to the landing between the fifth and sixth floors, removed the cord, which had dug deeply into the flesh of the neck, rolled up the yoyo and put it in his pocket. He relieved Barreto of his wallet, wristwatch, and wedding ring. As he left the building, the doorman hardly looked at him. Fuentes walked right by Barreto's wife, parked at the curb waiting for her husband. A little further down the street, he stuck the wristwatch and wedding ring in a drainpipe and gave the eight thousand cruzeiros he found in the wallet to a couple of beggars. ("A country full of beggars and rich thieves.") In newspaper accounts, the police were quoted as attributing Barreto's murder to a gang of thugs, led by a guy called Crablegs, which had been active lately in the downtown area. A few days later, Mateus came looking for Fuentes to tell him that he and his friends were extremely pleased with the performance, especially the fact that he had left a false trail for the police. Fuentes made a point of mentioning that he had thrown away the jewelry and given the money to beggars; he didn't want them to think him a thief. He had steady employment from then on. Though he knew there were people above Mateus who gave the orders—Mateus spoke of a "Main Office"—Fuentes didn't ask questions; they paid well and that was what counted.

It was on his third assignment that he met Rafael. The two of them had been contracted to kill three men who lived on Rua Araujos, in the Tijuca district of Rio. "What do you think these guys did that they want us to waste them, huh, Chinaman?" Rafael had asked, once they were alone. Fuentes turned his back and muttered, "Chinaman, your dick." The men lived alone in an old house. Fuentes and Rafael watched the place for three days. The men rarely went out. One of them did the shopping at a nearby supermarket on Praça Saenz Pena. The shutters remained closed regardless of the weather. It was Fuentes who came up with the plan.

The man who did the shopping, wearing jeans and a red T-shirt that said COME TO MARLBORO COUNTRY on it, was making his way along Rua Araujos with two sacks of groceries when they pulled up next to him in the car supplied by Mateus. Rafael leaped out shouting, "Hold it, police!" He pulled a gun out of his belt and repeated the order several times for the benefit of a few passersby who had stopped to stare. The man hesitated, glancing toward his destination: not far, but with shutters resolutely shut. "Okay, get in," said Rafael, pointing to the open car door. The man bent to set his grocery bags down on the sidewalk. "The bags come too," said Rafael. As soon as the car had sped off, the few witnesses to the kidnapping dispersed. It had not been an extraordinary enough incident to merit a great deal of attention. The grocery bags contained macaroni, eggs, cooking oil, meat, and quite a few cans of beer. Except for small change from the supermarket, the man's pockets were empty. "How much do you want?" he asked from the back seat where he sat handcuffed to Rafael. "Nothing," said Fuentes. He watched through the rearview mirror as Rafael buried his knife in the man's heart. They were driving the empty streets around Maracanã stadium. Rafael covered the body with a blanket. The two of them got out of the car and slammed the doors. Once Mateus' emissary arrived and drove off ("Mr. Marlboro's on his way to be turned into emergency rations," said Rafael), they headed back to Rua Araujos on foot. The two men inside the house would eventually become worried and one of them would have to go out in search of the third. Two hours later, a short man emerged and walked slowly toward Praça Saenz Pena. As soon as he was out of sight, Fuentes knocked at the door and said through the peephole, "A man got hit by a car in front of the market where I work and asked me to come tell you they're taking him to the hospital." Fuentes talked real fast so the listener would have trouble understanding him. "What? Where is he? What hospital?" Peering out through the peephole, it was impossible for the man to see Rafael. "He's in the hospital," repeated Fuentes. The man opened the door. He was around forty and held a gun in his hand. "Hey, what's this?" said Fuentes, feigning fear. "The manager sends me down here to give you a message from your friend and this is the reception I get?" "Just a minute," said the man, sticking the gun into his belt after getting a look at his visitor's jacket, SENDAS MARKET stamped on the front. Fuentes was on top of him immediately. The man was stronger than he looked, however; Rafael found them struggling in the living room and neatly stabbed him in the kidneys. Lying around the room were two Urco rifles and five .38 Taurus revolvers. Fuentes and Rafael waited in silence for the third man's return. They heard the turn of the key in the lock. Rafael wanted to show off his dexterity with the knife ("The Professor taught me everything he knows") and had asked Fuentes to leave this last to him too: "The other guy didn't count, it was from the back." The man came in to find two strangers in his living room. His hand darted to his waist. Rafael's move was extremely quick. Not a sound. The man tottered and fell slowly, eyes closed, the blade deep in his chest. Rafael bent over him and removed the knife. A gush of blood soaked the dead man's shirt. "All modesty aside, I doubt if anyone could've done it better, even the Professor," said Rafael. "Right in the heart." (In point of fact, I had been the only person to survive Rafael's knife. Hermes' assertion, on examining my scar, that my attacker must have been an incompetent, turned out, in addition to having its fortuitous, ironic aspect—Rafael had been his student—to be unjust. Rafael was extremely good at his craft.)

Arriving in Rio, Fuentes checked into the Hotel Bragança, on Rua Mem de Sá. It was modest and, because of the strength of the cruzeiro in relation to the peso, full of Argentine tourists speaking a mixture of Spanish and Portuguese. He could easily blend right in.

In the yellow pages, Fuentes chose an ophthalmologist with a Spanish name: Pablo Hernandez. Though he was of Uruguayan descent, to Fuentes' disappointment Dr. Hernandez did not speak Spanish. He examined Fuentes painstakingly in his well-appointed office on Avenida

Graça Aranha, in the Esplanada do Castelo district. Lens, iris, conjunctiva, optic nerve, muscles, arteries, and veins, all fine. The cornea, however, had been damaged. Hernandez pedantically explained to his patient that the cornea was an external transparent layer through which light—and with light, color, shapes, movement, etc.—penetrated the eye. The solution to his problem would be a cornea transplant. He should check with one of the existing eye banks.

"To get an eye from a dead person?"

"Yes, within three hours after death the eye can be packaged in a special receptacle, kept at low temperature, and taken to an ophthalmological surgeon to perform the transplant. But it's not easy to get a cornea from the eye bank."

One alternative was the donation of a cornea, from a friend, say, but such an arrangement required large sacrifice on one hand and much grace on the other: "One party altogether willing to give and the other to receive."

Another solution would be to buy a cornea, but you had to be careful. Hernandez had heard of a case in which the supposed seller was paid in advance and then didn't show up at the appointed time to "deliver the merchandise."

"How would I go about buying a cornea?"

"Check the newspapers, in the classified."

"Cornea for sale—female, age 24. Call 185-3944."

There was only one ad, in the *Jornal do Brasil*. Fuentes had also checked *O Globo* and *O Dia*. From his room in the Hotel Bragança, Fuentes dialed the number. A woman answered. The matter had to be discussed in person after eight P.M. She gave him an address in Cidade de Deus. Fuentes didn't know Rio well, and asked how to get there. She told him to take a bus from Largo do São Francisco.

"Where's that?"

"Downtown, just ask around. I can't talk right now, my boss is calling me."

The Largo do São Francisco was not hard to find, but there was an endless line and Fuentes had to wait for the third bus. Many of the people in the crowd, mostly women, but some men as well, carried old plastic sacks bearing the names of various stores, in which they had transported their lunch to and from work.

It was a relatively new building in a housing development, already in disrepair. The plaster was peeling, the grass needed cutting. A thin, light-skinned mulatto woman opened the apartment door.

"Is it for you?" she asked, when Fuentes announced that he was the person who had phoned. The bitch figures an Indian couldn't possibly have the money to buy himself an eye, thought Fuentes. (I already mentioned that he was a rancorous, easily offended man, with a tendency to find hostility where it didn't necessarily exist.)

"As a matter of fact it is." He was glad, at least, that she apparently hadn't noticed the scar on his left eyeball. It wasn't really even a scar, just a small discoloration, but he had supposed it was an obvious disfigurement, unavoidably noticeable.

"Ten million," said the woman impatiently. "And that's cheap. My daughter's never been sick a day in her life, she's got good teeth, perfect hearing. Terrific eyes."

A crack in the living-room wall ran uninterrupted from ceiling to floor. The roof was stained and blistered from water seepage.

"I'm going to think about it," said Fuentes. "I'll call you tomorrow." (It wasn't the money—he had that—it was the filth he saw around him. Terrific eyes—here?)

"That phone number's the place I work. I've got tomorrow off, and there's no phone here."

"Can I see the girl?"

"Marluci," yelled the woman.

Pale, with great round eyes, Marluci appeared in the living room dressed in cotton shorts and a faded shirt that said: COCA-COLA—THE PAUSE THAT REFRESHES.

"This guy's here because of the ad," said the woman.

"Why are you selling your cornea?"

"I have my reasons," said the girl.

"She has her reasons," said the mother, belligerent.

I can't buy this kid's eye, thought Fuentes. She's got the same straight dark hair I do. Could she be Indian? But hadn't Brazil killed off all its Indians? The girl was pale, anemic-looking. An eye is something you take from an enemy, yank it out and put it on ice in a little box and deliver it to the doctor. A little Styrofoam ice chest, as if it were ice cream. Was ten million a fair price for an eye?

"So?" prompted the woman, interrupting Fuentes' ruminations.

"I'll think about it."

"Don't worry, honey," said the woman, turning to her daughter as she closed the door. "Someone else'll come along." There's nothing in this world that isn't bought or sold, thought Fuentes, and she knows it.

Out in the street, Fuentes couldn't stop staring at the eyes of people passing by. He had never felt so indecisive in his whole life. The sight in his right eye—always stronger than the left, in which he was slightly near-sighted—seemed better than ever; but nevertheless there was a point to the left beyond which he couldn't see without turning his head. He held his left hand up to the side of his head, a wrong-handed salute. All he could see was the profile of his nose. He knew that this was dangerous.

Fuentes met Miriam (one of the cloak-and-dagger coincidences I mentioned earlier) in a supermarket on Rua Riachuelo, not far from the hotel where he was staying. He liked to walk around grocery stores looking at the merchandise on the shelves and watching the women doing their shopping. You could see all kinds of women in the supermarket—housewives, young girls, live-in maids—and also horrendous ones, and it was easy to remain inconspicuous ogling them, even for a man with only one eye. The women standing in line, the pyramids of colorful packages, all within arm's reach—Fuentes found it a fascinating spectacle. A tall bleached blonde in short-shorts flaunting her tight, round buns caught his attention. But soon he realized she was actually a transvestite; there were a number of them in that part of the city. Homosexuals, of either sex, neither attracted nor repelled Fuentes. He was indifferent; they were neutral persons in whom he was not interested and with whom he could have an unwitting social relationship.

Now Fuentes was watching a light-skinned freckled woman in low-heeled sandals who seemed to be absorbed in reading labels and packages. Fuentes, too, enjoyed reading what was written on the boxes and cans neatly lined up on the shelves. Earlier he had considered buying a can of peaches, but after reading everything on the label of each brand had lost interest in peaches and changed his mind. The woman Fuentes was following around the store seemed to be doing the same thing. At the moment she was reading detergent boxes, having already carefully studied canned peas, asparagus, mushrooms, and hearts of palm. In the intervals between displays she took off her glasses and idly pushed an empty shopping cart; her stride said that she knew she was pretty. The woman had a mature and pleasing body; with or without glasses there was a certain satisfied, dignified sensuality about her. It didn't take her long to realize she was being watched, and by a man who turned his head from side to side as he studied goods and people alike, as if he could see out of only one eye. She no longer had romantic illusions, having already gone through her quota of men of his sort; her heart no longer pounded madly, as it had when she was younger. But it was always wonderful and energizing to feel a man's interest, especially a man with the brute grace of the robust and unabashed. Unconsciously, she began to hold her body more carefully; her shoulders straightened, her stomach flattened (making her bust more prominent), her chin jutted forward to minimize the slight jowliness, a family weakness, that spoiled her profile. Their eyes met. He moved toward her and those dark pupils surrounded by brilliant white zoomed into close-up.

Suddenly she felt unnerved and inhibited, unexpectedly tongue-tied.

"You live around here?" A new note in his voice.

"Mmm-hum. And you?"

"I'm in a hotel on Mem de Sá. My name is Camilo."

"Mine's Miriam."

They were experiencing the euphoria that marks the beginning of a relationship sparked by reciprocal erotic overtones. As she walked, Miriam placed each foot carefully in front of the other. Fuentes managed to keep her on his right. They both studied the items on the shelves with less intensity—mainly interested in each other. Fuentes concentrated his one eye on Miriam, principally her body. A woman's face could be ugly (ugly faces are always, or almost always, expressive), but she had to have the kind of body he liked: thick meaty thighs, a trim turned-up ass, a flat stomach, breasts just slightly larger than the palm of his hand.

"What are you doing this afternoon?"

"I'm not sure."

"How about going out with me?"

"Where would we go?"

"You could come by my hotel and we could decide from there."

"Where are you staying?"

"The Bragança, on Mem de Sá."

"Uhh, that ratty place. They don't like women going up to the rooms. They always make trouble, the creeps."

"Don't worry about it. What time would be good?"

More relaxed once they had made their pact, Miriam and Fuentes went back to examining the stuff on the shelves. "It's incredible, isn't it? Have you been to Porcao, on Avenida Brasil? Or Freeway, in Barar, or Carrefour?" Miriam asked.

After they separated, Fuentes hurried back to the Hotel Bragança.

"Will you be here at four o'clock?" he asked the guy behind the desk.

"Yeah," said the clerk.

155

"A friend of mine is coming to visit. I want her to be able to come upstairs and I don't want any trouble."

"I'm sorry, sir, but the hotel has regulations, and unfortunately—"

"Look, buddy." Fuentes' body seemed to take up the whole counter. His wide eyes and soft but husky voice startled the clerk, who took a step backward. "This regulation of yours is illegal. She's coming upstairs and no one's going to bother her, you got that?"

"Yes, sir. I didn't realize she was a relative."

Fuentes said nothing more. Maybe later he'd give the jerk a tip, but right now he wanted it to be perfectly clear that if the lady was inconvenienced the piece of shit with a mustache would pay dearly.

"Don't worry, no problem, no problem," muttered the clerk as if he had read Fuentes' mind.

At five after four Miriam walked into the Bragança and up to Fuentes' room. She was wearing a red dress (not new, but it made her feel good) and high-heeled sandals. And makeup. Now you look like a whore, thought Fuentes, disappointed.

"You want to sit down?"

Miriam sat in the only chair in the room. Fuentes sat on the bed.

"Have you been here before?" he asked.

"No."

"Then how did you know they don't like women coming up to the rooms?"

"It's a long story."

"You don't want to tell me, don't tell me."

"I had a house of girls, you know how it is."

"In the Zone?"

"Mmm, they tore it down. But I didn't service the johns myself, I was the madam. The place was torn down. I hired a lawyer, but it didn't do any good. They tore down the whole street."

Fuentes had no objections to getting involved with a prostitute; all he worried about was catching something. He believed the majority of prostitutes were responsible

156

people, incapable of deliberately transmitting venereal disease to a client, but there was still the chance they were in the initial phase, without symptoms.

"I'm worried about catching something," said Fuentes.

"I'm clean. Went to the gynecologist just last week."

"Sometimes a woman doesn't know."

"I'm not a prostitute. I haven't even had relations with anyone for over two months. You don't have to worry, really."

Miriam grasped his arm. "Your arm is hard as a rock. You have anything else this hard?" There wasn't a trace of malice in her smile.

"It's even harder."

"The guy downstairs acted like I was invisible. Did you say something to him?"

"No. They must have changed the rules."

15

ON THE FOURTEENTH Fuentes told Miriam that he had to go to São Paulo the following day. They had rented an apartment together in Rio on Rua Riachuelo. They avoided talking about their respective "former lives." Miriam didn't want to know how Fuentes got all the money to pay their expenses. They spent the majority of their time in bed, sleeping and fucking. In between, they strolled downtown, usually in Santana Park, visited restaurants in the neighborhood, particularly Lisboeta's, went to the movies, or watched television. They were living like people on vacation, far from home, and Miriam knew it couldn't last forever. Maybe Fuentes' trip to São Paulo was a pretext to split up without having to explain. When Fuentes left early on the fifteenth he repeated that he would be back the next day, but Miriam had known too many men to believe the promises they made.

Fuentes arrived in São Paulo at lunchtime. He took a taxi downtown and ate a sandwich at a luncheonette. Then he sat on a bench in the Praça da República and carefully considered whether or not he should go to his apartment or wait until the appointed time to meet Benito and find out what was going on. In the end, he opted for a compromise: He would pass by Benito's newsstand and, if it looked safe, stop to talk with him. That way (if he was lucky) he wouldn't have to wait until eight P.M. He was anxious to get back to Miriam as fast as possible.

The newsstand was closed. Fuentes walked past without stopping and went into a drugstore a little farther down the street.

"Aspirin," said Fuentes. "A small packet."

From the drugstore he could observe the entrance to his building. As he was debating his next move, he recognized a woman walking out of the apartment building—a neighbor; they had met once in the hall and she had struck up a conversation. Fuentes crossed the street and headed in her direction.

"Well, hello, how are you?" said Fuentes as they were about to pass on the sidewalk.

The woman recognized him and stopped. "Just fine. I haven't seen you around lately. Been traveling again?"

"Just got back to town this minute. Hope nobody's broken into my apartment."

"Heavens," said the woman, staring at Fuentes' hands, as though she thought it strange for them to be empty, "I hope not either. That hasn't happened yet in our building; let's hope it never does."

"Everything's in order, then?"

"As far as I know," said the woman slowly, in a different tone.

"Well, I'm off. Have a nice day, now."

"You, too."

The woman took a few steps, looked back over her shoulder, and then continued on her way.

Fuentes returned to the drugstore.

"You forgot your aspirin," said the cashier.

"And give me some vitamins, too."

"Which one?"

His exchange with the neighbor had made Fuentes uneasy.

"Which vitamin?"

Talking to her had been a waste of time. If the building was being watched, she wouldn't be aware of it. And the fact that Benito's newsstand was closed—that was a mystery in need of solving.

"What do you want—A? B? C? . . ."

"B."

"Any particular brand?"

Fuentes paid for his purchases and left the store. He

159

had decided to spend the afternoon at the Ipiranga Theater, across from the Marabá, where he was supposed to meet Benito. But instead he crossed the street again and headed for his apartment building. No one at the front desk. He rode the ancient elevator full of graffiti ("You Queer," "Go Vasco!") to the eighth floor. When he got out, he stood still and listened to the sounds wafting down the hall. A baby crying, which usually irritated him, but now it was merely one of the sounds to be evaluated and identified, along with music, children's voices, dishes clattering, a soap opera on television. He placed his ear against the door to his apartment and concentrated like a doctor using a stethoscope. Finally satisfied, he opened the door and silently slipped inside.

Fuentes stood motionless in the dim living room, straining to detect suspicious sounds or images. He noted the smell of cigarettes in the air. The room was otherwise as he had left it. The only thing out of the ordinary was the smell of cigarettes. Which was why he looked around cautiously, trying to locate the source.

Benito was in the bathtub, missing his shirt and shoes, his thin body covered with circular burns. In the bathtub, too, Fuentes found a wad of cotton, a shirt that had been torn into strips, cigarette butts, and a box of matches. Shreds of cotton clung to Benito's mouth. Benito could not have resisted long; surely he had told his torturers what they wanted to know.

Fuentes meticulously examined the rest of the apartment. The television was still warm. He dragged Benito out of the bathtub and put his shoes on him, then dressed him in a clean shirt from the top drawer of his bureau. The outsized shirt made Benito look like a scarecrow.

Leaving the body laid out in his bed, Fuentes went downstairs. He was greeted by the doorman, who had in the meantime returned to his post.

Fuentes sat in the Ipiranga Theater and watched the same movie two and a half times over. When he left, at quarter to eight, it was raining heavily; traffic completely jammed Avenida Ipiranga. He crossed the street and walked into the Marabá. There were only a handful of people waiting for the six o'clock show to end. Fuentes wandered the lobby as if searching for someone who hadn't yet arrived. He was careful to look at people absentmindedly; Benito's killers were no doubt present, but he had no way of confirming it without arousing their suspicion. It would be best if they assumed he had fallen into the trap.

The six o'clock movie ended and the doors swung open. Gradually the lobby emptied; there were only a couple and two men left. After all of them had bought candy, the two men sat down on separate benches. The couple went in to take their seats.

"Where's the men's room?" asked Fuentes loudly.

The girl behind the candy counter pointed.

Without looking back, Fuentes walked toward the door marked MEN. Inside, a guy had just finished pissing and was washing his hands. Fuentes stood at the sink next to him and lathered up, observing the door through the mirror. One of the men from the lobby came in and headed for a urinal. Fuentes took a good look at him; he appeared to be middle-class, gray suit and tie. The guy who was washing his hands left the room. Before the door had closed behind him, Fuentes grabbed the man in the gray suit by the neck and slammed him backward, knocking his head against the wall. Then he dragged the man into a stall, closed the door, and stood him against the wall with his two feet in the toilet. He was bleeding from the head and having difficulty breathing. Fuentes placed his hands around the man's neck and applied pressure for two full minutes. Then he looked through the man's pockets: I.D. Lupiscínio Costa; twenty thousand cruzeiros; Taurus .38-caliber revolver. All of it transferred to Fuentes' pockets.

Fuentes left the stall, propping the body so its head fell forward keeping the door closed. The Taurus in hand, he waited for the next guy.

This one, too, wore a suit and tie. Seeing the gun Fuentes held aimed at his stomach, he raised his arms

161

slightly in front of his chest and said smoothly, "Take it easy, take it easy."

"Tighten your belt," said Fuentes.

"What?"

"Tighten your belt," he said again, punching the guy in the stomach.

The man tightened his belt.

"Tighter," said Fuentes.

"It's on the last notch."

"Now stick your hands inside, one at a time."

The man did as he was told, though he had trouble with the second hand.

Fuentes shoved him toward one of the stalls. "Get in there."

Fuentes closed the door behind them.

"Get in the toilet."

"I'll ruin my shoes," said the man.

Fuentes hit him in the face, not particularly hard. The man climbed into the bowl, slipped, and bent over, balancing himself precariously with his knees on the rim.

"Where's Lupiscínio?" asked the man.

"He turned into shit and went down the tubes."

The two talked softly, as if they were performing some lascivious act in the toilet stall and didn't want to be discovered.

"I've got a proposal," whispered the man.

"Yeah, what?" Fuentes whispered back.

"Can I get out of here first? My foot hurts."

"No. Talk."

To prevent himself from falling, the man was now leaning on Fuentes' shoulder. His breath smelled of the mints he had been sucking in the lobby.

"How about: I tell you what you want to know and we part friends?"

"Talk."

"Mateus sent us."

"Was Benito part of the contract?"

"No. Just you. He came by while we were waiting for you in the apartment. We asked about you and he said he

162

didn't know who you were, that he'd just come to clean the place, he was carrying sponges and stuff in a bucket. We leaned on him and he told us he was supposed to meet you here."

"That's all?"

"Sure. End of story. Your beef is with Mateus or the guys above him. I'm just a technician, like you. Okay? Friends?"

"Why'd you do that to the kid? He was scared shitless, all you'd have to do was yell at him."

"No way. It was a real job getting him to open up."

"I think I'll take your tie home with me," said Fuentes, loosening the knot.

"Take whatever you want. Just don't tell Mateus I fingered him."

"Don't worry about it. Is this silk?"

"A hundred percent. Only the best. I buy everything—"

He never finished the sentence. His tongue fluttered uselessly for a few moments between parted lips. The total constriction of the tie around his neck prevented any sound whatever from escaping his throat.

Fuentes went through the second man's pockets: Dirceu Guimarães; another Taurus; five thousand cruzeiros; Elo; Diners; Credicard. Fuentes took the money and the credit cards and left the gun. He tried to prop Dirceu in the same position as Lupiscínio, but even though Dirceu's feet remained stuck in the toilet bowl, his abdomen fell to the floor and his head appeared under the door, as if he were peeking out at the row of sinks.

Out in front of the Marabá, Fuentes hailed a cab to the bus station. While waiting for the bus he bought a package of crackers, which he ate, leaning against the wall, watching the hubbub of the station. He felt like strolling, but people who walk slowly draw attention to themselves and people who walk fast need a destination. Better to sit on a bench and read a newspaper or pretend to sleep— pretend, mind you. Fuentes wouldn't close his eyes in church, if one day he ever went to church. Two hours' wait for the bus to Rio. Fuentes didn't like traveling by

163

bus, because of the stickups that were common on Dutra Highway on the way out of town, but he didn't want to spend the money for a plane ticket. Actually, he was afraid of flying. But he didn't know that.

16

A MAN was talking to Wexler when I walked into the office. He was gesticulating wildly, and Wexler seemed quite interested in whatever it was he was saying.

"This is Mandrake," said Wexler.

"My name is José Zakkai. I came to see you, but I've been talking to your partner here while I was waiting. He told me, what shall I say"—pause—"a very strange story."

"You came to see me?" I asked.

"Privately, if possible."

I took him to my office.

"The name Zakkai doesn't mean anything to you?"

"No."

"How about Iron Nose?"

I'm relating events more or less chronologically, but once in a while I forget a particular episode that one of the characters told me, or sometimes even one in which I participated myself. It was very hard to reconstruct my conversation with Zakkai or, for that matter, the one he had with Lima Prado the only time they met. (In fact, I lifted the Zakkai/Prado conversation practically verbatim from one of the financier's notebooks.)

"That's me—Iron Nose," said my visitor, plopping down into an armchair as if he were about to embark on a long trip. "I can tell you're trying to categorize me, but don't bother, I'm not even sure myself if I'm white or black, Moor or Jew, and besides it doesn't make the slightest difference. I'm a man who knows things, I spend my days on the telephone keeping myself informed. The news-

papers don't say anything and television—bah, I agree
with Lenin: television is the opiate of the people. I call
bankers, parliamentarians, generals, journalists, cabinet
ministers, detectives like Raul, "ladies" who stick their
noses into closed spaces, to quote Balzac. I call people on
both sides of the curtain and by the end of the day I know
which way the wind's going to blow; then I raise the sails,
if you get my drift, and sell my spices to the dimwits, and
thus the product is converted into diamonds and postage
stamps, a fortune that can be transported in a virgin's
pussy if the need arises to flee some particular state of
affairs. But that moment has not yet arrived, 'tis the sea-
son to plant the boodle and harvest it all juicy and golden
from the entrails of the ambitious, as Mohandas Gandhi
once said. I no longer sniff, myself, and I don't sell what
you think I sell. An awful lot of people are getting collared
these days, and the legal vices play better, according to
Souza Cruz Tobacco. I know every big spender in this
world and they're all assholes. When I was a kid I'd watch
the snooty women go by in their cars, their fingers dripping jewels, and I died to have a pair of those hands holding on to my cock. It was during this same period that I
dreamed of getting to know Charlie Chaplin, but he died
before I had the honor. He died, fuck him. I never had an
idol. I considered Jesus Christ for a while, but, to quote
Archbishop Cardeal, he was a failure. Do you understand
what I'm saying? I sold peanuts, shined shoes, peddled
Chiclets, lead pipes, grass, snow, and limes that I stole
from vegetable stalls—not in that order. I've been a midnight dentist. I lived in the sewer with the rats. I've been
spit on, pissed on, and shit on. It was either die or turn
into the wonderful person I am."

I had let him talk on without interruption. Iron Nose,
who was a dwarf but carried himself like a giant, stood up
and turned his enormous head of frizzy hair sideways to
exhibit his profile. His nose was immense, with perfect
lines, just slightly more negroid than the rest of his face.

"I was prepared to confront adversity. I've just finished
a book, in fact, called the *Manual for the Frustrated,*

166

Fucked Over & Oppressed, in which I describe systemat-
ically and in great detail the dirtiest and most destructive
tactics to get even with whatever enemy, whether it's the
armed forces, the utilities, credit card companies, a bank,
the cops, your landlord, a local merchant—any person or
institution that uses its power to fuck people over. I can
see by your look you don't like me." (Actually, this book
was never written. Iron Nose liked to brag not only about
things he had done but also about those he was planning
to do.)

"You're wrong. I like people who know their true stature," I said.

Iron Nose considered my comment for a brief moment.

"I'm a dwarf, but I'm not marked to die."

I waited. I took a short dark panatela out of my desk
drawer and lit up.

"Is that a cryptogram?" I asked.

Iron Nose laughed, revealing purple gums and pointed
teeth like a dog's. "When Raul came to me I promised to
keep my eyes open, because I owe him favors from back
in my poor phase. So I discovered there's a contest on to
see who can fumigate the solicitor on the square, sub-sub-
contracted, naturally, to shield the mastermind. Green-
backs here, there, and everywhere. Not that I like opening
my Adam's apple, but as I said I owe Raul a few favors,
so here I am, like Desdemona, calling a spade a spade."

"Fumigate how?"

"Stiff—*revertere ad locum tuum*—return from whence
you came."

"Who are the various contestants?"

"They're into drugs and pornography. Women, submissive sluts, covered with semen from gigantic pricks, their
cunts like carnivorous plants split wide open, and sinister,
sexy black assholes like spurting oilwells, as Euclides da
Cunha once said. That stuff pays pretty damn good in this
bubbling country. Coke and cunts, that's the business
these boys are in. It's a cooperative they call the Main
Office; the camels are autonomous operatives unknown
to each other and small-time no-counts who just pass

167

off to the consumer at the end of the line, and if they're picked up don't know from nothing, 'cause they really don't."

"I find you rather metaphorical, as Mao Zedong would say," I said, trying to imitate Iron Nose's hoarse voice. "Why do they want to off the solicitor?"

"He should know."

"Do you?"

"I've said what I came to say."

"How about one last chance? A game of true or false," I suggested, thinking I had figured something out about how his mind worked.

"Five questions. Begin."

"The Main Office is a criminal organization which uses legal businesses as a cover and also for diversification of investments."

"True."

"The main figure in this organization is a guy named Roberto Mitry."

"Pass."

"Roberto Mitry is involved."

"True."

"How?"

"True or false questions only."

"Sorry. Roberto Mitry is a member of this criminal organization."

"True."

"And killed the women."

"Pass."

"One left," I said, thinking aloud. "You don't play fair." I dawdled, relighting my cigar. I was convinced the guy was telling the truth. The pleasure he took in the game was not that of someone who was cheating, but of someone risking everything and playing by the rules. Why had he come to see me? Not, obviously, to repay his old debts to Raul. What kind of organization was this Main Office? A guy like him couldn't be just an autonomous operative, much less a retail-level no-count. But figuring out what went on inside the organization was, in a situation as hot

168

as this, less relevant than finding out the reason for his coming to see me.

"I think I'll leave the last question for another time," I said.

"Throwing in the towel?"

"I never was very good at this game."

"It was your idea."

"You're on the outs with the Organization."

"True."

"And you want me to be your ally."

"False."

Iron Nose got up, placed a finger to his lips, and walked out of my office, leaving me in deep thought.

17

THE FIRST TIME she came to my apartment she'd been struck by the pictures of women all over the place. Four large posters in the living room alone, and an even bigger one in the bathroom: a pale, dark-haired woman sitting behind a chessboard. She thought it best, at first, to ignore them, but finally, as we sat on the couch making conversation like strangers in the dentist's office, she had motioned at the photographs and said, "Trophies, I presume?" Not that they bothered her, really. How could she object, given my past? On the contrary, the idea that I was well versed in that department appealed to her, for the simple reason that she had decided to rid herself of the (bothersome? anachronistic?) condition of being a virgin. The correct thing, of course, would be to wait until she got married, as the women in her family had always done; but she didn't want to get married or didn't want to wait or whatever—and with my obvious experience, I seemed just the right person to help her achieve the desired aim. I was attractive and I was in love with (or at least enthusiastic about) her. The way I had approached her as she came out of the Exercise Club had been a good omen. During her workout a few minutes before, as a sort of prodrome (in her uncle the doctor's vocabulary) of what would come after, she had been staring, riveted, at her body in the mirror extending the full length of the studio, and had suddenly come to the conclusion that it was high time she "gave" herself to a man. That was how she verbalized the decision to herself, this idea of presenting her virginity to someone as if it were a very special, valuable gift, undoubtedly a romantic vestige of her provincial origins, of which she was conscious and perhaps even proud. She waited for a while to make sure I was the right man to receive such an offering. She could never "give" herself to a stingy person, for example; generosity was the most crucial of virtues. Arrogance and foolishness were also to be avoided. But I struck her as kind and intelligent, and my face, apparently marked by a secret suffering, inspired confidence, in spite of the pictures on the walls. "They're friends," I had said. "My best friends have always been women." She never knew their names, with the exception of the chess player in the bathroom, Berta Bronstein, Jewish like my partner, L. Wexler. That first night we made love her heart beat so wildly she thought it might pop out of her mouth. She considered changing her mind and leaving, but that would have been a cowardly thing to do and the memory of it would persecute her the rest of her life. Better to just get it over with and then go home to bed. I held her hand, implacable, like her mother the day she walked her to school the very first time. She was wearing a blue dress, she'd never seen a blue like that again, soft, like felt, and her mother had gripped her hand tightly, as I was doing that night, in a strange house, looking at her with an ugly, obstinate expression. She couldn't remember how she had managed to get undressed, it couldn't have been too easy, that much she knew, with a bra (an item she'd given up wearing long ago), a sweater (though the temperature didn't require it), long pants, and a leather belt that had left a mark on her stomach. As if by a touch of a magic wand, we were lying in bed naked and I was stroking her hair and then her knee, which gave her goose bumps all over.

The bus turned into Avenida Brasil and the thought of her destination made Ada leave off reminiscing. She was anxious to see me. She hadn't been able to let me know she was coming, since there had been no answer at my home phone and the office was closed because it was Saturday.

When she arrived at my apartment, a short girl with the round face of a foolish child opened the door.

"Is Attorney Mandrake in?"

171

"No. Would you like to leave a message?"

"He is in town, isn't he?"

"Uh-huh. He went out to get some beer. Would you like to come in and wait?"

"No," said Ada, picking up her suitcase and turning her back to the girl.

My apartment was on the top floor of a four-story building with no elevator. Ada walked slowly down the stairs, on the verge of tears. A woman in my apartment could only mean one thing. "My best friends have always been women!" What a farce. She sat down on the stairs and cried, even though she knew her nose would get red and her eyes swollen. Men weren't worth a plugged nickel, they were all the same.

She picked up her suitcase and climbed the stairs a second time. She rang the doorbell, long.

"He hasn't come back yet," said the girl.

"I'll wait." Ada squared her shoulders and entered.

"Would you like to sit down?"

"No." Ada stood in the middle of the living room, her suitcase in her hand.

"Well, put your bag down at least, and give your arm a rest."

"Don't get fresh with me, you little snot," said Ada.

"I know you're his girlfriend," she responded, ignoring Ada's hostility, "the one with big eyes and ribs that show, right? My name is Bebel."

Bebel held out her hand. Ada set her bag on the floor and stood with her arms at her sides, unsure what to do or say.

Meanwhile, I was having a beer at a bar on Praça Antero de Quental.

The bar was packed. People stood around drinking and noshing—hard-boiled eggs with dyed-yellow shells, *linguiça*, fried pork rinds, chicken gizzards, fried sardines, mortadella, campesino cheese. Three customers were having a heated argument as to whether the minister of planning was mainly stupid or mainly a son of a bitch. There was a moment, though, when the only important thing was choosing a piece of fried pork rind from the glass plate on the counter. There were a few women in the bar. They were discussing tans. "When someone says you look terrific it means you look like shit." They also discussed cellulite and the pill. The owner of the place was a dogged type who made his living standing behind the cash register eighteen hours a day watching over every nickel. (His son attended a good private college, etc.) A wild-eyed fellow walked in, accompanied by a mess of a drunk, and tried to buy a chicken gizzard without money to pay for it. I ordered him a gizzard and a draft for his friend. The crazy guy, a mulatto maybe twenty years old, stared at the gizzard—red with tomato sauce, impaled on a toothpick—a long time before eating it. The drunk, white with a scrawny blond beard, sucked up the draft in a single gulp. Then he sighed and asked for another.

"People always say, Is it for food? If it's for food I'll give you something. But I don't want to eat, I want to drink and I say, No, lady, it's for drink, and then they don't give me a dime. What's the matter with them, don't they know that for a drunk like me drinking's more important than eating?"

"Of course they don't," I said. "They don't know anything about anybody else." I drained my glass. I was not a real beer drinker, but I was out of wine; the only place in the neighborhood you could buy wine on Saturday was at one of the bakeries that also sold assorted grocery items, and for various obscure reasons I staunchly refused to buy wine at a bakery. It's not that I found beer distasteful, but that it required such quantities to reach a satisfying state of inebriation.

When Ada, instead of Bebel, opened the door to my apartment, my first reaction was embarrassment. I was happy to see Ada, in spite of her long face, but also irritated, because I don't like surprises, not even that type. I detest watching other people suffer, and when I'm the one

173

responsible, even involuntarily, for their pain, the guilt lasts for a long long time. I put the sack of beer on the floor and sat next to Ada on the couch. We were both tense; she was hostile.

"Your little friend went home," said Ada.

"Ah, Bebel. She's the daughter of a client," I said, relieved that she was gone.

"A client. Now you're drinking beer?"

"Always did."

"I don't remember that."

I grabbed another can out of the sack, opened it, and took a swallow.

"The wine's gone. I'm glad you came back."

"I'm not so sure."

"Please don't look like that."

"I can't help it. What was that girl doing here?"

"I already told you."

"You didn't tell me a damn thing."

"She came to talk about her mother. Her mother disappeared. Now she's back. It's complicated, it's all connected to that case with the masseuses."

"And you went to bed with her?"

"No, of course not, don't be ridiculous. She's a client's daughter. Are you going to stay here with me?"

"Yes. And I don't want to run into any more clients' daughters, okay?"

"Okay."

We sat in silence. I kissed her on the cheek.

"I'm going to take a shower. I'm all dusty from the bus trip."

While Ada showered, I examined the implications of her return. It wasn't Bebel that concerned me but the revelations Iron Nose had divulged. If my life really was at risk, as the dwarf said, then my apartment was not a safe place for Ada. I didn't want to tell her this and risk scaring her off again, but if I didn't give her a reasonable explanation she might think I was trying to push her away because of Bebel.

When Ada came out of the bathroom, she seemed to have forgotten her annoyance.

174

"I've put on some weight, huh? It's all this time without any exercise."

"You're beautiful."

"You think so? Did you miss me?"

"All the time. And you?"

"I couldn't take it anymore. All of a sudden I just decided I had to leave. My mother tried to talk me out of it, but it didn't work. I arranged for a substitute at school and, well, here I am. Pouso Alto's a drag, you saw what it was like. All my father's friends could talk about was politics and coffee, and the younger people go on and on about the new cars they've bought or are planning to buy. But even if Pouso Alto were the greatest place, I would have left anyway, I missed you so much." She could not stop talking.

We were wrapped in each other's arms when the phone rang. I answered it.

"Don't think for a minute that I'm giving up on you, you rogue. I only left 'cause I felt sorry for *her*. You'll hear from me at your office."

"Who was that?" Ada asked after I hung up.

"I don't know. They didn't say anything. It happens all the time with this phone."

Some people seek relief from their tension in food. I find my point of equilibrium in sexual activity. After spending a good, long time in bed with Ada I felt positively cheerful. I put on my swim trunks and went to the beach. Raul was coming to lunch that day.

Raul arrived before I got back. Ada recognized him through the peephole and opened the door. She liked Raul and was glad to see him.

Raul had two wrapped bottles of Periquita under his arm. Ada had purring Betsy in hers. They kissed hello.

"What's this? Wine?"

"Yup."

"He's drinking beer now."

"I don't believe it." Raul smiled. He had a crooked smile.

175

They drank coffee. Ada said, "I'm going to marry Mandrake."

"Terrific. For him."

"For me, too. I love the guy, Raul, I can't live without him. No, don't laugh, or I'll get mad."

"It's just nervousness."

"He's going to change; he's going to be all right. He was never the same ever since, well—since that day. Marriage will be good for him." Ada, too, had been walking around unable to focus on anything other than what had happened. But one day, there in Pouso Alto, she was watching a cow graze and suddenly she said to herself, Every obstacle in life that we surpass, especially the most horrifying ones, should make us only that much more conscious of the pleasure of living. "Looking at that cow, I realized how good it was just to be alive! Nothing else matters, nothing at all, if you *know* that you're alive, if you know *what it is* to be alive. At that moment I gave up lamenting, I gave up suffering for fear, love, anxiety. It's all part of being alive. It won't do any good to call this line of thinking immoral or impudent individualism or any other damn thing, it's just love of life."

"I think (of the cow), therefore I am (happy)."

"Oh, Raul, you're worse than Mandrake."

As soon as I arrived, still damp and sandy from the beach, I opened one of the bottles of wine. Ada said she felt like joining us.

"No more yoghurt?" I teased.

"Besides," she said, "I want to hear what the two of you talk about."

I told Raul about my conversation with Iron Nose. When I got to the part about Zakkai's warning ("They want to fumigate me") his face clouded.

"A bunch of hooey, right?"

Raul didn't answer.

"Do you trust the guy, Raul?"

"I'm scared," said Ada.

Raul paced the living room. Something seemed to be bothering him deeply. "I already got the guy off once," he

176

said, in a sorrowful and irritated voice. "I mean, if it wasn't for me the Nose would be behind bars until the middle of the next century. He's involved in all kinds of stuff: motels, gambling, drugs, erotic books, porno flicks. Plus nightclubs, restaurants, and a chain of luncheonettes and video arcades. How does it all work? Shares in the clubs, restaurants, and motels are owned by a partnership called Goodtaste. The chain of luncheonettes belongs to a company called Fastfood. The publisher and film company are also a limited partnership, this one named Pleasure. And a firm named Fun owns the arcades. Goodtaste, Fastfood, Pleasure, and Fun—all in English no less. The partners in Goodtaste are, let me see"— Raul took a piece of paper out of his pocket and read— "José 'Iron Nose' Zakkai, Pedro Paulo dos Santos, Joaquim Silva, Nadir Alves Castro, João Gambacorta, Elisio Pinto Braga. Recognize any of them?"

"No."

"Fastfood is made up of exactly the same partners. Ditto Pleasure and Fun. Nadir's a retired Army colonel. Gambacorta was a dentist. Elisio Pinto Braga used to work at the Ministry of Industry and Commerce, until he got fired; he was an obscure economist. None of these guys had sufficient resources to invest in these business ventures. Iron Nose owned a small gay nightclub in Copacabana, which went bankrupt. Nothing is known about the remaining two, Silva and Santos—two of the most common family names in Brazil. So where did all the money come from to build motels and open luncheonettes? We assume it's drugs. Second-level employees say there was a problem with Fastfood; it looks like the chain of luncheonettes is changing hands. Inside information on Goodtaste indicates that the same thing is going on with the motels, which is probably their most lucrative area. Legal, that is. As far as the illegal business goes, we know nothing, or very little. Goodtaste, Fastfood, Pleasure, and Fun all function under the control of a secret holding company, which actually works like the kind of superbank that finances known figures in the numbers racket as well as

177

international drug dealers and invests part of its earnings in the businesses that function as fronts but are no less lucrative."

The three of us: pensive, drinking wine. Raul couldn't sit still. Every other minute he'd leap up and go back to pacing the living room.

"You're really worried about this fumigation thing, aren't you, Raul?" said Ada. "Which makes me terrified."

"Probably just an unfortunate metaphor," I suggested.

"All the principals are already under investigation. They seem to have a couple of traits in common: They're discreet men with few friends and no social life to speak of. Gambacorta lives on Rua Maria Quitéria, married, no children, and only leaves the house for a morning stroll in Praça Nossa Senhora da Paz. Colonel Nadir lives on an estate in Teresópolis. Monday, Wednesday, and Friday he swims for about an hour at a local country club. Tuesdays he practices target shooting, also at the club. He stays inside the rest of the time except for occasional work in his garden. He's got a wife and two kids and is close-mouthed by nature. Elisio lives in a large apartment on Morro da Viúva, Flamengo, surrounded by minicomputers and other electronic gadgets. He's single. An old woman who's been with his family since he was an infant takes care of the apartment. He never goes out except to the movies. The Feds haven't managed to get phone taps on these guys yet; they say they're up against obstacles and bureaucratic hang-ups. Which could be a lie."

II
FAMILY
PORTRAIT

WHENEVER HE visited the enormous dark house, bigger and all the more gloomy because he was a child, there was always a certain smell in the air that came from the furniture and dusty draperies and remained inside the closed rooms. The old woman always wore ancient clothing and a string of pearls, her mottled fingers weighed down with ugly rings. She gave off an aroma of mothballs mixed with age, spent flesh. Certain rooms were off-limits to him, so that he wouldn't muss or break things: carved wooden oratories, crystal, china, sideboards crowded with knickknacks. The old woman liked him and kept a tin of colorful hard candies that she handed out to him, with a distant air, one at a time. As she did (was it always when she was giving him candy?), he would hear a howling coming from somewhere in the house. The candy tin trembling in her hands, the old woman would tell him it was the dogs, but it sounded to him like some other kind of animal, desperately sad. It was a long time before he discovered the secrets hidden in those dark rooms, in the cellar, in the closed minds of the women of that family, in the trunks full of letters and papers locked in the attic. In the strongbox. But discovering the truth had not made him a better or worse man than he was before: "I left a part of me behind in everything I saw." *C'est la vie.*

Now that he was an adult, the old woman appeared constantly in his dreams. She was Athena and had made him go mad, putting a sword in his hand. He was surrounded by herds of sheep and cattle, thinking they were men; after immense slaughter, he decapitated a sheep and cut out its tongue—No, it was Menelaus' head, and he tied another sheep to a pillar and whipped it with a horse's halter, screaming insults, calling it Ulysses, traitor, liar.

Recovering from his fury—still in the dream—he took the sword, the same one Hector had traded for the purple baldric, and stuck it upright in the earth before him. At his birth they had thrown a dog's hide over him, thus making his body invulnerable, with the exception of neck and armpit. He knew what to do. After asking Hermes to con-

181

duct his soul to the Elysian Fields, he threw himself upon the sword. It bowed into an arc as if to evade its task and it was daybreak before he succeeded in killing himself by driving the blade into his armpit.

18

WHEN JOSÉ Joaquim de Barros Lima was born, son of
Portuguese immigrants, in Rio de Janeiro in 1845, the
population of Brazil was estimated to be eight million,
three and a half million of whom were slaves. He had an
impoverished childhood, helping his father deliver coal.
By virtue of much hard work and ferocious austerity,
which deprived them of almost everything and possibly
caused the tuberculosis that killed his mother before she
was forty, the couple managed to buy their own coal yard
and finally satisfy their greatest ambition, which was to
send their son to study at Coimbra. Little else is known
about Barros Lima's parents. No photographs, letters or
other documents survive to register their passage through
the world. Five years after arriving at Coimbra, José Joaquim returned from Portugal with a law degree and the
slight accent he would have the rest of his life. In Rio, the
young attorney became friends with José Maria da Silva
Paranhos, Junior, a colleague his age who had been
awarded a degree in São Paulo in 1866, the same year
José Joaquim finished his studies at the University of
Coimbra. Their friendship deepened over time. José Maria
left Brazil and lived abroad as a diplomat, but the two
men corresponded frequently.

Barros Lima was already an attorney of considerable
prestige at the age of forty-two when he married Vicentina
Cintra, daughter of Senator Abelardo Cintra, an ardent
supporter of abolition and republicanism. The year they
were married saw the abolition of slavery, and soon after,
in 1889, Manuel Deodoro da Fonseca and the Army did

183

away with the monarchy. With the Proclamation of the Republic and the strengthening of his father-in-law's political position, Barros Lima's law practice became the most prominent in the nation's capital. His friend José Maria was also achieving great renown as diplomat and statesman; he served as Brazil's chief negotiator and successfully defended the nation's interests in the dispute with Argentina regarding the Mission Territory, as well as the Amapá boundary dispute with French Guiana. When José Maria, by then known as the Baron of Rio Branco, took charge of the Ministry of Foreign Relations, he invited his friend to serve as legal consultant. Barros Lima was one of the main advisers to Rio Branco in the diplomatic undertaking that led to Brazil's occupation of the 152,000 square kilometers belonging to Bolivia, which, annexed to the Republic, came to be called the Federal Territory of Acre.

The boy coal dealer, son of immigrants, was clearly a realized man. In Coimbra he had participated in the turbulent intellectual polemics involving Antero de Quental, who initiated the rebellion against romanticism in Portugal and introduced to the university the study of Proudhon, Michelet, and Hegel. Barros Lima would never forget the image of the poet's face—pale, framed by a wild, curly beard—as he held forth in the debate between formalists and realists that had almost transformed the old university into a battlefield. Barros Lima wrote his own first verses at Coimbra, inspired by Antero's *Odes Modernas*. Arriving in Rio during the height of the Paraguay campaign, he attended soirées at which the war was merely a pretext for literary and patriotic diatribes. Later, he became friends with important writers like Machado de Assis and Fagundes Varela. But poetry was to be the source of great frustration and disappointment to Barros Lima. In spite of a generous preface written by Machado de Assis, the reception of his first book, *Poemas Modernos*, was limited and cool, not only because his verses were mediocre but because everyone's attention was focused on the emergence of a young Bahian poet named Castro

Alves. Even so, when the Academy of Brazilian Letters was established, it became Barros Lima's dream to gain membership to that exclusive literary elite. When finally he became a candidate, he was sure that he would be elected, for in addition to his friendship with de Assis, the Academy's president, and promises he had received from various other members, Barros Lima had arranged for the Academy, which had no fixed meeting place, to be quartered in the Silogeu Brasileiro Building. Even with all this to his credit, he was defeated in his bid. Embittered and betrayed, Barros Lima gave up writing poetry and avoided bookstores and literary salons completely. His new obsession became investiture as a justice of the Supreme Court, which would be the crowning achievement of his illustrious career as lawyer and jurist. And his nomination was in fact finally signed by President Wenceslau Braz, but Barros Lima died the night before his swearing in. In the same year, 1918, his friend the Baron of Rio Branco would also die, wreathed in glory. Both were seventy-three. "The Terrible Enemy has harvested one of the strongest," declaimed the orator standing beside Barros Lima's bier, "and all of us suffer pain and remorse. But Death failed in his perverse design, striking down with unmerciful dagger, in incontinent, devouring rage, this superior soul, for his name shall remain forever inscribed in the history of our nation, and, moreover, the great Barros Lima died a happy man, conscious that his debt was paid, bequeathing an example for future generations."

In fact, Barros Lima had not died a happy man. His frustration at not having been granted (as so many bad poets before and after him had been) the consolation of membership in the Academy and his difficult and tardy nomination to the Supreme Court were not the only reasons for his suffering. Barros Lima's family, no different from those of all men, great or small, had given him more grief than happiness. His wife was an apathetic woman who addressed him as Dr. Lima on the few occasions on which she spoke to him at all. Pretty Vicentina cut an opulent, even elegant, figure, particularly when squeezed

into one of her Devant Droit corsets by Madame Tourche-
beuf, in Pompadour silk, always black, with embroidered
bouquets, purchased for 110 milreis at the Grand Estab-
lishment of Black Cloth on Rua Uruguaiana. Barros Lima
had always wanted to have an affair with a soubrette
from the Trianon Theater, which turned out to be one
more frustration. It was this small-time actress he
thought of the day he died; her name—Penha—was the
last word he spoke, intriguing those standing around the
deathbed, who, in the absence of any other explanation,
chose to assume that he was referring to the saint of the
same name.

Barros Lima's daughters, Laurinda and Maria do Socorro, did not love him. Laurinda was a mild girl, and as
was fashionable at the time had learned to speak French,
to paint, to embroider, and to play waltzes and polkas on
the family's German Bechstein, but her relationship with
her father was ceremonious and cold. At sixteen she married José Priscilio Prado, a seventeen-year-old youth from
a wealthy São Paulo family. It was a hasty wedding,
owing to Laurinda's untimely pregnancy. The two had
met at a party while the boy was vacationing in Rio and
saw each other only three times. José Priscilio was already back home in São Paulo when Laurinda's delicate
condition revealed itself. On being informed of the unpleasant news, the Prados (José's uncles, since the boy
was an orphan) agreed to the moral reparation demanded
by the offended family and the wedding was expeditiously
set for June fourteenth, permitting precious little time to
prepare a trousseau. Especially a trousseau to the stan-
dards of fashion dictated by Paris: The skirts, long or
short, should be flowing or pleated, and slightly clingy at
the hip; the *tailleurs* jacket was worn long, closed by a
single line of buttons, with an opening in back or on the
sides; the most fashionable trim was cotton braid; for the
traveling outfit batiste and linen were the preferred fab-
rics, and both the Directoire and Empire styles were losing favor. Low shoes were beginning to supplant the high-
button variety, especially the Molière design, patent

leather with a square gold buckle. The color de rigueur was mauve, in tones from violet to heliotrope. Head-hugging cloche hats were all the rage, covering neck and ears, and decorated with a garland of flowers and a pink faille ribbon. The most popular stone was the emerald. The wedding of Baroness Mauricio de Rothschild established its desirability, and thereafter all brides wanted an emerald surrounded by diamonds or set alone, *en cabochon*. Parisiennes, everyone knew, always carried a small gold mesh bag, which Laurinda assiduously searched for and found. She appeared in the Church of São Francisco in a stunning rose-colored dress of Liberty silk, with an embroidered mantle that was open in front but trailed down in back like a royal train. Orange buds were clustered on either side of her head, Princess Lointaine–style. The antique lace veil fell away to show the bride's beautiful face. She wore Swedish leather gloves and kidskin slippers over silk stockings; her underclothing was immaculate white, as were all the undergarments in her trousseau, made of fine linen and trimmed with luxuriant Valenciennes lace. Since full-dress tails were not worn for daytime weddings in Paris, the bridegroom sported a gray frock coat, with a light tie and patent leather high-top shoes. Unfortunately, the crowd was not what Barros Lima had hoped. True, the church, though quite spacious, was standing room only. But by one of those unlucky coincidences, Afonso Pena, the President of the Republic—whose presence had been expected—passed away that very day, and as the vice president, Nilo Peçanha, was being installed that afternoon, the principal authorities sent representatives in their place.

Barros Lima's other daughter, rebellious and eccentric Maria do Socorro, had always caused her father a great deal of grief. At seven she suffered a convulsion of unknown origin, and her mother insisted she wear the Hercules Electric Belt, by Dr. C. A. Standen of New York, which, according to the brochure accompanying it, cured nervous conditions, rheumatism, dyspepsia, lumbago, sciatica, paralysis, neuralgia, and acute neurasthenia. It did nothing for Maria do Socorro, and finally a Dr. Pinto da Rocha, who called himself a crenotherapist, prescribed a visit to the potent waters of Lambary; after a month of hydromineral baths the girl was apparently well. As an adolescent, though, she had a relapse. Maria do Socorro smoked La Reine cigarettes on the sly, dressed as a man, and suffered from euphoria. This extraordinary behavior led her parents to place her under the care of a Dr. Pedro Barbalho, who had studied in Vienna. Barbalho managed to win the girl's trust, and as soon as she told him what she had been doing in school with a friend of hers he counseled her father to keep her at home under strict supervision. According to Barbalho's written case history, Maria do Socorro and her little friend Silvia were devoted to *masturbatio feminae delectae,* cunnilingus, and *tritus mutuus genitalium appositorium.* The diagnosis was read to the father in Latin to cushion the shock. Dr. Barbalho also referred to tribadism, reciprocal manustupration, and other rare and terrifyingly suggestive words. All these external symptoms earned Maria do Socorro one of the labels fashionable in medical jargon of the day—neuropathic—which justified, *erga omnes,* the measures of segregation that were taken. Sequestered at home, Maria do Socorro spent her days reading. All books entering her room were subject to prior inspection, to ensure that she not read literature that undermined good and moral behavior. One day Maria do Socorro scrawled on the wall of her room, with charcoal, in big letters, *Ne cherchez plus mon coeur; les bêtes l'ont mangé.* The same day she confessed to Barbalho that she masturbated daily; her doctor took this as a sign of hypersexuality, which could possibly lead to neurasthenia. He feared that what was developing was a case of gynandria, as referred to by Krafft-Ebing, an extreme condition of degenerate homosexuality in which women become interested in "masculine" subjects such as politics, sports, and business. Barbalho reread Goltz, Eckard, Schleirmacher, and Kraussold, but the masters understood masculine perversions better than their feminine counterparts. According to Dr. Barbalho's diagnosis, Maria do Socorro was in a state of transition called paranoid sexual metamorphosis, in which the subject believes that he/she is changing sex. And in fact, Maria do Socorro's breasts had become smaller, her pelvis seemed narrower, her voice had acquired a serious, husky quality, and a new smell seemed to emanate from her body. This last was confirmed by the laundry lady, who commented that the girl's clothing definitely had a stronger, more manly odor.

Meanwhile, Laurinda's misstep and subsequent wedding plans released Maria do Socorro from being the focus of the family's worries. The entire household was in an uproar with preparations. Barros Lima exhausted his savings to pay for the festivities, dowry, and trousseau. Vigilance over Maria do Socorro's reading material diminished. Without anyone suspecting they were perverse (containing main characters who were lesbian), the books *La Religieuse, La Fille aux Yeux d'Or,* and *Mademoiselle Maupin* were purchased and delivered to her. She suffered acutely, soaking her pillow with tears, over Diderot's unfortunate heroine. This only confirmed her belief that she should reveal her secret side to no one.

A few days after Laurinda's wedding, Barros Lima invited Socorro to accompany him to the inauguration of the Municipal Theater of Rio, since Vicentina did not want to attend. *Le Refuge,* the latest theatrical novelty from Paris, was to be performed. Wearing a dress of silk mousseline, Socorro sat beside her father in the box, comporting herself with the modest elegance befitting an aristocratic *jeune fille.* A month later, she was permitted to return to the Municipal Theater to attend a lecture by the writer Anatole France. On that occasion, she asked permission to read the much-talked-about poet Luiz Delfino. As it happened, the only copies of some five hundred of Delfino's sonnets, which were to be published by Casa Laemmert, had been destroyed in a fire at the printer's. This apparently did not upset the bard, who claimed that five hundred sonnets weren't worth a great deal and, besides, he had five thousand more in his house on Rua

Jockey Club. A friend of the illustrious poet, Barros Lima requested a few of the unpublished sonnets for his daughter's perusal, and Delfino sent the girl the gift of nearly a ream of sonnets in his own hand. All this taken into consideration, it was decided that Maria do Socorro was cured and that Barbalho's services were no longer required.

Except for the family home on Rua São Clemente, Barros Lima possessed nothing to speak of when he died, which gave the lie to rumors circulated by his political enemies that he had gotten rich on shady business dealings with Rio Branco. At the time of her father's death, Laurinda was living in São Paulo and had three children, a boy of ten named Fernando, and two girls, Maria Augusta and Maria Clara, nine and seven respectively. An English governess looked after the brood. During the Great War the Prado family businesses had prospered more than even before; Laurinda came to own two residences, having bought a fine city house on Rua São Clemente in Rio near her mother, where she stayed when she came at least once a month to deliver a generous quantity of money so that her mother and Maria do Socorro could maintain the comfortable life they had lived when Barros Lima was alive. A profound change had come over Laurinda. Except for the untimely pregnancy, she had always been timid and conformist, but in São Paulo she had blossomed into a dynamic and independent patron of the arts; and her salons—in both cities—became the center of society and the intelligentsia of the day. Her husband, José Priscilio, was a compulsive gambler and lost prodigious amounts of money at poker, but it was said that he had so much money that neither his gambling nor the whims of his wife could dissipate the family fortune.

Maria do Socorro, meanwhile, could finally lead the double life of her dreams. Dressed as a man—her tiny breasts, slim figure, and haircut à la garconne (the height of fashion) aiding her success as a transvestite—she frequented the luxurious bordellos on Rua Taylor. The prostitutes with whom she established an intense if somewhat restricted sexual exchange never suspected she was a woman. On the contrary, they fell in love with that exotic young man, his mouth always perfumed with Odol *(Das Beste für die Zahne)*, who dressed formally but never undressed and was nevertheless capable of creating the most delirious libidinous experiences. These were Maria do Socorro's salons, equally full of talk about poets—Baudelaire, Rimbaud, Schiller, whom Socorro read in the original and later translated. Some of the prostitutes were French, and others Polish, and could read German. Socorro's favorite, a young Polish woman named Wanda, wrote her own melancholic verses describing her childhood in Cracovia. These literary interludes almost always occurred at the end of the night, once the clients of the house —among them senators, businessmen, government officials, and retired big shots from the provinces—had gone home. The women, still decked out in the glamorous floor-length satin and silk dresses with plunging necklines they wore to receive their guests, drank champagne and listened attentively as young "Mário" recited his poems.

When performing her public feminine role, Maria do Socorro tried to behave like a proper young woman of society, but in spite of her efforts she was still viewed with certain reservations. She smoked in public (Turkish cigarettes purchased at the London Smokeshop), drove her Pierce-Arrow convertible at breakneck speed, and went riding horses at the Horseman's Club of Rio de Janeiro. The two sisters got along quite well until the visit of King Albert and Queen Elizabeth of Belgium to Brazil. This royal visit was considered of utmost political importance, a definitive sign that Brazil now belonged on the roster of great potentials, and society was aflutter preparing to greet the King who had behaved so heroically during the Great War that had ended only two years before. Both the Municipal Theater and the Monroe Palace were strung with thousands of lights. A schedule of formal calls and receptions was organized for the Belgian monarchs. Laurinda exerted all her prestige so that one of the banquets in honor of the visitors, who were staying at the Guanabara Palace, would be scheduled at her house on São

Clemente. She succeeded, and an invitation to Laurinda's banquet became an honor hotly sought after by all Rio's high society. But Maria do Socorro declined to attend her sister's gala, claiming that she wasn't interested in meeting the King, or the Queen for that matter. This marked the beginning of the break between the two sisters. Earlier, Socorro had provoked Laurinda's ire when summoned to preview the redecoration of the mansion. Laurinda was bursting with pride over her new furniture, but to Socorro such antiques were a thing for the nouveau riche, and she made a point of saying so. "All that contact with those guinea Paulistas has obviously been bad for you, my dear." This, followed by the disdain with which Socorro greeted her invitation to the royal reception, soured their relationship once and for all. Offended, Laurinda began to consider reducing the monthly allowance she sent to Socorro and her mother. Some months later, when the terrible tragedy occurred, the two sisters were not speaking.

Maintaining salons both in Rio and São Paulo was quite a feat, not only in terms of financial resources and energy, but also the intelligence and sensibility required. Rivalry between the two cities was large. On one hand Rio, the metropolis, political and cultural capital of the nation, and on the other, São Paulo, the City That Couldn't Stop, where a new kind of bourgeoisie was emerging with sufficient money and leisure to stimulate or participate in the adventure of creating. Laurinda knew how to deal with this intrinsic conflict: She remained neutral, both in Rio salons when people sneered at Paulista provincialism and in São Paulo when their counterparts discussed the decadence and indolence of the Cariocas. By the beginning of the third decade of the century, Laurinda's social life was at its peak. Rui Barbosa had abandoned political life; the dismantling of Castelo Hill had begun, and with it the demolition of the oldest part of the city ("We want wide, geometrical avenues"); the great sculptors Kanto, Bernardelli, Correa Lima, Grazianni, and Tadey were producing outstanding examples of funerary art, exhibited in the

192

cemeteries of São Francisco Xavier and São João Batista. All this and more was discussed at Laurinda's salons. Alceu Amoroso Lima's comment "The twentieth century belongs to São Paulo," published in the *Revista do Brasil,* provoked jubilation in one and mockery in the other. Literature was one of the main themes: the Parnassian movement (decried), Imagism, Vorticism, Acmeism, Expressionism, Surrealism, Dadaism, Symbolism, Romanticism, Suprematism, Modernism, Futurism ("How vast is the world of literature"). Up-and-coming poets came to Laurinda's to recite their verses—Manoel Bandeira ("What a shame he's going to die so young, he has tuberculosis, oh, didn't you know?"), Menotti del Picchia, Guilherme de Almeida, Mário de Andrade—and many years later, when Modern Art Week of '22 (which had not generated a great deal of interest at the time) came to be seen as an important cultural event, Laurinda was fond of claiming that the idea had been born in her salon on Avenida Paulista. ("Anita, Oswald, Pagu, all of them were habitués.") Patron Laurinda's library in the mansion on São Clemente boasted thousands of bound volumes, all with the ex libris done by the young painter Di Cavalcanti, a design she later discovered to be quite similar to the ex libris the artist had done for Ronald de Carvalho. ("Shamelessly inspired by Beardsley.")

Then the first calamity. Laurinda's guests were enjoying a concert by pianist Maria Carreras, during an evening soirée on São Clemente. A young prostitute on Rua Taylor killed her lover in one of the rooms of the brothel. When the police arrived at the scene (from the newspapers: "The hetaera, weeping profusely, was embracing her gallant, sprawled across the bed, dead from a gunshot wound"), it was discovered that the young man killed out of deranged jealousy by his Polish whore was in fact a young lady. And this young lady was— Horror of horrors! The newspapers cooperated (friends of the family), but the news circulated secretly from mouth to mouth, as is usually the case with rumors and shameful truths, to the hypocritical consternation and secret joy of all.

The house on São Clemente was closed and Laurinda stayed away from Rio for a long time. Vicentina reluctantly went to live with her daughter in São Paulo. With age, the matriarch had grown very fat, and fine blue veins crisscrossed her milk-white face, sinuous lines like rivers on a colorful map. At parties, Vicentina was apt to sit in the corner for hours, all dolled up with rings, brooches, chains, and pendants, unmoving, silent, like a gigantic doll. When she did speak, she seemed drowsy and incoherent. Her mother's presence was for Laurinda a martyrdom endured with resignation.

The thirties—with the constitutional revolution in São Paulo, the rise of Vargas's gauchos from the south, and the New State—were not propitious years for the Prado family business dealings. As if gambling was not enough, José Priscilio added cocaine to his list of vices. Laurinda, a grandmother twice over, no longer courted by her visitors, longed for the turbulent passions of bygone days, and reread with great pleasure letters from her old lovers, which she kept under lock and key in a strongbox in her room.

On the fourteenth of June, 1940, the second calamity occurred. Priscilio arrived home before dawn, having spent the night playing poker, lay down in bed beside the sleeping Laurinda, and shot himself in the head. It was their thirty-first wedding anniversary. It was also the day Paris surrendered to the German Army. The pillars of Brazilian society, staggered by the fall of the city that represented the epitome of culture and civilization, where they went periodically in search of spiritual and bodily nourishment, were too numb even to comment on a subject as promising as the scandalous death of one of their notorious members.

José Priscilio Prado was bankrupt. One of his uncles promptly paid the many debts he left behind, but the entire Prado family ignored the appeals of Priscilio's spendthrift wife, and Laurinda had to sell the mansion on Avenida Paulista and move to the one on Rua São Clemente in Rio. Her son Fernando, who in 1931 had married

194

Luiza Montilio, daughter of a well-known homeopathic doctor, also relocated to Rio, where he found a modest position in City Hall. Laurinda's daughter Maria Augusta found herself abandoned by her husband, a Frenchman named Bernard Mitry (who called himself a count), as soon as it became evident that the family was bankrupt. Bernard returned to France without a word of farewell. Maria Augusta, and her son Roberto, went to Rio to live with Laurinda. The youngest daughter, Maria Clara, "had problems," as they said euphemistically. She suffered from outbursts of aggression during which she attacked anyone within reach. She also howled frequently as if she were a wolf. Maria Clara, incarcerated in the cellar of the mansion on Avenida Paulista, now accompanied her mother to Rua São Clemente, where there was also a cellar, as discreet and isolated as the first.

All these facts and events were amply and minutely described in *Family Portrait,* a five-hundred-page book by Basílio Peralta, published in 1949. The book did poorly, both financially and critically, not receiving so much as a brief critical notice in the press. The Lima Prado family was no longer important. The new industrial bourgeoisie had given rise to other, more powerful and attractive clans. Because of an acute paper shortage, the thousands of leftover copies of *Family Portrait* were sold by weight to be reprocessed. Basílio Peralta died of cancer in 1951. His book could be considered a rarity if anybody cared. The copy in the National Library disappeared, no one knows how or when. At least one copy survived, however, in the possession of Thales Lima Prado, grandson of Priscilio and Laurinda de Almeida Prado, "cousin" of Roberto Mitry. The book came into my hands at the same time as the Notebooks. Without these written sources, I could not have portrayed the financier's life in such detail—his love life, business transactions, etc. (including of course the Main Office). I have used his own words, directly from the Notebooks, wherever possible, in an attempt to preserve the literary effects he intended; after all, Lima Prado considered himself a man of letters. Both his strange conversation with Zakkai, where Iron Nose recounts the episode of the toothed vagina, and his first meeting with Mônica, where the scatological basis of his desire is first revealed, have been reproduced exactly as they originally appeared.

19

THALES LIMA PRADO believed—and I share this point
of view—that, if he chose, he could write an even more
comprehensive version of the story than Basílio Peralta's.
He had in his possession innumerable letters, official certificates, correspondence of his grandmother's, and sun-
dry papers that would never have passed through
Peralta's hands. In addition, some very important events
had taken place since 1949. Neither Thales himself nor
Roberto Mitry appears in *Family Portrait*. Maria Clara is
barely mentioned. All that is said of Fernando, Thales'
father, is that he came to Rio and got a job in City Hall.
(The impoverished children of "good" families, just like
the incompetents of rich families, always manage to find
good civil service jobs, where they do nothing.) The out-
line sketched in the Notebooks indicates that if one day
Thales Lima Prado had decided to write the family saga,
he would have produced a very interesting, if slightly pe-
dantic, volume. He loved mythology and English poetry,
particularly Yeats and Eliot. Phrases from several of these
poets can be found in the pages of the Notebooks. "Man
created death" appears most frequently. I thought about
this phrase for quite some time. I believe that in a certain
way it explains Lima Prado. Man created death. Because
he knows death exists, man created art—a Nietzschean
thought. The name of the German philosopher also appears in the mess of notes. "Birth, copulation, and death"
is the second most frequently cited phrase, to which I
have also given a great deal of thought. Birth, copulation,
and death. After all, this would perhaps tell the story of
my life. All our lives.

Lima Prado inherited the house on Rua São Clemente but had not yet had time to explore all the crannies of attic and cellar. (If his grandfather had not squandered the family fortune, he would not have had to spend his youth in military academies, nor would he have gotten stuck in that fortification of the lower middle class, the Brazilian Army, but would already have assumed "my true vocation —thinker, man of letters.") Peralta's book ended with the events of 1949 (actually nothing happened in 1949), one year before the suicide of Thales' father, Fernando Lima Prado. Thales was thirteen by then and aware that it was not his father who had sired him but his uncle, the French con artist Bernard Mitry. His cousin (that is his brother) Roberto Mitry also knew this. Everyone knew, and everyone pretended ignorance. Including Laurinda. (It was Laurinda who finally told him the truth: He was not her grandson.) But Laurinda loved Thales and detested her true grandson, Roberto. It was lamentable, poor inoffensive Fernando. In addition to being sterile he was impotent and had the bad luck to marry an adulteress. But "adulteress" was too inexact, legalistic, and biblical a word for his mother. Luiza Montilio Prado was not an evil woman. At least she had not abandoned her family, as Bernard had, upon learning that the money had run out. Of course it's rare for a woman to do such a thing; like any woman, Luiza had been conditioned to stay with her young. The fact that she had stayed with him instead of following her lover meant little to Thales; it represented neither self-denial nor sacrifice, but rather a biological reflex. In any case, if not for the fact that both Bernard and Luiza had been unfaithful to their respective mates he, Thales, would not have been born. And what difference did it make whether he was son of *a* or son of *b*? He considered himself merely the result of the combination of defects and virtues and other characteristics transmitted generation after generation via couplings that were, after all, only the result of the instinct to preserve the species.

A life made of many bad memories. But there were good ones, as well. Oddly enough, he felt a certain longing for the days he spent in the military, serving in various cavalry units. Longing for the thrill of riding a good horse. Longing to enter the arena to jump, longing to feel his heartbeat quicken, to know his face was pale, to feel, despite the heat of exertion, his body covered with cold sweat. The anxiety that came before the challenge, the risk, the obscure, amorous, inexplicable communion between two animals, man and beast, instinct taking precedence over reason. The bittersweet odor of the muscular bulk of the horse drenched in his white steaming, frothy sweat in the steeplechase. His own sweat always cold—a man maintaining his thermic equilibrium regardless of physical exertion. That's why he, man, was a resistant animal. One day, after hours of hard riding during which man and animal pressed their resistances to their respective limits, Thales witnessed the death of the horse. He felt with his own hands the quadruped's body burning with exhaustion, while his own face was ice. His aunt, Maria Clara, had howled in the cellar where she was incarcerated for fifty-nine years; sometimes, imagining she was copulating with Jesus Christ, she beat her head against the wall until she lost consciousness; sometimes she went days and days without eating or drinking; sometimes she ate her own feces. What other animal could endure such suffering for so long a time? If the ridiculous Dr. Barbalho were still around, he would mumble something about coprolagnia and claim that Maria Clara desired mystical mortification, like the nun Antoinette Bouvignon de la Porte described by Professor Zimmermann in *Die Wonne des Leids*, Leipzig, 1885. It was in order to hear the voices of the angels that she ate feces mixed with her food.

Lima Prado had learned a few things from those women. An appreciation for secrecy, for one thing. When his mother died, they discovered a trunk full of jewelry with marbles as gemstones, the cover to a gold watch, a gigantic emerald, the portrait of a man who was neither her husband nor the brother-in-law but had been her lover, and two love letters in an almost illegible hand, possibly from the fellow in the picture. The letters were signed with the initial J. The women in that family!

His grandmother was even more intriguing than his mother. Laurinda died at home at ninety years of age when she fell coming down the stairs, but up until her death her health was still so robust that she hoped to realize the marvel of having been born in the nineteenth century and dying in the twenty-first.

A few days before she died, Laurinda called Thales to her house on Rua São Clemente. They spent the afternoon talking. The mansion was in a pitiful state; the gardens were almost completely destroyed; bushes and field grass grew where there had once been roses, geraniums, and rhododendrons. Only the larger trees—mango, fig, and ipê older than their mistress—had not suffered; on the contrary they were more exuberant than ever and produced abundant and welcome shade in the ravaged garden. Inside the house time and lack of care had wreaked even greater devastation. The wallpaper, imported from France, had come unglued in several rooms and dangled from the wall, covered with dust; the seventeenth-century jacaranda wood chairs in the sitting room lay in pieces on the floor; the huge Persian rug that covered almost the entire living-room floor was stained and tattered; the spines of the books in the extensive library were motheaten and crumbling. In the so-called gallery/study, the jacaranda table and chairs with leather seats and backs displaying the coat-of-arms of the Captaincy of Bahia de São Salvador were swarming with termites and covered with dust. The dining-room furniture made of holy wood was also in terrible shape; the bannisters on the stairway leading to the upper level, which had come from the chancel of the Church of São Pedro, O Velho, had been crudely patched by a slipshod carpenter. A seventeenth-century bench from the Church of São Francisco in Alagoas now served as the plant stand for a huge vase of dead greenery. "I don't care about these things anymore," Laurinda said. "This house is full of rare, sacred objects, most of them stolen from churches—there are more than ten triptychs alone—but none of it interests me anymore. What matters now are the memories, and they're right here inside this old trunk," and she knocked the side of her head with her hand. That day she also opened the strongbox and lifted out a pile of photographs. "This is the man I loved the very most. Albert. I took him to the pier at Mauá Square when he boarded the ship back to Belgium. I remember as if it were yesterday, Albert in his grand uniform on the main deck of the dreadnought *São Paulo* waving goodbye. We wrote to each other secretly until the day he died, a mountain-climbing accident. I have all his letters here in this strongbox. One day you'll be able to go through and read everything. It will take years." She smiled. "In addition to the strongbox there are drawers, boxes, trunks, wardrobes, shelves, endless piles of papers, books, photographs. . . . Do you know who this is?" It was a picture of a fat man wearing a hat: "For Laurinda. Respects from Paulo Barreto." Another photo of men and women dressed to the nines, tuxedos and floor-length gowns, sitting in folding chairs with BRAHMA written across their backs gathered around tables with ice buckets and bottles of champagne: "Saturdays, at the Palace Hotel, the new bourgeoisie of the twenties, sipping champagne in chairs from a beer hall. Dreadful." A picture of the grand opening of the Urca Spa Hotel; on the back was written: "Guest rooms. Physiotherapy, under the direction of Prof. Dr. Gustavo Armbrust, located on Avenida Portugal, a picturesque neighborhood built by the company." Lots of people in costume: the crossing of the equator aboard the ship *Arlanza*. A small short-haired woman wearing a white hat: "Greetings, Berta Singerman." "This is General Pershing, that's me dancing with him on the deck of the American warship *Utah* during a social offered to Rio society. Here's Pershing in full-dress uniform, look how elegant he is, how he stands out surrounded by fat little Brazilian generals. You've heard of Erté—one of the most famous fashion designers—this is one of his creations, at the Hotel Madison in New York. I believe he's still living, somewhere in the world, older than I am. This half-nude woman was the star of the movie *Let No Man Put Asunder*. This is the whole gang, just look at us, on the beach in 1925, suits and ties and straw hats. That skinny kid with the felt hat is Dr. Lameiro. Look how long our dresses are; you can't even see the ankles, and only one woman's wearing a bathing suit. Nowadays they go to the beach with their breasts hanging out. Well, it's the truth, isn't it?" "It's the eighties now, Grandmother." There was a photograph of seven people seated at a table looking straight at the photographer, only one of the faces was obscured by a flower arrangement. The two in the center were bride and groom. The bride's veil concealed her hair and forehead completely, making a wave of fabric down her neck, with a string of pearls just barely visible. She had pale skin and a small mouth with thinnish lips, but they looked fuller because of the lipstick she was wearing. The groom was also dressed in white; he had a round folded-down collar and a long black tie that matched his wavy hair and a pearl tiepin. He was handsome and looked like he had been skinny when younger but had put on weight with age. Sitting next to the bride was a dark Italian-looking man, also in white, with a vest, turned-up collar and black bow tie; to his right, a woman in a dark dress and a huge black wide-brimmed hat. Beside the groom sat another woman with a similar hat and beside her a stout man also in white with a black bow tie; and, finally, the woman whose face could not be seen. Except for the bride, the three women's hats looked embarrassingly alike. A piece of paper was glued to the back of the picture: "Wedding of Senhorinha Gabriela Besanzoni Lage, the amazing world-famous contralto, to Sr. Henrique Lage, director of Lage Brothers, Incorporated, president of the National Coastal Shipping Company. The religious ceremony, which took place in the lovely Lage family residence on the Island of Santa Cruz, was performed at 11:30 by the Reverend Monsignor Rosalvo Costa Rego, vicar-general of the Archdiocese of Rio de Janeiro." Laurinda added, "Gabriela is wearing the pearls

202

Henrique gave her, and his Oriental rose-pearl tiepin was her gift to him." "How do you remember all this at . . . How old are you now?" "You know perfectly well I'm eighty-nine. And I remember a lot more than that. I remember the Maestro Salvador Ruperte playing a *meditazione* on the organ, accompanied by Maestro Fittipaldo. After the ceremony there was a banquet with three hundred and forty place settings. D'Annunzio sent such a beautiful telegram that I asked to have a copy. It's right here—*'Invidio Orfeu d'oltremare che inghirlanda un'Euridice assai piu melodiosa e deliziosa del l'antica. Vi mando una stella della notte di Brescha e una rosa del' vittoriale.'* No one talks like that anymore. Poets these days are rude and foul-mouthed; the more modern they are, the worse. Now people don't use anything but English or swear words. This fellow sitting beside me is President Alessandri Palma of Chile, on his visit to Brazil. And here, holding the wineglass. You know who this is, don't you?" "Grandfather." A pallid-looking man, with dark straight hair and large dreamy eyes. "Your fake grandfather. You know what he's drinking? Gin. A wineglass of gin. That was how he took his cocaine, mixed with gin, it was all the rage. The Divine Powder they used to call it." "Did a lot of people use the Divine Powder?" "No, very few; I only knew two or three. Alvaro Moreira wrote a book called *Cocaine* in 1925, but it didn't do very well. Look at this party at the Hotel Glória. I'm dressed as the Princess of Egypt." "What about Maria Clara? I remember when I was a boy I'd come visit and you'd give me candy and I could hear her screaming in the cellar. What was she like?" "Every family has a lunatic, and ours certainly had more than its share, but I don't like to talk about that. Besides, you're not a blood relative. As a Mitry and a Montilio, you're free of our curses."

Lima Prado's jottings were made in pen and ink, three colors: blue, red, and green. Observations about his days in the Army were in green (an irony, no doubt); his secret

203

activities were in red; and family topics were in blue. There was no chronological order, or even logic, to the notations. I had a hard time putting everything in order and understanding what was autobiographical and what was fiction. He would have been an interesting writer, I repeat, if only he'd had the time to dedicate himself to that arduous profession. He liked to address himself to old photographs. "I stared for hours at a picture of a pale girl with fleshy lips; her mouth is closed but between her lips, precisely in the center, is a minuscule opening that gives the impression she's a dainty woman who never clenches her teeth unless it's absolutely necessary, who lives a tranquil life, and whose mandibles give way to her tongue."

20

AS USUAL, at nine A.M. Thales Lima Prado arrived at the building downtown on Praça Pius X occupied by Achilles Financial Enterprises.

The Achilles financial consortium was made up of the following businesses: Achilles Bank & Trust Co., S.A.; Achilles Investment Bank; Achilles Credit, Financing & Investment, Real Estate Trust, S.A.; Achilles Brokerage & Personal Securities, S.A.; Achilles Bonding Company & Currency Exchange, S.A.; Achilles General Insurance, S.A.; Achilles Administrative Enterprises, S.A.; Achilles Real Estate Development, Achilles Foresting Group, S.A.; Achilles Tourism, S.A.; Achilles Hotels, S.A.; Achilles Data Processing, S.A.; and Achilles Mining Group, S.A. Several of these businesses had minority capital holdings in dozens of other commercial and industrial companies.

His dark brown leather briefcase in hand, Lima Prado rode the elevator to the eleventh-floor corporate offices of Achilles. As usual, he politely greeted the elevator man as well as the receptionist and secretary. On his desk he found the news bulletin prepared by the Communications Section, with a summary of the main stories covered by the media the previous evening, which he glanced at superficially. If a particular subject merited closer study, the section chief would have prepared a special memo in the concise and objective style that was standard at Achilles. Lima Prado still had an hour before the morning's first interview. The office boy, dressed in black pants and an immaculate white dolman, entered and served black coffee in a porcelain cup. He and the cook were the only ones

205

who had access to the kitchenette contiguous to the president's office. The cook was busy preparing Lima Prado's lunch, which invariably consisted of a grilled steak or piece of roast meat and steamed vegetables, with a pear or apple for dessert.

After coffee, Lima Prado went into his private bath, also contiguous to the office. On the counter next to the sink sat *Collectionneurs d'Armes de Poing*. This book never left the bathroom; Lima Prado attributed to it mysterious laxative powers. *Bien que les pistolets européens le plus anciens remontent aux toutes premières années du XVI Siècle, il fallut attendre 1537 pour trouver la première arme de poing susceptible d'être considerée avec suffisamment de garanties comme étant française. Il s'agit d'un pistolet de style germanique, portant l'inscription "Vive Bourgogne 1537" sur la poignée* . . . And Lima Prado began to defecate with pleasure. It was always at this point—*Vive Bourgogne*—that his intestines began stirring. When he was done, he crouched over the special-order bidet made of English china and laboriously washed his anus with medicated soap. Lima Prado never used toilet paper, no matter how soft.

His secretary informed him that his first appointment had arrived. A well-dressed man with a briefcase walked in. As usual, the interview was not to be interrupted, regardless of who might wish to speak with the president.

"So?"

"All our research indicates a state of perfect equilibrium. There's no way to tell, at the present juncture, who will win. It's possible that the picture will be clearer a few months from now, but the right time to"—he hesitated—"to contribute is now."

"Fine. There are five parties, right?"

"Five, yes."

"I want you to contribute to all of them. But manipulate things so that it's at their invitation."

"That shouldn't be difficult. Your name is neutral and they all need money, with the exception of the government party."

"In addition to institutional donations, which as I recall you've guaranteed will not be reported, we'll contribute to individual candidates as well. And don't leave out the radicals. They do accept contributions, don't they?"

"Corruption knows no allegiances."

"This is not corruption, Gontijo."

"You're right, sir, of course. Sorry."

"Fine, get me the list of suggested names as soon as possible. And I don't want anyone else involved in this. You report directly to me, is that clear?"

"Of course. I've already made the first contacts and I'm working on the preliminary report."

"Verbal. I don't want anything on this subject in writing."

After Gontijo left, the secretary buzzed to say that Mr. Romualdo Magalhães was in the waiting room. Lima Prado instructed her to send him in.

Romualdo was a burly young man who looked uncomfortable in his clothing; his collar seemed to pinch his neck and he constantly pulled at his tie. Lima Prado motioned for him to sit in the chair next to the president's desk and he did.

"This conversation is just between the two of us, is that clear?"

Romualdo nodded his head.

"I want no one, that means no one, to know I am contracting your services."

"Don't give it a thought. No one will know."

"Do you know of a discreet pool somewhere?"

"Can't we use yours—if you don't mind my asking?"

"No, we can't. I don't trust the servants."

"A pool at a club would be much more obvious, if you'll permit the observation."

"All right. We'll use mine. I just hope you'll succeed where the others have failed."

"If it would be all right, I'd like to ask you a question. What do you feel is your main problem?"

"I sink. I can't float. It's as if my bones were made of lead."

(At times I wondered whether this episode was really important. But I figured that Lima Prado's difficulty in learning to swim—considering that he was an excellent horseman—must have had some significance.)

"It sounds psychological."

"I don't care if it's psychological or any other damn thing," said Lima Prado, irritated. "I'm willing to pay you a fortune—a fortune that will guarantee financial independence for the rest of your life; all you have to do is teach me to swim. If it's of any interest to you, I was in analysis for many years, and it was my psychoanalyst who terminated treatment. We dealt with the subject exhaustively over many sessions. Period."

"When would you like to begin?"

"This afternoon."

"This afternoon? I—"

"This afternoon."

"Fine. Just let me make a note of your address."

"Get it from my secretary," said Lima Prado, dismissing Romualdo.

Finally, the last appointment of the morning. He was tall and thin, though round and fleshy in the face. Graying at the temples, horn-rimmed glasses. He carried a black attaché case and resembled all the other important executives who frequented the office.

"You've heard the saying: Either do it right or don't do it at all," said Lima Prado.

"Sure."

"Sometimes one bit of foolishness can mean the loss of a big project, an important deal."

"We're not doing anything foolish. *I'm* not doing anything foolish."

"Relax, Mateus. I'm not blaming you for anything. We've worked together a long time, I have confidence in you, always have. And we're friends, above and beyond our mutual interests in the Organization. I've dedicated my life to the Organization, when what I really wanted to be was a man of letters, as they used to say, or one of those erudite monks who spend their lives reading a lot and eating very little. But here I am worrying about administrative problems. What I mean is that there have been some small things, unimportant I realize, but which indicate that we need to pay more attention to certain details of the business. Our great success all these years has perhaps made us a trifle negligent, careless, and this is not good, Mateus, this is not good. How is it that Zakkai managed to get so much leverage? I know you had nothing to do with it, it's not your area; but everyone was wrong about Zakkai, you included, and when I said I didn't trust him you people all but called me a racist, a naniphobe— but have you ever heard *me* call the guy a dwarf, the way all of you do, or a dirty nigger? Well, have you? Hmmm?"

"No."

"I discovered Hermes, and has he given us problems? Elisio I didn't know beforehand, but just looking at him I knew we could trust him. Has he given us problems? Or Gambacorta? And then there are all the others, competently doing their jobs without asking for more than they already get, which is a lot, don't you think? They're all rich. But Zakkai, an outsider, wants more, and gets more each time, and we end up with our hands and feet tied behind our backs. It makes me nervous, Mateus. I don't like people to squeeze me; I've been that way ever since I was a boy. I go crazy when anyone hounds me, and that's exactly what Zakkai is doing."

"There are ways to put a stop to that."

"Sure. But this is a complicated game we're playing. They could get to me through Zakkai. I don't mean me-me, but the heart of the Organization. To Achilles. Do you understand what I'm saying?"

"Zakkai doesn't know anything about our connection to you and Achilles."

"Look, Hermes is reliable. You're reliable. Hermes could be subjected to the worst kind of torture, one that fits his most secret and irresistible fear. And we all have our own secret personal fear, as Big Brother knows; but even so, Hermes would rather die suffering horribly than to turn me in."

"I would, too."

"You, too; you, too, I know. I know. But people do foolish things. Not you; I'm not referring to you. The foolishness I mentioned earlier."

"I don't know what you're referring to. If it's the contract on that lawyer—"

"No, not that. That was a mistake, ineptitude on the assembly line. There was no need to create that whole rigmarole to get back the videocassette. Which we ended up not getting back, incidentally. We stirred up the lawyer for nothing. What's his name again?"

"He's known as Mandrake."

"Seems like an impulsive guy, running off to do all sorts of unpleasant investigating. I know the type, not the sort we want in our way. And your people were stupid to go after him based on a false assumption. But that's not what I was referring to, no. No, I'm worried about Roberto. Roberto Mitry."

"But he's not even part of the organization, he doesn't know anything. He's only involved in Achilles business."

"Maybe he knows, without even knowing he knows. And talks, without knowing what he's saying. And the worst is that he may be the one who has the videocassette, which only has value to me, and sentimental at that."

"But he's your cousin. Your friend."

"The Organization is a more important friend. Unfortunately, Roberto is a risk that must be eliminated. It's a shame. A real shame."

"Hermes can take care of that."

"Hardly necessary for a job that should be as easy as taking a stroll on the beach. Let's not waste the Professor on this."

"Our team is short-handed," said Mateus. "We've lost Fuentes, as you know. The Feds are on his tail, so we thought it best to eliminate him. That's always been standard procedure. Dirceu and Lupiscínio were supposed to take care of it. Fuentes didn't know them, but he put both of them away. In São Paulo. I still don't have details. So, of five permanent operatives, we're left with only two—Rafael and Silvio. I don't know if I'll use one of them or someone new. Hermes is working with two more recruits."

"That's your area."

"You know the training phase takes time."

"It's your area."

"But we've already got a backlog—the lawyer, the Bolivian, and now Zakkai and Roberto—and I just think that—"

"Mateus, Mateus, that's your area. You set up the method and the priorities. All I ask is that Roberto be first on the list. The rest you can take care of as you see fit. Do we understand each other? Another thing: The situation in Bolivia has gotten complicated with Zuazo in power. None of our people have had unauthorized contacts with the Nazis, have they?"

"Altman and Fiebelkorn? They're a couple of cachexic septuagenarians dying of old age. There's been no contact with them—I'm not even sure they're still good for anything—nor with the Italians. I saw Pagliai, in Caceres, and Delle Chiaie in Santa Cruz de la Sierra. Demented fanatics, those two. The Bolivian police let the Italians and Americans extradite Cherubino back to Italy, but he was already in a coma and died. Just Caccola left to go."

"The others will take care of him. You did well not to get involved. Meza and Gomez took off for Argentina. We'll have to restructure the Bolivian operation. Here are the new contacts." Lima Prado handed Mateus a piece of paper. "Memorize the names and instructions and destroy it. Don't do anything for the time being. Fernandez is in charge. He has good friends in the new administration, but he said to wait. He'll be the one to give the green light. In the meantime we'll work with Colombia. Inform Buschetta that we guarantee the Italian supply. If the Sicilians would just stop creating problems . . . they're just too

211

dramatic. To them the world's an opera. Do you like cold roast beef with cauliflower? That's what we've got."

"I eat anything. I'm thinking of going on a diet, anyway, try to take a few inches off this paunch."

21

AS USUAL, Evilásio was to withdraw immediately after serving dinner; his solemn presence had a way of constraining the guests. He selected from the wine room several bottles each of Rausan-Ségla (his boss enjoyed suave red wines), Château d'Yquem, and Krug champagne, this last for the ladies who preferred a bubbly *vin de joie,* the closest thing to the carbonated soft drinks they were used to. That's what the boss said, but Evilásio was tired of watching the men drink champagne just as avidly as the women.

That afternoon Mitry had been paid a visit by his barber, a gentleman who carried the accoutrements of his profession in an executive briefcase. The barber was well aware of his capricious client's requirements for a haircut: His hair must look as if it had not been so much as touched by scissors. Mitry interrupted the barber's work constantly, asking for a mirror to be placed behind him so he could monitor his progress. Then, at a given moment that the barber could never anticipate, Mitry would abruptly stand up and announce that the haircut was over. The barber always protested (politely), since like any professional, he liked to put the final touches on his work for that finished look; not doing so, he feared, would make it hard to justify the high price he charged. His client's hair was thinning and a bald spot was beginning to form at the crown, but the barber kept his silence. Science had not yet discovered a way to avoid the problem, and the last thing he wanted to do was provoke the mercurial temper of the man sitting in front of him with this disturbing news.

After the barber left, Mitry retired to his bathtub. Evilásio had drawn the water, adding aromatic bath salts, and placed beside the tub a book (*Le Mobilier Chinois*), a battery-operated tape recorder, and a tape of Lully's opera *Rolando*. Mitry dozed in the lukewarm perfumed water, listening to the enchanted trumpet frighten the Saracens; when his fingers began to wrinkle he stepped out of the bath, dried himself, and went to bed.

Now he was spying on his guests, for whom he had not the least affection. They were all the same, high-born or low, rich or flat busted, educated or ignorant, white or black; they were all there for the express purpose of gorging themselves on free delicacies. Mitry had no illusions. But he was a gregarious being who didn't like to eat, drink, smoke, or snort alone. And he felt a certain complacent respect for two of his guests—the two little strumpets perched on the sofa in the main living room looking around at his art objects with studied indifference. They were young women from the lower middle class on their way up the ladder, well dressed and well tanned. Their names were Titi and Tatá. In the armchair facing them, drinking whiskey (standard executive practice), sat Alvaro Monteiro. He leered hungrily at the two girls. Rumor had it that Monteiro was a weapons dealer to Middle Eastern nations. A couple who had just come back from New York, both handsome and less than intelligent, were asking indiscreetly for the white stuff. An already inebriated guest was saying that Xantipa (which was what he had just facetiously dubbed his wife) had not been able to make the party because she was sick and that he hoped by the time he got home she'd be dead. The chief executive of a conglomerate of contractors who worked for the government was saying that if he didn't fork over ten percent he would never get a single contract, adding, "It's been that way since 1950." Mitry, dressed in a silk shirt open to the waist and revealing his flabby paunch, hairy chest, and thick gold chain, watched and listened to his

214

guests with undisguised disdain. Finally, he came out from behind the Chinese screen and joined them in the living room.

"Titi, Tatá—I've made you wait so long, darlings. Monteiro, I see you've already made the young ladies' acquaintance. This, girls, is the largest supplier of planes, tanks, and cannons in the world. He's the one who wins all the wars. Right, Monteiro?"

"Not all of them. You have wonderful paintings," said Monteiro, anxious to change the subject.

Stationing himself in the middle of the room so that everyone could hear, Mitry pointed out his treasures as Evilásio poured predinner champagne into crystal flutes: "Scliar, Visconti—extremely rare—da Costa, Tarsila, Millôr, Cícero Dias, Krajberg, Anita, Di, Volpi. If you'll forgive a short burst of immodesty, I have to say I own the best in Brazilian art." To Monteiro: "I happen to have a whole room of Guignards. Interested?"

"Later," said Monteiro, sipping his whiskey, unable to take his eyes off Titi's mouth. "Which one are you, Titi or Tatá?"

"Titi."

"Your gums look like iridescent coral. I've never seen such beautiful teeth."

"Isn't that nice."

"Titi is one perfect little animal; all she lacks is the pedigree. Isn't that right, love?"

Titi drained her glass without responding.

"What are you chewing on, Mitry?" asked Monteiro.

"You really are into mouths, aren't you? Ginseng root." Mitry stuck out his tongue; on the tip was something that looked like a small piece of dark cork.

"Taste good with champagne?"

"I'm not drinking champagne. I'm saving myself for the dinner wines."

Evilásio served French *pâté truffé* irrigated by Château d'Yquem, various meats and cheeses accompanied by Rausan-Ségla, and fruit with liqueurs. "We always had wine with meals," said Mitry. "My father ordered them

215

directly from France. He was an elegant man, my father, perhaps a bit . . . a bit . . ." He stopped, searching for the right word. "A bit archaic. There was always a good Château d'Yquem on the table. Ah, the dissipations of youth! How lovely it used to be to get drunk." Mitry held his glass up to the light. *Une précieuse liqueur d'or liquide.* My father, my father . . ."

He left the sentence unfinished.

Evilásio served coffee, verified that the time had come for him to withdraw, and retired to his small room in the depths of the apartment.

The guests made themselves comfortable in the living room and looked at their host entreatingly. There was still something missing to complete the party.

"Happy dust! Goofball! Green dragon! Bernice!" exclaimed the couple who had just come back from New York, demonstrating that they knew the American slang for the missing ingredients.

"Which one do you like better, Titi or Tatá?" Mitry asked Monteiro, ignoring his guests' broad hints.

"Titi."

"At the end of the hall, to the left, there's a suite. Mirrors, hot videotapes. All yours whenever you want it."

Titi stood up, ready.

"Later," said Mitry, "after the pièce de résistance. I'll be right back."

He returned with a silver tray on which he had arranged several small mirrors with fine lines of white powder and a crystal vial full of colorful pills.

"You're not going to indulge?" asked Mitry when he noticed Monteiro pass. "It's a combination I invented myself, give it a try. Or would you prefer to shoot it? Or maybe a speedball? I've also got the Big D."

"No," said Monteiro.

"You're not scared, are you? Of getting addicted? Or going nuts, or impotent, or dying? All myths, my friend."

"Perhaps," said Monteiro.

"Or are you afraid of opening up your head and discovering something new?"

216

"Perhaps."

"It's the only way to experience total freedom," said Mitry, snorting a line and popping a pill in his mouth. "People like you covet prestige, a good reputation, and passively accept the loss of autonomy that goes with it."

"Perhaps," said the weapons dealer for the third time.

"What the hell kind of conversation is this?" said Tatá with unexpected belligerence. "Why don't you put on some music?"

"You don't know what you're missing. It's a way of transcending, of going beyond. Try it, nothing could go better with your profession of middleman to destruction." Mitry's eyes had taken on a reddish glow that flashed when he turned his tead. Tatá began dancing. "I'd like to show you my best canvas, a masterpiece the likes of which no one else in Brazil possesses. You come, too, my bitchy little poodle." Mitry pulled Monteiro and Titi by the arms and led them to a large room with only one very large painting on the wall.

"See? One of the *Three Studies of Lucien Freud*. Bacon's just a genius. Lucien is a pig, an amorphous pasta that projects itself out of this transparent cube which bisects his body and permits us to foresee all the parts of his decomposed integrity." Mitry grabbed Monteiro's arm roughly. "Now before you say that that's just a bunch of alkaloid rhetoric, I want you to take a good look at the foot, the nose, the hands—Jesus Christ, the hands, he doesn't have hands!" Mitry flicked on another spotlight to bring out the painting's yellow and brown tones. "Look at the nose. Just think what Lucien does, sitting in that wicker chair in black socks and gloves and molten hands. Look at his chamois-colored shoes, his face—red, white, and gray—and the soft blue and green tones of the cancer that go so well with decomposing things."

"Lovely," said Monteiro. "Look, Titi and I are going to head for—you know."

In the suite, Monteiro and Titi sat down on the bed.

"You really want to?" asked Monteiro.

"Why not? Today could be the day it clicks. Who knows?

I always get to a certain point and then I just float. What I want is to hear trumpets, bells, the whole works."

Monteiro felt his penis stiffen. No time to lose; a couple of times in the past he had not taken advantage of the moment and his cock had gone back to its debilitating slackness. Hurriedly, sweating profusely, Monteiro pushed inside the passive Titi. After he came, he quickly climbed off, feeling relieved, like someone who has just fulfilled an obligation. Lying on his back, already bored, he said, "I have to get up real early tomorrow." He looked at his shoes on the floor. "Did you hear trumpets?"

"More or less. I mean you were terrific, obviously it's *my* problem. Aren't you going to give me something to remember you by?"

"Of course. I'll write down your phone number and call to arrange everything."

Monteiro put his shoes on and, still nude, asked, "Have a pen?" He began dressing.

"No. But you know what? Never mind, forget it."

Mitry and Tatá were the only ones still in the living room; the other guests were nowhere to be seen. Naked, Tatá was singing and dancing.

"I've got to go," said Monteiro. "I have to be up real early in the morning."

"But you just got here," said Mitry, delirious. "I am a promiscuous pansexual! I look around me and what do I see in every corner of my solar city? Nothing but hypocrites chasing after success and money, searching for eternal youth." Mitry pinched Tatá's ass. She went right on smiling and gyrating like an unhinged robot. "The newest dream of the powerful—that flesh should have the durability of synthetic rubber! The new lie! The new corruption!" Flailing his arms over his head, Mitry yelled threateningly at Monteiro: "A new kind of madness is raging in the world!"

"I have to get up really early," apologized Monteiro.

"You ate, you drank, you fucked, and now you're going back to your missiles."

"Men are poor sons of bitches," said Titi.

Next door to Mitry's apartment building, from inside a car parked on the sidewalk, Rafael watched the reception area. He had shown up early enough to observe Mitry's guests arrive. Now it was four A.M., the perfect time for a break-in. People who go to bed late had already turned in, and people who get up early hadn't yet awoke. Rafael watched Monteiro and the others leave; by his calculations that left only the two girls still upstairs with Mitry.

He adjusted his tie, buttoned his dark new suit coat, and lifted a large, colorfully wrapped package out of the back seat. Under the box, secured with masking tape, was a knife. Carrying the package with both hands, he approached the glass doors of the building. Inside, behind a small desk, the doorman sat listening to the radio. Rafael knocked on the glass. The doorman motioned for him to pick up the phone to the left of the door.

"Delivery for Mr. Mitry," said Rafael into the receiver.

"Just leave it outside," said the doorman.

"Outside? Are you crazy? This is far too valuable an item to leave here outside."

"Mmm. Well, this is no time for deliveries."

"Hey look, I'm on my way to the airport to catch a plane. I don't have time for fun and games. This is a gold and platinum vase, it cost a fortune. I have to deliver it today or Mr. Mitry will be furious. And you have to sign the receipt."

Rafael watched as the doorman hung up the phone, removed a revolver from the desk drawer, and stuck it in his belt. Then he opened the door.

"Please, be careful." Rafael shifted the weight of the package onto the doorman's chest. As the doorman struggled with both hands, Rafael ripped the knife off the bottom of the package and pressed the blade to the doorman's throat.

"Not a word or you're dead," said Rafael.

The doorman stood stock still, balancing the package in

219

his trembling hands. Rafael slipped the gun out of the man's belt.

"Let's go, back there. Slowly. Turn off the lights. Not a peep."

Once in the dark hall, Rafael took the doorman by the shirt collar and said, "Now pay attention. If you cooperate, nothing will happen to you. I want to get into the penthouse. You're going to come upstairs with me, ring the bell, and get them to open the door. If they get the least bit suspicious, I promise you'll die like a swine." Rafael drew the knife blade slowly across the doorman's nose.

In the elevator Rafael asked if there was anyone else in the penthouse besides the two girls.

"Just Evilásio, the butler. He's an old man."

"The suspicious type?"

"I don't know."

"We'll go in the back way. If he doesn't open the door, you know what happens. You live here in the building?"

"Yeah."

"With your family?"

The doorman was silent.

"Answer me." Rafael pricked the man's neck with the knife.

"With my wife. Ground floor, in back."

"You try anything funny, she gets it too."

The elevator stopped. They got off.

"You got a phone in your apartment?"

"No."

"Does the one at the desk make calls outside the building?"

"Yes."

"Tell the old man that your wife is sick and the phone at the desk isn't working and you need to call an ambulance. When he opens the door, don't go in right away, stand back and give me a minute, you got that?"

Rafael hid around the corner from the staircase. The doorman rang the bell.

"He's probably asleep."

"Ring again," said Rafael from his hiding place.

This time the doorman held the button long and hard, a buzzing that seemed as though it would wake the whole building.

"Who is it?" asked Evilásio through the door.

"It's me, João. My wife is sick and I need to use the phone. The one downstairs is broken."

Evilásio opened the door. Four quick steps and Rafael was out of his corner and holding Evilásio by the collar of his striped pajamas.

"Silence," he said.

Turning pale and beginning to shake, Evilásio let himself be pushed back into the apartment along with João. The doorway led to the pantry area with white Formica walls that reflected the cold light from the ceiling fixture. Rafael cut the lines of the two wall phones. Then he led the two men into Evilásio's small windowless room. He had them lie down on the floor and tied them up.

Rafael locked the door behind him and proceeded into the dining room. He walked calmly and casually; if someone were to surprise him they would think he was one of the guests. The apartment was brightly lit, and signs of the recent visitors were everywhere—cups, bottles, ashtrays full of cigarette butts, sofa cushions scattered on the floor.

Mitry was snoring gently with his mouth hanging open in the extra-wide double bed in his room. Beside him lay Titi and Tatá, asleep in each other's arms. The Professor had taught Rafael the correct use of the knife in his hand. Though he had originally planned on using a Cassidy with a fourteen-centimeter blade and a black Micarta handle, at the last minute he opted instead for an ordinary Tramontina purchased in a cutlery shop on Praça Tiradentes. After the job was completed, he would leave the knife at the scene. Mitry was shirtless, belly up, which called for the ice-pick grip, counterindicated in any other situation.

Rafael leaned over Mitry's body, carefully brushing aside the metallic regalia covering his left nipple. He gripped the knife firmly, barely fifty centimeters away from his chosen target, the muscles in his forearm tense, biceps relaxed. He had never had such a perfect opportunity to execute an utterly clean, explosive stroke. The knife came down fast and hard, its blade plunged into Mitry's chest up to the hilt. The sound of metal tearing flesh and Mitry's short, mild exhalation hung in the air a few seconds. Leaning on Mitry's chest with his left hand, Rafael removed the knife, which was no easy task, because of thoracic suction. He went into the bathroom and washed the blade. He removed his clothes and shoes. Completely naked, he returned to the bedroom. With the Professor's instructions in mind, Rafael now gripped the knife with his palm turned under, thumb and index finger pressing against the guard, wrist slightly twisted backward. He was going to slit the girls' throats. But first he contemplated their two sleeping bodies. The one on the left had a leg and an arm draped over the other girl, who was on her back, and their faces were very close, almost touching. One was wearing a string of pearls, which would not make the operation any more difficult. Rafael gently climbed onto the bed and, perched on their legs, began cutting their throats in rapid horizontal strokes. The bodies shook convulsively and gurgled for a few instants, blood spurting all over the pink satin sheets from the deep slashes. Rafael's arms, chest, and face were also bloodied. There was no time to lose. Darkness was already dissolving; the gray of dawn was visible out the window. Rafael rinsed off under the shower and dressed. When he came back through the bedroom the bodies were already cold. He began his search for the videotape. On a shelf in one of the living rooms he found hundreds, lined up side by side like books.

22

THE DEATH of Roberto Mitry received ample coverage in the newspapers. Editorials energetically condemned the escalating violence and citizens' lack of security. The other hundred and fifty and some odd homicides that occurred that month in the greater Rio area, in which the majority of the victims were poor blacks and mulattoes, had received only routine press attention; but Mitry's murder was a fascinating bit of news—a rich society man killed in his bed with two nymphettes. The papers published glamorous pictures of Titi and Tatá topless on the beach in Ipanema; Mitry on board his yacht in Angra dos Reis; the building on Vieira Souto where the millionaire lived; and the interior of his apartment, with special emphasis on the valuable objets d'art. There were interviews with the doorman João, Evilásio the butler, the girls' mother, and Raul, the detective in charge of the investigation. There were accounts of the sex and drug orgy that apparently took place the night before the triple homicide —some of the papers called it a massacre, others used the word carnage. There was lots of speculation about the mysterious guests at the party, and hints that some were famous. People like to read about the sordid episodes of the famous.

I met Raul at the morgue. Mitry's death had left us perplexed. Raul had gone to the apartment on Vieira Souto as soon as he heard about the murders.

"Mitry was killed in his sleep. The expressions of horror on the girls' faces indicate that they were conscious of being killed. We believe there was only one assassin, and that he's right-handed. It's obvious, from the nature and condition of the wounds, that it was an expert, someone very, very handy with a knife. There was blood all over the shower stall, probably the victims'. We're still waiting for the results of the lab tests for confirmation. Tests are also being done on sperm from both girls' vaginas. No fingerprints were found on the weapon, which was left at the scene."

A man in an apron approached. "Dr. Sette Neto is waiting."

"Sette Neto?"

"That's right."

"I thought he died."

Raul and I crossed a long, white-tiled room with stainless steel tables on which naked cadavers waited for autopsies.

"I'm sure somebody told me he died," said Raul.

"Guys like that never die."

"Those were the days . . . remember?"

"How could I forget? Such pleasant memories," I answered.

We found Dr. Sette Neto in his tiny office surrounded by diplomas and certificates. He looked older but had all his hair, gray now, but still stiff and shiny and slicked back to his scalp like a helmet. He wore glasses and had put on weight, a flaccid adiposity that made him look rather sickly. Either the bags under his eyes were darker or his face was paler, I wasn't sure which. He gave Raul an ironic look and said, "Lacassagne's scarlatiniform rash. Still have that prodigious memory, hmm?"

"No, Professor, I've forgotten everything."

"And you, you were in the same class, yes . . . but not such a good student—no offense. Are you in police work too?"

"He's an important lawyer."

"That's life for you," said Sette Neto. "Well, here's the information you asked for." He consulted the handwritten notes in front of him on the table. "The male victim's heart and left lung were perforated with one stroke. The weapon was a knife with a double-edged blade approxi-

224

mately fifteen centimeters long and a little over three centimeters wide. The women's necks evidence multiple lesions, between the larynx and the hyoid bone, and also on the nape. One appears to be missing a piece of the neck, not uncommon in this type of lesion. Both carotid arteries, as well as the phrenic and pneumogastric nerves, are severed, and in one case the medulla also. There's an interesting contrast here in the killer's apparent attitudes—clearly this is the work of only one attacker —toward his victims. The male victim was dealt only one lethal stroke. But after inflicting lethal wounds on the women, the killer continued madly slashing away. Very interesting. Perhaps it can be of some help in your investigation. It certainly seems to indicate the existence of passion. And of course that would figure into the psychological profile of the killer."

"You think he was a psychotic?" asked Raul.

"We're all psychotic," said Dr. Sette Neto, removing his glasses. "No, that's not it really. There are men who are potentially capable of slitting a woman's throat without being quote-unquote psychotic, and there are psychotics who aren't capable of slitting the throat of a chicken. Rigid labels just don't work. What I mean is that it's not all that difficult to tell who, given the opportunity—knife in hand and neck at the ready—slices and who doesn't slice. And, on slicing, the passion put into the motion also tells us a lot about him, or her: his vision of the world and of the 'other,' his cosmic ideology, his interpretation of reality. It's a theme that has fascinated artists since man developed language complex enough to express the intricacies of his essence. All the great characters in literature, when you stop to consider it, are killers. Starting with Cain—the Bible's full of murders—and right on down: Ulysses, Oedipus, Electra, Othello, Macbeth, Raskolnikov, Sorel. I could go on and on." Sette Neto held his glasses up to the light, examining the lenses. "Raul, when you catch a killer, aren't you curious about what makes him different from others? The ethos, the pathos . . . They're always different, aren't they?"

"It would be great to discuss this further, Professor, but

225

there are people waiting for us at the station," I said. I could not stand it in there one more minute.

"A pity," said Sette Neto. He walked us to the door, clearly disappointed. "The autopsy report will be ready tomorrow."

From the morgue we went to Amarelinho's bar in Cinelândia. We took a table on the street.

"The old duffer's full of theories, all right—too full, for my taste. Once doctors get talking, they just don't stop. And the smell of cadavers, no matter how much ozone they spray around, it makes me sick. Hey, you see that cornice up there, well there used to be an eagle—"

"You've already told me that story dozens of times. And there was also some pigeon—right?—that shit on your head. And meanwhile, the sinister Pigeon Breeders Association . . . I know it all by heart."

"Okay, Mr. Know-it-all, then do me a favor and sketch out the cosmic ideological profile of the killer—epistemologically speaking, of course."

We sat drinking beer until nightfall.

23

LIMA PRADO made a point of insisting that he was not a Nazi, but nevertheless Hitler might well have been the greatest man to live in the twentieth century. Humanity was beginning to recognize this slowly, in spite of efforts by Jews and their allies from both camps, plutocrat and communist, to insure that the memory of this great German would continue to be execrated by ongoing campaigns of defamation and calumny—"to use the tired nomenclature of the penal code."

Lima Prado regarded the man in front of him and went on: "You know how Jews manipulate things, with their partners of circumstance; they control the flow of information, the media; they dominate the arts, education—not to mention international finance, of course. Was the Holocaust, the Final Solution, so monstrously extraordinary, then, considering the atrocities committed by the Jews later in Palestine? The Beirut bombing was worse than Hiroshima, at least in terms of the duration of the terror involved. And what about the massacres of Chatila and Sabra? Eichmann didn't kill anyone with his own hands, either; he merely closed his eyes, like Sharon. Hiroshima lasted but a minute; the bombing of Beirut went on for weeks and weeks, with the civilian population blown to bits by fire and fragmentation bombs—in streets, garages, schools, hospitals, under the bed, in the cemetery."

The man with Prado, a respected senator, considered replying to all this absurdity, this semi-astute mountain of half-truths, but decided it more politic to keep silent and register his disapproval merely by maintaining a rigid chin.

"But in spite of this master plan," continued Lima Prado, "including the mobilization of a fantastic amount of money the world over, the truth is beginning to come out." Even the film industry, another area controlled by American Jews, has begun to produce movies in which Hitler no longer appears as the stereotypical insane killer. Recent historical works written with strict impartiality showed how much Hitler had contributed to the strengthening of Germanic culture. The swastika was little by little becoming a symbol for youths worldwide, and Hitler the man—the great military leader who confronted the bellicose powers of the East and the West, fabulous orator capable of stupefying multitudes with the sincerity of his immense eloquence, writer who analyzed as no one had before the frustrations and aspirations of a great nation cruelly humiliated and driven to retaliate in order to free itself from the savage oppression of the so-called democratic nations—Hilter was beginning to be understood and loved by young people everywhere.

Lima Prado and the senator were sitting on the veranda of the Yacht Club of Rio de Janeiro. It had rained the whole previous night, and day had dawned clear and sun-drenched, so that it was possible to see great distances in the clean air. Things stood out in extreme clarity: the green vegetation in the hills, the white sails of distant boats in Guanabara Bay. The senator was drinking whiskey, Lima Prado a gin and tonic. As usual, Lima Prado had brought his own flask of gin; he didn't trust drinks served in public or private places. On the infrequent occasions when he attended social gatherings, he always drew the attention of the other guests by serving himself from a pocket flask. The truth was he was afraid of being poisoned; but because he didn't want people to suspect this, he had invented the justification he repeated now for the senator: "Hogarth is the only gin I can stomach; it's made of special juniper berries, caraway, coriander, and cassia bark, according to the original recipe of the Dutchman Franciscus de la Boë, who invented gin. But it's impossible to find it in Brazil."

"What's the brand again?"

"Hogarth."

"Mmm, of course."

Lima Prado smiled, not even trying to disguise the sarcasm on his face. He was treating the senator with the lack of consideration he typically reserved for those to whom he donated money. (Hogarth, William: British painter of the eighteenth century, reformer and moralist, creator of several narrative engravings denouncing the evils of gin. Lima Prado was in fact drinking Bols, a brand of gin relatively easy to come by.) He was in a particularly caustic mood because, above and beyond everything else, this meeting had obliged him to shave two days straight, which irritated his sensitive skin. As usual, no matter where he was, he was wearing a black suit, white shirt, black tie, black shoes and socks. He owned no fewer than twenty-two black suits.

Imagining that in the sporty atmosphere of the club Prado's formal attire signified mourning, the senator—himself dressed in a print shirt of the middle-aged variety that fit him poorly (as happens with parliamentarians and executives when they dress informally)—felt an obligation to mention Roberto Mitry's death, which up until then he had been avoiding.

"A terrible thing, your cousin's death. I don't know if you were aware of it, but some time ago I made a speech in the Senate—it was featured in the press—about urban violence in this country. I've done a lot of research on the subject and I've come to the conclusion that the demographic explosion, first, and then the uneven distribution of wealth that followed are the principal causes for the escalation of violence in our cities. There are other factors, of course, such as the inefficiency of the police and the moral decadence of society. When I was a boy, calling someone a thief was the worst offense, the worst insult imaginable; violence was confined to a few less-than-respectable areas of town. Nowadays it's a different story, and we see the same problem the world over. It may sound old-fashioned, but there's just no shame anymore, no dignity, no propriety. People no longer have the built-in brakes to restrain them from antisocial, immoral, yes immoral acts." He looked at Lima Prado and thought he detected a slightly scornful expression, which caused him to change course. "Just consider the case of your cousin."

"My cousin?"

"Citizens today are not even safe in the seclusion of their own homes. Did he have any children?"

"No, Roberto was single. I'm his closest relative."

"Terrible, just terrible."

The senator seems to have forgotten, thought Lima Prado, that he's spent ten years in the Senate legislating, directly or indirectly, on behalf of his own self-interest.

"As long as the negative example of the elite exists, it will be very difficult to improve the social fabric of the country." The senator's voice took on the ranting cadence he habitually adopted on the floor of the Senate. "The lack of leaders, two dictatorships in less than fifty years, all this has destroyed traditional values and prevented new ones from emerging. The elite—and by that I mean entrepreneurs, professional liberals, the military, intellectuals, religious figures—are not capable of, or willing to come up with, the courage and clarity necessary to lead this country into true democracy, with liberty and social justice. The risk is that we will emerge from a dictatorship of the right only to fall into a dictatorship of the left—which, as you know, would be worse." Another pause. Nihilism was not befitting a senator. Criticize and denounce, okay, but don't forget to be optimistic! "We must trust in Brazil. This is a great and still fledgling nation, while Europe is on its deathbed and the superpower imperialists are at the apogee that precedes irremediable decadence."

Feigning interest in what the senator was saying, Lima Prado unobtrusively slipped his hand into his jacket pocket where he had placed two clippings from the newspaper: "Why take unnecessary risks? Visit the kind of extremely discreet and luxurious hideaway a man like you deserves. Unlimited pleasure in a dreamlike atmosphere. Call for appointment." And: "Only one client per day. What I have to offer doesn't exist in the best houses of Paris or Bangkok. Utterly unforgettable."

"I've got to make a phone call," said Lima Prado, interrupting the senator's lecture.

From the phone booth he could see the senator drinking whiskey and eating cashews compulsively. There were a lot more interesting things to do than listen to that fool. He looked like a ventriloquist's dummy, his dark eyes unmoving behind thick lenses and his outsize teeth and gray lips opening and closing in a mechanical grimace. There was someone in the phone booth next to him. The receiver to his ear, Lima Prado waited for his neighbor to finish before beginning to dial.

"I read your ad."

"Want to make an appointment?"

"Unlimited pleasure. What does that mean?"

"Why don't you come and find out?" The woman was trying to hide her impatience; she probably got lots of calls that amounted to nothing.

"I'm very shy. And real awkward in waiting rooms."

"This isn't a dentist's office."

"Will I be taken care of right away?"

"Sure, that's why you make an appointment. You sign up, you show up, you get it up."

"But I want a good long one. Don't schedule another client right afterward. I'll pay double."

"No checks, okay?"

"Can I call to confirm in a little while? I have a few things to take care of first."

The senator continued his gustatory labors, whittling away at a platter of assorted snacks that had been placed in front of him by the waiter. Even from a distance, Lima Prado had the impression he could hear the man's jaws working.

The phone rang many times before someone finally picked up.

"I read your ad."

231

"Wait a minute, just let me turn down the stereo." She sounded young, happy. "That's better. I'm crazy about music."

"Why Bangkok?"

" 'Cause it sounds mysterious. I don't even know where it is. Isn't Bangkok where they had the thousand and one nights?" She laughed. Young and innocent.

"Are you free?"

"For the moment. You want to make a date?"

"I'd like some information."

"The apartment's in Copacabana, near lifeguard station number five. I'm blonde, I like music. What else? What about you?"

"Me?"

"Yes, you."

"What do you want to know?"

"I can't make a date till I know something about you. I only like charming men, men who like music like me."

"I'm charming."

"But do you like music?"

"Sure."

"Promise?"

"Promise."

"How old are you?"

"In my forties."

"Pretty old, huh?"

"What about you, how old are you?"

"Ah . . . eighteen. What's your name?"

"Ajax." A dumb idea, but it was too late. Why? Pallas Athena with blue-green eyes. Parthenos. (It took me a while to identify it, even though I already knew ancient Greece was one of Lima Prado's interests.)

"Ajax? Sounds like a detergent. Mine is Mônica."

The plate of snacks was licked clean, the whiskey bottle half empty.

"While you were on the phone I recalled a phrase of Cromwell's: Democracy is strong in England because in

232

this country men of integrity have the same audacity as the rabble. Which is not, unfortunately, the case in Brazil. Here men of integrity are cowards. The most qualified people just want, by any means possible, to make their fortunes—and I'm not referring to you, who were born rich and have demonstrated great public spirit—but it's true all over the country, even in the poorest states. Great individual patrimonies have been established, not always honestly, millionaires out of nothing, unscrupulous men who take advantage of the situation the country is in to line their own pockets. The recent history of Brazil can be summarized in five words—unbridled power, fear, stupidity, and corruption. Pitt the Elder said for the first time in 1770"—the senator returned to his eloquent parliamentary mode—"that power corrupts, and Acton, another Englishman, coined the expression 'Power corrupts, and absolute power corrupts absolutely,' a word game that works better in their language. But really, as I've said before, power doesn't corrupt men; men, the fools, should they achieve a position of power, corrupt power. Fear, yes. Fear corrupts, as someone whose name I can't recall at the moment confirmed"—too much whiskey, thought Lima Prado—"fear of losing power, the fear this government is experiencing, that's what makes people most corrupt. If you'll permit me a circumlocution, in Brazil power creates the corrupt and corruption creates the powerful."

"The government, the church, the press, the entrepreneurs, the military, the intellectuals—none are exempt, my dear senator. Now if you'll excuse me, I have to make another phone call."

Dadá was not at home; she had gone to the hairdresser's. Lima Prado asked the governess how the children were. The youngest, six-year-old Rogério, had a cold. The daughter had gone to ballet class with one of the maids. The doctor had stopped in to examine the boy and prescribed a medicated syrup which the chauffeur was sent off to buy at a pharmacy in Leblon. As he talked, Lima Prado fingered the shape under his shirt. Across his chest in a sheath hung a custom-made knife designed by

233

Roderick Caribou Chappel, one of a kind, a gift from Hermes, who had been the sergeant under him in the Special Services—NUSS.

He returned to the table. The senator did like to talk. "Time offers us new perspectives, modernizes symbols, gives new strength to the truth. Don't you see Getúlio's vision in the Brazil of today?"

The exciting prospect of a rendezvous had left Lima Prado feeling confident. Anticipating what was going to happen once he was alone with Mônica, and wishing to bring this interview to a close, he asked the question that was the reason he had summoned the senator to a meeting in the first place: "What about the license—when will it be official?"

The senator took a slug of whiskey. "We'll get it, don't worry. But it's not easy. You saw the last announcement from the Central Bank, didn't you? As you can imagine, it's created certain problems for us."

What would Mônica look like? "I saw it, but I don't think it should prevent the minister from deciding, and soon, in our favor. He's made plenty of nepotistical concessions that were riskier than this and nothing happened except a few feeble remarks in the press. Achilles is solid. We need this license to grow. You're his friend; talk to him."

"I already did. More than once. He's resisting."

"Forgive the abruptness of the suggestion"—Mônica was waiting; he could quiet his impatience no longer—"but I've heard the minister is sometimes responsive to certain pecuniary incentives. If that's a fact—"

"That's an issue that's been talked about a lot in this country," the senator cut in. "In fact we were just discussing—"

"Does he take money or not?" pressed Lima Prado. What about Mônica's body? The smell of her breath? "Let's be frank. We're old friends; we trust each other. Does he or doesn't he?"

"I don't know. But if he does, it's probably done in a very indirect way. He's very smart. I don't like him, but I do recognize his genius."

234

"I'm willing to play by his rules. I'll deposit the money wherever they want in whatever currency they want, the first half in advance and the second half after the license is granted. I'm the one who runs the risk, since I'm in his hands instead of the reverse. He knows how it's done. Do we understand each other?"

After leaving the senator, Lima Prado headed for his rendezvous with Mônica, accompanied only by one bodyguard, Captain Virgulino, who was not a captain, in fact had never even served in the armed forces, but was dark, skinny, wore glasses and looked like the famous bandit Lampião. He was a silent young man who had come to work for Lima Prado at eighteen straight from the National Foundation for Juvenile Correction, where he had been deposited at age eight as a delinquent.

Captain Virgulino accompanied Lima Prado into the building, alert as always and thoroughly prepared to kill or die to protect the life of the man he considered his benefactor. They took the elevator upstairs.

"I want you to get a look at the young lady's face and then wait for me downstairs. Check back in two hours."

The door opened: a girl in jeans, tennis shoes, and a T-shirt on which was written I and NEW YORK, with a red heart between the two.

Lima Prado was surprised and confused. "Is Mônica here?"

"That's me." Captain Virgulino looked at the girl's face and without a word turned and walked away. "And you're — What was it again?"

"Ajax." Another wave of foolishness washed over him.

"That's right," she said, laughing. "Come in, come in."

He had not expected someone so young; she looked about the same age as his sixteen-year-old daughter. But what really shocked him was the resemblance between Mônica and Cila. The eyes were the same, wide and luminous green, and the mouth was identical, the upper lip protruding slightly, distinct lines defining the shape of the

235

mouth and making it sensual and naïve. His heart pounded with eagerness, but he kept it in check.

"Who was the guy with the glasses?"

"My secretary. He wanted to meet you and now he has. He'll never forget your face. Is this apartment yours?"

"It belongs to a friend of mine, an older woman, but she only comes at night. Why won't he ever forget my face?"

"How old are you?"

"Fifteen. But what difference does age make? Mozart wrote a symphony when he was eight—a symphony, can you imagine? The world's full of child prodigies. I'm one of them. Do you like music?"

"Yes."

"If you didn't, I'd send you away. People who don't like music can't be good people, I don't give them the time of day."

"I like it a lot."

"What an awful suit. You look real pale in black. I've got a Japanese kimono that will look great on you. We can pretend we're in the *Teahouse of the August Moon*. Did you see it on TV?"

Locking himself in the bathroom, Lima Prado changed into the red kimono Mônica had given him. He was careful to hide the Roderick Caribou Chappel in the pile of clothing he left folded up on a stand next to the bidet.

Mônica had also changed into a kimono.

"You sit on this mat while I make tea."

They drank tea with creme crackers.

"Do you think the Japanese eat creme crackers with chopsticks?" asked Mônica, smiling. "Now I'm going to dance for you."

Mônica took off her kimono and began dancing as if she held a fan in her hands. Her body was so perfect and her movements so natural that Lima Prado was dazzled. He could not take his eyes off her. A butt like Cila's! Butt, buttocks, bottom, *bunda*, buns. Noticing which part of her body Lima Prado was fixated on, Mônica stopped, moved closer, and turning her back to him, asked, "Want to touch it?"

The dorsal muscles outlined a convex vertical curve that followed the backbone and ended in the cleft separating her firm gluteals: the part of the body that can, like no other, represent the decadence, fragility, ugliness of a person or, on the other hand, the beauty, energy, abundance.

With the exception of Cila, he had always found (in greater or lesser quantity) pimples, protuberances, or patches of roughness on the various bottoms he had contemplated and caressed. Delicately running his fingertips over Mônica's warm satiny flesh, he tenderly separated the two firm muscular hemispheres, admiring the light-skinned furrow, golden fuzz, and rosy sphincter. He recalled the immense field of sunflowers disappearing into the horizon that he had seen on his first trip to Spain, when he was an adolescent. His head filled with colorful images of Goyas he'd seen in Toledo.

"Put it in slowly," she said, straining her neck to look him in the eyes. Now they were in bed. The incision. The crypt. Gently, he entered Mônica's body until he felt the firm curve of her large gluteals pressing against his pubis. "All the way," breathed Mônica. One of her breasts was nestled in the palm of his hand, and he kissed and licked her slender, diaphanous neck, swaying forward, then backward, smelling the strong fragrance of flowers and tree resin—her hair grazing his nose. Once many years ago, while he stood watching a seventh of September military parade, the classmate in front of him, blue uniform skirt and white blouse, had exuded the same good aroma he smelled now on Mônica's neck. Memories, like light bulbs. Suddenly Mônica said something that made his body shudder as if he'd felt an electrical shock. Human defecation always made him nauseous. Now, a mystery revealed was creating a new mystery and a new astonishment. He both wanted her to repeat what she'd said and was afraid that she would. *Humanum nil a me alienum puto?* He, the man of letters, had always considered this axiom an ingenuous apology for the vices and weaknesses of humankind; and now, in the grip of the tumultuous delirium Mônica's phrase had inspired, he saw the aphorism in a new light. (A surprise behind each new discovery!) Antoinette Bouvignon de la Porte. The cave. Shivering with anxiety he asked her to repeat it. "Ay, I'm going to cover your prick with shit," she said again. His body trembled with passion and he came with a pleasure he had never before experienced. Then he lay still, clutching her body like someone who had awoken in the middle of a dream. After a while, even though she asked him to stay inside, he withdrew, disengaged his body, and got out of bed. In the bathroom he crouched on the bidet and closed his eyes. The smell from his cock was like subterranean earth that had never seen the light of day. He soaped himself carefully, eyes still closed, afraid to look. It seemed as though the cavernous smell would never go away, as if it were radiating from an inexhaustible fountain in the basin where he was sitting. Finally, after minutes of scrubbing, he rinsed and stood up. A towel was draped over the edge of the bathtub; smelling it to make sure it was unused, he noted with pleasure the smell of the hot iron that still clung to the fabric.

Mônica was lying in bed, face down.

"The thousand and one nights were in Baghdad," he said.

The buzzer rang. Mônica jumped out of bed.

"It's your secretary," she said, after looking through the peephole.

When Lima Prado got home he found Romualdo waiting for him.

"Your pool is heated," said Romualdo with admiration. The swimming instructor was also impressed with the size of the house, the gardens, the number of imported cars on the patio, and the number of security men with walkie-talkies stationed at strategic points around the grounds.

Accompanied by his secretary, Captain Virgulino, Lima Prado went inside and returned shortly in a black bathing suit that made his body look even more ashen than his business suit did. He had given orders to the chief of security that no one was to watch the swimming lesson. Even so, two chambermaids peeked out of a second-story window, smiling to see the boss climb into the shallow end of the pool and, following Romualdo's instructions, lie in the water holding on to the edge while he kicked his feet. Lima Prado wasn't worried about the chambermaids. It was his wife he didn't want watching.

"Now put your face in the water and then lift it out again, breathing the way I showed you."

"I can't."

"Any kid can do it," said Romualdo, trying to conceal his nervousness.

"I can't," said Lima Prado, standing up in the pool. "Isn't there some way to learn to swim without putting your face in the water?"

"Sure there is." Romualdo laughed awkwardly, afraid that it sounded as if he were about to tell a joke. "You're not trying to become a champion, right? Only champions have to put their faces in the water."

Romualdo considered himself an expert. Swimmers who did water ballet with their heads out of water must have learned to swim correctly first, and then learned to hold their heads up, he reasoned; then, too, at the beach he frequently saw people swimming with their faces out of the water, heads turning from side to side synchronized with the movement of their arms. They had simply taught themselves to swim—probably starting by treading water, then playing around with the dog paddle, and finally picking their arms up and imitating the circular stroke they had seen real swimmers use. It was a terribly ugly way to swim, but that was how he was going to teach his student. Yet what if this guy was as crazy as Romualdo's cousin who had never been able to learn to ride a bicycle? Romualdo was tempted to jump in the pool and push his student's face underwater, to give him a shock like they do with stutterers. Maybe that would cure his inhibition.

"You're going to have to learn to tread water. Just pre-

239

tend you're pedaling a bicycle and at the same time move your arms back and forth like this."

Lima Prado tried to do as Romualdo instructed, but he constantly touched his foot to the bottom of the pool and gave his body a little push upward.

"That's it, you're doing it, you're treading water!" exclaimed Romualdo, unaware, or pretending to be unaware, that Lima Prado was supporting himself from underneath.

At that moment Dadá appeared at the edge of the pool.

Lima Prado stood utterly still. The water was up to his neck. "Did you want something?"

"I'd like to talk to you."

Lima Prado's voice was cold, controlled, but his irritation showed.

Dadá sounded slightly distracted and jittery. "You'll never learn, why waste time trying?"

Lima Prado climbed out of the pool. From across the yard, the chief of security caught his eye and made a discreet gesture toward the lady of the house, as if to exonerate himself. The chambermaids had disappeared from the window.

Without a word to Romualdo, Lima Prado walked into the house, followed by his wife. Leaving a trail of wet footprints behind him on the wood floor and carpets in the living room, he went upstairs. At the door to his room he turned to Dadá and said, "When I'm ready, I'll call."

"You do that," said Dadá crossly. She came from an aristocratic family and considered good manners a virtue to be cultivated.

Good manners included not turning into a repulsive fat matron like her mother. Of course Dadá no longer had her schoolgirl figure, but she felt she was still attractive and elegant. Her face, after plastic surgery, was like an eighteen-year-old girl's; and if it weren't for the cellulite in that dangerous thigh area, you could almost say she was winning the battle against the march of time. Certainly she was still capable of turning the head of many a man; it was just that she didn't have much of a chance—sigh—

to prove it, surrounded by bodyguards. Her tennis instructor, for one, looked at her with admiring eyes and stammered during those fleeting moments when they were alone. Also the art history professor who came to the house twice a week to give private classes to her and a small group of friends—he never took his eyes off her cleavage, and when she crossed her legs he would suddenly trail off in midsentence.

The telephone rang. It was Lima Prado, ready to talk with his wife.

He was waiting for her, doing isometrics in front of the mirror. His musculature was extremely well defined; even when he was relaxed, the muscles in his abdomen were visible under the skin, muscles art student Dadá saw as "half half-moons, chiseled out of a block of marble."

Dadá had always admired her husband's body, but it had been quite some time—

"How much did you lose?" Lima Prado flexed his biceps, varying the angle between upper arm and forearm.

"No, it's not that. You know what happened? I'm so embarrassed, but I bounced a check and to guess who—Amelinha Calamandrei."

"You've got to be more careful with your account."

"I think I need a larger monthly allowance."

"You can buy whatever you want with credit cards."

"Credit cards aren't money."

"Poker isn't a game for women."

"What is?"

"Canasta, bilboquet."

"I don't like canasta. What's the other one?"

"Is there anything else, besides the money?"

"No." Furious, Dadá stalked out, slamming the door.

How could he, Lima Prado, have married someone who didn't know what bilboquet was? What good was it to be well born if you didn't even know what bilboquet was? He picked up a book. Birth, and copulation, and death. That is all, that is all. Is it all? It was. After a few pages he got sleepy. Reading his favorite poets always made him feel peacefully drowsy; a laziness came over him that was serene and at the same time sharp and penetrating. Tranquillity for some people meant not feeling untranquil, just as for others feeling good merely meant not feeling bad. What would be the right word for the opposite of pain? Just as perfect synonyms didn't exist—and this made even more sense—neither did perfect antonyms; nothing was either exactly the same or exactly opposite. That was life—on an island of crocodiles or in the city of Rio de Janeiro. And with that he fell asleep.

24

THE CONVERSATION between Lima Prado and Zakkai (as well as that between Prado and his partners in the Main Office) was set down in the Notebooks in a clear and linear manner. Lima Prado did an excellent job of capturing the way Iron Nose talked. Having spoken with Zakkai myself several times, I know this is exactly what he was like—a high-flying chatterer.

"I was reclining, watching a volleyball match on TV, it's the only sport I like. Soccer irritates me, in spite of the fact that it *is* a game for small men. But I wasn't watching the game, really. I was naked—I like to go around naked—and that particular day I was looking at my cock with great concern, looking at that thing, *that mark.* I had been with her, such a monumental woman, until less than half an hour before, and there was my cock, as if it had been hanged, it was bizarre, it looked like commercial *linguiça,* the kind that have knots in between the plastic skin, but it was my cock. I said, My God—I think I said, My God, I like bringing invented people, beings from the fantasy world, into the real world—My God, I said, paralyzed, contemplating that recently hanged but miraculously still-living sausage. In those days I had various vices. One of them was eating chicken innards—heart, liver, gizzards, feet, no, not feet, they're not innards—and another of my vices was thinking, but at that moment I wasn't really thinking, not about my battered cock or about anything else for that matter, I was just looking,

243

bewildered. . . . I know we're not all that intimate for me to be telling you what I'm about to tell you—we really only know one another superficially—but you said, when I first walked in here you said that you'd *heard* of me, my reputation preceded me, and later you claimed that all women are the same, and in order to prove to you that all women are *not* the same I'm telling you this story, which if it does nothing else at least will serve to cut the tension, because there is tension, isn't there, between the two of us?"

(The day before, Mateus had come to Lima Prado with the news that Iron Nose was requesting a meeting with him. Mateus had told Zakkai that he was merely an assistant to the president of Achilles, and that he didn't know whether or not he would be able to arrange an interview. The Notebooks do not clarify what it was that led Lima Prado to consent. A reference to the videocassette, perhaps? In spite of being a partner in one of the firms controlled by the Main Office, Zakkai ostensibly knew nothing of the involvement of Achilles or its chief executive in that organization. There was a notation in red: "Z-videocassette.")

"It was raining the next time I found myself in her company. We were driving down Avenida Brasil in her blue Volkswagen listening to music. She bounced up and down as she drove, dancing and singing along with the music, and even though it was a song she'd never heard before, she was so quick that she got each line right immediately, on key, with all the right words, practically synchronized. Bouncing up and down in a blue Beetle. Finally we got to the motel. Straight off in the entryway I stumbled into a hatrack. Of course no one wears hats anymore, but there it was, holding out its arms for hats, and there also was a spacious round bed and mirrors and a TV and buttons for the stereo equipment and air conditioning mounted on a steel plate in the wall. She handed me a mint and stretched out in the bed, still dressed in jeans so tight they looked like armor. I said, Take off your pants, and when I saw she wasn't moving I added, Take off your pants, sweetheart. Slowly, with studied movement, watching herself in the ceiling mirror, she began pulling off her pants, not by the waistband, as a less athletic woman would do, but by the cuffs. Then, reflected in the mirror, those phenomenal thighs came into view, shocking I would call them if an over-the-hill dwarf could be permitted to talk like a surfer. I grazed that endless stretch of warm, smooth skin with my hand. She opened her legs, supine and imploring, and said, Come, gripping my cock tightly and inserting it into her vagina. And so I was hit once more with that combination of ecstasy and horror. In spite of this, or perhaps because of it, I took a long time to come. But even so, she kept wanting more. I drew my poor flayed cock—which, all modesty aside, is enormous, which, ditto, is normal for a dwarf—out of that cave and stuck in my middle finger, which is actually not middle-sized but rather large." Iron Nose held out his hand to show Lima Prado. "Are discoveries a matter of chance? Never. Cabral knew exactly where he was going. People are always dying to discover something, and finally, after so many days, on that particular day when I stuck my finger in that hot and viscous canal that resembled a rudimentary meat grinder more than anything else, I discovered something surprising. And that something was the *vagina dentata,* the toothed vagina of the ancients, which I'd always thought was a literary fiction or an invention of the architects of sexual repression, but there it was, right at my fingertips, and I mean that literally. It was grinding my finger to bits after having already devoured my prick. The *vagina dentata!* Heavens! My soul filled with terror. Now, because I'm a dwarf and on top of that black and on top of *that* old—though I know I don't look it—because of all of the above I couldn't really say to her, Hey, your vagina is a real shocker. I mean how could a man, much less a man of my peculiarities, ever confess

245

such a thing? Besides, fear, under those circumstances or any other, to be quite frank, was something I had only experienced once before in my life, and then it was because of a smell. That's another interesting story I'll also tell you today, if time permits. It was a smell from hell, one that would give anybody goose bumps, and I mean I've been places even rats won't go—but I'll save that for later. So I told her I was hungry, and I picked up the phone and ordered a steak and fries. First, of course, I asked if she wanted anything and she said no, nooo, and kept rolling from one side of the bed to the other, moaning and calling to me like a tiger in heat. I waited for the steak in the entryway near the door, wearing my pants and shirt but barefoot, making excuses to her through the door to the effect that when the waiter came I couldn't very well answer the door naked, urging her to have a little patience. It was a waitress who brought the food. She made a face when she saw me, sort of embarrassed, as if dwarves didn't fuck like everyone else—and it's well known, I repeat, well known, that dwarf hard-ons are bigger than anyone else's—and she kept staring at the floor as she put the plates and silverware and everything on the table in the entryway. I don't know how she did it, staring all the while at the floor. She was fat and ugly and maybe she thought that in addition to having no right to be there dwarves brought bad luck. After she left I distinctly heard her 'knock wood' to shake off the bad omen; I heard the tap-tap-tap on the wooden doorframe downstairs outside the garage. Suddenly from inside the room came an incredibly loud wail, a really jarring, excruciating sound, half machine, half animal. It was as if against my will my legs were being commanded to move by someone else; I went back into the bedroom. She was lying on her back with her legs as far apart as physically possible, as if she was having a terrible cramp or a convulsion, she looked like a metal doll, teeth clenched, eyes closed, face contorted with pain. She was saying something from between her teeth, it was hard to make out, but finally I understood. She was begging me not to let her die. How was I supposed to know what to do? But I did, it was

246

divine intuition, to quote Luther. Only one thing could save her! I picked up the steak and slowly, tenderly inserted it into her pulsing vagina. As that carnivorous crack devoured the beefsteak I heard her breathing begin to return to normal. Her muscles relaxed, her face became beautiful once again. She really is a knockout of a woman, eyes like agate. Finally she fell into a deep sleep. I sat beside her on the bed, immobile for fear I would disturb her. After she woke much later, she got up and took a shower. Later, after leaving the motel, we stopped on that little hill down at the bottom of Avenida Niemeyer and stood gazing out at the sea. It was rough, the waves crashed violently against the rocks and tens of thousands of insignificant invisible drops of spume wet our faces. There are no two women alike. Get it?"

"A very interesting and well-told story," said Lima Prado, "if we take into consideration that you aren't a specialist. What *is* your specialty, Zakkai?"

"Survival. When I was born my mother took one look at my hands and fainted. I had webbing between my fingers. Can you imagine? A mother expecting her baby to be adorable, perfect, and instead . . . I also had a spinal defect and didn't speak my first word until I was eight. But here I am"—Iron Nose held out his hand, palm up, spreading the fingers as far apart as he could—"a first-class chatterbox, though I still haven't grown much. And yours?"

"My what?"

"Your specialty."

"I usually say that I'd like to be a man of letters, a species now extinct, but unfortunately I'm a man of commerce, which is still, after all, quite a civilized calling. Speaking of commerce, I'd like to clarify something from earlier in our conversation regarding the subject of women, which is that the company over which I preside, Achilles, has only a small, and for that matter indirect, interest in Pleasure. When Mateus told me you wanted to speak with me I agreed to do so, but I don't believe that I should, or can, express an opinion as far as this business of passing control of Pleasure to your group."

"I have no group. I'm alone in this."

247

"But as you see, in any case, there is nothing I can do for you. I did enjoy your story of the toothed vagina, though—such a significant archetype. Do you have other stories like that, about women who break down barriers—you know what I mean."

"Women who go for black dwarves? Sure. But what about your cousin Mitry's murder? Have the police come up with anything yet?"

"I don't know. The police are not notably efficient. Thousands of homicides remain unsolved. It was probably a robbery."

The two were silent for some time, each waiting for the other to take the initiative. Iron Nose's loquacity had run out.

Lima Prado stood and nodded his head in a gesture of dismissal.

The meeting with Zakkai took place in the morning at the Inter-Continental in São Conrado, a suite rented especially for the occasion. After lunch (a grilled steak of approximately fifty grams and an apple, which he peeled and ate only after carefully checking that the skin had no holes or cuts), Lima Prado received the participants of the second interview. Gambacorta arrived first. As an ex-dentist, he valued punctuality. Then came Nadir, the ex–Army colonel. Elisio and Pedro Paulo dos Santos arrived almost simultaneously. Mateus was last.

"Something to drink, gentlemen?" asked Lima Prado.

No one wanted anything.

"This year," began Lima Prado, "has been our best yet, and I must congratulate all of you. Certain businesses prosper in a time of crisis, and ours is one of them. But even with these favorable conditions, we would not enjoy success of this magnitude without your dedicated and competent collaboration."

"Next year should be better still," offered Elisio. "The world economy will be up against serious obstacles. Inflation, unemployment, recession—"

"Those present today represent the essence of our Organization. Which is why it is my duty to inform you of certain problems. First, in the international arena. The arrest of Delibes and Wolf, those two nincompoops—to borrow a word from their own Americanese—could mean trouble. Delibes, as you know, is an executive in the automobile industry, Wolf a famous Hollywood producer. The FBI is going to become interested in investigating people they never dreamed about before. They got Delibes by chance; that must have been some surprise. So how could this lead them to us? Our principal contact in the States is J. C. Abercrombie. In Germany, Otto Hermans. In France, Jean Bianchon. All of them presidents of middle-sized banks, but men with prestige in the financial community. Efficient, reliable, untouchable—like Delibes, if you see what I mean. But the worst is yet to come. I have a meeting with Abercrombie in New York next month, and one thing that concerns me is that he's asking for control of the retail trade. The last time I saw him I warned him about the risks involved. I said, Okay, Jack, it's true there's more money in retail, but it makes you much more vulnerable; you'd be like a foot soldier penetrating enemy territory. But he didn't want to hear it. And recently he's left his wife, dyed his hair, and started dressing like someone who goes to nightclubs. Plus he got married again—to an ambitious social climber—and he told me he's thinking of spending his next vacation in Rio so he can have some plastic surgery done by Pitangui. It may be that he's losing control, the most important control of all: control over himself. And now the worst of it: Delibes was picked up in company with Bill Hendrick, and I happen to know that Abercrombie financed Hendrick in two ventures. Hendrick may attempt to plea-bargain, as they do in the U.S., admitting his guilt and exposing the others —that's the way they try to reduce their sentences. Abercrombie is a trump up Hendrick's sleeve. Will he play it? Or will he claim entrapment and try to get them to drop the case as Delibes's lawyers plan to do? We wait and see. Then there's Bolivia. No new developments there. Fernandez is doing what he can. Trusting in the corruptibility of mankind, especially Bolivians, I believe that in a few months it will be business as usual."

"If Bolivia goes communist we might as well cross it right off the map," said Pedro Paulo.

"It's still too early to talk like that. Anyway, it wouldn't be an irreparable loss," said Nadir. "The day is coming when marijuana and cocaine will be legalized. Don't forget, there was a time when tobacco smokers were excommunicated by the Pope! The fact that drinking alcohol can lead to physical dependency, increased tolerance, withdrawal syndrome, and worker incapacity and absenteeism hasn't stopped it from being legal all over the world."

This line of thinking appeased Nadir's conscience.

"As you know," continued Lima Prado, "there are, and have been for quite some time, in addition to the Mafia, other international institutions—terrorist organizations, religious groups, political interests—that are getting involved in the drug trade. I'm still unsure how this may affect us and our associates. I do know, and this I guarantee you, that our Organization will resist and overcome this competition or any other. We're solid. Efficient. Which is not to say that any organization is free of problems, particularly in the areas of communication and decision making. Order has to be based on some form of power; where there is no power, chaos sets in. That's how the universe came into being. I could decide things unilaterally, but I choose to consult you, to consult the assembled group, 'we few, we happy few, we band of brothers.' "

He looked around him to see if they had appreciated the quote, but their faces showed only reverent attention. "I think it's fair to say that we're happy working together, don't you? That we're brothers. And that's because our work is well organized. Always has been. That's where our strength lies. And now that a problem has come up, I've come to consult my brothers. So. Zakkai. Zakkai. Zakkai always was an outsider. I'm not even sure why he was accepted into the group, since he never really won our trust. But now is not the time to discuss that. You've all heard about the unfortunate episode of the videocassette my cousin left at the apartment of a prostitute who was subsequently murdered. The cassette disappeared and Mitry went around acting foolishly. He's no longer a problem. But the fact that Zakkai wanted to talk to me is not a good sign, not good at all. Achilles itself has always been above suspicion."

"Mitry talked?"

"Mitry assisted in the transference of funds to foreign banks, that's all. He could have told this to Zakkai if they were, as we suppose, friends and confidants. But that would hardly be enough of a reason for Zakkai to come looking for me. I believe he has an intuition, nothing more. He might have the videotape, or know about it, but that doesn't matter in the least. The tape itself isn't worth anything. You guarantee that it wasn't at Mitry's?"

"Our operative examined every tape in the house; they were all labeled. The one you wanted wasn't there."

"But regardless of what Zakkai knows or doesn't know, there's only one course to take. Agreed?"

They all nodded in agreement.

When his visitors had gone, Lima Prado called the desk and asked to speak with his driver. "Captain Virgulino, go pick up Dona Mônica."

While he waited for her arrival, Lima Prado took a letter out of his pocket. The paper had yellowed, but the words, in the elegant script of an accomplished student of calligraphy, were still bright blue. *Undoubtedly written with a Belgian steel-tipped pen and imported German ink,* Lima Prado jotted in his Notebook. The previous day he had visited the house on São Clemente to check on the progress of construction and continue examining Dona Laurinda's papers. With much difficulty, and the help of a locksmith, he succeeded in opening the beautiful Chatwood strongbox (it must have been at least a hundred years old), but he still had not had time to look over the innumerable papers he found inside along with antique

251

jewelry, old currency, coins from various foreign countries, bonds issued by Rio de Janeiro Tramway, Light and Power, and stocks from the Port of Pará, from Equitativa, and other companies. There were also many letters; he had picked out and read one of them, the contents of which had troubled him. Because he was on his way to an important appointment, he had not had time to search through the various piles to find another one with the same handwriting on the envelope. Now, he reread the letter.

My Dear d. Laurinda,

I regret that you have discovered the truth. If I have been an accomplice in concealing this shameful and sad event it was not to defend the honor of the Lima Prados or to protect them from scandal, as none of those around me, nor the dubious dignity of the family, merits my connivance. What I did I did for the poor child, as it would be a misfortune for him to know the terrible truth of his origin. I raised him as if I were his real mother. Would Maria Augusta have done the same? Don't you find it ironic that I, who was always considered the intruder, have performed this service for the Lima Prados, without anyone knowing—such a protective gesture—considering all the affronts I have had to suffer?

Yours,
Luiza Montilio Lima Prado

Then he wasn't Luiza's son! When they had told him his father was not Fernando but Bernard Mitry, it had not really bothered him. The Frenchman was an interesting character, and had always treated him kindly as a boy. Fernando, on the other hand, was a taciturn man who had hardly ever said a word to him. Lima Prado couldn't remember ever once being alone with him; he had no memories, really, of Fernando from his entire childhood. His childhood. And once—how old was he?—he had seen his mother kiss Bernard on the mouth, hard. Bernard had patted him on the head, sat him in his lap—the rest was

252

foggy. Bernard carried him downstairs. No, his nurse had carried him downstairs.

When Captain Virgulino arrived at Mônica's apartment, she opened the door wearing only her underpants.

"The boss sent me to get you."

"Come on in."

"I'll wait outside."

"I'm going to take a bath."

"He said now."

"You don't scare me."

Captain Virgulino came in and shut the door.

"Go put something on."

In her few short years, Mônica had learned to interpret men's various looks. This was not a man. The look in his eyes were less expressive than an ape's.

She went into her bedroom and dressed.

"The boss. The boss. Doesn't he have a name?"

Captain Virgulino opened the door.

"João? José? Manoel?"

Captain Virgulino stepped out into the hall.

"Alfredo. Antônio. Otávio. Gabriel." Mônica named names all the way to the hotel. Captain Virgulino didn't pay any attention to anything she said. He led her to the suite where the boss was waiting and went back downstairs to the lobby.

"Is something worrying you, sweetie?" asked Mônica.

She had put on a silk dress, very short, purchased in an exclusive boutique. It looked like a natural part of her body, her beauty and energy (*attributes of the soul,* recorded Lima Prado). Beauty and energy which she exuded like waves of heat and light.

"How are you feeling, Mr. X?"

He felt like his head was underwater and he couldn't breathe.

The nurse had carried him down the stairs. Or was it

253

really Bernard? Bernard smelled of cologne and pipe tobacco. His mother's dress was open, he could see her
breasts. But she wasn't his mother. Luiza Montilio's
breasts. A shiver ran up and down his spine.

"I'm not feeling anything. What's this Mr. X business?"

"Well, I don't know your real name, and I'm not too
crazy about Ajax."

Mônica had tried to find out who he was. She had written down the license plate number and after a lot of tip-
ping and a lot of flirting at the Registry had managed to
get the name in which the car was registered: Hector In-
dustries. This name was not in the phone book.

She got no further, which irritated her. If he was hiding
his true name it must be because he was a very important
guy. She had started paying attention to the pictures of
people that appeared in the newspapers and on the TV.
No luck.

"Don't you trust me?"

"I don't even know my father's name."

"Ah, ah."

"Or my mother's. End of discussion."

"I really want to go to Hippopotamus tonight and break
in the new lamé dress I bought."

Lima Prado had prohibited Mônica from going out at
night. She spent her days at home waiting for him to call.
Her only friend was the hairdresser she visited once a
week. Friend and confidant. "What good is it for this guy
to give you everything in the world if he keeps you a prisoner in your apartment? You'd be better off going back to
tricking," Joãozinho had told her. At night Joãozinho's
name was Jane. He had shown Mônica his big silicone
breasts one day—"Pretty, don't you think?"—and said the
only reason he still had his penis was because "at the last
minute I got scared." His boyfriend was the jealous type,
too. "Married, two kids, and he's exactly the same, wants
to keep me at home, but I told him, If you want to keep
me under lock and key, then give up your bogus wife and
come live with me, because I'm your true wife."

Lima Prado's voice got soft. "We already agreed you

wouldn't go to Hippopotamus anymore, didn't we? Furthermore, you're a minor and it's illegal for you to hang out in nightclubs."

"If you want to keep me prisoner, then give up your bogus wife and come live with me, because I'm your true wife."

"I did not bring you all the way over here to have this discussion."

"Then why, Mr. X?"

Lima Prado gently gripped her by the neck and said dreamily, "You know why."

She thought about saying, No, I don't, Mr. X, but she detected in Lima Prado's face a sadness that restrained her. Silently, she took off her dress.

25

CAMILO FUENTES, a can of peas in one hand, a can of hearts of palm in the other, turned his head to read with his good eye what was written on the labels. In São Paulo he'd had no trouble seeing well enough to kill Benito the newsdealer's two assassins, but the small print on these labels was giving him trouble.

"Do you think there's such a thing as canned fresh peas?" A pause. Minuscule letters. "Do you think I should buy a cornea?"

"They're all cheats. Listen to this. Ingredients: peas and salt. It's got to be a lie, don't you think?" asked Miriam. "There's a whole lot of crap in there they don't tell you about."

"At least this one's a little more up front." Fuentes read from the hearts of palm label: " 'Contains acidulent H Two.' All this canned stuff is full of chemical preservatives, it's just that the food industry doesn't like to talk about it." Fuentes turned to the other can. " 'Swift peas are the only brand that truly melts in your mouth. Fresh-canned right at the place of harvest, they retain all the nutritional qualities of fresh peas. Always succulent, flavorful, and tender as if they'd been shelled in your own kitchen.' The creeps. Shelled in your own kitchen. So what about the cornea? You think I should buy it or not?"

Fuentes and Miriam were at the Freeway supermarket in Barra da Tijuca. Bright and early that morning they had left the apartment, walked down Rua Riachuelo to the intersection of Avenida Mem de Sá, near Largo dos Pracinhas, and on to the Carmo de Lapa Church, so that

Miriam could pray. Then, on Avenida Augusto Severo, they caught a bus to Barra. It was quite a distance to the Freeway, but both of them liked to watch the city go by out the bus window. They made a habit of shopping at grocery stores in far-off neighborhoods, which sometimes required as many as three separate buses.

"Well? Should I buy it or not?"

"Look, this one's all in English," said Miriam, holding up a different brand of hearts of palm.

"That's just to prove it's good enough even for the Americans to eat. You didn't answer me."

"I don't know."

"You don't know? You want me to be half blind the rest of my life?"

"Do you have the money?"

"Sure."

"Then buy it."

"I keep thinking about the girl."

"What girl? What girl?"

"The girl selling her cornea. I'm just not sure it's fair for her to give up one of her eyes so some guy with money can have two."

"But she wants to sell it, right?"

"She's being forced. By poverty."

"So why doesn't she sell her little pussy like everybody else?"

"Not everybody."

"What does she need so much money for, anyway? And don't tell me what a poor little thing she is. I don't buy it."

"Are you mad at me?"

"No one can even tell you're blind in one eye."

"I can. That's what counts. And it's not that I want to be handsome or any of that crap. The rest of the world can go fuck itself."

"Me included?"

"It feels really lousy not to be able to see on one side."

"Me included?"

"You included what?"

"I can go fuck myself, too?"

257

"You're different." Until meeting Miriam, Fuentes had despised all the Brazilian women he'd been involved with. But he respected Miriam, a prostitute no less.

"Ex-prostitute," Miriam corrected him. "Since I met you I haven't turned a trick, or even pimped. That reminds me, I have to get in touch with my lawyer. He never liked what I was doing with my life, he'll be happy."

"He'll be happy you're not tricking anymore?"

"Uh-huh."

"What'd you ever have a lawyer for, anyway?"

"I told you, remember? City Hall wanted to tear down my place in the Zone and I hired him to fight for me. The government can really screw you if you don't have a lawyer defending you."

"Did he get anywhere?"

"No."

"Great lawyer."

"It wasn't his fault. He's fantastic."

Miriam sang my praises all the way down the long aisle of canned vegetables. Fuentes listened in silence. It wasn't long before he realized she was talking about the same lawyer whose apartment he had invaded in the company of Rafael. He considered telling her, but she spoke of me with such affection that he decided it was better to say nothing.

They boarded the bus back downtown.

"The family was overjoyed when I was born," said Miriam. "I was white and had straight light hair—the only one. But being light-skinned and pretty only helped me become a prostitute. I mean, I don't really know for sure if a white girl's better than a mulatto, commercially speaking. Plus, they told me I got into the life because I wanted to. I was twelve years old."

Fuentes was gazing out the window at the scenery.

"I didn't like it, but I didn't leave it, either. Now, let's say I could go back to being twelve. You think I'd manage to do something else with my life? Or does everyone have a destiny and there's no running away from it? Like one person's born to be a madam, another a whore, another a nun, or a television star, or a nurse. Do you think it works that way? Like on the soaps?"

"All that destiny stuff is a bunch of crap," said Fuentes, turning away from the window.

"I don't know. I think when we're born it's already decided, even the number of times our hearts are going to beat. The time comes for us to die, ready or not, that's it."

"No one's ever ready."

"But they die."

"And who decides?" Fuentes looked straight at her.

"God."

"God doesn't exist."

"Then who made the flowers and the stars and the fish? Tell me that—who made all this?"

Fuentes turned back to his window.

"There was once, one time I decided to leave it all behind, and I went and got a job as a live-in maid. The woman I worked for was terrific; when she bought a color TV she gave me the black-and-white one. They were real nice to me there and I didn't even have to work very hard. I could have stayed if I wanted. Well, couldn't I?"

"Washing someone else's bathroom?"

"It's better than selling an eye."

They were silent the rest of the way to the apartment on Rua Riachuelo.

A man was waiting for Fuentes at the door to their building and followed them upstairs. He was a musclebound mulatto with gray hair, named Arlindo.

"The cops are looking for you in São Paulo and on the Bolivian border. And there's some other weird types trying to track you down. A guy called Iron Nose."

"Who?"

"Some dwarf—black, rolling in dough. One of his men looked me up. And Rafael's been asking about you. Have you seen Chinaman? he asked me. You called Chinaman?"

"Only by that bastard."

259

"Well, I didn't tell him you called me; I said I had no idea where you were. I told the guy the dwarf sent that I'd see if I could get hold of you."

Miriam brought three cans of ice-cold beer.

"What about you, what've you been up to?" Fuentes clapped Arlindo on the shoulder.

"Selling dope with cow chips. Things have been tough lately."

"That's bad stuff."

"Yeah, I know. I don't like dealing adulterated merchandise. But the kids don't even notice."

"Let them smoke their shit," said Miriam. "The high's the same."

"Who's the guy working for the dwarf?"

"First time I met him. I asked the guy, How'd you know I'm a friend of Camilo's? But he didn't answer. And I don't know the dwarf, either, just by reputation."

"They killed a guy in São Paulo for that."

"For what?"

"For being a friend of mine."

"This is a different fucking story. We're talking about Arlindo, from Santo Cristo."

"I don't like it."

"What don't you like?"

"None of it. I don't know anybody in Rio. How'd they know I'm here? Like this dwarf."

"The dwarf wants to meet you at the Garcia Circus. It's on Praça Onze, near Benedito Hipólito. You know where that is?"

"I do," said Miriam.

"A circus"—Fuentes laughed—"the perfect place to meet a dwarf."

"He said to give you this ticket. It's a box seat, for Thursday, nine P.M. You're supposed to show up alone and sit down and wait for him."

"And what's he look like, this Iron Nose?"

"I told you, I never met him. Anyway, all dwarves must look alike, except this one's black. How can you go wrong?"

"I don't like being in the dark."

"Think of it this way, you'll be in the black. Not a bad pun, huh?"

Fuentes didn't answer.

"Oh, I almost forgot," said Arlindo, pulling an I.D. out of his pocket. "We've got you born in Mato Grosso. I figured that'd be good because you know the area and there's Indians all over the place."

"Do I look like an Indian? Huh, Miriam?"

"Sort of. A hell of a handsome one."

"Your name is Carlos Fagundes."

"Was it enough money?"

"Ten thousand short."

Fuentes wrote out a check.

Fuentes sat for a long time, the fake I.D. in his hand, his face tense. Arlindo had left. Miriam knew that at times like this Fuentes didn't want to be disturbed.

"I think we should move out of here."

Miriam waited.

"Get a place right downtown."

"Remember that girl we met at Sendas?"

"No."

"Sure you do. We were in the supermarket; she had a baby in the carriage with her. Her name's Regina. She worked under the name Xuxa, until she met that guy and had his kid. Anyway, you weren't paying any attention that day, but she said she was moving out of her house in Gamboa. They're going to live in Goiás, where Elomar has a farm. It's a pretty shabby neighborhood, but the house is real cute."

"I like living around poor people," said Fuentes.

They took the Gamboa bus to the intersection of Rua Marechal Floriano and Camerino, walked to the Praça dos Estivadores and from there down São Felix to Regina's house, which was on an alley called Madre de Deus.

A man opened the door. "Looking for someone?" A farmer's twang.

261

"Is this Xu's—I mean Regina's?" Miriam knew that Elomar didn't like people calling his wife Xuxa.

"That's right. Regina, there's some people here to see you."

The two women hugged and kissed and exchanged greetings while the men looked on awkwardly. The house hadn't been rented yet. Elomar, the farmer, didn't want to rent it at all, but Regina thought it would be a shame to close the place up and not get anything out of it.

"I love it here, this little alley. There's nothing like this in Goiás," said Elomar.

"When you come to Rio, you can stay with us. There are two bedrooms, right? We'll leave one all set up for you," said Miriam.

Elomar brought out a special bottle of *cachaça*, home-brewed on the farm.

Fuentes arrived at the Garcia Circus at eight-fifty Thursday evening. It was packed; there was only one empty box, right next to the ring. The lights dimmed. The orchestra struck up a raucous fanfare.

"Good evening." Unnoticed, Iron Nose had slipped into the box and sat down next to Fuentes.

"I love the circus," he said. "Everyone's born with a certain vocation and a certain aptitude, and those who satisfy neither are very unhappy people, as Sigmund Freud once said. My vocation was to be a clown, a position for which, it may be said in passing, I am more than qualified."

Fuentes had inclined his head slightly and was listening, but without looking at Iron Nose.

"If, as in my case, vocation and aptitude are one and the same, it's either terrific or a total disaster," the dwarf continued. "I ought to be disconsolate, dying of jealousy, watching these two wonderful characters accept their applause," he said motioning toward the two clowns who had just run out into the ring, "but I'm not suffering and I'll never suffer, and do you know why? Because, in addition to vocation and aptitude, some men—not all—are born with indestructible energy. Do you know who said that?"

Fuentes did not answer. But he moved his face a millimeter, showing that he was listening.

"*I* said that." Iron Nose's words were swallowed by the orchestra, and he paused, leaning close to Fuentes' ear, and said, "I have that energy. I have it like no one else in the world."

Fuentes pulled away and fixed his eyes on the woman above them walking across a tightrope.

"Now you—an intelligent man, I know—must be asking yourself, Did this guy summon me here to listen to his philosophy of life? In addition to being a dwarf and black and a frustrated clown, is he nuts? No, my friend, I summoned you here to warn you that war has broken out and to invite you to be my ally."

"I fight my battles alone," said Fuentes, still fixing his gaze on the performance.

"War is older than mankind." Again, Iron Nose waited for the music to diminish. "I've studied this subject quite thoroughly. Those who try to fight alone get fucked. I've studied war among animals and war among men—among savages, among Greeks, among pagans, and among religious fanatics. When it comes to war, those without allies are destroyed. Always."

Fuentes stared straight ahead.

"On your own, you are one man. They'll get you in the end"—pause—"Carlos Fagundes."

Fuentes stared at the man next to him in astonishment. How could Iron Nose have discovered the fake name on the I.D. he had bought only two days before?

"A couple of my people have been following an uppity mulatto named Arlindo. The objective was to get to you."

"Well?" asked Fuentes.

Their eyes met, glinting, a challenge, light reflected from the ring.

"So that's my proposal, all you have to do is decide. Shall we unite to destroy our enemies?"

263

Iron Nose had learned that Mateus was recruiting two hit men for a "clean-up" operation; the dwarf knew, via the same informant, that Fuentes was on the list and, furthermore, that the other hits were to be: "some lawyer called Mandrake" ("No, I don't know him," answered Fuentes), a dealer named Fat Carlinhos ("Nope, not him either"), and himself, Zakkai.

"I'll pay you three times what they did. Let's see what you think of my plan."

Iron Nose and Fuentes talked until the first act was almost over. Iron Nose left before the lights went up. Five minutes later, Fuentes went to the refreshment area and ordered a beer.

When the rest of the audience started back to their seats, he headed for the exit. It was raining outside, and Avenida Presidente Vargas was empty. Fuentes carefully examined the deserted street. A taxi approached and he flagged it down, telling the driver to take him to the Praia Bar restaurant on Flamengo Beach, the corner of Buarque de Macedo. He walked into the bar and checked to see if he was being followed. Then he took another cab back downtown, via Rua do Catete. At Rua do Passeio he got out and hailed a third cab to Rua Riachuelo.

Next morning, Fuentes and Miriam moved to the house on Madre de Deus Alley. Since they had only two suitcases, it wasn't difficult to take various taxis, using the same careful diversionary tactics.

26

AT FIVE A.M. in front of the gates to the Brazilian Jockey Club, next to Miguel Couto Hospital in Gávea, a man stood immobile as a statue. Even so, an attentive observer would have noticed the small but constant twitching of the little finger on his right hand. The man did not have to wait long. A modest dark blue Chevy pulled up to the curb and he got in.

Recognizing the occupants of the car, the Jockey Club guard opened the gates and the car entered and turned left, heading toward where the grooms, exercise boys, jockeys, handlers, and trainers did their daily work. It was a brilliant morning; a refreshing breeze wafted down from the trees of Tijuca Forest. Several horses were already circling the dirt and grass tracks. Some, ridden by exercise boys with legs extended and flying free, their saddles mounted on small blankets with foam rubber padding, were working out in a contained gallop. Others, piloted by genuflecting jockeys in saddle and stirrups, were being clocked at top speed against the stopwatch.

A man approached the Chevy. "Good morning, sir."

Lima Prado got out of the car, accompanied by Hermes, and greeted the trainer of his stable of twenty-three horses, a man named Moreira.

Moreira wanted to talk to the owner about Pascal, a sorrel with a star on his forehead, and Conselheiro, who was registered in the studbook as a dapple-gray. Most of the thoroughbreds at the Jockey Club were sorrels, chestnuts, or blacks. A few were dapple-gray. The horses in Regiment Andrade Neves, where Lima Prado and

265

Hermes had met, as major and sergeant respectively, had also been homogeneous, but Hermes grew up in a part of the country where there were bays, pintos, roans, palominos, dark grays, Appaloosas, "all the colors of the world."

Conselheiro was an ugly dapple-gray, small and frail, who had been "virtually laughed out of the paddock" before his first race, but had turned out to be an exceptional horse, going on to win the Triple Crown. Now he was being prepped for the Brazilian Grand Prix, but because of his physical frailty he trained only twice a week, and on the smaller dirt track, because it was closest to the barns and thus required a shorter walk. The days he didn't train he got his exercise swimming in the pool.

Pascal was large and muscular. His coat was short and so shiny it looked as if he had been painted with a brilliant cinnamon-colored varnish. His record, though inferior to Conselheiro's, was impressive. Both horses were being attended to by grooms. Pascal, wearing a loosely held bridle but otherwise unharnessed, looked perfectly relaxed. Conselheiro, in a bit and a tight curb chain, was being contained with difficulty. He quieted down when Lima Prado reached out and patted him on the neck.

"He's really attached to you," said Moreira. "But then, when he was a colt, you'd come down to the barn and feed him with a baby bottle."

"How's he doing?"

"He doesn't like to eat, sir. That's his problem. He won't even look at corn, and he's not real crazy about oats. The only thing he'll touch is alfalfa. Conselheiro's a difficult horse, but you know that; you know him better than anyone."

"Corn's fattening," said Hermes.

"Of course," said Moreira, trying to curb his irritation, "but mixed with oats, five-to-one, it would be good for him."

"How much straight oats is he eating?" asked Lima Prado.

"Eight kilos. That's not much. I've never seen a horse

266

with spirit like his, but a horse needs more than spirit to live on."

"What about Pascal?"

"Eighteen kilos of oats, five of corn, and incredible amounts of alfalfa." He looked straight at Hermes: "And not a gram of fat on him." Then, to Lima Prado: "Could I talk to you in private?"

"You can talk in front of them." Lima Prado's gesture included Hermes and Virgulino, who had joined the group after parking the car.

"I'm thinking about putting an apprentice on Conselheiro for the Grand Prix," said Moreira hesitantly.

"Who?" It was a shocking suggestion.

"He's a novice, sir. His name is José Pinheiro, we call him Pinheirinho."

"You're actually suggesting that a novice mount Conselheiro in the Grand Prix?"

"Sir"—Moreira's voice was trembling—"Conselheiro hasn't raced in two months. This kid is the only one who's worked him this whole time, he won't let anyone else mount him. Not even Juvenal, and they won several races together. I don't know what's going on with Conselheiro, but he only wants the kid."

"Horses are capricious creatures," said Lima Prado. "Have you tried putting a lamb in his stall?"

"Horses are worse than women," said Hermes.

"We tried, sir, but it didn't do any good. He paces back and forth all night long."

Summoned by Moreira, Pinheirinho approached the group. He was wearing jeans, tennis shoes, and a white T-shirt.

"How old are you?" asked Lima Prado.

"Seventeen."

He looked younger. "Where are you from?"

"Magalhães Bastos."

"A suburb," explained Moreira.

"I know where Magalhães Bastos is. Why did you decide to become a jockey? Did you ride a lot as a kid?" Lima Prado's son didn't like horses. Nor his daughter.

"I don't think he even saw a horse until he came to Rio," said Moreira.

"In the movies I did." Pinheirinho smiled.

"Why did you decide to be a jockey?"

"I like horses." Another smile.

Moreira should have sent the kid to the dentist. One of his incisors had a large rotten spot. Lima Prado didn't like the idea of one of his jockeys going around with a rotten tooth.

"He came to the training school last year. He's got the gift, sir—good balance, peripheral vision, fast out of the gate. No one has reflexes like this kid, he's better than the masters I've seen in action—Leguisamon, Zuniga, Rigoni, Marchand, any one of them."

Still restrained by the groom, Conselheiro turned his head and gave the boy a wide-eyed look. Lima Prado and Hermes, who had spent years in close proximity with horses, could see in the animal's eyes the pleasure and excitement he felt with Pinheirinho nearby.

"Why the whip?"

"No reason, sir. For looks. He doesn't like to be hit," answered Pinheirinho. "And I don't like hitting."

"Horses don't like people who whip them," said Moreira.

"I want to see the two of you in action," said Lima Prado.

After Moreira nodded his permission, Pinheirinho handed him the whip, told the groom, "You can let him go," and holding Conselheiro by the withers, leapt onto the horse in one light and agile move.

In spite of the blanket between boy and horse, it seemed to Lima Prado that Pinheirinho's and Conselheiro's bodies at a gallop became one inseparable mass. Lifting the binoculars from Moreira's neck, he watched their course around the track. Perfect communion. Which is something that perhaps can only be attained between man and animal, he thought, and never between two men.

"It's going to be a scandal. The fans will be appalled," said Lima Prado.

"Then you mean . . ."

"I mean that a novice is going to be riding Conselheiro in the Brazilian Grand Prix," said Lima Prado. "Name of Pinheirinho."

After watching the groom bathe Conselheiro with a hose, Hermes and Lima Prado sat down under the arbor near the main pool, closely watched by Virgulino from his post at the bar. At that hour there was no one in the pool area, not even the mothers who would soon be arriving with their charges at seven for the first children's swimming class. Lima Prado breathed deeply, appreciating the clean morning air, a motion that was imitated at a distance by Virgulino, who never took his eyes off his boss.

"This is the best moment of the day," said Lima Prado.

Erect in his lacquered wood chair, motionless except for inclining his head slightly, Hermes examined the locale with a professional air. The sun sliced through the wooden latticework, painting brilliant white stripes on the two men. A horse galloped by on the dirt track that ran alongside the pool. "Doesn't it make you nostalgic?" asked Lima Prado. Hermes nodded his head in agreement. They sat silently with their memories for a while.

"Do you know why I chose you, out of all the sergeants applying for the position on NUSS? Have I ever told you?"

"No."

"Because of your name. Do you know who Hermes was, in mythology?"

"No."

"Someday I'll tell you about it. Did Mateus talk to you?"

"Your trainer never explained what the problem was with the sorrel."

"I'll ask him about it later, can't be too important. Have you talked with Mateus?" Lima Prado's respect for Hermes showed in his voice. It was also the reason he had invited Hermes to meet with him personally at the Jockey Club, instead of just sending a message.

"He talked to me."

Lima Prado waited. He had always been patient with the laconic Hermes.

269

"The dwarf dropped out of sight."

"I knew he would. He opted for guerrilla tactics: attack and retreat. A hard man to figure. Have you met him?"

"No."

"Sometimes I think I even like him."

Mothers and children began to arrive for swimming class. Some of the women were dressed for tennis and accompanied by uniformed governesses instructed to look after the children. They stood watching the preparations for class, beaming at their offspring.

"There's nothing more idiotic than mothers and children at swimming class. Just look at the imbecilic expressions on their faces," said Lima Prado.

"Who's going to take care of the lawyer? Rafael?" Hermes' voice was so expressionless that it was hard to tell he was asking a question.

"Mateus told me you don't want the assignment, and I understand. Gratitude is a noble sentiment."

"My debt is paid. He knows that."

"Then what is it?"

"I don't know."

"The years we spent in the Army left marks that will never disappear. Loyalty, esprit de corps . . . You must unconsciously feel that the man's still part of your group. After all, for months—"

"Years."

"He helped you unselfishly. And managed to get you acquitted in a difficult case."

"Whatever. I don't want the job." Pause. "Does it have to be done?"

"You told me he was a hedonist—I know, not in so many words—a generous, happy-go-lucky guy, incapable of bearing a grudge over a long period of time, who would forget all about what happened—oh, the stupidity of Mateus, or excessive zeal or whatever—but my information is that the lawyer is still investigating this thing on his own. He's out for blood, intent on discovering who wronged him and his woman. Yes, it has to be done. I believe it's been assigned to an operative named Rafael, but I'm not sure; you know I don't get involved with the assembly line."

The children in the pool were doing everything they were told. At the teacher's shrill command, they put their faces in the water and paddled across the pool, lifting their heads to breathe only every four strokes. They looked happy playing in the blue water. Irritated, Lima Prado abruptly stood up and made for the tennis courts, accompanied by Hermes and followed at a distance by Virgulino. Two young women were trying, without much luck, to hit the ball back and forth at least two times successively.

"You have to find Zakkai. Find him and finish him. If you locate the videocassette, so much the better."

Hermes looked at Lima Prado dully. "Search and destroy," he agreed. As they used to say in the Army.

27

RIO CONTAINED an immense number of people—Mateus didn't even try to guess how many—capable of filling out the team of operatives working for the Main Office. Though perhaps of interest for other purposes, Mateus obviously didn't include in this list pickpockets, juvenile housebreakers, drug dealers, teams that snatched purses on buses and in stores—the vast legion of child delinquents who at this initial stage might demonstrate at least a certain daring. But he followed the development of some of them, waiting to see if they matured and escaped the daily risks of their apprenticeship in the streets. Also excluded from the list were those juveniles who had passed through this initial phase to become unintelligent, routine thieves. The person Mateus was looking for had to have the right instinct to kill, because everyone had the wrong one. He also needed to have a certain capacity to hate. To despise both rich and poor, weak and strong, ugly and handsome. Mateus' great discovery, Camilo Fuentes, was like that; but unfortunately Fuentes could no longer be counted on. If younger men were prone to be nervous, older ones—greater experience notwithstanding—had lowered resistance and had either already developed their own scams or had retired. Mateus himself intended to quit at forty-five, which wasn't far off. But right now he needed to find someone with the same qualities as Fuentes. This person could be recruited from the police, though the Main Office had not yet put a cop under contract but merely hired them occasionally for specific passing assignments. He could be drawn from the military—

they were generally disciplined and loyal—but military men tended to have heavy consciences. It was not easy to find a truly qualified professional. Mateus perused the list of names he had written down and sighed. He thought of better times.

After being released from the Foundation of Juvenile Correction, Mateus had toyed with various professions and finally began working with a group of eight men who supplied protection to the merchants in São João do Meriti. The leader of the group, who was known as Captain Eronides, had been expelled from the military police for homicide. Eronides took pride in never having killed an innocent person. "You have to be absolutely sure the guy's a thief, only then do you go out and do justice on the pig." As part of the team, Mateus participated in the deaths of forty-eight "hoodlums and crooks." There were other, similar groups active in the area; they were called the "Mineira police," and none was as respected as Eronides' group. Mateus quickly gained prominence in the eyes of captain and cohorts alike. "This kid is smart, real smart," Eronides would say. "I just get up early and don't know how to stand around doing nothing," responded Mateus. By the time the sun was up he had already studied what had to be done that day. He knew he was no genius, but he saw that Eronides, who was less intelligent than he, had a house, a summer cabin, a car, and a savings account. It was Mateus who suggested to Eronides that they enlarge their parameters to include Belford Roxo. He personally directed the "elimination" of the main group that had been active there. Finally, Mateus proposed to Eronides that in addition to the merchants the group should supply protection to numbers people and drug dealers in the area. "Are you crazy?" said Eronides. "We've always drawn a moral line. We take care of business people and their families and keep our heads above the slime." Mateus drew the S & W from his belt and held it to Eronides' head. Eronides looked at him and said, "You don't have the fucking balls to pull the trigger, you piece of shit." With Eronides' death, Mateus took charge of the group.

273

He was ambitious and had the capacity to perceive people's true motives and to understand the most complex situations. Soon after offering protection to the cocaine middlemen, he himself realized that his group didn't have sufficient strength for the job. It was around this time that he met Hermes, who invited him to come to work for the Main Office, where he could earn much more. It wasn't long before he had gained the trust of Lima Prado. "Money buys, money relaxes, money cheers, money strengthens," said Lima Prado the first day they met, "but money isn't everything. Remember that."

In order to get to sleep I had to just lie in bed and let sleep come when it came. Anything could snatch me back from sleep—reading, television, videotaped movies, music. When I was a kid we had a very large clock. During the day I never noticed its ticking. But at night, when I was in bed and my mother had turned out the light for the third time, ordering me to sleep, I couldn't stop hearing that constant tick-tock, imagining what I would do, and become, when I grew up: Beau Sabreur, the Scarlet Pimpernel, Pardaillan—perhaps the origin of my interest in *Persev*, the blade of steel?—fantasies lifted from books. The family doctor advised, "All this child needs is sleep: sleep in which to dream." He didn't know that I dreamed wide awake, and so I took to pretending to be asleep and kept right on dreaming. For two whole months I didn't sleep a single night.

"Okay, let's say I believe you," said Wexler.

"It's the God's honest truth," I insisted. "Two months without a wink of sleep."

When Betsy Bean was at BB's (Berta Bronstein's) house in the country, this is how she would catch a bird: She stood perfectly still, watching the birds pick at things on the ground, slowly and patiently evaluating their flight, the speed, direction, etc., and then, at a determined and unexpected moment, she chose one and pounced—not where the bird was but where it would be—and caught it between her teeth midflight. "Oh, let the poor thing go, oh—" the witnesses would exclaim (they only realized much later that Betsy had ripped its little head off), and, oh! oh! they were fascinated by Betsy's feline agility and accepted, oh! oh! in their heart, the right of the cat to do what she felt led to do with that other, winged, animal.

Now Betsy was trying to leap to the top of the TV, where she liked to stretch out, listening to the voices and feeling the heat, and she almost botched the leap, her claws noisily scratching the screen.

"Things change," I said. "Nothing escapes time."

Wexler had never lived with a woman. He loved Ada, but Ada was his friend's woman. And Wexler was a Jew, and as a Jew had an extremely active conscience, a strong sense of right and wrong, a responsibility to justice.

"As a people we are, and have been for thousands of years, the subject of people's envy."

"Because you're better." Wexler ignored the intentional irony in my voice.

"The fact is that no one has suffered the way we have."

"The blacks."

"Don't be ridiculous. How can you compare the discrimination against blacks, which began in the sixteenth century, with ours?"

"It's a whole new reality."

"They have Africa, an entire continent. And us?"

Betsy stretched herself out on the rug. I knelt down and stroked her belly. She tried to turn over, but a claw caught the carpet. This had never happened when she was younger; her reflexes now were just not the same. That morning Betsy had walked into the bedroom meowing the minute I opened the door. Since Ada had moved in, the bedroom door had been kept closed at night. I had always let Betsy sleep with me, but somehow it seemed too much to have both of them in bed with me. (To be honest, I really liked sleeping alone.) Anyway, Betsy was gently carried to her basket in the pantry every night, and the bedroom door closed. And every morning she came into the bedroom meowing furiously and jumped in bed to smell the sheets. When I tried to set her on my lap her claws caught in the fabric.

"Her loss of claw retractability must correspond to our loss in short-term memory. Look how white she's getting, look at her face. Time." Pause. "In this order: fish, vegetables, warm-blooded animals, end of the world."

"With or without the bomb?"

"With or without the bomb."

"What about insects?"

"That's a good question."

"What about the women?"

"What women?"

"Your women. I don't know how you can spread yourself so thin. And I'm not even referring to the ethical dimension of promiscuity."

"Of course not, you moralist."

"Just consider the logistics: Ada, Bebel, Lilibeth. Isn't it confusing? Hasn't it ever confused you, just a little? BB, Eva. That black woman. Et cetera."

"Some people are so fascinated and attracted by the Other that they cannot be satisfied with superficial contact, subliminal signs, secret imagination, compensatory contact. No, they need to get to the bottom of it, to expose themselves, grab hold, explore, exhaust, burn. See this wrinkle between my eyebrows? It's the mark of a man who loves women ardently."

It was Sunday morning.

Ada came back in shorts and tennis shoes, her face flushed from running. Her thighs glistened with sweat.

"Am I late?"

"No, no, of course not." Wexler was merely flustered that so much of Ada's skin was showing. He kept his eyes on her face.

"Who else is coming?"

"Raul."

"I'm going to take a quick shower."

Berta Bronstein didn't sleep in the nude, because she didn't like anyone to see the little bulge that appeared when she lay on her side. Ada's body was perfect in any position. I followed her into the bathroom. She hadn't changed a bit since the day I first met her coming out of exercise class. No, she had not gained weight in Pouso Alto. Nor had she lost any. The tooth that had been knocked out that cursed day had been replaced. She was still an attractive woman. But looking at her, I realized I didn't feel the same way as before. How long had this been going on?

"What kind of sad look is that?" Ada put a shower cap over her hair and stood there with her arms raised.

"I like your upper pectorals." I touched her chest, above the breasts.

"I know you love to look at women with their arms raised like this. You've told me more than once. Why do you think I've been fiddling with the shower cap all this time? But tell me, what are you thinking?"

It was more than simple desire, what I felt before, seeing her like that. It was a sense of astonishment, of surprise, that fervent nakedness, alive like nothing else alive. So . . . where had the feeling gone? How could it have disappeared?

"Hey, is it okay if I put my arms down now?"

I hugged her. I kissed her on the face. I felt like crying.

"Promise me you'll get rid of that knife?"

"What knife?"

"Do you still love me?"

Intuition? But she seemed so relaxed, looking me straight in the face, studying my eyes.

"More than ever. I like you more each day."

"Like?"

"Love."

I felt—or had the impression, perhaps mistaken—that my voice did not sound very convincing. "I love you, I love you, I love you." I heard the doorbell ring. "That must be Raul." Ada's arms held me tighter.

"Forget it. Wexler will answer the door. Kiss me."

I kissed her lightly, on the cheek.

"No, a real kiss," said Ada.

"A real kiss will give me a hard-on and then I won't be able to go back in the living room."

Ada's mouth searched for mine hungrily.

277

At that moment, in Praça Onze, in one of the Garcia Circus trailers, which served as dressing room and residence for the clowns, two men were talking.

"Friends are more important than money. I won't forget what you've done for me."

"A part-time job as a clown?"

"The two apartments."

"In the Springs? No big deal," said Amândio Ferreira, a thickset Portuguese with a square face who was not much taller than his interlocutor. The Portuguese had worked for the circus as a stagehand and now as front man. Whenever a circus came to town Amândio was hired to take care of the paperwork required by City Hall. He had arranged the permit that allowed the Garcia Circus to remain for three months in that location.

"I need to lie low for a while, and I know they'll never look for me here, or in the Springs. The guy who's after me is a powerful man, but time is on my side. Why? I'm not sure. It's what my rat's instincts tell me. And then there's the matter of the videocassette."

"The videocassette?"

"I have no idea what's on it, but there are people willing to do anything to lay their hands on the thing. It vanished. I want you to place this ad in the classifieds of *O Globo* and *Jornal do Brasil*."

"Lost videocassette," read Amândio. "Willing to pay top dollar. Absolute secrecy. Write Videocassette c/o Classifieds at this newspaper."

"The idea is to drive the big guy crazy. I don't expect whoever's got it to come forward. He'll lay back for a while; it's as if the thing is cursed or something, like the hot items from King Tut's tomb."

"Who is this guy?"

"In ancient times the VIP's used to be buried with their treasure, jewels, gold. Sooner or later the thieves got everything."

"The only gold that'll be buried with me is this tooth," said Amândio.

"They'll get that, too. There are squads working all the cemeteries in Rio. I myself made my living for a time as a midnight dentist, pulling teeth out of cadavers in São João Batista."

"Oh, Nose, you've done it all."

"Except be a clown."

A little later, carrying a briefcase made of cardboard, Iron Nose crossed Rua Santana, which ran along the vacant lot where the circus was set up, and entered the Loud Springs Building. Stepping off the elevator on the eighteenth floor, he walked the long corridor full of doors until finding the one he was looking for. He removed a key from his pocket, opened the door, went inside, and locked it behind him.

It was a one-bedroom apartment, with a living room, kitchenette, and bath. The only furniture in the living room was two armchairs and a sofa. In the bedroom he found two single beds, pushed together, with stained mattresses and no sheets. Iron Nose lay down on one of the beds and closed his eyes.

He wished he had a woman there in bed with him, a blonde with fine hair that fluttered in the slightest breeze, transparent blue eyes, white skin, and tiny hands. But just as guard dogs performed better when they were hungry, he knew that privation would make him more vigilant.

He didn't sleep long. Someone was knocking at the door. Fuentes.

"The job was done with a Tramontina. It's a kitchen knife you can buy anywhere."

"That much I read in the paper."

"But what you didn't read is that I know a guy who's partial to that particular tool. The guy's a pro, he owns lots better specimens, first class in fact, but sometimes he uses an ordinary piece like that. His name's Rafael, we worked together for Mateus."

"Rafael. I've heard of him. They say he's pretty good."

"Maybe. He's a coward and he's mean."

"But he's famous."

"Who wouldn't be, after killing a half a dozen people?"

"Mateus never mentioned Lima Prado?"

"Nope."

"It had to be Lima Prado who ordered the hit on Mitry. Burning the archives. The guy's a gangster, but if I said so no one would believe it. It would be like saying the Pope raped an eight-year-old girl."

"You think any Pope ever raped an eight-year-old girl?"

"Maybe. Back in the old days. So what about Rafael. Will he be tough to locate?"

"I don't know."

"What does he like? Women?"

"Money."

"Who doesn't."

"Roses."

"Roses—you mean flowers?"

"He grows roses someplace, to sell."

"Then it'll be easy to find him. I've got contacts in the Flower Market. If he's squeezed, will he talk?"

"I told you, he's a chicken."

"What about that character everyone calls the Professor?"

"Rafael says that's who taught him how to use a knife. Who knows if it's true. No one's ever met the guy. Except maybe Mateus."

"Well, it's those two cronies who are after us, according to my sources. There are probably others, but I've got my people, too. You don't mind if I don't say who, do you?"

"No interest to me. I'll do my part, you do yours."

"I already made the first deposit in your account. You can stop by the bank and check."

"I already did."

"Another thing. There's a whore on the sixth floor. I want you to make a little visit. The cops are on your tail, and this way if they pick you up—it's a long shot, but we have to be prepared for anything—you've got an excuse for being here. She's expecting a guy named Roberto. That's you. Give me two days for my people to find Rafael.

280

Stop back Monday, same time. First visit the skirt, then come upstairs. Today and Monday."

Fuentes went down to the sixth floor as instructed and rang the buzzer. A woman opened the door partway, the chain still on.

"I'm Roberto."

"Took you a while, huh?"

The woman closed the door. He heard the noise of locks turning before it opened again.

The television was on. So was the air conditioner in the living-room window.

"It's five thousand. Up front."

"Five thousand?"

"But I do everything. E-v-e-r-ything. Want a whiskey? My name's Aurora, by the way." The woman went to the refrigerator in the corner and took out a tray of ice. She ran it under the sink.

"I don't drink," said Fuentes, examining the apartment.

"But I do." She sang, "I'm a drinker and I'm alive, there's people who don't about to die."

Aurora was around thirty, a bleached blonde. She had skin like someone who got a lot of sun on Sundays and none during the rest of the week. She dropped the ice cubes in a glass and half filled it with Drury's Special Reserve.

"You have a rubber?" asked Fuentes.

"What do you want a rubber for? I'm clean." She sang, "Brand-new woman, so pretty and tender, makes the man moan, but he feels no pain."

"You ought to be on the Chacrinha amateur hour."

"I already was."

"Beep! Beep!"

"Me get the horn? Obviously you don't know a thing about music. I'll have you know they let me do the whole number and I got a ten. And an invitation to make a single for Phonogram."

"What about the rubber?"

"Fresh out. This isn't a drugstore."

"I'll tell you what. Here's the money. You buy a rubber and I'll come back on Monday."

"But that's not fair. I don't like leaving my customers hanging." She counted the money, one-thousand notes, five of them.

"Monday we'll make a double album," said Fuentes.

"We could do other things today."

"Monday."

"You want to hear the songs I'm going to record?"

"Monday."

"There's a samba, by Zé Pixe, called 'Maxi Suffering,' that's going to explode on the charts."

"Monday."

"Are you really coming back?"

"Absolutely. Monday."

28

THE LETTERS were written on linen paper that was beginning to curl. The blue ink appeared to have been applied deliberately, as if Luiza thought slowly, or held her feelings in check, subordinating them to the slow rhythm of her hand. "I didn't hate the boy. There is a terrible curse on this family. I think Fernando is as mad as his sister."

Lima Prado considered the weak light that still angled in the window. Because of construction, the electricity had been turned off in the house on São Clemente. He would have to leave soon or be left in total darkness.

"Fortunately, the boy is normal, praise be the Holy and Most Merciful Virgin. It was not God's will that the offspring of this sinful incest should be stigmatized with the sickness of his parents." The letter.

The house darkened. Lima Prado sat unmoving in his chair next to the strongbox. The old woman had kept the trust from him all those years. She had led him to believe that his father was Bernard Mitry, when it was really Fernando after all. And his mother was Maria Clara, the mad aunt howling in the cellar. "Mortals will learn many things by seeing; but no man, before seeing it, shall be able to read the future or his own destiny." (Lima Prado was given to quoting Greek thinkers. Also found in the Notebooks: "My eyes have seen what my hands have done.") A crazy person would not have such intelligence, such a good memory. Crazy people knew that they were crazy. Crazy people were known by others as crazy people. None of this was the case with him. He would be better off worrying about the Brazilian Grand Prix, which was to be run the following day. And about his date with Mônica that evening.

Moving slowly but even so tripping several times over objects left around by the carpenters, Lima Prado made his way out of the house. On the veranda sat a guard with a flashlight. When he saw Lima Prado he got up.

"I'm leaving now. Good night."

"Night, sir."

Captain Virgulino was waiting for him in the courtyard next to the car.

"Take me to the girl's apartment." He got in and leaned back, stretching his legs. "Thus, as our eyes await the last day . . ."

Mônica was in a foul mood. It was no fun at all to hang around the house waiting for Mr. X to call or visit. He had given her jewelry and money, but what good were they when she was locked up and couldn't see anyone? At first she had believed there was something to be gained from the relationship, but now she just felt aggrieved and unhappy. Even sex was no longer pleasurable with Mr. X. What made sex good was liking the person; otherwise it quickly lost its attraction.

"What's up, White Tornado?"

"White Tornado?"

"Ajax, the White Tornado, the cleanser that kills dirt on contact. Haven't you seen the commercial?"

"I never watch television. You shouldn't talk to me like that."

"Like what?"

"Please." His hand felt for the Roderick Caribou Chappel hung across his chest.

"Like what, Ajax? Argh, what a ridiculous name."

"Please."

"It's too much."

The following day Lima Prado arrived early at the Gávea racetrack. He went directly to the stable, where he met the trainer Moreira.

"How did he sleep last night?"

"All right, I guess. He never sleeps well, sir. He's nervous by nature. I looked in several times during the night. Once I found him staring at the moon, as if he knew the moon was the moon. Sometimes I think there's something human about that horse."

"How about Pinheirinho?"

"The kid's calm as can be. Hard to believe he's about to run the Grand Prix."

"Where is he?"

"Go find Pinheiro," said Moreira to a stablehand.

"I've got a lot of money bet on that horse. Should I be worried?"

"No, sir. Not unless it rains something awful. But it won't. God is great." Moreira looked up at the cloudless blue sky.

"What about Cronópios, the Argentine?"

"He's no match for Conselheiro."

"Or the Chilean mare?"

"Celestina? She won't even place."

Pinheirinho walked up to them carrying an Uncle Scrooge comic book.

"How's it going, my boy? Today's the day. All set?"

"You bet. Conselheiro's in top form. The others don't stand a chance."

"I'm having lunch here, Moreira. If you need me for anything, you know where to find me."

The stands started filling early. Lima Prado was joined at his table by Apolônio de Almeida Pinto, a retired Supreme Court justice and friend of his grandmother's.

The judge was wearing a white linen three-piece suit, in spite of the heat. His huge bald spot glistened intensely.

"The crowd gets more common by the year," said the judge. "What you see before you is riffraff in sport clothes, women of dubious suitability and even more suspect gentility. Horses are switched to trick innocent bettors. The most unimaginable fraud is committed, involving owners and trainers alike. And don't you think for a minute that these are the senile ramblings of a ninety-year-old man. I may have turned ninety this month, but I'm as lucid as ever."

"My congratulations," said Lima Prado.

"Do you know the first time I saw a horse race? The twentieth of June, 1903. My father took me to the Grand Cruzeiro do Sul. I was all of ten years old. The President of the Republic was there with his entire family. And do you know who was chief steward? Dr. Lauro Müller. The minister of industry! What a difference, eh, between then and today. Yesterday, a minister of state of the eminence of Lauro Müller as steward! And today—"

"Today it's a photofinish."

The President of the Republic arrived fifteen minutes before post time. His appearance on the speaker's platform was announced over the loudspeakers. There was applause, not particularly warm. Lima Prado had met the President once before, at a meeting of the Brazilian Horseman's Society. Today the President chatted briefly with Lima Prado, asking after his horse Conselheiro; then he went on greeting the other people crowding around him on the platform. The Jockey Club bleachers were standing room only. It was expected that in spite of the current economic crisis the day's betting would break all records.

When the odds for the Grand Prix came up on the board, Conselheiro was listed second, right behind Cronópios, the horse from Argentina. Rumor had it that Conselheiro was no longer favorite because he was being ridden by an apprentice. Sitting on the platform, in close proximity to the President, ministers of state, and other powerful figures, moments before his horse was to run the "greatest test of Latin American turf," Lima Prado felt enormously bored. He also felt something he couldn't quite define, related to the fact that he was the incestuous child of the woman who howled in the cellar on São Clemente when he was a boy.

29

ON MONDAY all the papers gave front-page coverage to Conselheiro's victory in the Brazilian Grand Prix, which "confirmed the excellence of domestic thoroughbred breeding." There were pictures of the horse, of Pinheirinho, the apprentice-turned-overnight-sensation, and of the President congratulating Conselheiro's owner, "industrialist Thales de Lima Prado," this last a photograph whose rarity—it was the first of that powerful man ever to appear in the media—went unnoticed by all the journalists.

Fuentes and Iron Nose had arranged to meet at one o'clock in the apartment on Rua Santana. First Fuentes stopped at Aurora's apartment. He had phoned from the street to let her know he was on his way and did not want to run into any other client in the apartment.

"Come with me, I want to show you something," said Aurora, leading Fuentes into the bedroom. On the night table were three stacks of small cardboard boxes.

"There's a dozen boxes, three rubbers to a box. You think that'll be enough?" Aurora knew that some men didn't like jokes in bed and had only one thing in mind—penetration, invading the woman with their flesh and sperm. Here was one of them, except that to complicate things even further he also had antiseptic preoccupations.

Fuentes picked up one of the boxes, read everything that was written on the outside (including the small print), opened it, removed one of the plastic envelopes containing a prophylactic, and read what was written on that.

"All this and you're still scared?"

"Women always scare me."

"A man your size. You'd think you'd be just like Viní-cius." She sang, "As long as I have a tongue and a finger, no woman will scare me away."

"That's a Vinícius song?"

"It was never recorded."

Fuentes looked at his watch. This woman did not appeal to him. He was going to have to throw away five thousand more cruzeiros. It was the dwarf's money, but it bothered him to throw money away, even somebody else's.

"You've heard of *fleur-de-rose?*" asked Aurora.

"Who?"

"A rim job—where have you been all your life? You must be a virgin, or close to it."

"That's right, I am."

"No kidding—word of honor?" Aurora didn't believe him, but there was always a remote possibility that it was true, and the idea excited her.

"Just take a look at my face."

"Then you're lying. Virgins are tender young kids with pimples."

"That's baloney. Just like when I was a kid they told me jerking off makes you go blind or grow hair on the palm of your hand."

"And you didn't go blind."

Silence.

"I did. In one eye."

Aurora leaned to look into Fuentes' eye. "You really can't see anything, not anything at all out of it?"

Fuentes thought of the girl who was selling her cornea. Marluci. Had she sold it yet? He should have closed the deal with her.

"Well?"

"Well what?"

"Lie down." Aurora tried to push him. "Jeez, you're heavy."

289

Fuentes took a wad of bills out of his pocket and counted out five thousand cruzeiros.

"I didn't work, so I shouldn't make anything. It's not fair."

"Sure you did. You lost time on me." Fuentes threw the money on the sofa. The bills scattered as they landed.

"Want a cup of coffee?"

"No. I'll call when I want to see you again."

"What's with men, anyway?"

"What's with women?"

"I'll give you a special discount price."

"The price is fine."

"My customers are crazy about me. You don't know what you're missing. It's not right. Hey, you could at least say goodbye."

"Goodbye." Fuentes slammed the door.

He rang the buzzer upstairs, three long and two short, as Iron Nose had instructed.

The two stood in the living room next to the closed door and talked briefly.

"Did you see the whore?"

"Yeah."

"I found out where our friend grows his flowers. Friburgo. A helicopter is waiting for us at Santos Dumont. You leave first. There's a cab out front, the driver's a Portuguese named Amândio. One of my people. Get in the back seat and wait for me."

Before getting in the cab, Fuentes surveyed the scene carefully. A policeman wearing the visored cap of a traffic cop was preventing other cars from pulling up to the curb. The taxi with the Portuguese driver seemed to be invisible to him. The meter was running. A man stood on the curb holding a black briefcase, but it appeared that he was merely waiting for a chance to cross the street, which before long he did.

"Amândio."

"Get in."

Fuentes noticed that the driver avoided looking at him in the rearview mirror. Fuentes could see his forehead and eyes buried in deep sockets below heavy, untamed eyebrows. A thick neck. Sometime in his life this man had done heavy physical labor. These Portuguese were hardy, Fuentes thought. An announcer on the car radio was talking non-stop. Then he played a song. Then went back to talking. Fuentes felt himself becoming impatient and irritated.

"I don't like waiting for people," said Fuentes when Iron Nose got in the car.

"Neither do I. Circumstances beyond my control."

The cab drove down Avenida Presidente Vargas to Avenida Rio Branco. Traffic was slow.

"If there's anything I hate, it's being stuck in a car. I can understand your irritation. Once, during one of those March floods, I spent a whole night in a car on Avenida Brasil. I thought I'd go nuts," said Iron Nose.

"Why didn't you get out and walk?"

"Swim would have been more like it. I'll tell you why. Because there was a package in the trunk, a fifty-kilo package, a fifty-kilo package of metal, a fifty-kilo package of yellow metal, a fifty-kilo package of precious yellow metal, a fifty-kilo package of precious yellow metal called gold. You know who used to talk like that? Carlos Lacerda, the greatest orator in the history of Brazil. Before your time. Do you know how much fifty kilos of gold is worth? Of course there *are* things worth more, by weight, like, for example, certain snake venoms. But gold is gold is gold. You know who used to talk like that?"

Fuentes merely stared at him.

"Don't look at me like that. We're allies. I know I talk too much. When I was prisoner on Avenida Brasil, surrounded by water, I talked the whole time, and you know why? Because I didn't start talking until I was eight years old. My mother, and everybody else, thought I was mute. Natural compensation. This fucking traffic isn't moving.

I didn't say babá—you know, babytalk for nurse, though I don't suppose you had a nurse, me neither, I daresay it's the rare dwarf who did—or mama, or dada, or cha-cha-cha. Was that before your time, cha-cha-cha? So you see I was mute, even though only temporarily. Imagine the suffering of the few people who managed to suffer for me. And when only a few people suffer for someone, their suffering is greater, although, granted, less spectacular and far-reaching. When a famous movie star dies, mobs of people scream their lamentations, but actually each one only suffers a little. The thing is that all together it adds up to a veritable earthquake of pain. But imagine just for a moment a widow whose only child dies. An event that would not have the slightest repercussion in the world at large—goddamn traffic—but that single mother's pain would be greater than the epidemic of suffering of those hundreds of people lamenting the death of their idol, and all idols have feet of clay and hemorrhoids. Another thing that happens with ex-mutes is that they talk like they're high, half out of their minds. Talking makes me drunk, and the more I talk the more drunk I seem. In the old days, my frowning friend, words used to provoke hard-ons and tears, they caused revolutions and made people kill themselves, but now they just make people look stupid, like you —no offense. Goddamn traffic."

Finally they arrived at Santos Dumont Airport. As soon as they boarded the helicopter that had been waiting for them, the engines revved up and the machine lifted off.

"Look . . ." began Fuentes. He paused.

"You don't know how to address me, do you? Just call me Nose."

"Okay, Mr. Nose—"

"Mr. Nose! Nose, Nose, nose that never ends, nose that if it fell off the world would lose a friend. You know who used to talk like that?"

"Look, uh—Nose—don't you have a name?"

"José."

"Look, José—"

"No. No one calls me José. Only me, myself, and I."

"Look, Nose, you talk and talk and talk. My whole life, all I've heard is lies. Lies, that's what words are."

"That's an Indian idea. Indians can't even think without stepping on someone's toes."

"Blacks can?"

"Not them either."

"And whites?"

"No. It's been like that for a long time. No one knows anything about what matters to people's happiness. Astronomy's doing just fine, thank you, as well as physics and chemistry, but we dwarves, and blacks, and Indians, and even whites, are in an ever-worsening situation. Something has to be done about it before the great catastrophe, the hecatomb, understand? I'm quibbling, I know, but we have to create a new world for the weak. More power to the weak! I can talk for hours on this subject!"

"But I don't want to hear it."

"That's your privilege."

The rest of the journey went by in silence.

The helicopter landed in a clearing beside a parked car. A man standing next to the open car door waved. Iron Nose and Fuentes jumped out of the helicopter and into the back seat of the car. The man who had waved sat in front next to the driver. Both he and the driver were black and wore navy blue suits and ties.

"Does he have any security men?"

"No. A half-dozen employees, but they're all gone by now. You'll find him alone."

Iron Nose gazed out at the scenery. "You couldn't get me to live in a place like this, not over my dead body. Too much oxygen. Did you bring the box?"

"It's in my pocket."

Iron Nose began to laugh, small giggles that soon turned loud and convulsive. Fuentes did not react.

"What an idea! It wouldn't have occurred to me in a

293

hundred years," Iron Nose managed to say through his guffaws.

Finally they arrived at Rafael's country place. A one-story building was visible from the road, an old-style farmhouse behind a stone wall. The rose garden was out back.

"You two wait here," said Iron Nose as he and Fuentes got out of the car.

The gate was unlocked. They walked up to the front porch. There was no doorbell, so Iron Nose knocked.

Rafael opened the door. He did not appear surprised to see his visitors.

"How's it going, Chinaman?" he said. "Who's our friend here?"

"Iron Nose, at your service."

"I never knew the famous Iron Nose was a dwarf. Come on in." He stepped back.

The living room they entered contained two tables littered with papers, a telephone, a large antique typewriter, and a sharp pair of scissors, open. In the middle of the room stood an old file cabinet painted dark green.

"Nor did I know that you cultivated roses."

"I have more than a hundred and fifty different species. My interest in roses started with my mother. We had a house in Bangu where she planted lots of roses." His look went from Fuentes' face to Iron Nose's and back to Fuentes. "My mother had the prettiest roses I've ever seen, to this day. And I think they're the most sublime flower of all." Rafael scooped up the scissors from the table. "I'll go outside and cut you a few—"

Rafael lunged forward, but Fuentes was quicker. He grabbed the typewriter with both hands and hurled it against Rafael's chest.

When he came to, Rafael's hands and feet were tied. Fuentes and Iron Nose sat there looking at him.

"What's going on, Chinaman? Fuck, have you gone nuts?"

"We'd just like to ask you a few questions," said Iron Nose.

294

"You're an ugly son of a bitch, you know that, Mr. Nose?"

"If you were a woman, I'd be worried." This guy was not acting scared, as Fuentes had predicted.

"Was it you who did the job on Vieira Souto? The twins and the playboy?"

"Hey, I get my orders from the top. I'm a soldier, just like you."

Rafael described in detail the deaths of Mitry, Tatá, and Titi.

"Don't you use the Cassidy anymore?"

"That knife's got a past, Chinaman, a history, you know that. I decided to give it a rest so it doesn't get ruined. I'm going to leave it to my grandchildren. But hey, China, you don't have to tie me up to ask questions. Tell the dwarf here that I'm okay. What do you say?"

"What about the videocassette?"

"What videocassette?"

"The same one we were looking for at the lawyer's. When you stuck your knife handle up his girl's ass. The Cassidy."

"Bygone waters don't move the waterwheel."

"What about the videocassette?"

"Chinaman, Chinaman, why stir up a fight? There's no way this dwarf here can give you cover."

Fuentes removed a small red box from his pocket that had a label that read *Faria Homeopathic Healing Center, Variolinium 200a., 10 packets.* Inside were three large hard-shelled cockroaches.

Fuentes plucked out one of the cockroaches, which struggled between his fingers, legs and antennae squirming. Rafael's eyes widened and he paled visibly. Fuentes bent over him and, holding his chin, began stuffing the insect into his mouth. Rafael locked his teeth and tried to wriggle free from Fuentes' grasp. The two struggled for some time. Squashed against Rafael's closed lips, the cockroach had turned into a slimy pulp that dropped down his mouth and chin. Fuentes stood back and watched Rafael writhe on the floor like a poisoned rat, scraping his mouth on the floorboards.

"The videocassette?" asked Fuentes.

Rafael was throwing up, violent spasms that drowned out the question.

"Give him a minute," said Iron Nose.

An acrid, repulsive smell filled the air.

They waited.

Rafael rolled away from the pool of vomit. Lying on his side, with his eyes closed, he looked like a cadaver, except for the fresh blood running from one of his nostrils.

They waited.

Rafael opened his eyes. His gaze met Fuentes', each trying to understand the other.

"The videocassette?" said Fuentes.

"The problem is he's not a coward," said Iron Nose. "But you and I may be the only ones in the entire world who don't mind cockroaches. I saw the way you picked it up. There was a killer on the loose in Rio once—I had nowhere to live at the time and was sleeping in doorways —who went around pouring gasoline on tramps and beggars while they were asleep and then setting them on fire. He killed a bunch of people. I had this feeling, see, that he was going to get me, this premonition. And he almost did. I woke up soaking wet, covered with gasoline, with the guy standing over me, calm as could be, looking as if he was about to light the oven. I ran like a maniac. After that I slept in the sewer. The roaches crawled all over me, but I knew they wouldn't do me any harm, at most just suck a little piece of lip here, a bit of finger there. At least I was safe with them, death was outside on the street: It had two legs, two arms, and a head, like me, created in the image of God our Saviour Jesus Christ."

"What about the videocassette?" It seemed to Iron Nose that Fuentes' voice contained a certain disgust. A day of surprises.

"I didn't find it, Chinaman."

"Don't call me Chinaman. I've told you that a million times." There was no rancor in his voice now. Both of them were tired. They had reached the end.

"Did you look real good?" asked Iron Nose.

"The pretty boy . . . he had thousands of cassettes . . . but that one . . . a black case . . ."

"He didn't find it," said Fuentes.

Iron Nose picked the scissors up off the floor. He held them out to Fuentes.

"Finish him off."

"I don't kill people who are tied up."

Rafael closed his eyes.

"Well I do," said Iron Nose.

30

I HAVE become involved in many extremely complicated cases in my life, cases full of unbelievable coincidences and sinister, indecipherable mysteries. Perhaps the Mitry case was the worst of all, the most confusing. I became aware of certain episodes—like the death of Rafael, for example (the murder of a "small-time flower grower" by unknown assailants did not arouse the interest of the press or even of the police, who treated it routinely and never ascertained the true circumstances of the crime)— only long after the fact. Lima Prado's Notebooks proved quite difficult to interpret; the effort involved in translating this virtual Rosetta Stone would have been worthy of another *Letter to m. Dacier*. To add to all this, I was going through a very trying period in my personal life. I was blessed with the delights of Ada and her sumptuously prominent quadriceps, the languid elegance of Lilibeth, Bebel's perverse naïveté. I believed that I loved them all, and that I needed the variety of scripts, rhetoric, fantasy, and sexual conquest they provided. "Liking women the way you do is more neurotic than hating them," Wexler told me. Perhaps I was a bit neurotic during the fetishistic phase with the Randall, overcome by *animus necandi*. The world around me was the world of Mitry. "A new kind of madness is raging in the world," he had said before he was killed. I was fornicating, waiting for death to arrive. "After more than six hundred years, a triple conjunction of Saturn, Jupiter, and Mars is occurring in the fortieth degree of Aquarius," said Bebel, repeating what the sages of the University of Paris had told Philip VI. "Another

Black Plague is on its way, let's take advantage of it." The end was near for those who had all their teeth, as Zakkai, the Iron Nose, would say later.

Setting aside the ethical question—it's not that I disregarded this angle of the problem, but rather that having several women actually did not weigh on my conscience —it was easy for me to rationalize, claiming that human beings should have the freedom to exercise their capacity to love more than one person, etc. Even so, there were complex problems involved, mainly on the practical level. After all, each day contains only twenty-four hours; and I had to work, at least a little (allowing Wexler to carry me on his shoulders), and sleep, at least a little. Between those two activities alone I lost ten hours a day, five for each. The fourteen remaining hours were taken up with my lovers.

None of the three was prepared to accept this situation.

"Okay," said Bebel, "the skinny one has seniority, so I'll give you a little time to settle accounts without hurting her."

Lilibeth, as she ran her hand over my chest: "Who scratched you like this—that woman who lives with you?" (Aging Betsy no longer had control of her claws; after she'd been on my lap for a while and I went to set her down, a senile fear came over her and she'd dig her claws into my chest.) "A cat, a four-legged feline?" exclaimed Lilibeth. "You expect me to believe that? Don't you understand how awful it is to have your lover all scratched up by some other woman?"

Ada knew nothing. She was the first, as Bebel said, and if she found out she would leave me. Ada wanted to get married and have children. The idea depressed me. Some men are born to be husbands, fathers, heads of households. I just couldn't see myself in any one of those roles. Meanwhile, women always wanted to marry me and have kids. For a time, as a defense, I pretended to be married to a woman named Hortensia, native of Pindamonhangaba, where she frequently spent time visiting her family. Berta Bronstein quickly discovered I was lying and made me give up that infantile imposture. Berta was really amusing. No, Berta was not really amusing. But if she wanted me right now, I'd go running and jump into bed with her.

Ada's heart beat fifty-two times per minute (she was an athlete); Bebel's seventy; Lilibeth's, seventy-eight. The smell of Ada's armpits, when she was not wearing deodorant, excited me. That was all I knew about the women I loved. I knew more about Betsy, the Siamese.

Lilibeth opened the door (she called my office daily saying she needed to speak with her lawyer, but when I went to her apartment we never discussed any legal topic that I can remember) and said, "Guess who's here?"

It was Val, her husband. Lilibeth had ("following your advice") given up her initial hostile intentions, and the two had arrived at a kind of peaceful coexistence. They no longer lived together, and after the legal waiting period would apply for a divorce. Val was wearing a silk robe.

"So you're Mandrake? I've been so anxious, I mean *so* anxious, to meet you. Lili hardly talks about anyone or anything else."

"He slept here, but it was in the guest room," said Lilibeth. She had noticed that I had noticed that Val was wearing a robe.

"There's nothing I like better than sleep," said Val. "Do you know how many hours I slept last night? Eleven. I could've slept another eleven, but I promised Lili I'd make lunch for you. It's going to be a fish *moqueca,* my own creation. Two kilos of grouper, two kilos of shrimp, a kilo of mussels, half a kilo of squid—it has to be the tentacles, all those little legs, you know, it looks like a gigantic spermatozoa. Anyway it's the tentacles that give my *moqueca* its special flavor—two cups of olive oil, a cup of *dendê* palm oil, two large onions, a bunch of parsley, scallions, cilantro, three garlic cloves, juice of two limes, half a cup of vodka, a teaspoon of black pepper, two *malaguêta* peppers, grated ginger, and coconut milk. When I made this dish for Nureyev he went absolutely nuts over it, that's why I call it Moqueca à Nureyev, which also explains the vodka. Everybody else uses white wine. Then there's the preparation. Would you like to know the secret?"

"No, thank you."

"I find your lack of interest extremely rude."

"Val, Mandrake doesn't have the sensibility to be a chef, that's why he's not interested."

"That's not true," I said in my defense. "I know how to cook lots of different things."

"Really, what things?" asked Lilibeth.

"Goulash. Beet soufflé."

"Beet soufflé? How awful!" said Val. "The only palatable use of beets is in borscht."

"Why don't we have a chat while Val works on his *moqueca*," said Lilibeth.

"Fine. What shall we chat about?"

"You know."

I followed her into the bedroom.

"The Nureyev Val was talking about is not the famous Russian ballet dancer," said Lilibeth. "Did you think it was?"

"I didn't think anything."

"He's just a friend of Val's who's the spitting image, a face and body—he has a beautiful body—just like Nureyev. Have you missed me?"

"I've missed you."

Even without lipstick Lilibeth's lips were dark, opaque, the color of a blood blister. Without makeup her white face had the phantasmagoric look of a Japanese geisha in a samurai movie.

I sat on the edge of the bed. Lilibeth sat on the floor and leaned her head against my knees. A demonstration of submissiveness. But Lilibeth was not a submissive woman. I think she imagined that all men liked to subjugate women and was trying to please me.

"Get up, come sit over here. Do you know why I have a cat instead of a dog?"

"No, and I don't want to," she said, sitting beside me.

"We could have a little white wine before lunch," I suggested.

"First you have to do something to deserve it. Nobody gets anything for free around here."

"That will be a real sacrifice," I said.

Her areolas were the same color as her lips, but the skin on her body gave off the luminous whiteness of women who had breasts with pink halos.

"Tell me you love me."

Just like Mercedes, the federal investigator killed by Fuentes. Just like Ada. Just like Sofia. Just like everyone. People wanted to be loved.

"I know you love me," said Lilibeth, fondling me, "but I want you to say it. I want to hear it. Go on, say it."

"I love you."

Even with so many women on my mind, I had not forgotten Fuentes, Rafael, and the lethal Main Office: I still carried the Randall in its leather sheath. But sometimes I felt like I really didn't understand what was going on, mostly with my own behavior.

"I love you."

The *moqueca* was delicious. Also the wine, a German Schwarze Katz—any wine named after a cat had to be good.

"What do you think I should do with my money?" asked Val. "Open a savings account, buy gold, dollars, gems, stamps? I told you, didn't I, darling?"

"Uh-huh."

"We don't want our money to rot, after all."

"The thing that rots beyond repair is blood," I said.

"Oh, oh," said Lilibeth.

"It's terrible having money to invest," continued Val. "Ah, heavens, so many alternatives!"

302

"So?" said Lilibeth.

"So, what?"

"What would you do with your money?"

"I don't have any."

"What if you did?"

"If I did, maybe I'd be just like all the speculators who do everything they can to save their stash and the world can go fuck itself."

"I don't want the world to go fuck itself," said Val. "I adore the world. I adore life. But inflation is eating away at my money. The little that cost me so much to inherit. Another thing"—he stamped his foot—"I did not sleep in the guest room. You got that?"

"That doesn't mean anything," said Lilibeth quickly.

"After all, I am her husband."

"Now who's being rude?" said Lilibeth.

"But it's true, isn't it? Where did I sleep, darling, hmmm?"

"You've ruined my appetite," said Lilibeth, pushing back her plate.

"I'm sorry, I'm really sorry," said Val, getting down on his knees and placing his hand on his chest dramatically. "Tell me you forgive me. You too, Mandrake. It was so tasteless of me it's not even worth mentioning, isn't that right, sweetheart?"

"That's right. It was very awkward of you."

"But not offensive."

"No. Just awkward."

"Then eat my *moqueca*."

"Do you know how to make rice-and-octopus-with-broccoli?" I asked.

"Val is a terrific cook," said Lilibeth.

"Men are much better cooks than women," said Val. "All the great chefs are men."

"Orwell says that men are merely more organized and process the orders in the sequence that they come to the kitchen," I said.

"Women don't have the military mentality that men do, thank God," said Lilibeth.

"Does Orwell understand cooking?"

"He worked as a *plongeur* in Paris," I said.

"*Plongeur*? What's that?"

"It's a kind of dishwasher."

"A writer and a dishwasher. Really impressive."

I tried to imagine Val and Lilibeth in bed together. I wasn't jealous. He was her husband; he was homosexual; he was ridiculous. What I felt was a sort of diffuse bitterness.

I called the office to say that I'd be late, that Wexler shouldn't wait for me. I called Bebel (in a whisper so the others wouldn't hear me) to say that I'd be stopping by her place.

Val was sleeping in the hammock on the terrace when I said my goodbyes.

"You're not mad, are you? Poor Val, he came over and I realized it would be good for him, psychologically, to sleep with me. It was really quick, less intimate than a handshake. Then he turned over and went to sleep. You understand, don't you? It was a gesture of compassion on my part. He's feeling so lost."

"I understand."

"The *moqueca* was good, wasn't it?"

"It was."

"He's a great cook."

"I have to go, I'm late."

"Then tell me you love me."

"I'm not in the mood."

"Then you *are* mad."

"No I'm not."

"Don't make me unhappy," said Lilibeth.

"I love you."

Bebel told me she knew all the synonyms for love—"care for, desire, admire, fancy, cherish, revere, adore, esteem, relish, treasure, enjoy."

"Relish. I like that. Of course there *are* more, aren't there?"

"So tell me."

304

She wanted to hear the strong ones.

When I first arrived, I'd found a surprise visitor there as well: Bebel's mother, Rosa.

"I came to see how my daughter's getting along. When she lived at home she insisted on every convenience; now she might as well be a barefooted Carmelite. This place doesn't even have air conditioning. So, you two are still seeing each other?"

Rosa's deeply tanned skin looked even more leathery than when I'd last seen her. She was still lighthearted, agile, nervous, pacing around the living room.

"Whatever happened with the case of that poor girl Cila?" asked Rosa. "Have they come up with anything? The police are so incompetent I can't imagine they'll ever get to the bottom of it. After all, it shouldn't be all that hard."

"Oh, no?"

"Of course not."

I waited.

Bebel lit a cigarette, impatient. Irritated with her mother for not agreeing to leave before I arrived, even before she got a chance to look around. It was Rosa's first visit to the apartment her daughter had rented on Rua das Laranjeiras. The noise from the street was so loud that we had to raise our voices to talk.

"The police suspect her lover," I said, trying to egg her on.

"But who is he? Do they know?"

"No. But you got a look at him that day, didn't you?"

"My life would make a novel," said Rosa.

"Did you or didn't you?"

"Of course I did. Through the mirror in the vestibule. He didn't know it, though."

"What did he look like?"

"He was fat—real fat, tall and red-skinned. He looked like a gringo."

"Why didn't you tell the police? Considering that he's the one who probably killed Cila."

"I didn't want to get involved. You can tell your pals on

the force if you want, but don't bring me into it or I'll deny everything."

"You see what kind of woman she is?" said Bebel.

"I've learned to mistrust men . . . and women."

"I gave you back your letter, so you could tear it up, remember?"

"I don't know who's worse, you or her."

"Shut up, little girl."

"No, I won't shut up. Besides, it's time for you to go."

I nudged Bebel out of the living room.

"Bebel, your mother may be about to give me some very important information and you're upsetting things."

"I hate that woman."

"Just do me a favor and stay here while I talk to her in the living room, okay?"

"Are you sure you don't want me to stay in the living room while you talk to her here in the bedroom? She likes dirty words too."

"Please."

"You don't deserve any favors. Have you left that woman yet?"

"We'll talk about that later."

"Well, have you or haven't you?"

"I haven't had the chance yet. You said yourself not to hurt her."

"You've already had plenty of time to use the anesthesia of your choice. I'll give you one more week, do you understand? One week to give her the pink slip."

"Fine. But right now just please stay in here and read your Donald Duck, okay?"

"It's Simone de Beauvoir, you jerk."

"I'll be right back."

Rosa was not in the living room. I checked the bathroom, then the kitchen. She was gone.

31

THE NOTEBOOKS contained a genealogical tree sketched by Lima Prado. It began with Barros Lima and Vicentina Cintra, disregarding, as Basilio Peralta had also done in *Family Portrait,* the Portuguese immigrant couple who first established the family in Brazil.

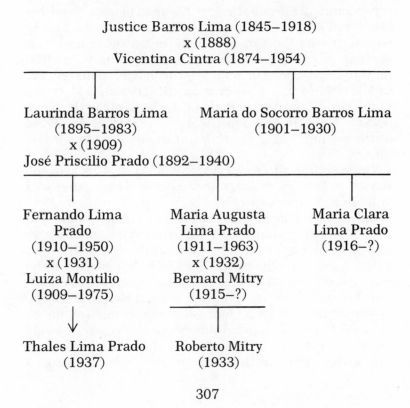

Justice Barros Lima (1845–1918)
x (1888)
Vicentina Cintra (1874–1954)

Laurinda Barros Lima   Maria do Socorro Barros Lima
(1895–1983)   (1901–1930)
x (1909)
José Priscilio Prado (1892–1940)

Fernando Lima   Maria Augusta   Maria Clara
Prado   Lima Prado   Lima Prado
(1910–1950)   (1911–1963)   (1916–?)
x (1931)   x (1932)
Luiza Montilio   Bernard Mitry
(1909–1975)   (1915–?)

Thales Lima Prado   Roberto Mitry
(1937)   (1933)

Certain discrepancies existed between Lima Prado's version of the family tree and information included in Peralta's book, for example Laurinda's age at the time of her marriage. According to Lima Prado, his grandmother was born in 1895 and married in 1909, at fourteen, not sixteen, as Peralta claimed.

Lima Prado never added a new family tree to the Notebooks showing Maria Clara as his mother.

Sorting through the contents of the strongbox in São Clemente, Lima Prado found receipts for payments made to the São Pedro Clinic, an institution for the aged in Tijuca. The receipts referred to the internment of Maria Clara Lima Prado.

He was alone in his grandmother's room when he found the documents from the institution. He rose from his chair and stretched out on the worn floorboards, feeling weary. It was the sort of fatigue he'd experienced as a student in military school after participating in his first military exercise. He had fed the horse, removed the saddle and bridle, lay down on the ground, and stared at the sky ("Like Andrei Bolkonski," he wrote in the Notebooks). Now, in the São Clemente mansion, he stared at the ceiling, lost in another immensity—the one inside him.

The most recent receipt was dated six months ago, one month before his grandmother's death. His mother was still alive, he was sure of it.

Lima Prado folded the last receipt from the hospital, put it in his pocket, and closed the strongbox. For the very first time he felt like taking a look at the cellar. He went to the door beside the pantry, opened it, and paused at the top of the stairs. The electricity had been reconnected, and he flicked on the light and started slowly down the stairs. At the bottom he found a vestibule and two doors. One led to a huge room full of broken furniture, various tools, even two birdcages. Behind the other door was a windowless room with a narrow bed, a bureau, and a small table. On the table he found a music box, which, when opened, played a few strains of a piece of music that he recognized but could not identify. He turned the key on the bottom of the music box and sat down on the bed to listen to the entire piece. So it was here that Maria Clara had lived, howling. . . . Had she been allowed to wander, adrift, from one room to the other, as mad people like to? Lima Prado felt as if he were in a daze, unsure what to do, which direction to go, almost as if he were chained to the floor. Finally he gave a start and fled the room, bounding up the stairs.

"Is something wrong, boss?" asked Captain Virgulino when Lima Prado appeared, breathless, on the porch.

"No, no, I'm fine," said Lima Prado.

(In this section of the Notebooks Lima Prado had written in large block letters: WHAT'S IMPORTANT IS NOT THE FACT BUT THE SYMBOL. HANDSEL. It was in blue ink, which indicated a family subject. At first I interpreted this entry to mean that he longed to see his mother's insanity as merely a fact rather than a "sign," but I later decided it was just the opposite. Lima Prado had construed his mother's illness to be the earnest money in a contract—the price of freedom: freedom in exchange for sanity. His was a tortuous and obscure logic. As was mine.)

"Visitors are allowed only on Thursday afternoon and Sunday morning."

After this pronouncement the receptionist went back to reading her magazine. The reception area of the São Pedro Clinic was dim and resembled the lobby of a cheap hotel.

"My name is Thales Lima Prado. I would like to speak with the director."

"He's not in right now. Just stepped out."

"Well, then with whoever's in charge."

"That would be Dr. Zuomira. What was your name again?"

"Thales Lima Prado."

The receptionist picked up the telephone.

"Dr. Zuomira, there's a man here— What was your name again?"

"Thales Lima Prado."

"A Mr. Prado would like to talk with you." Pause. "What is this in regard to, Mr. Prado?"

"It's about a patient."

"It's about a patient," repeated the receptionist. "Okay." She hung up the phone.

"Dr. Zuomira will be right with you."

Dr. Zuomira was a short, thin, colorless woman with a pointy chin and an oversized head. She was wearing a white lab coat, white pants, and bright blue running shoes.

"You wanted to speak with me?" She pressed her lips together as she talked, looking first at the floor, then at the ceiling, like a frightened squirrel.

"Yes, it's about a patient. Maria Clara Lima Prado."

"Please step into the office."

Dr. Zuomira closed the door. "Have a seat," she said, pointing to a sofa and two chairs upholstered in green vinyl.

"Are you a relative of Maria Clara's?"

"I'm . . . her nephew."

"What did you say your name was?"

"Thales Lima Prado."

"It's all here in the files," she said, pulling a folder out of an enormous file cabinet. "Your aunt's been with us for over thirty years." Dr. Zuomira thumbed through Maria Clara's file.

"What exactly is my aunt's problem?"

"Paranoid schizophrenia . . . with complications of senility. She does fine in her own little world, but out there it would be dangerous for her."

"Can I see her?"

"Visits are permitted on Thursdays and Sundays."

"I want to see her today."

"It's against regulations, I'm sorry."

"I'm asking you to make an exception," said Lima Prado, trying to catch Dr. Zuomira's wandering eyes.

"She hasn't had a visitor for years. You've never come before to see her. Why the sudden urgency?"

"I learned only today that she was here. I've been away."

"I'm sorry, but the clinic does have regulations." Dr. Zuomira fixed her gaze on the wall.

"I happen to be president of Achilles Bank & Trust. The bank could be very helpful to the clinic, in case we reached an understanding here."

Dr. Zuomira's eyes veered from the wall. "Achilles Bank & Trust? I've got an account there."

"What a coincidence."

They walked down a long hallway, passing several other wards before reaching Maria Clara's. Poverty has a smell, age has a smell, death has a smell. They were all three mixed together in that hallway, hovering in the air like a thick, rancid invisible fog that seemed damp on Lima Prado's skin and in his nostrils.

"She used to have a private room, but the payments stopped coming some time ago. So after waiting and waiting and receiving nothing, Dr. Wladimir had her moved out to the ward—where treatment is also very good, of course. Dr. Wladimir is a very humane man. . . . It's a losing proposition, a clinic like this. He's always taking money out of his own pocket—"

"Is your name Zuomira or Zulmira?"

"It was supposed to be Zulmira, but they registered it wrong. The same thing happened to my sister. Her name was supposed to be Anesia but she ended up Aresia. Can you believe it? Only in Brazil!"

Every time they passed one of the wide arches leading to a ward they were hit by a suffocating gust of foul-smelling air. Finally they turned and walked through one of the archways.

"Here we are," said Dr. Zuomira.

311

The ward contained about twenty beds, all of them occupied by old women dressed in gray nightgowns. A few were sitting up in bed, but most were lying down.

"You happened to arrive at naptime," said Dr. Zuomira, ignoring a grumbling woman tugging at her arm. They stopped next to the bed of a fat, lethargic-looking patient whose toothless mouth hung wide open. She was still as a statue—not even her breathing was perceptible.

"Is she my aunt?"

"No. This one here."

The woman in the adjacent bed was skinny, very pale, and had snow-white hair. There were dark blotches around her eyes, but the rest of her face was smooth and clear, with hardly a wrinkle. She sat staring vaguely forward, her head unmoving, face expressionless. As Lima Prado approached her bed her head turned slowly, in exaggerated slow motion, until finally her eyes rested on those of her son. A smile gently spread along her closed lips and then seemed to become fixed there, enigmatic.

"They all love visitors, even the ones in the most advanced stages," said Dr. Zuomira.

Lima Prado felt his body lean slightly forward, as if about to take a step. But suddenly he flinched. Someone had grabbed hold of his arm. It was a tall, cadaverous woman.

"This is a warehouse of old people," she said. "Something has to be done about it."

"Go back to your room, Dona Santinha," ordered Dr. Zuomira.

"I wrote a letter to the President and he didn't answer. I turned on the television and he didn't answer," said Dona Santinha.

"This gentleman is visiting his aunt. Please don't interrupt."

"Stacked up horizontally," continued Dona Santinha. "You've got to do something." She squeezed his arm, hard.

A nurse approached. "Let's go, Dona Santinha."

"Children are so very ungrateful," said Dona Santinha as she was led away.

"She's right about one thing, though," said Dr. Zuomira. "Children never do come visit their parents; they really are ungrateful."

"Not all of them," said Lima Prado, looking at his mother. Maria Clara's lips still formed a frozen smile. She looked as if she were made of wax.

"Yes, all of them," said Dr. Zuomira. "That's what the world's like nowadays."

Lima Prado could endure the ward no longer. He felt nauseous and afraid that he might have to vomit at any moment.

"Talk to her. Old people like it when you talk to them."

"Some other time. I'm not feeling too well right now."

He left the ward without looking at his mother again. The doctor followed.

Dr. Zuomira gave him a few drops of something to take with water and had him lie down on the sofa in the director's office. Once he was feeling better, Lima Prado made arrangements for Maria Clara to be transferred once more to a private room. Later he would find her a better hospital.

He was enormously relieved to be out on the street again.

"Do you have a mother?" Lima Prado asked Virgulino after getting in the car.

"You know I don't, boss. Never did."

32

"ONE DAY when I arrived at her apartment the doorman let me go up without buzzing her on the intercom as he usually did. I rang the bell and Fafá opened the door, but Cila appeared suddenly, extremely nervous, and stopped me from coming inside. I asked her if there was someone there. She turned white and told me to go away. Please, she said, I'll explain everything later. I want to know who it is, I said. Please—she was whispering and so nervous she began stuttering—I'll explain everything later. Is it him? I asked. Cila nodded her head. She looked so awkward and unhappy, and—since I'm not cruel like the majority of people—I felt sorry for her and left. Though I must admit that before leaving I called her a cheap tramp, a common whore, but that's what she was. It wasn't the least bit unjust. A common whore."

That's what Rosa Gonzaga Leitão told me the day Bebel and I located her at the country house on Arcas Highway where she was hiding. She said she'd arrived at her lover's apartment and found her with the mysterious "protector" (from whom Cila swore she had separated). That was the last time Rosa saw Cila alive.

I believed what Rosa told me that day. As it turned out, she was lying to me.

The story of Rosa's life was not terribly extraordinary. When she was twelve her father left the family and moved in with a woman in Cachambi. Rosa's mother, Nelly Abdalla, began making homemade candy and other sweets, which Rosa sold at suburban bus and train stations. The business prospered, and by the time Rosa turned fifteen they had several young boys peddling candy for them on the street, a job that Rosa considered humiliating. She was a pretty girl, quite popular at the Saturday night dances at the Magnates Club near where she lived in the Rocha district. At sixteen she was chosen Miss Magnates and became a contestant for Miss Rio de Janeiro, which she lost to "a blue-eyed blonde from Ipanema who didn't look the least bit Brazilian." The loss shattered her mother's dream that Rosa would become Miss Brazil, and finally, Miss World. Nelly Abdalla's disappointment was so great that she wasted away with some illness the doctors were unable to diagnose, dying several months later. At the time, Rosa had a boyfriend who was a partner, along with three friends, in a small luncheonette in Rocha that specialized in chicken (The Golden Chicken). The boyfriend, who had not been thinking of assuming any obligations other than the one he already had to the chickens, felt obligated to ask Rosa to marry him. Since she hated the candy business and had no intention of spending her days stirring great cauldrons of sticky goo, she figured it made good sense to get married. The couple rented a small apartment in the same neighborhood. Suddenly with the whole day to herself (her husband Ary, whose nickname was Bolinha, didn't want her to work), Rosa matriculated at the Waldemar Paulino High School, which was so notorious for the ease with which a diploma could be earned that students had dubbed it Pay and Pass.

After two years of marriage, Rosa and Bolinha took a sixteen-day charter excursion by bus through the south of Brazil to Montevideo and Buenos Aires. Their route took them south on the Rio–Santos highway, affording glimpses of Angra, Paraty, Ubatuba, Caraguatatuba (places Rosa had read or heard about), finally arriving in São Paulo, where they stayed overnight at the Rio Othon Hotel. Rosa had never seen the inside of a luxury hotel before and felt intimidated by such conspicuous wealth. Bolinha claimed he had once stayed in a hotel of that class, though he couldn't remember where. From São Paulo they continued to Paraná and Santa Catarina, driving through several cities so full of German immigrants that they looked foreign, which Rosa and Bolinha found very confusing. The group spent what the guide called a "technical overnight" (an excuse for the hotel, which was not good) in Criciúma, the following day moving on to Torres, Porto Alegre, and Pelotas. Only four days of traveling and they felt as if they had been on the road for months. After lunching in Pelotas, the tour group crossed the border into Uruguay at Arroio Chuí. So that was Chuí, of the expression "all the way from Chuí to Oiapoque," thought Rosa. For the first time in her life she was standing on non-Brazilian soil and it thrilled her. In Uruguay they visited Punta del Este and Montevideo, where they stayed at the Victoria Palace. It was on the boat trip to Buenos Aires that Rosa met the man who was to become her second husband. He was tall, wavy-haired, mustachioed—and audacious: the complete opposite of Bolinha. Ivonildo, or Nildo as he was called, was traveling with his wife, a bleached blonde every bit as dauntless as he. They lived in Copacabana, Rio, and had joined the excursion in Montevideo. At the tour group dinner in La Boca, the Italian section of Buenos Aires, Nildo and his wife showed off their talents dancing the tango. For the remainder of the trip, to Asunción and back through Iguaçu Falls, Nildo entertained the entire busload, singing all the Brazilian pop hits in his booming baritone. During one of the brief moments they managed to be alone together, Nildo asked Rosa for her phone number.

The day after returning to Rio, Nildo called. They arranged to meet downtown on Avenida Rio Branco next to the Municipal Theater. Nildo drove up in a Puma and spirited Rosa off for lunch in Barra; they ate shrimp fried in the shell and drank beer. But when Nildo suggested they go to a motel, Rosa protested, insisting that she wasn't the type of woman he thought, and stalked out of the restaurant. Nildo was impressed. It was the first time he'd taken a woman to lunch in Barra without going to a motel afterward. And, moreover, Rosa had had the courage to confront all the difficulties of finding her way back to Rocha alone.

316

Nildo owned a small women's clothing factory. "The last thing women will stop buying is clothes," he always said when anyone mentioned Brazil's current economic crisis. Women were consumers and women were tramps, that was what Nildo had learned in the clothing business. But Rosa was different. She'd returned all the presents he sent her, including a silk dress and a Seiko quartz watch. When he called her she insisted, again, that she was not the kind of woman he thought she was.

The truth was, Rosa had about had it with Rocha, Bolinha, and The Golden Chicken. Nildo was an industrialist, a man of the world, and Rosa was, in fact, very interested. But she had come to the conclusion that men only respect women who do not surrender. She also believed that men were not to be trusted when it came to matters of a sexual or emotional nature.

Finally Nildo made the right proposal: they would live together. No furtive encounters in motels. Ercília, the bleached blonde, made a terrible scene, and apparently carried a revolver in her purse for three months, but never went further than threats. Bolinha accepted the situation.

Nildo and Rosa got an apartment in Leblon. The economic crisis was worsening, but Nildo had been right: The clothing business continued to prosper.

Rosa met Gonzaga Leitão at a luncheon in honor of a textile tycoon at the Rio Country Club. Married to Nildo for two years, she had become a completely different woman. No more the little girl dazzled by the big world, Rosa wore elegant, if trendy, clothes, and knew when to speak up, which she did with confidence. She had enrolled in the University, where she was majoring in literature.

Leitão, executive vice president of Achilles, recently widowed, was taking advantage of what he called his "new freedom." Life with his wife, who died of stomach cancer, had been "living hell": She was jealous, aggressive, and vulgar. Now here was this charming young woman in short boots carrying on an intelligent discussion about writers and books. What a shame she was married to that jackass.

Rosa used the same tactics on Gonzaga Leitão that had

brought such good results with Nildo. Men were all the same, after all. When Leitão presented her with a beautiful and expensive aquamarine, Rosa returned it, saying that if he wanted to give her something he should give her a flower. Impressed, Leitão sent her a rose.

When Nildo found out that Rosa was leaving him, he beat her up. But he left it at that. Killing your wife was one of the few things that could have a negative effect on the clothing business.

Gonzaga Leitão and his first wife had not had children, and he was very happy when Bebel was born. Without her first two husbands realizing it, Rosa had intentionally avoided pregnancy. It was just the opposite with Leitão; she did everything she could to get pregnant—including soliciting the help of other men, according to some of her closest and dearest friends. In addition to earning a degree in literature, Rosa decided to become an artist, to "develop her personality." She painted faceless madonnas at first; later she moved on to abstract works. She had a few exhibitions, with the support of Achilles Bank & Trust. Before long she had found her niche in the "exclusive" society of Rio de Janeiro.

A rather unremarkable tale of opportunism; with small variations here and there, it resembled that of many great ladies of society.

Rosa's ambition did not stop with Leitão. She set her sights on her husband's boss, but quickly realized that Lima Prado was a special case. The old tricks she had used on Bolinha, Nildo, and Gonzaga did not apply; this was a man she could trust. And so she slept with him, knowing he would never leave his wife. Lima Prado was the first and last man with whom Rosa would enjoy sexual pleasure.

Rosa had lied to me when she told me about her last visit to Cila's apartment. She had not become furious upon discovering Cila in the arms of "her old protector." Rosa had indeed become furious, but for a different reason. She and the "ex-protector" had, in fact, arrived together, unexpected, for an afternoon of pleasure at Cila's apartment and discovered Cila in bed with one of the employees from the boutique Messina. It didn't bother Rosa if Cila had sex with her "ex-protector"—with or without Rosa's participation—or with any other man. But with another woman—that was something Rosa could not accept.

For quite some time the two had been arranging trysts with transitory third partners, chosen by him or by Rosa. But the affair with Cila, which had begun as the result of a classified ad in the newspaper, had lasted longer than usual. The "protector" had bought the apartment for Cila and supplied the investment for Messina, which Rosa had taken great care to set up. Cila was truly extraordinary in bed with the two of them. She completed the perfect trio as none of the innumerable others before her had been able to do.

Cila and her employee were lying in bed naked and completely taken by surprise by Rosa and the "protector." "You're nothing but a common whore," Rosa screamed, pulling Cila out of bed by the hair.

From the pantry, Fafá heard the entire scene going on in the bedroom. (She and the doorman were two other consummate liars, but I only came to know this much later, when the segment involving Cila's death was finally clarified.) Cláudia, the salesclerk, was also screaming and wailing. Only the "protector" remained calm. He was not, as Rosa had told me, "fat, tall, and red-skinned," but thin, short, and pale. His name was Thales Lima Prado, which is another thing I did not find out until much later. It was there in the Notebooks, in one of the passages that took me a long time to decipher.

Lima Prado contemplated the scene the women were making and finally rescued Cila from Rosa's clutches.

"That's enough. You, get dressed and get out of here."

Sobbing, Cláudia threw on her clothes and left as fast as she could.

That very night Cila was murdered.

Considering things logically, a posteriori, I was intrigued by the fact that Cila had not been killed in the

319

same way as the others. Why hadn't Lima Prado strangled her and left a *P* carved on her face, as he had with Elisa/Gisela and Carlota/Danusa and possibly others in Brazil and the world?

Simple: It was not Lima Prado who killed Cila, but Rosa.

The last reference to Mônica in the Notebooks says only, "I gave Mônica a topaz." Even after the case was closed —I had established a date after which I would consider it closed, because stories as complicated as this one are endless, and that date was the day I got back the gold unicorn, a gift from Berta, which Rafael (I thought) had ripped off my neck the day he and Fuentes had invaded my apartment—I kept searching for Mônica. I finally did manage to locate her, and she clarified something that was not mentioned in the Notebooks, or which I'd never managed to decipher correctly. Mônica really was quite beautiful. Damn, she was still just a child. I was more impressed than Lima Prado when I first saw her. She looked younger than fifteen, had an absolutely perfect body (like a plastic doll), seemed very intelligent and utterly amoral—shocking, really, but she did help me to understand what was understandable about that complicated affair. Our meeting is a whole other story, and no less complicated, but one that I would rather not relive at the moment.

In spite of all I had suffered at the hands of women, they still interested me. At the very moment the battle between Zakkai and Lima Prado was reaching fever pitch, I, too, was heading toward the culmination of the as-yet-undeclared war between me and my three lovers. One day Bebel complained of what she called my "sultanism." "Sartre had plenty of women nibbling at his heels," I told her, "but that didn't upset Simone de Beauvoir." "No?" said Bebel. "She just told the whole world after Sartre died that he used to piss in his pants." But Bebel did not tell me, and neither did either of my other darlings, that the three had met secretly and that at this secret meeting, after overcoming their mutual mistrust and jealousy, they had placed me in judgment, without my knowledge, as if I were some defendant of unknown whereabouts, which at the very least amounts to unfair obstruction of the defense. The verdict was that I was insensitive, insane, and incomprehensible (in both senses —incapable of understanding or being understood) and that an ultimatum would be delivered: I had to choose one of them or forfeit all three. And this in almost the twenty-first century! But before the final demand was made (in point of fact, it was never delivered to me in a clear and objective way), I did have several indications of what was coming.

"The wish for fidelity, or, if you would prefer, exclusivity of desire," said Lilibeth one day, "is not a result of jealousy or possessiveness. You have to understand that a man who parcels himself out among several women, even a man as passionate and imaginative as you, is in the end incapable of giving any one of them the minimum amount of satisfaction she needs. I wish you would get it into your legalistic, reasonably shrewd head that we women are inexhaustible." It was true. At least for the three of them. (And others, too, I remembered: Eva, Berta.) The indicators were beginning to appear, but without my understanding their true significance. Ada began spending more time in front of the mirror, for example. A small degree of narcissism is natural in these promiscuous, schizophrenic times, which is why I wasn't overly worried to notice a slight accentuation of this quality in the woman I lived with. It took me a while to see that she was actually withdrawing from me.

I recounted to Ada an episode from Greek mythology involving Zeus and Hera. In an effort to justify his infidelities, Zeus claimed that his wife Hera's pleasure in the sexual act was infinitely greater; this gave him the right to his small pleasures with other women. Hera maintained the opposite, that it was Zeus who enjoyed greater sexual pleasure. The famous seer Tiresias, whom Aphrodite had transformed into a woman (for having said that another goddess was more beautiful than she), was called to resolve the dispute. "And do you know what Tiresias, the only being ever to have experienced sex as, alternately, man and woman, replied? If sexual pleasure were to be measured in parts, said Tiresias, nine would go to the woman and only one to the man. . . ." "That's the silliest thing I ever heard," said Ada, turning back to the mirror. "I bet you made the whole thing up." I tried to explain that Zeus was right, that myths often contain a lot of wisdom, that women's greater capacity for pleasure (and love)—repressed and negated for centuries—had been established thousands of years before in Greek mythology. The issue here was not multiple orgasms or any other Reichian nonsense, but something beyond *voluptas corporis, libidinum plenum*: It was the ability to create Great Feeling that made woman superior to man. Which explained why, even as we suppressed and negated feminine sexuality, we men needed to accumulate our small and assorted pleasures in an attempt to approximate the feeling experienced by women, which we could only imagine and envy. I was drinking wine, and when I drink wine I get high ideas. I asserted these and other Grand Concepts with exaggerated vehemence but without, however, making a favorable impression on Ada.

While my love life was deteriorating, Fuentes and Miriam were approaching perfect harmony, if such a thing exists between a man and a woman. Fuentes had always felt great contempt for the women he was involved with, but his relationship with Miriam had taken some pleasant and unexpected turns toward the ceremonious. Once when they went to lunch in Lisboeta he pulled Miriam's chair out for her (this remarkable gesture of courtesy almost went unnoticed), and he had gone on to demonstrate consideration and respect in other ways. It was only in bed that their relationship remained primal, him dominating by virtue of sheer animal force. But even in that area, little by little Miriam was introducing Fuentes to the delicate delights of more subtle pleasures. One day, as

322

they gazed into each other's eyes (the three that they had between them), Fuentes said to Miriam what he had never before said to any woman: "I care for you." As soon as he completed the contract with Zakkai, he would change his life. Zakkai had claimed, "You and I detest the contumely of the powerful; their insults are the hardest to bear of all. This is our struggle." But Zakkai craved power above all else; Fuentes merely wanted to avoid being humiliated, at the hands of the strong *or* the weak. He had given up trying to understand Zakkai, "a man who got a kick out of playing the clown." All this certainly merited more focused reflection on my part, but I was not particularly perceptive at the time, reflection having given way to emotion. Zakkai believed that with Lima Prado's death there would be no one left in the Main Office with the leadership capacity to unite the group around a common objective, which would permit him to take command. "The Mafia knows what it's doing," said Iron Nose. "You settle or you die!"

Meanwhile, Wexler, who was doing more and more work (and me less and less), was acting so jittery that I proposed he take a week's vacation. All the powers of attorney were in both names, so it would be no problem for me to follow the civil cases in progress. He strongly resisted, but ended up agreeing. I could never have imagined how much that vacation would make me suffer.

33

IRON NOSE wrenched the blade of the scissors from Rafael's chest. The single stab wound had not caused its victim to die immediately; Rafael's head rocked back and forth as if vigorously negating something. Curious, scissors poised, Zakkai watched Rafael's flailing head, prepared for another lunge. But the head abruptly stopped its wagging and fell to one side.

"The bastard didn't want to die," said Zakkai. "Now let's look for the tape."

"I don't think it's here."

"It's here, I'm sure of it. Let's start looking."

"Be my guest," said Fuentes. He sat down in a chair and watched Zakkai search the living room. Opening drawers, throwing the contents on the floor, Iron Nose talked non-stop.

"Life is sacred, said the Pharisees as they chomped on beef and horse meat. The life of a monkey, I would maintain, is worth more, is more rare, than the life of a man, that mammal which is competing with the rats in the race for proliferation." Iron Nose picked up a picture of a woman that had been clipped from a magazine. "I've met whores with beautiful bodies who think they're going to stay that way their whole life. Beauty is the least durable of possessions. The Pope is scared to death—the Church is well informed, they have spies all over the world. Every night the Pope gets handed a pile of documents in Latin that come from every corner of the globe, and he reads them and shits all over himself, clutching his crozier of gold and precious gems. And the presidents and dictators of the great powers and the banana and oil republics, they understand the atrociousness of the future—that's why they do what they do, madness, treachery, depravity. Here in Brazil it's going to be something truly fantastic."

"You hate all the whole human race," said Fuentes.

"The human race is a pile of shit."

Zakkai continued throwing things all over the floor.

"So what's so terrible that's going to happen here?"

"*Crudelissimum supplicium.*"

"What the hell does that mean?"

"Cruel torture. Especially of the people who still have all their teeth. That's how the encyclical Saint Peter didn't have the courage to send to the bishops begins."

A bee landed on Rafael's nose.

"We've got to get out of here before dark," said Zakkai.

"Go look in the kitchen," suggested Fuentes.

The videocassette was inside a cannister labeled flour. A shiny hard plastic case less than twenty centimeters long and ten centimeters wide; two openings and a clear cover permitted a view of the spools of tape inside.

They returned to Rio as they had come, by helicopter. From the airport they took a cab to Rua Santana. On the way Iron Nose asked Amândio to advise the circus owner that he would not be able to work for the next two days.

"I have a feeling I'll never go back to the ring," said Zakkai. "I'll miss the lights, the laughter. But my clown days are over. The time comes when you take a certain road and then it's too late to leave it."

"I don't know," said Fuentes.

"What don't you know?"

"I think you can always turn off one road and take another."

"The world doesn't let you. All you can do is travel every inch of the road you're on and wreck whatever's in front of you."

It took a while for Amândio to get back with the TV and the videocassette player. He had to buy them at an all-night shopping center in the Zona Sul. Iron Nose hooked up the two gadgets according to instructions in the manual.

"People have literally died to see, or not to see, this tape," he said, holding up the plastic case.

"Now nobody else has to," said Fuentes.

"There's still the last phase to complete, though. If it weren't necessary to kill, we wouldn't. But we agreed to two more. That's what's in the contract."

"And then it's over. I'm going to move someplace real quiet with my woman." Pause. "I've only got one eye."

"Camões only had one eye. Cyclops only had one eye. People with one eye possess the greatest of treasures. Because a real treasure is something you can't afford to lose. You take good care of that eye. How'd you lose the other one, anyway?"

"Distraction."

"It happens. And your woman?"

"Huh?"

"You two have children?"

"No."

"I have great respect for couples who don't have children. And now, the end of a great mystery."

Iron Nose turned on the TV and the videocassette player.

"All I have to do is press one button and the show will begin," said Zakkai.

"I'm not interested," said Fuentes.

"People died, lots of people," said Zakkai.

"Fuck it," said Fuentes, walking toward the door.

"It's not a good idea to go wandering around at this hour. Go pay the whore a little visit."

"She might be busy."

"So unbusy her. Be back in a hour. If things heat up, is the saber all you need?"

"You're expecting something to happen—tonight?"

"You never know. I'm going to take a look at the movie, and I don't want some curse grabbing me by the leg."

326

Fuentes went downstairs and rang the buzzer outside Aurora's apartment. He heard noise behind the door, but no one opened up. He pressed the buzzer again.

"I'm with a friend," said Aurora through the half-opened door. "You didn't tell me you were coming."

"Tell him to leave. Tell him your man came home."

"He is my man. I mean, more or less. I don't exactly have a 'man.' "

"So?"

"You're not going to put me off like the other day, are you?"

"No."

"Go downstairs and have a beer while I work it out, okay?"

In the lobby Fuentes met Amândio.

"How's it going?" asked the Portuguese.

Fuentes said fine with a movement of his head. "Want to go for a beer on the corner?"

"I can't leave. Neither can Pires." Amândio pointed to a guy out on the sidewalk. "The Nose said enemy forces could attack at any moment. You like the knife? Sharper than a razor, eh?"

"It's fine. But I call it a machete."

"Ha, the Nose calls it a saber. Me, I prefer a rod." Amândio patted a bulge at his waist.

"Makes a lot of noise," said Fuentes.

"Now that's true," said the Portuguese.

There were a fair number of people, including several women, standing around drinking beer or soda in the corner bar. A guy who was obviously on drugs and could not manage to hold his drink in his shaky hands came and stood next to Fuentes. Without hurrying, Fuentes moved to the other end of the counter.

A woman approached him.

"In the mood?"

"No."

A police van pulled up outside and three military police got out. Two of them entered the bar. The one outside had a machine gun.

"Identification," said one of the M.P.'s.

"You can't ask for no I.D.'s. We're just sitting here peacefully," began the drugged-out guy at the end of the bar. One of the M.P.'s grabbed him by the belt and dragged him outside to the van. They opened the doors and threw him in back.

Fuentes calmly took out his fake documents—I.D. card and work card—and placed them on the bar in front of him. He sipped his beer. If they were civilian police he'd be worried. The Feds and the guys on the Vice Squad knew him. One of the M.P.'s whispered something to one of the women; she went outside and whispered something to a cop in the front passenger seat of the van. Meanwhile the M.P. in the bar was checking all the men's documents (the women had not been asked to show theirs). A black guy was also seized and tossed in the van. Fuentes realized it had been stupid to come have a drink in a place like this. Iron Nose had warned him. A good way to get fucked, he thought. All's to be feared where all's to be lost, as an old smuggler friend in Corumbá used to say. Fuentes hated the police, especially the rude and insolent M.P.'s. He knew that their superiors, who made top dollar in payoffs and lived in fancy apartments in the Zona Sul, were even worse. But it was these infamous scumbags in their blue uniforms that he hated most.

"You live around here?" asked the M.P. who was examining Fuentes' identification.

"Down the street."

At that moment Fuentes noticed Amândio's friend Pires walk into the bar. A rapid look passed between him and the owner.

"He's a regular, officer. No problem," the man called from behind the bar.

Eventually the M.P.'s got back in the van and slowly pulled away.

"How much do I owe you?" asked Fuentes, indicating his beer bottle.

"Don't worry about it," said Pires.

Amândio was still in the lobby.

"They prowl around all night long, busting the fuck-ups, hassling easy marks and whores," said Amândio. "You going back up to the Nose's apartment?"

"No. But he knows where to find me."

"Me too."

Aurora opened the door immediately.

"Took you a while."

Fuentes walked inside. He checked the kitchen, bathroom, and bedroom.

"The suspicious type, huh?"

"Got any beer?"

"Sure, Antarctica. Want one?"

"Yeah."

Fuentes sat on the couch with the bottle in one hand and a glass in the other. Before long the bottle was empty.

"Want another?"

"Sure."

As he drank the second, Aurora kneeled down and, with some difficulty, pulled off his pants.

"I don't have a rubber this size, no way. You'd have to go to the zoo and borrow it from the elephant."

"I want a rubber." Fuentes was not about to risk getting a venereal disease. He had heard that gonorrhea resisted all treatment. Sexual diseases were sickening.

"It's a mania with you, huh?"

"What do you mean?"

"Thinking everybody's got the clap."

"Guess it works, I never caught it."

"Why don't we stop talking and start fucking."

Fuentes didn't like women to talk like that. It was one thing for men, but women shouldn't curse, it was ugly.

"What's wrong?"

329

"I'm just killing time. I've got to leave soon." Fuentes stood and picked up his pants.

"I send my friend away and now you tell me you're just here killing time!"

"That's right."

"What good is a big cock like that if you don't use it?"

"Look, I don't want to fight with you." She had placed herself directly in front of him. Fuentes backed off.

"Fucking impotent." Without much conviction.

"You shouldn't talk to people that way. The guy could be nervous. Or really fucking impotent. And then he might get nasty. Did you ever think of that?"

"I even dreamed about you," said Aurora, disconsolate. "Want to hear the dream?"

"I have to go."

"We were flying above the ocean and we looked out a little window and saw a whale down there, swimming along."

"That's all?"

"That's all. I dreamed it twice. You're sitting next to me and we're holding hands. I've never ridden in an airplane and I'm scared. In the dream."

"It's growing, this dream."

"No, that's really it. Nothing else. Do you understand dreams?"

"No." Fuentes sat back down on the couch.

"We're holding hands like this." Aurora took his two hands in hers. "I've got a little coke left. Want some?"

"No. That stuff's poison."

"Then I'll get a rubber."

When the buzzer rang, Fuentes slipped out of bed silently and peered out the peephole. It was Amândio.

"The Nose says you should get upstairs. Urgent."

"I'm on my way."

"Are you coming back?" asked Aurora as Fuentes dressed.

"I'll call."

330

Amândio and Fuentes went upstairs. Zakkai was waiting.

"I called our friend. We made a deal, he's coming over to pick up the tape. But I don't trust him. I can't believe he's really going to throw in the towel just like that. Amândio, I want you upstairs here, in the hall. When the man comes you check him out. Only one comes inside."

Zakkai handed the machete to Fuentes, who set it on the floor, leaning against the chair in which he was sitting.

"Don't you even want to know what was on the tape?"

"No."

"My business is commerce," said Zakkai. "The first merchant deserving of the name in Brazil was a converted Jew, an ancestor of mine named Fernão de Noronha. In 1502 he was awarded the concession for brazilwood. Every year he had to send a fleet of six ships to explore three hundred leagues of coastline and build settlements. Then he'd fill each ship with five thousand logs of brazilwood, plus slaves, parrots, and parakeets. Do you like parrots?"

"I hate them. They talk too much."

The buzzer rang. Zakkai opened the door.

Amândio and another man came inside.

"He's clean," said Amândio.

"Who are you?" asked Zakkai.

"My name is Hermes."

"Where are the papers?" asked Zakkai.

Hermes took a step to the side, putting him directly in front of Amândio. He was wearing a coat and tie, with his hands folded in front of him like a priest. He fixed his cold gaze first on Zakkai and then Fuentes. Suddenly his hands separated and his right arm flew down and back. The old Applegate trick.

It all happened so fast that none of them knew what was happening. Least of all Amândio, whose stomach was perforated with one violent backward thrust. As Amândio fell, Hermes rotated the grip on his knife in a gesture too fast for Zakkai and Fuentes to follow. Now the

331

blade became a horizontal extension of his forearm, glinting red in the dim light of the living room. A Loveless special, which had belonged to a past president of the Knifemakers Guild of America.

"It's the Professor," said Fuentes, rising to his feet, machete in hand.

For a few moments the two men looked like figures in a wax museum.

They studied each other, frozen. Hermes knew that the easiest opponent was one moved by either hate or fear. He could see immediately, however, that Fuentes was not experiencing either of those emotions. This adversary possessed what Cassidy had told him during his training was the greatest quality in a fighter—"cold hate." Rather than dissipating the indispensable mental discipline of the combatant, this singular hate strengthened it. Hermes also saw and admired in Fuentes' total utter immobility the control he was exercising over his physical and mental energy. Easy opponents began moving immediately, especially muscular ones like the man in front of him. And upon moving—whether the movement was accompanied, as in the case of Asian-style fighting, by a shout aimed at frightening the adversary, or by making faces in an attempt to distract, and regardless of whether the movement was rapid or slow-motion—in the motion itself the enemy created openings, showed who he was, revealed himself. But this antagonist remained motionless, his arm parallel to his body, the point of the machete resting on the floor.

Of course Hermes also remained absolutely still, in the stance referred to in NUSS as "Battery Position"—right elbow almost touching his side, knife gripped firmly, thumb up, the hand on the same horizontal line as the right knee, which was slightly forward and flexed, left arm partly extended, left hand open with palm facing the adversary, chin imperceptibly tucked. Hermes observed Fuentes' body as a whole, not fixing on any particular part, neither the hand holding the weapon nor the eyes. (If he had known that Fuentes had only one working eye he would have been more confident.)

In a corner of the room, with his back against the wall, stood Iron Nose, also frozen.

Hermes knew that people wielding machetes liked to strike horizontally. If Fuentes did this, Hermes would execute a *passata sotto,* rapidly changing position and piercing him deep in the liver. A horizontal thrust always left the right side exposed.

Slowly Fuentes began raising the arm that held the machete. But instead of stopping with the elbow extended and his hand at face level, as he would if he were going to attack on a parallel with the floor, he continued the movement until the blade was over his head. And then stepped backward with his right leg.

Hermes knew that with Fuentes in such a position the *passata* wouldn't work. It was going to be a one-stroke fight, without the preliminary swipes, cuts, and incisions that commonly preceded the mortal thrust in knife combat. According to the vade mecum of Araujo, then, he had two options: parry or avoid. The parry would have to be done with the forearm, the blow of the machete merely mutilating him, which was better than dying. The problem was not the risk of losing an arm or the improbable risk of losing consciousness—he would feel no pain, a mutilating blow did not hurt—but of losing his balance, which could prevent him from responding instantaneously with a lethal *stoccata.* Thus, the advisable alternative was avoidance, which would mean getting out of the line of the descending machete in a perfect dodge, that is, without suffering any lesion at all. This done, it would be possible to counterattack immediately, finding the opponent's carotid or chest, whichever seemed better, while he was "off balance and vulnerable." But there were further problems: Someone handy with a machete would not make a thrust in a straight line, but would make the metal describe an arc as it approached its target. Knife versus machete! It was an unpleasant situation, not for its deadly aspect but for its intrinsic heresy.

The broad sharp machete came down with incredible velocity. Hermes' reaction was fast enough to save his head. But he could not prevent the machete from falling full on his shoulder, lacerating the trapezoid and small rhomboid muscles and fracturing collarbone and shoulder blade. The knife still secure in his hand, he fell backward onto the floor, his face expressionless, pallid. The padding in his suit jacket had lessened the blow slightly, preventing the blade from slicing more deeply. Hermes felt the silence become more muffled, as if he had stuffed cotton in his ears. But even so, he heard the whistle of the blade cutting the air before colliding with his temple.

At that moment I was at home feeding Betsy. The doorbell rang.

It was Bebel.

"Ada might get home any minute," I said. "She's at a party."

"This won't take long," said Bebel.

"I was feeding Betsy. What a smell."

I held my hand up to Bebel's nose. She followed me into the kitchen. While I finished chopping sardines, Bebel and Betsy paced back and forth across the room, the cat rubbing against my legs.

"Old cats love to eat," I said.

"I love to eat. We begin to get old the minute we're born," said Bebel.

"Everyone knows that. But actually the moment that aging sets in is when we start to *really* love to eat, the way old cats do. It's an absolute truth."

"There are no absolute truths, only obsolete. I believe those were your exact words."

"Would I make a lousy pun like that?"

"Mandrake, I'm here for a very specific reason. I came to tell you that it's all over."

"All what?"

"Everything. Me, Lili, Ada. We no longer feel love for you. Just charity. I came to tell you, for all three of us."

"Love and charity are the same thing. In Latin," I said, because I didn't know what to say. I needed to control myself so Bebel wouldn't see what I was feeling.

334

There was an old lawyer at the courthouse who used to say that there's no situation so bad a woman can't make it worse.

"So it's a conspiracy. I can't believe that Ada's mixed up in this. Why didn't she come talk to me?"

"It would have been too painful. She thinks she still loves you. But she doesn't want to see you anymore."

"But all her things are still here."

"Not all of them."

There was still a small piece of raw sardine in my hand. Distracted, I slipped it in my mouth.

"It's dirty, it's treachery," I said, spitting out the sardine, "for you three to do a thing like this to me."

"We're not trying to crucify you, or punish you. We're not interested in making you suffer. We just want to define our true roles."

"Why do there have to be roles, anyway? That's what's wrong with the world these days. Forget the roles, let's just be ourselves."

"Don't give me the sly shyster act, please."

A writer named Edith Wharton once said that the use of dialogue in fiction was one of the few things with respect to which a definitive rule could be established. Dialogue, she said, should be reserved for "culminating moments." I recalled this and resolved to remain silent, surrounded by the rotten smell of fresh sardines. (Like many lawyers, I aspired to write for a non-magisterial audience; as a lawyer I made my living off words, either oral or written. So what would be more natural than for me to write a novel according to Mrs. Wharton's specifications, in which there was not one word of dialogue? But that's another story.)

After a time, as Mrs. Wharton foresaw, Bebel, as any reader, felt suffocated by my silence and longed for a little dialogue.

"What kind of face is that?" she asked, stroking my cheek.

"I stink of sardines."

"I like the smell."

335

"Really?"

"No, I was lying. Go take a shower."

While I was under the shower, Bebel came into the bathroom.

"I swore to them that I'd give you the message and leave. That I wouldn't expose myself to . . ."

I kept soaping my body and kept quiet. I felt like singing "I Took a Boat up North" (how bizarre!) but contained myself.

Then she said, "Ada went on a trip with Wexler."

My partner's vacation. *A waycher mentsch diment . . .*

I said nothing. Soap got in my eyes; it was beginning to sting. Through the translucent glass I watched Bebel walk out of the bathroom. I dashed out of the shower and locked the bathroom door. I sat on the toilet seat and stayed there. I stayed there.

When I came out, Bebel was gone. I lit a short dark panatela and lay down in bed, wrapped in a towel. Betsy came and lay down on my pubis. Betsy didn't like cigars. Or maybe she did. She definitely didn't like wet towels. But she stayed there, blinking once in a while with sleepiness.

"Really," I said.

When I got up, much later, I dug out the Randall and posed in front of the mirror. First I attempted the moves Hermes had taught me. Then I held the knife by the haft with both hands, like Tatsuya Nakadai, watching my face in the mirror, the point of the double-tempered and sharpened blade pricking my stomach. Me, who had never had serious ontological worries, kneeling with my ass on my heels, thinking to be or not to be.

I returned the Randall to its leather sheath and buried it in a bottom drawer full of rarely worn clothes. I wanted nothing more to do with revenge. Why had they done this to me? Cretins. Lilibeth, the little socialite, would never find another man like me. She deserved her dear Val and his fish *moqueca*. The New Black Plague would take care of Bebel, with a little help from obesity. Ada I didn't even want to think about. I relit the panatela that had gone out and was sitting in the ashtray on the night table. The best revenge would be to live a long, long time.

34

"What did you do with the bodies?"

We were sitting in the office of the holding company that controlled Pleasure, Fun, and Fastfood.

"What bodies?"

"Hermes and Amândio."

"I forget, it was so long ago," said Iron Nose. "Well, when I saw the two of them were dead, I picked up the phone and called someone to get rid of the bodies. No problem."

"No problem?" I meant to be ironic, but didn't quite pull it off.

"Hermes was good, but he had bad luck with Fuentes. He came expecting to fence, something artistic. Instead he was up against that crude Bolivian, so he got screwed."

"There was nothing in the papers," I said.

"They got a pauper's burial. Nobody asks any questions. A dead pauper's better than a live one; a dead and buried one is better yet."

"But Amândio was your friend. You let them—"

"He was dead. He wasn't anybody's friend anymore. He wasn't suffering anymore, he didn't know from nothing. A dead man is beyond everything."

"What about Fuentes?" I asked.

"I think he got married. Disappeared. Brazil's a big country."

"Do you know what really happened with Lima Prado?"

"Only what was in the newspapers. And what his business partners—my business partners—told me. Quite incredible, really."

Iron Nose's face told me nothing. He could have been lying. Or not.

"And what about the videocassette?"

"There was nothing on it. I played the whole tape and all I saw were those little lines you get on the screen. Nothing."

"Then all those people died for nothing?"

"That's life. But you're confusing things."

"And you're lying."

"My dear sir . . ." Iron Nose seemed to be enjoying himself.

"I have Lima Prado's Notebooks. Did you know that?"

"Mmm. Raul told me. As far as I'm concerned you might as well use them to wipe your ass."

Iron Nose had never heard a sound like the one of Fuentes' machete splitting open Hermes' head. It was so violent a blow that a chunk flew off and hit the wall. The sound hung in the air in two sonorous parts, first cracking like wood breaking and then a deep muffled sound that Iron Nose attributed to the brains being expelled.

For a while Zakkai stayed put, leaning against the wall. Then he went over to Amândio's fallen body. Amândio was dead.

"Where's the bathroom?" asked Fuentes.

In the bathroom he washed his hands and face and combed his hair.

"The war's not over yet," said Iron Nose.

(It was, but he didn't know it.)

"For me it is," said Fuentes, drying his face with his handkerchief.

"This isn't the person I wanted," said Iron Nose, picking up the phone. "Hello? It's the Nose. I have two hams to unload. Mmm. In Baixada. Mmm, the merchandise is here in the Springs. You can get the key from Pires downstairs in the lobby."

Iron Nose turned on every light in the small apartment and inspected all the rooms. He picked a pen up off the table in the living room.

"Let's go," said Zakkai.

"What about all this?" Fuentes motioned toward the machete leaning against the wall, the two bodies on the floor.

"My people will take care of it."

Perhaps that's the way it happened. I couldn't be sure. I could imagine, speculate, deduct—I had done nothing else since the whole thing started. In any case, I was very close to the truth.

Lima Prado received a lengthy phone call that day. Mônica was with him at the time, but all she heard him say was "Yes . . . yes," holding the receiver tight to his ear as if he were afraid she might hear what his caller was saying.

His wife and children were traveling in Europe. That morning he had told all the servants and security guards to take the day off, without giving any explanation for this unexpected turn of events. He did not want witnesses to Mônica's visit. Why had he invited her there? She said it was his idea. It could only have been for one reason. He was planning to use the Roderick Caribou Chappel.

Mônica doesn't remember exactly what day it was. "I think it was a Thursday, but I don't know the date." Captain Virgulino picked her up and delivered her to the mansion. "I'd never seen such a big house, not even in the movies."

Captain Virgulino left her at the front door, which was opened by Lima Prado himself. "A vestibule the size of a train station."

"Are you finally going to tell me your name?"

"Thales Lima Prado."

"What?" said Mônica, visibly disappointed. The name meant nothing to her.

He repeated it.

"What do you do?"

"I'm a financier."

340

All that mystery for nothing, she thought. Her lover was not the owner of Casa Sendas Supermarkets or Mesbla Department Store or Brahma Beer or any other company whose name appeared on television.

Lima Prado acted strange that day, she recalled. "It was like he was sleepwalking." But it wasn't drugs—she knew the symptoms.

After the phone call he said, "I think you should get dressed and leave."

"I just got here," said Mônica.

"Go on," said Lima Prado hoarsely. "Captain Virgulino will take you home."

The driver was waiting at the door.

Halfway home, in Ipanema—the mansion was in Gávea Pequena, and Mônica lived in Copacabana—she asked Captain Virgulino to stop at a bakery, from which she emerged in twenty minutes with a package. He left her at the door to her building and returned to Gávea. The round trip must have taken the better part of an hour.

When he got back, Virgulino went looking for his boss to report that he had "delivered the girl." Captain Virgulino found Lima Prado on the floor of his bedroom, still clutching the Roderick Caribou Chappel, its blade buried deep under his armpit. He was unconscious but still alive and bleeding profusely. Recovering from his shock, Captain Virgulino called the Miguel Couto Hospital, but by the time the ambulance arrrived Lima Prado was dead.

Raul was notified and arrived at the house in Gávea Pequena after the medical examiner had already done his work and the body had been removed to the Institute of Legal Medicine.

He found the Notebooks lying on a table in the kitchen next to a bottle of rubbing alcohol. Lima Prado had intended to burn them, but for some reason had not.

35

THE NEWSPAPERS no longer devoted much space to the continuing mystery of Lima Prado's death. The initial repercussions had been great, divided opinions generating many heated discussions. Mrs. Dadá Lima Prado insisted that her husband had been murdered and hired a famous lawyer to investigate the case. But the media soon lost interest; the crime had already yielded all the news it could and had been squeezed dry in the process.

It was two o'clock Saturday afternoon. Wexler had just called to say that he wouldn't be back for another two weeks.

The doorbell rang. It was Miriam. She paused in the doorway.

"Come on in," I said. I had to take her by the arm.

Miriam took a long time to get started. She and Fuentes had moved to a little farm near Areias, in the state of São Paulo, to start a new life.

"Do you know where Queluz is?"

"Uh-huh."

"Close to there."

They had decided to plant corn and beans, and put down roots. "It's a pretty place. There's no electricity, at night you can see all the stars in the sky."

Miriam began to cry. "The little calves are so cute," she said between sobs.

I waited.

"They came in a jeep. Camilo was fixing the roof. They had rifles and machine guns and even after he'd rolled off the roof and fallen on the ground they just kept shooting,

342

it was horrible. He was such a mess you couldn't recognize him."

Miriam opened her purse.

"Just the night before he gave me this, to give back to you. He asked me to tell you he's not a thief. He never stole anything else in his whole life, just this little thing."

My gold unicorn. Cupping it in my hand, I thought of Berta. And all the other women in my life.

Miriam had just left when Raul arrived. He was wearing his suspicious, provocative cop-face.

"I'll say it one more time," I said. "Lima Prado killed himself. He plunged the knife into his armpit, just like Ajax's suicide in Greek mythology, which Prado describes in the Notebooks. He left us all to join Hermes in the Elysian Fields."

"Tell me, have you ever heard of anyone killing themselves like that?"

"Ajax."

"That's mythology! It's absurd, it's illogical."

"Lima Prado was an absurd and illogical man." (I didn't have the courage to say he was mythological.)

"Look, Mandrake, this story is very confused. You say Lima Prado killed the masseuses, but how can I even be sure of that?"

"It's there in the Notebooks."

"The way you interpret it. Nobody can really read and understand that crap. I had those Notebooks for a while, remember? I don't believe you can even decipher his minuscule, crabbed handwriting. The business of Rosa killing Cila is another one of your 'interpretations.' In fact, the only thing I know for sure is that Lima Prado was one of the top dogs in the drug trade, but I'll never even be able to prove it."

"Fine. *Ad argumentandum tantum:* If he didn't kill himself, then who did?"

"Zakkai. Working for Gonzaga Leitão."

"Rosa's husband?"

"Leitão was getting squeezed by all the power struggles going on inside Achilles. After Prado's death Leitão

343

gained control of the organization and turned over—or sold cheap—Pleasure and the other companies to Zakkai. Now Achilles is only involved in legitimate financial activities."

"Right. Usury, speculation, financial swindles, et cetera."

"Like any bank."

"Which means that crime pays, you cynic."

"All these years as a cop have made me something worse than cynical."

"Which is?"

"Lucid."

I raised my wineglass. I looked at the precious glittering liquid. "Do you at least agree that it was Rafael who killed Mitry and the twins?"

"I do."

"And who do you think killed the masseuses?"

"It could have been anybody. It could have been you, Mandrake."

I lit a short dark panatela.

"Open another bottle," I said, "and tell me more."

"Are you forgetting that one of them came to see you in your office, and the other went out with you—in both cases the night before they were found dead?"

"You're a cretin, you know that?"

"A lucid one. Wexler says your inordinate love of women is very close to hate."

"But I didn't buy the Randall until after they'd been killed. And I didn't know how to use it before, either. Still don't."

"Anybody can draw a P. And we're born knowing how to choke someone. You devised the idea of deciphering the Notebooks because that way you could make up any story you please."

"I have witnesses."

"Who?"

"Hermes."

"A corpse for a witness?" Raul had not heard the irony in my voice. They were all corpses.

344

"You've gone off the deep end, Raul."

"I know. Did I tell you I'm going to move back in with Ligia?"

"Ligia's a good woman."

"Too good."

The bell rang.

"Expecting someone?"

"A friend."

I opened the door. The young lady came in.

"Well, I better get going. Lucid, you hear? Lucid," said Raul. " 'Night, señorita."

"Who's he?" she asked after Raul had left.

"A friend."

I waited.

"It's been so long. . . . Still remember me? I've lost weight, don't you think?"

I laughed. "Yeah."

"Still love me?" asked Bebel.

"I do."